THE
HIDDEN
SAINT

THE
HIDDEN
SAINT

A NOVEL

MARK LEVENSON

Author Photo Credit: AnneBeth Litt Levenson

First edition

ISBN: 978-1-68512-050-4

Cover art by Level Best Designs

This book was professionally typeset on Reedsy.
Find out more at reedsy.com

To my parents, of blessed memory, who taught me how to live.
And to my wife and children, who make living worthwhile.

Advance Praise for The Hidden Saint

"An ingenious, compelling mix of horror, fantasy, suspense and Jewish mysticism. Think Tolkien, albeit benefiting from a yeshiva education."–Jonathan Kellerman

"Has a sense of timelessness that makes it feel at once mythic and intimate. It has all the best pieces of history and fantasy woven into a single sweeping epic."–Mary Robinette Kowal, Hugo-award winning author of *The Calculating Stars*

"Astonishingly original. A literally spellbinding tale that is as much a poignant elegy as it is a wildly imaginative tragi-comic entertainment."–Steve Stern, author of *The Frozen Rabbi*

"This spellbinding novel brought me to the edge of my seat more times than I can count. It made me think deeply, feel profoundly, and pray hard – for a sequel."–Ruchama King Feuerman, author of *In the Courtyard of the Kabbalist*

"A terrific read, impossible to put down. An unforgettable world of demons, imps, werewolves, a golem, and a hero who triumphs over unspeakable evil."–Greg Stout, author of *Gideon's Ghost* and *Lost Little Girl*

"A riveting read that weaves together an extraordinary tale from threads of the Bible, Kabbalah, Star Wars, Game of Thrones, and even Frozen."–Rabbi Yakov Saacks, author of *The Kabbalah of Life*

"A hero's journey through the magical landscape of Kabbalah and Jewish

i

mysticism."–Izzy Abrahmson, author of *The Village Twins and other tales of The Village Life*

Chapter One

Miropol, Tzardom of Russia, in the year 5505 of the Hebrew calendar, corresponding to the year 1745 of the common era

T he boy raced across the heath to see his bride. Overhead, thousands of sprites, each no bigger than a bee, caught the moonlight with their wings, sending streaks of gold across the darkness. As he ran, words of the Sages came unbidden to challenge him: *If three travel together at night, the evil spirit does not appear. If two together, the spirit appears but does not attack. If one alone, the spirit attacks.*

He was one person alone at night.

Still, for six whole days, he hadn't seen Rachel, not even a glimpse. Everyone knew it was bad luck to see the bride in the seven days before the wedding, and Adam was nothing if not cautious. But on this night, his desire to see Rachel was an unquenchable fire against which caution had no chance. After being chaperoned—no, dogged—by his parents the past few days, the freedom of the night and the thrill of the cool wind against his face were exhilarating and helped to drive away his fears. No harm would come to him, he told himself, surely not tonight.

The enforced separation of this week—a separation from Rachel longer than any he could recall in his seventeen years—had been an ache on Adam's soul. He couldn't remember a time without Rachel and, for all practical purposes, there had been none. As children, they had played together in the courtyard of the synagogue during services, around each family's weekly

1

Sabbath table, and in the meadows that ringed the village, until they reached adolescence, the age at which tradition isolated boys from girls, and their largely separate lives began in earnest. Still, they had found their ways.

When Adam was called to the reader's table or to the Holy Ark itself during Sabbath services, he would gaze up at the women's balcony and, no matter how crowded it was, see only her face. Adam and Rachel continued to trade glances and smiles during chance encounters at the smithy's, or at the well, or on busy village roads during market days. Once, when Adam was bringing food and firewood to the Widow Baile—in secret, so as not to embarrass her—he glimpsed Rachel through the snowy trees, likewise engaged in a clandestine act of kindness. *Soulmates*, he thought then. Once, at the leaven bonfire before Passover, a particularly malevolent imp had dislodged an ember that shot like an arrow to Rachel's dress, setting it aflame. Almost before she could realize the danger, Adam had dashed to her side and smothered the fire with his jacket. He had made a silent promise then that he would never allow her to come to harm.

So, when their parents announced that the children would be wed, it merely confirmed what Adam had already known: Rachel was his predestined bride. The teaching of the Sages was true: *Forty days before a mother conceives, the angels call out: "This one will be married to that one."*

His "that one" was Rachel.

Adam tripped, scattering his reverie like dust and sending his tall, thin frame to the ground with a painful thud. As he lay there on barren earth, his shoulder aching, his nose suddenly prickled. What was that smell? Something both sour and sweet. Imps? Had an imp been having its fun by tripping him? He knew that wherever a sin had been committed, an imp was born. Much had happened on the heath about which no one spoke. Imps were a distinct possibility.

I should have waited; the wedding is tomorrow, after all, Adam thought as he picked himself up. He brushed bits of leaves and dirt from his black coat and breeches and replaced his cap over his mop of curly black hair.

He scanned the lifeless, sandy earth, which was relieved here and there only by patches of rough grasses and low shrubs—and rocks, some as big as a shed. And then he saw it: about twenty feet away, small against the ground, the slimy green skin that flashed in the moonlight. The imp, no bigger than a mouse, dusted itself off and stood up, its harlequin-hued cape flapping in the breeze. Adam glowered at the creature and prepared to go after it; he had caught imps before and this one didn't look particularly tough. Then he noticed its stub of a tail where a long, snake-like appendage, useful for keeping an imp upright, should have been, evidence no doubt of a past encounter the imp was lucky to have survived. Tonight, the imp probably had lost its balance and fallen before Adam tripped over it.

The imp's gaze was locked on Adam, its black eyes sparkling like diamonds.

Adam sighed. "Go on," he said with a wave of his hand. "Get out of here and don't trouble me again."

"Thank you, boy," the imp called out in a high, raspy voice that Adam strained to hear. It started to turn away, then looked back at Adam. "The heath at night is no place for a human. Take care!" And then, with the uncertain, jerky motion of a pull toy across an uneven floor, the imp limped off, slipped into a crack between two rocks, and was gone.

Adam stared at the spot where the creature had gone to ground. Imps could be great trouble, but he supposed they too had their place in the Almighty's creation, although he'd be dashed if he knew what it was.

He ran on, past a copse of ancient oaks. One path led to another and, a few minutes later, he came to the village of Miropol. Adam crept without a sound past the market square and the modest timber-and-plank houses with their steeply gabled roofs, passing a cowshed here and a chicken coop there, praying that none of the animals would awaken and then awaken their owners. The last thing he needed was to be discovered seeking out his bride. A glimpse, just a glimpse, was all he wanted. The village's main road took him to a two-story house with covered porches on both floors. During the day it looked inviting enough; now, with the windows shuttered against the night and all that it held, the house looked cold and forbidding. Adam stared up at Rachel's window. How could he get her attention—without getting the attention of anyone else? He hadn't thought of that while running across the heath. Perhaps a light tap on the window...

He picked up a pebble the size of a pea and threw it upward. It hit the shutters with the tiniest *ping* and bounced into the night. He squinted; did the shutters part? No, just wishful thinking. He threw another stone, this one the size of a grape. It hit with a louder *bang* than Adam had anticipated. He flinched, then crouched behind some bushes. He could just imagine Rachel's father responding to the noise with his musket. Better to give up, go home.

And then the shutters slowly opened.

Adam gazed up. His recklessness had been rewarded. Rachel leaned out slightly over the windowsill, her honey-colored hair framing the long, alert face that sat above her elegant neck like a jewel on a pedestal. By the light of her candle, Adam could see her eyes sparkle as she looked out into the night. She spied Adam and those eyes widened. Was it surprise—or disapproval? Adam felt a blush creeping up his neck and he stood awkwardly, staring up at her. She thought him foolish, maybe even improper, in having violated tradition by coming to her on this night. He had made a mistake. He shouldn't have come.

He opened his mouth to call to her, as if uttering her name might make things right, but she put a finger to her lips warning him not to. Her lips now parted in a sweet smile and Adam wondered how he could have thought she'd disapprove. No, she didn't think him foolish at all. Not a word passed between them but, in that mutual gaze, each saw the other's promise of eternity.

Adam grinned, a smile so broad he almost lacked the teeth for it. He'd gotten what he'd come for.

He quickly retraced his steps to the heath. As soon as he had passed the last houses on the way out of the village, he began to whistle, a loud, clear clarion call to the heavens. He always whistled when he was happy or excited, and now he was both. He knew it was foolish beyond measure to draw attention to oneself at this time, in this place, but tonight he was invincible. He had seen his Rachel and tomorrow they would be wed. Adam scanned the vista carefully for any sign of lurking imps and ran all the way home.

Early the next morning, Adam and his father took their cart to the village, to the synagogue, for morning prayers. As they rode, Adam slipped his hand into his pocket. He fingered the small wooden flute he'd carved for Rachel. He would give it to her that afternoon, after the wedding ceremony, in the seclusion room, when they would spend their first moments alone together as man and wife. Maybe she would play a tune and he would whistle in accompaniment. Rachel seemed to enjoy his whistling; she always came to hear him when he was attracting a crowd to his father's booth on market days.

He might even sing a song to her, something from Psalms:

Tremble and do not sin; commune with your own heart upon your bed and be still.

No, he shook his head, not quite right for a wedding day. Maybe:

Praise the Lord from the earth, you sea-monsters and all depths; fire and hail, snow and vapor, stormy wind...

No, he grimaced, definitely not right. Perhaps something from the Song of Songs. One of King Solomon's verses floated through his head:

Behold, thou art fair, my love; behold, thou art fair.

Thine eyes are as doves behind thy veil.

He blushed so hard he could feel the heat rising through his face. He could never sing that to Rachel. All these years, he had never even flirted with her, and now he would start serenading her? Maybe Rachel would laugh at him. No, there wasn't a cruel bone in her body. Still, he could imagine her stifling a laugh in an attempt to be kind. Agh, he could be such an oaf at times. Clumsy too. He squirmed on the rough wooden bench. It struck him how little he knew about women, and what he knew about his mother was hardly of use.

The wooden plank on which he sat slapped him as the cart lurched over a rut in the road. He looked at his father, who was concentrating on the path and murmuring now and again to the horse.

"Papa," he began.

His father glanced at him. "Yes, Adam?" He turned back to the horse. "There is something on your mind?"

"Oh... nothing." He pulled on the wisps of black hair that had recently made a home on his chin.

His father cast him a discerning look. "I too was nervous on the day I wed your mother," his father said, his voice managing to be both gentle and gruff at the same time. "It's the way of bridegrooms."

Adam nodded and again fingered his incipient beard.

At the synagogue, Adam mumbled the familiar words of prayer unthinkingly along with the other worshippers, until absolute quiet settled suddenly on the men as they began the silent recital of the eighteen benedictions. Adam stared at the prayer book in his hands, the black words on the white page swimming before him. Why was he worrying about what he'd *sing* to Rachel? Singing was the least of his troubles. The seclusion room was where he would be alone, truly alone, with Rachel for the first time. They would touch. Would they kiss? Would they do more than that? He didn't know. If not there, then certainly that night. He felt queasy. What if he hurt his bride? What if he inadvertently committed a sin? He groaned to himself.

After the service, as he wrapped and put away his phylacteries, the villagers smiled and offered their blessings. Adam nodded as though he heard them. On the ride home, his father again concentrated on the path and on the horse. Adam sat utterly quiet. When they reached the farmhouse, his mother had his father's breakfast of bread and porridge waiting. For Adam, she had only an apologetic smile; he would fast today, this most holy of holy days for him, his personal Day of Atonement, when all his sins would be forgiven. Fasting was just as well to Adam; he had no stomach for food.

Later, when his mother called to him that it was time to get ready, he washed by the basin in his room, then donned his black satin caftan and broad-brimmed black hat. He entered the parlor and saw his father waiting for him, the older man's attire identical to his own, except for the sable trim on his collar, sleeves, and brim. His mother came in from the kitchen in her emerald-green dress, her hem skipping against the floor. She poked a few exposed strands of hair under her green and white head scarf, then reached up to touch her son's face. She stepped back, admired his transformation from boy to bridegroom, and beamed.

"What a man you are!"

Adam flushed. A man? More likely still a boy, a boy who knew nothing.

She patted the ivory brooch near her collar as though confirming its presence and then the three of them set off for the synagogue, travelling along the road that skirted the heath. It was longer than crossing the heath itself, but the only way possible in the cart. When they were halfway there, Adam felt his pockets, first routinely, then in dismay—the ring! He'd forgotten the plain, thin brass band which he had purchased for a ruble from the smith three days before. He searched his pockets again and all he came up with was the little flute.

He called to his father, who pulled sharply on the reins, bringing the cart to a sudden stop.

"What do you mean you forgot the ring?" his mother asked, alarm in her eyes.

"So we'll go back for it," said his father, beginning to coax the horse to turn around in the narrow road.

"No," said his mother sharply. "If we return to the house, we'll all be terribly late." Her hand pulled nervously on her brooch. "Everyone will wonder what happened. I'll go to the village; you two go back to the house."

Adam looked from one parent to the other, his heart sinking. His mother couldn't drive the cart alone and, if his father drove alone, his mother would never manage the walk in time. He drew in his breath, afraid to propose the only solution.

"Better that you two should take the cart and go to the village to explain," he said. "I'll run back to the house, get the ring, and take the shortcut over the heath."

"You can't be alone today. You're a bridegroom. It's bad luck," his mother blurted, her thin face alive with her fear.

His father shook his head slowly. "I don't like it either." His mother started nodding, until he continued: "But I suppose it's the only practical way."

7

Yes, he would be careful and quick. Yes, he would be fine. Yes, they should leave him now, before any more time passed. Reluctantly, his parents set off in the cart toward Miropol. Adam, alone, ran back toward the house.

By all calculations, it should have taken Adam less than an hour to get the ring and arrive at the synagogue. But he didn't appear after an hour, nor after an hour and a half, nor after two. Enough was enough for Rachel's father. The delay was unprecedented: A groom who doesn't appear at his own wedding! Some grew fearful, others increasingly vexed. Adam's mother sat by herself and moaned, clutching the brooch at her throat as she saw the future slipping away. Several men were dispatched by wagon to find Adam and bring him to the synagogue. His father's concern for his son mixed with a growing sense of embarrassment. This would not soon be forgotten by the community. How could his son do this to Rachel, to the village, to his parents?

By the time the villagers reached the house, it was empty—and vandalized, with heirlooms smashed, furniture overturned, holy books thrown from their shelves. The men looked among the debris for an unconscious or wounded Adam but didn't find him. A search was organized immediately. It lasted for days but the people of Miropol might have saved their trouble. Adam was not to be found anywhere around the house, on the heath, in the woods, nor anywhere else in or around the village.

Days became weeks, became months, became years. They never saw him again.

Chapter Two

Lizensk, Kingdom of Poland and Grand Duchy of Lithuania, twenty-five years later

Sarah's eyes flashed open. Lying in her thin bed, she turned in the direction of Adam, whom she could hear muttering again in his sleep. After a few moments, her eyes adjusted to the darkness and she looked at him across the stool's breadth they kept between their beds during the monthly period of separation. His pale face was coated with sweat although the room, to Sarah, felt cold. He brought his hand up past the thin growth of his beard, the black now well-flecked with gray, to the faded scar that ran across his right cheek, as though feeling it for the first time. Now, his whole body twitched, its long, gaunt frame moving like a marionette in the hands of a most inexpert puppeteer.

His thin mouth, quivering at the corners, turned into a frown. As if in sympathy, so did Sarah's. He was burdened with his secret pain and so was she with hers. Her right hand moved to touch the inside of her left wrist, then moved slowly up the inside of her arm. She could recall Adam's gentle touch, the touch that used to accompany their intimacies, the touch that had been lost somewhere along the way to the monthly, perfunctory relations that followed her visits to the ritual bath.

She shifted in her bed. She should rise. There was plenty to do today in preparation for Hersh's wedding tomorrow: clean her son's coat, hat, and breeches; complete the cooking; invite the village poor. She imagined that Adam's day would remain largely unchanged. He would rise and go to morning prayers. His morning would be spent at the synagogue teaching a class and deciding questions of law that the villagers put to him. Was this stew pot rendered impure by an inadvertent drop of milk? What should be done with that one who couldn't repay a loan? Who was responsible when Ruven's cow fell into a hole dug by Shimen and had to be destroyed? In the afternoon he would visit the sick and give coins to the poor from the communal fund. Likely, she wouldn't see him until well into the evening. After all, the job of a village rabbi required him to be available to his flock whenever they needed him. And when he did return home, he still wouldn't be there, not fully, not to her. Now, in his troubled sleep, she could feel the pain that his diffidence caused even to him.

But if he could no longer muster affection for her, at least, thank God, he showed it to their children. She recalled how Adam had spent many a Sabbath afternoon at the table with Hersh, conveying crucial lessons of the faith in a sweet, loving voice. One week it was how, because we are created in the image of the Holy One, Blessed be He, we must be kind and forgiving to each other, just as He is to us. Another time it was how each person is commanded to repair his wrongs—a bad habit perhaps, or an injury done to another—and, in so doing, to help repair the imperfect world in which we live. Sarah smiled at the thought of those overheard conversations, of the praise and encouragement that Adam heaped upon Hersh when it was clear that the boy understood his father's words.

She smiled, too, thinking of how he showed affection to their precious Mendel and Leah. Just the other day, Adam and the twins had been playing blind man's buff, the eight-year-olds giving their blindfolded father gentle buffs—just taps, really—as he tried, or pretended to try, to tag them. Their laughter had been contagious and Sarah, watching and listening from the window, found herself laughing as well.

But then, without thinking, little Leahele had asked, "Papa, what games did you play when you were little?" Adam had stared at her, stumped, as though he hadn't understood the words. Thank God he hadn't gotten angry, as he sometimes did when Sarah asked about his childhood or, indeed, about any of the years before he and Sarah had met. Adam hadn't answered his daughter, just as he never answered such questions from Sarah.

Whether he could not or would not answer such questions, however innocently asked, Sarah didn't know. For a long time, the distinction had mattered to her. But she did know that the shadow into which he so often retreated seemed to be growing larger and darker.

How different it all was from the day that the shy, orphaned student from the academy had come as a guest to her father's Sabbath table. He had not looked at her except when he thought she wasn't watching, but her peripheral vision had been better than he imagined.

"'Where there's no Scripture, there's no bread,'" her father had called out suddenly, quoting the Sages and commanding the attention of the twenty guests crowded into his dining room. "We have the bread, thank God, so we need the Scripture. Who can give us a thought?"

Half a dozen students had brayed like donkeys as they tried to outdo each other in showing off their erudition. Her father had not been impressed. "You, Adam!" his voice had rolled like thunder down the length of the fine table to the one boy who had tried to look inconspicuous. "A thought."

Adam had looked up quickly and blinked twice, as though confronted by a brilliant sun. But he hadn't faltered. "On the first verse of the Bible, the rabbis inform us that the first act of creation of the Holy One, Blessed be He, was the creation of the alphabet, and that by combining and recombining the letters into words, He brought into existence all that was to be."

"Excellent!" her father had bellowed. "May you be strengthened. And from this we learn what?"

Here Adam had paused. Sarah could see from his expression that he knew the answer. What was he waiting for? And then she knew: he was waiting for her.

"Father," she had interjected, with a boldness that surprised the others—and herself, "from this we learn that just as the Holy One, Blessed be He, created His world through His words, so we create our world through ours."

"Well done, Sarah!" her father had commended her, his face beaming with pride. "May you, too, be strengthened."

She had turned and smiled at Adam, who had become as red as the wine and busied himself with the soup. But after a moment he had met that smile with a crooked, embarrassed grin of his own, a smile that was all the more genuine for seeming so seldom used, a smile just for her.

That shyness had been a welcome contrast to the brashness of the others. Adam's awkwardness was temporary, she had told herself; it would soften after the wedding. *She* would soften it. For the first few months, his awkwardness *had* softened or, at least, she had thought so. But after their first anniversary, it was clear to her that his manner had instead congealed into a stiffness. She saw that stiffness in the way he sat at the breakfast table when he did return from morning prayers, averting his eyes, his shoulders perpetually stooped with some unseen burden. She heard it in his silence when one warm word would have given her much comfort during her own, increasingly frequent, moments of sadness. Oh, when was the last time they had drawn strength from each other by studying holy texts together? She couldn't remember.

At such thoughts Sarah faulted herself, not her husband. Adam provided for her and the children, at least as much as was within his power, which was far from the case with some husbands in the village. There was chicken on their table every Sabbath, where others, she knew, had only turnips. And he had never, ever, laid a hand on her or the children in anger. She knew she expected too much of Adam too much of the time. But as a girl, she had also seen the loving looks and heard the gentle words between her father and mother and had assumed that was the natural way between a husband and a wife. Was she wrong?

The memory of Adam's uncertain smile was a welcome reminder of what had been, and an unwelcome reminder of what was no more. For years, Sarah had tried to fight her husband's aloofness. Now, she felt only helplessness, her daily dose of pain. Maybe, she considered, their marriage was some sort of divine test. If so, she took comfort from the tradition that the Holy One, Blessed be He, never gave a person more pain than he could endure. She just hoped that the Holy One had calculated her measure of pain correctly.

Sarah turned over in her thin bed, away from her husband, and tried to return to her own troubled sleep.

Chapter Three

A dam looked across his reading stand at the two dozen men who sat in groups of twos and threes at the tables and benches that filled the little synagogue. The sun had long since set, the evening prayers concluded. Candles now burned from the wall sconces and on the tables, multiplying the shadows of each man and creating the impression, at least on the walls, of a hundred students or more. As he watched the shadows dance, Adam fancied that they were the shades of Lizenskers who had prayed and studied in this little room over the centuries, and maybe they were. The little synagogue was certainly old enough for that. Some said it was of incalculable age, having been not constructed by their ancestors but rather discovered by them, beneath the earth, and merely excavated.

Now, before the evening turned to night, was the time for study. A large volume of the law was opened before each group of men. These books told them what the Holy One, Blessed be He, expected of them: Which animals they could eat and how they must slaughter them. How many witnesses were needed at trial and how they should be examined. Which actions—cooking, writing, and cutting among them—were forbidden on the Sabbath. Who was permitted to make a binding vow and under what circumstances. Which times of the month they could have relations with their wives and how the women would prepare for that holy act.

Adam liked being the rabbi of Lizensk. He liked teaching Scripture and law to the villagers. He liked answering the villagers' questions on religious practice. And he liked that the job was more or less his for life. More, because there was once, he knew, a Lizensk rabbi who so loved giving sermons from

14

the pulpit that he continued to do so for months after his demise, until an exorcism could be successfully performed. And less, because he knew of another of his predecessors who had publicly rebuked an ignoramus who turned out to be a witch or a demon—there was no consensus on this point—and, for his trouble, was turned into an apple tree. To console the transformed rabbi as best they could, the villagers used his fruit, along with the traditional honey, to help celebrate each incoming new year. The tree still stood outside the synagogue and Adam, glancing out the window, could see it now. And it still bore apples although, with each passing year, the fruit proved increasingly bitter.

"Continuing from where we left off last evening," said Adam, gazing out at the men, his eyes alight with more than the reflected glow of the candles, "we learn from the Book of Courts that 'whomsoever saves a single human life,'" he bent over to consult the massive tome, "'Scripture regards it as though he saved the world entire and whomsoever destroys a single human life, Scripture regards it as though he destroyed the world entire.'" Adam straightened. "Why should this be so?"

An ancient, arthritic hand rose from the back of the synagogue.

"Per... per... perhaps, Rabbi... it's because the Master of the World... created all of humanity... from a single soul," said Gimpel Carrots, the sexton of the little synagogue, his words escaping like drips from cracked crockery as he struggled to complete the thought. His second name had been bestowed upon him by an impatient teacher who, focusing on his thick red hair, had once shrieked "Gimpel Carrots-for-brains!" The name, in shorter and less insulting form, still stuck after most of a century, long after the bush atop his head had dwindled to a few vague clouds of, remarkably, still-red hair.

"Very good," Adam told him, smiling. He addressed the others. "And why should the Master of the World create humanity in such a way?"

"So that no one should say that his forebears are better than anyone else's forebearers," this came from Daniel the Tanner, a somewhat disheveled and perpetually malodorous young man.

"Excellent!" said Adam, drawing enthusiasm from the growing enthusiasm of his students. He looked about the room "Anything else?"

"So that the disreputable among us cannot say that their fault lies in their blood, that they might not improve themselves," sniffed Eliezer the Bookbinder, looking pointedly at Daniel. Eliezer was the closest that Lizensk had to a dandy—with a ruffled shirt and velvet suit that more properly belonged on the fashionable promenades of Prague or Warsaw than the hamlet of Lizensk.

"So that the exalted among us cannot say that their virtue lies in their blood, that they might not fear sin," shot back Daniel to the exalted Eliezer, to the laughter of all the assembled. Eliezer gave Daniel a look of mock offense and then, with a shrug, joined in the laughter. In a village so small and isolated, no one could afford to stay mad at anyone else for long. The mood in the dim little synagogue brightened considerably.

"*Schnapps!*" someone called out and a bottle and stack of small tin cups appeared as though by magic. Adam never approved of liquor in the presence of the holy books and nearly objected, but caught himself just in time. The liquor would warm the men on the way back to their homes. More, it was a way for the men to celebrate, to honor the good fortune of their rabbi. Adam would not be ungracious.

"A t... t... toast to the father of the groom!" called out Gimple Carrots, his bony, slightly palsied hand rising like a reed buffeted by the breeze.

"To the father of the groom!" the room echoed, the men raising their cups toward Adam. He was pleased but could feel his face flush nonetheless. He was never comfortable being the center of attention. Tomorrow, at least, that would certainly not be an issue.

"To the rabbi! To Hersh!" called the men. "To life!"

And from a glance at the walls, it seemed to Adam that the shades of Lizensk were celebrating as well.

Chapter Four

Sarah, in her simple, dark blue dress, forced herself to smile and nod at the wedding guests from her high-backed chair in the center of the room. She knew there was no reason to be nervous, that the women's party was going exactly as planned, and that the ceremony itself would, too, but she found herself nervous nevertheless. But of course no one noticed her fidgeting; all eyes were on the bride, Miram, sitting next to her. Sarah and Miriam's mother, Feige—sitting on the other side of the bride—were merely the attendants. The women of Lizensk, now bedecked in their Sabbath finery, kept pressing closer toward the three of them, each woman hoping to receive a blessing from the bride. Goodness! Sarah fanned her neck with her handkerchief to stir a breeze but succeeded only in pushing the warm air toward her. Feige's home was large, but not large enough to contain them all, at least not comfortably.

One of Miriam's friends called excitedly to her, and Miriam pulled back her veil with a sweep of her hand. Her auburn hair fell away from her face, revealing large brown eyes that sparkled with anticipation and dimples that appeared and disappeared with the animation of her full, bright face. The Sages had once debated as to whether it was permissible to say that every bride was beautiful on her wedding day, when surely the compliment could not always be true; however, Sarah was certain that even the most discriminating Sage would have applied that appellation to this bride on this day.

One by one, Miriam's friends approached her and leaned down so that their whispered words could not be overheard. But Sarah, sitting so close, could not fail to overhear.

"Please, Miriam, ask the Holy One, Blessed be He, for my good health," rasped a thin, pale girl with dull eyes and listless blond hair.

"Of course I will, Golda," said Miriam. She closed her eyes and her lips moved silently as she beseeched the heavens for her friend.

"Miriam, a husband. Please pray that the Almighty sends me a husband who doesn't require a large dowry. I'll say yes, I promise," whispered another, a girl that Sarah recognized as coming from a family that, with seven daughters, could ill afford any dowry for their youngest, let alone a large one.

"Yes, Fruma, gladly," said Miriam, sealing her promise by embracing the girl's hands with her own. She closed her eyes, moved her lips, then looked again at her friend. "May it be this year."

While Miriam continued to pray on behalf of the others, Sarah found herself praying as well—for Miriam. Let her son Hersh provide for his wife, she asked silently of the Holy One, Blessed be He, just as Adam had provided for her and the children as best he could. Just as Adam had never raised his hand or his voice in anger against her or the children, let Hersh do the same. As Adam never let his eyes stray, so too let Hersh's eyes rest only on his wife.

As Adam... Sarah faltered now. She tried to think of other blessings to bestow on her soon-to-be daughter-in-law. Yes, Adam was a good husband—no one would say otherwise—but was it not also true that her husband moved through their home and their lives like a ghost? Dear God, she continued, her clasped hands buried in the folds of her blue dress, let Hersh always offer Miriam a kind word at day's end. Let Hersh's eyes light up upon seeing her unexpectedly. Let Hersh linger to talk with her after the Sabbath meal had been eaten and the dishes cleared away. Her throat suddenly felt tight.

Sarah wanted to speak to Miriam, to offer a blessing directly, but her attention was diverted by Basya, the doctor's wife, offering Sarah good wishes of her own. And Miriam too was occupied; out of the corner of her eye, Sarah could see that she was blessing an old woman dressed in tatters, one of the paupers with whom the wedding couple and their families shared their good fortune. Sarah smiled: The old woman had even come with a gift for Miriam, a necklace that she helped the bride to put on as she mumbled her thanks for the other's blessing.

Basya and the beggar woman retreated at the same time and Sarah seized the moment. She put her hand on the young woman's arm. "May every hope you have for your marriage be fulfilled," she said softly. Then she pulled Miriam close and hugged her, so that the young woman would not see the tear she could feel rolling down her cheek.

Just then the village women broke into song and danced around Miriam, Sarah, and Feige. They each moved two short, skipping steps to their right, twirled in place, took two short steps back to their left—their arms rising and falling like willow branches caressed by the wind—then repeated the movements over and over. Moments later the dance changed. Each woman made a hop toward the three women seated in the center and bowed deeply in a smooth, undulating motion. As the circle contracted and expanded with their movements, it resembled nothing so much as a beating heart.

Sarah's gaze moved from woman to woman. Here was Hindie the chandler's wife, with whom she had once quarreled over candles that were not quite long enough to burn for the required period on the Sabbath Eve; well, that was a very long time ago. There was Dvoire the Midwife, who had helped deliver the boy who today would become a husband. Sarah smiled as she looked at Yutke and Basya; they might be two old gossips but, although they moved more slowly and with less agility than the others, they were doing their part to bring joy to the bride. Some of these women were her friends, others were not, but they were all her community. And today she felt the affection they exuded for Sarah, Feige, and especially Miriam.

The women held out their arms, entreating the three to dance in the middle of the circle. Sarah smiled and shook her head, then tilted her chin toward Miriam and Feige. A bride and her mother deserved a special dance alone. She would join them later, after the ceremony. She watched as Feige and Miriam spun around each other in the center of the circle. Miriam's gown grazed the floor and her wedding belt, a gift from Hersh, caught the light and sent it shooting across the room like little bolts of lightning. How lovely, Sarah thought. And how lovely her own little daughter, Leah, looked, dancing on the periphery in the red velvet dress with lace collar, front, and cuffs that Sarah had spent hours sewing.

While the dancing continued, Leah slipped through the crush of women and rushed to her mother. Her eight-year-old eyes were wide, her smile bright, her face dappled with freckles like light through lace curtains. At her breast she clutched her favorite doll, Royzie, another freckled little girl, this one with a perfect porcelain head.

"Can we welcome Miriam to the family now?" Leah pleaded with her mother.

Sarah hesitated. "Not yet, Leah, dear," she murmured. One didn't take for granted what was still in the future and Miriam was not yet part of their family. To do otherwise was to invite bad luck and attract evil spirits.

"Mother, please let me welcome Miriam to the family!" Leah's voice quivered, squeezing her doll, whose head nodded as if to second the request.

Sarah barely suppressed a smile. Ah, how could she deny her? What harm could there be, really, in welcoming Miriam to the family before, rather than after, the ceremony? She couldn't bear quashing her daughter's sweet enthusiasm.

"Very well, welcome her now," Sarah replied, putting a gentle hand on her cheek. "If there's a sin in it, I take it upon myself."

Leah ran to the woman who would soon be her sister-in-law. Miriam was at the side of the room, deep in conversation with two of her friends. Leah cleared her throat twice before she caught the bride's attention.

"Sister Miriam," said Leah with all the formality the eight-year-old could muster. "On behalf of my mother, my father, Mendel, and me, welcome to our family." Then, she relaxed, noticed the doll in her hands, held it up, and added: "And Royzie welcomes you, too!"

Miriam's smile lit the room.

"What a dear, dear sister you will be," Miriam said to Leah. "Thank you!" She leaned forward and kissed Leah on the cheek. As she did so, Leah noticed something glistening just beneath the collar of the wedding dress and instinctively reached for it: a small green jewel on a thin gold chain.

"What a pretty necklace!" said Leah. She couldn't stop staring at it. Was the jewel merely catching the light or glowing on its own? "Where did you get it?"

"Necklace?" Miriam asked. "What necklace?" She quickly reached up toward her neck and fingered the jewel as though for the first time. "I don't know," she said after a moment, and with some confusion. "Was it a wedding present from Hersh?"

Chapter Five

Several streets away in the little synagogue, Adam watched from his bench as the men danced a far faster, rowdier version of the women's circle dance at Miriam's home. They held their hands on the shoulders of those on either side of them and raced about the circle, their feet executing complex moves that became a blur. The smaller men in the circle held on to their fellows that much tighter, for one missed step could send them flying across the room. Every few minutes, another pair of men would jump into the center of the circle to perform more elaborate steps—kicking high over each other's heads, whirring together like a two-man top, or circling at a languorous pace, arm in arm. The men's long black coats flapped like flags as they danced, fur hats regularly took flight, and ritual fringes and sidelocks took on erratic lives of their own.

Adam stood, his arms folded across his chest, enjoying the jubilance of the others without wishing to join them. He took in the joy of this day, the laughing and singing, the food and drink. He closed his eyes and a teaching of the Sages came to him: *The world is a wedding... The world is a wedding.* The pleasures of this world, like the pleasures of this wedding—the herring and the brandy, the lively tunes of the wedding musicians, the villagers on display in their finest clothes—were meant to be enjoyed. But the pleasures of this world, like the pleasures of this wedding, were fleeting. Was there no more? He knew that the bride and groom, at the center of it all, understood what the others might forget: that despite the distractions, this was a day of great holiness, a day when the world would change because two souls would become one.

And what was true for this bride and groom on this day was true for the world entire, every day: Life's pleasures were there for enjoyment, provided one didn't let them obscure the holy mission at the core of human existence. *The world is a wedding.*

Adam looked across the room and spotted his son Mendel, the boy's plump cheeks looking eminently pinchable, but the rest of him looking a bit forlorn. No doubt he missed his twin sister, Adam thought, feeling his son's loneliness as his own. There were Sarah's cousins, engaged in intense conversation that was either debate over a point of law or the imparting of the latest family gossip. Beyond them, Feivel the Merchant, who would soon be his son's father-in-law, was passing a glass of schnapps to a seated, much older, man: Feivel's own father. A troubling thought came to Adam. Where were *his* cousins, *his* own father? Did he even have relatives?

If only he could remember. His first memories began at the academy. He had called himself an orphan but was that even true? If it hadn't been true back then, it was likely true now, after the passage of so many years. If only he knew his parents' names and those of his siblings, if he *had* siblings. How had he performed at school? What sicknesses had befallen him as a child? What favorite foods had his mother made just for him? Where others had memories, he had only shadows, glimpses just beyond the peripheral vision of his mind that intruded upon his prayers, his studies, his time with Sarah and their children, just at the times he knew he should be closest to them. He chased after these shadows constantly. But one day, he feared, they would turn and chase after him.

Adam's spirits rose as he glimpsed Hersh step into the circle of dancers wearing his black satin coat and belt, and his large black satin hat. His son was tall and broad—taller and broader than his father, certainly—but moved with a grace that belied his bulk. His face, always strong and handsome, was lit by the twin fires of his blue eyes, and by a mouth arranged in a generous, radiant smile. A moment later Hersh was joined by his future father-in-law. In the face of Feivel's commanding presence, the other men instinctively stepped back, broadening the circle and giving Feivel and Hersh more room, which they immediately put to use. The two men faced each other and grasped each other's arms. Their legs rose high in the air and hit the floor with tremendous force. The steps continued as the two spun in clockwise circles, faster and faster, their bodies moving with the precision of the most intricate automata.

"Come, Rabbi Adam, you must join them!" Eliezer the Bookbinder, wearing his best velvet jacket, slapped Adam on his back, a familiarity he would never have attempted without the three shots of schnapps coursing through his veins.

Adam gently shook his head. "I prefer to watch from here. I'm not much of a dancer."

"Perhaps you could stick to the slower steps," urged the dandy of Lizensk. "Everyone wants to see you dancing. There's a time to watch and a time to do. And this is the time to do." Then, Eliezer moved closer to the circle of men, leaving Adam by his books.

Just then, his son rose above the crowd like a king, albeit a nervous one, as the men hoisted him up in a chair. Adam turned Eliezer's words over in his mind as the men swarmed around Hersh. *There's a time to watch and a time to do.* Well that was obvious enough. The trick, of course, was knowing the one from the other.

Adam gazed up at Hersh. His son's face was flush with excitement, his hands gripped tightly about the chair. The young man alternately laughed and roared that he was about to fall. And in witnessing his son's joy it seemed to him that Hersh would make a fine husband—in contrast to Adam himself. He knew he was not the husband that Sarah seemed to need. He knew it in a thousand tiny ways although, for the life of him, he couldn't think what he might do or say differently.

"It will yet be heard in Judea and Jerusalem: the sound of joy and the sound of gladness, the voice of the groom and the voice of the bride."

The rousing rendition of the wedding song yanked Adam from his gloom. It was time to celebrate, he reminded himself as Hersh returned to his seat of honor at the long table arranged along one wall. His brother, Mendel, sat next to him. Mendel was transfixed by the antics of the wedding clown, who juggled an increasing number of bells that rang merrily as they flew through the air in big, swooping circles. Mendel's thin, pale frame shook with laughter, his lively brown eyes glistened, his gap-toothed grin grew broader.

Meantime, the guests had taken to toasting the young groom.

"May you fall in love every day—and always with your bride! Amen." Drink.

"May you have many children, all beautiful, all scholars, all wealthy—and all renowned for their gratitude to their parents. Amen." Drink.

"May the roof over your heads never fall in and may you and your bride never fall out! Amen." Drink again.

Adam watched as Hersh poured a small glass of schnapps for his little brother. Adam was about to intervene, celebration or no, when Mendel took his first sip—and spit out the drink amid a barrage of coughing, his face turning red and his eyes watering.

Hersh found his brother a cup of water and a cloth for his face.

"Pay attention, Mendel," said Hersh, with mock solemnity. "Watch how a groom carries himself. It will be your turn before too long."

"I don't need to get married," Mendel insisted with all the fervor an eight-year-old could muster. "I have Leah. She's my twin. That's better than being married."

Hersh clapped a hand on Mendel's back. "Not entirely," he said, plucking the schnapps cup from his brother.

A moment later, Hersh was by his father's side. "Isn't there a law that a father must dance at his son's wedding?" Hersh asked of Adam with a smile. The men had broken out once more into dancing and Hersh was entreating his father to join them. Adam smiled weakly but said nothing.

"I'm the groom," Hersh reminded his father. "On this day I get what I wish. And what I wish is to dance with you."

Adam smiled, shook his head in exaggerated capitulation, and joined his son in the center of the circle. He held his son close. Hersh searched his father's face and frowned.

"Papa, you look troubled," he said. "What's wrong?"

Adam smiled up at the boy—no, at the young man—before him, who seemingly never doubted himself. "When you marry off your firstborn, you'll show me how I should have looked today," he answered, his words wistful but without reproach. He squeezed his son's shoulders and his eyes glistened. "My Hersh is so strong, so certain. Have I ever told you how much I admire you?"

Adam kissed his son on the cheek.

The musicians struck up a new tune: a wedding march. Adam smiled once again at his son. "It's time."

Chapter Six

A shout went up across the room and grew louder as more and more men joined the boisterous singing and clapping. They formed a horseshoe-shaped line around Hersh and Adam, with Feivel stepping in time to the music to join them. The village men led the three out of the synagogue, still singing.

"Blessed is He who created joy and celebration, bridegroom and bride, rejoicing, jubilation, pleasure and delight, love and brotherhood, peace and friendship!"

The violins and horns and flutes laughed and sobbed their tunes, flavoring their joy with an undercurrent of something else, something bittersweet.

The human torrent flowed down the street, wending its way through the village, to Mill Street, and finally into the house of Miriam and her family. They brought Hersh to the center of the room like an ocean wave depositing a trident's horn on the shore. There she was, veiled, seated, still, and gazing up at her groom as though she'd done nothing for days but wait for him. His mother sat to her left, her eyes gleaming with moisture. Miriam's mother sat to her daughter's right and daubed her eyes with a white lace handkerchief in a futile attempt to dam the steady flow of tears. And in the center of these women was his jewel.

Hersh stood before his bride, not moving, not speaking. His joy was too powerful for words.

"G-g-go on," cried Gimpel Carrots, standing with the men just a few feet away and waving his cane encouragingly, "M-m-make sure she's the right one!"

Thousands of years before, the wicked Lavan had tricked his nephew,

Jacob, into marrying his daughter Leah instead of her sister, Rachel. Ever since, the wedding ceremony had included this final meeting between groom and bride to prevent another such deception.

Hersh grinned and did as he'd been told.

The crowd pressed closer, giving Hersh and Miriam scant room.

Hersh leaned down, lifted Miriam's veil and looked into her bright, brown eyes, taking in her shiny auburn hair. After today she would cover it beneath a scarf, and only he, of the menfolk, would be able to glimpse it. He beheld Miriam in her white brocade dress and veil and forgot to breathe. She was a queen, his queen, and God help the man who ever tried to switch her with another. He lowered her veil with deliberation, inch by inch, until her lovely face was entirely swathed in white.

All too quickly, the cheering and singing began anew, the men sweeping up Hersh and escorting him out of the house. The river of joyfulness came crashing down the street and toward the village square. Four of Hersh's friends carried the wedding canopy, a prayer shawl tied to four poles and held aloft. Hersh and his family took their place under the canopy, open on all sides as a reminder to the newlyweds that their home should be welcoming to all guests. The villagers stood tightly packed all around like impenetrable waters about an island.

And then the waters parted. There stood Miriam, her mother and father on either side of her. Feivel had his daughter on his arm, his face red with an expression that looked to Hersh to be both happy and slightly sad. Miriam went to the center of the canopy and stood next to her groom. The seven blessings were made over a silver cup of wine and the wedding contract was read, binding Hersh to work for, esteem, feed, and support his wife, and to attend to his husbandly duties as befitted custom and tradition.

He placed a plain gold band on Miriam's right index finger, the finger whose artery, the Sages said, leads straight to the heart. Miriam circled Hersh seven times, the traditional prescription for tearing down the walls around a groom's heart, just as the ancient Israelites circled Jericho seven times to miraculously tear down its walls. As she passed around him, Hersh could feel the brush of her dress against his fine Sabbath trousers, tickling his leg.

Hersh watched with great anticipation as, finally, his father placed a glass goblet on the floor. Hersh brought his foot down hard; the sound of breaking glass cut through the air like a musket shot. Even at such a time, the broken temple in Jerusalem could not be forgotten, although the joyful shouts of "good luck!" that sprang from everyone's lips quickly dissipated that sad memory.

The villagers swarmed around Hersh and Miriam, this time escorting them through the streets toward Adam and Sarah's house, where they would be alone as man and wife for the first time. Leah and Mendel sang and clapped and followed the others, Mendel licking his lips at the thought of the wedding feast to come.

Suddenly, Leah cried out "Royzie! I forgot Royzie!"

"Don't worry, we'll find her," Mendel tried to calm her. "Where did you leave her?"

"In Miriam's house, I think," said Leah, her eyes beginning to tear. If anything had happened to her dear little Royzie…

"Then it's all right," said Mendel. "Let's go and get her."

The two children separated from the ebullient crowd and scampered to the big house on Mill Street. Leah was about to knock, then stopped. "Nobody's here," she reminded Mendel. "They're all at the wedding."

"That's all right," Mendel said. "Just go in. Aren't they family to us now?"

Leah opened the door and was about to step inside when she heard a raspy, high-pitched cry behind them.

"An imp!" Mendel shouted excitedly, pointing as a small, slimy-skinned creature in patchwork jacket and trousers darted into the tall grass against the side of the house. "I see an imp!"

"Well, you won't catch it," his sister said in an authoritative tone, pulling on his arm. "You're coming inside with me."

"This one I can catch," he insisted. "It's up against the side of the house. It has nowhere to hide." Then like a hound on the scent of a rabbit, Mendel ran off.

"Well, just wait for me here," she called after him. "I'll be right back."

Leah crossed the threshold and shut the door behind her. She looked under the chairs in which her mother, Miriam, and Feige had sat just half an hour before. The flowers on the white bridal chair had already started to wilt. She looked under the tables and chairs pushed to the walls of the parlor. She looked behind cushions, on bookshelves, even in the drawers of cabinets she knew she shouldn't open. Royzie wasn't anywhere. In a fit, she stomped her foot.

Leah heard a sound too faint for her to identify. Slowly she made out a voice, a woman's voice, lilting and pleasant. Somewhere upstairs, a woman was singing. Leah's first thought was to flee. But the woman's voice was so gentle, so sweet, that Leah moved without a thought toward the stairs. Who knew? Perhaps the woman had her Royzie or could tell her where to find it.

Leah reached the stairs, then climbed them. She was in the upper hallway and could hear the singing clearly now. It was a lullaby—and one that she recognized, one that had often worked its magic on her when she was younger.

Sleep, sleep, little one, my jewel, my gold,
Without a care in your head, you'll never grow old.

Leah stopped at the door through which the singing came. It was open but a crack. She pushed it open wider. In the darkness of the room, no one was visible. The singing stopped.

"Come here, little one," said the same sweet voice, sounding almost as musical as the lullaby.

"Who's there?" asked Leah in a small, uncertain voice, holding tight to the doorknob.

"Come here, Leahele," the voice urged. "It's all right."

It must be all right, thought Leah. *She knows me.* Leah took a step into the room, still holding onto the knob like a first-time swimmer holding onto the dock. Her eyes adjusted very slowly to the darkness—darkness that should still have been hours away.

She squinted and made out the woman's form. What little light spilled into the room from the hall revealed the woman's silky black hair and her pale skin. Now, Leah could make out her harsh, angular face. But it was the eyes, the shiny green eyes, that so fascinated the little girl. Leah stepped closer. And closer again, her hand releasing the knob. Like the swimmer losing his grip on the dock, Leah was at sea.

"I'm glad you came," said the woman. "I have something. I think it's yours."

The woman raised one arm. Leah cried with delight. There in the woman's hand was her doll, her Royzie. Leah ran to the woman, all her worries forgotten. The woman offered the doll to Leah, who hugged it against her chest.

"Thank you, thank you," said Leah, squeezing the doll so it could not get away.

"What a darling little girl you are," said the woman, her eyes riveted on Leah. "What lovely hair... " She brought her hand to Leah's head and caressed the girl's blond hair, as gently and lovingly as her mother had ever done. The woman leaned toward Leah and drank in the smell of the hair. She kissed Leah's head. Leah smiled.

"What beautiful skin," the woman continued, caressing and kissing Leah's forehead.

Leah continued to smile. Her lips felt strange, as though she could not stop smiling even if she wanted to. She felt numb, as though her body were no longer hers. Her smile lost its meaning as Leah's consciousness began to slip away.

"What sweet eyes," said the woman, kissing Leah on each one.

"And what a luscious little mouth." The woman kissed Leah full on the mouth. But there was nothing gentle about this kiss. With her lips firmly over Leah's, the woman sucked hungrily on the girl's soul, tearing it, wrenching it from her, attempting to absorb it piece by piece. Leah's body flailed and convulsed at the force of the rape, like reeds thrashing violently in a storm. Royzie slipped through her fingers, hitting the floor with a crash that splintered its porcelain head and sent the shards flying across the room.

Leah's eyes rolled up into her head.

From deep within her, Leah screamed at the intense pain and violation of the assault, the scream muffled by the mouth of the woman still affixed to her own. Her soul kicked and jabbed and scratched at the vicious animal that pulled at her, that ripped her away from her body. Leah's soul fought to retain her hold on her little mind, clutching onto whatever bit of the girl she could, trying so hard not to let go, even as she slipped further away.

Mendel wiped his sweaty forehead, breathing hard. In his eight years, he had caught moles, squirrels, and even rabbits, but he had not succeeded in catching his first imp. He threw his new cap down in disgust. Not only had he lost his prey, but at this very moment everyone else was off at the community hall, eating the puddings and stews and cakes for the celebration. There was even chocolate, or had been. He smacked his forehead with his palm. It would be just his luck to miss it. Leah should have been out by now. He would just leave her, he sulked. That would serve her right. Leah and her stupid Royzie. But he couldn't leave her, not his sister.

He picked up his cap and brushed it off—he could just imagine what his mother would say if she saw it dirty—then stepped into the house. The parlor was empty. How odd it looked with all the guests gone and the furniture still pushed into the corners.

"Leah?" he called out, his voice sounding hollow in the large room. If she was playing hide-and-seek with him...

He heard a sound above him, something hitting or falling against the upstairs floor. Leah had no business being upstairs in this house. He loved hide-and-seek, but not here, not now. They needed to leave, whether she'd found her silly doll or not. He climbed the stairs and looked down the long hallway, trying to guess from which room the sound had come. He could imagine his sister jumping out and shouting "boo!" Well, he wouldn't act surprised, not a bit. He walked along the passage and stopped before an open door. He peered into the darkness of the room behind it. Why so dark? The hairs on his neck prickled.

"Leah, Miriam's family is coming back," called Mendel without conviction, trying to draw his sister into the hall. "If you don't come right now, we're both going to get into trouble."

All was quiet. Mendel took a step into the room.

"Leah? Stop it! Come out now!"

Mendel made out the outline of a woman. A wedding guest? If so, she had to be one of Miriam's guests because he didn't know her. Something lay on the floor and she was holding the part of it that extended upward. *Leah's Royzie!* But no. It was too big to be a doll…

"Leah!" he cried out. "What happened to you?" He looked up at the woman. "What's wrong with my sister?"

"She's sleeping," said the woman in a voice soft and pure and sweet as milk. "See for yourself."

"But why would Leah sleep on the floor?" He ran to his sister and grabbed her by the shoulders and shook her a bit. "Leah?" he pleaded. But she just lay there, her little mouth slack. Mendel lifted his head toward the woman.

"Why won't she answer me?"

"Little boys always have so many questions."

"I'm not a little boy. I'm a big boy," corrected Mendel with indignation.

"Of course you are. That's why you need to take care of your sister."

Leah's face lolled to one side, the eyes empty. It had taken a moment, but Mendel's instincts had finally kicked in. He began to back away from the woman.

"Come here!" she demanded.

"No. What have you done to Leah?"

The woman's green eyes fairly lit up the room. "I'll show you," she said.

Chapter Seven

With their bodies twirling, arms raised and waving about, legs alternately stomping and kicking into air, the villagers escorted Hersh and Miriam to his parents' house, where the bride and groom would be alone for the first time as man and wife. The walk must have taken ten minutes or so, but it seemed to Hersh that they were transported there in just a moment. They entered the house while the villagers continued on to the communal hall for the wedding feast. Only Shimen and Sender, two friends of Hersh since childhood, remained outside the front door in the traditional role of marital guards, to ensure that no one intruded on the new couple.

Hersh shut the door behind them. He must have slammed it, because the resounding thunderclap surprised both him and Miriam. He gave his bride an exaggerated look of mock embarrassment, then smiled with warmth that was unmistakably genuine. They climbed the stairs to his bedroom, now transformed into their post-wedding seclusion room. A round table with a white linen cloth—one of his mother's finest, he knew—stood in the center of the room. Atop it sat plates with fish dumplings, vegetable puddings, roast chicken and beef, stuffed duck, his favorite pastries and a pot of tea. His gaze fell on the bed, covered with fresh linens, and he just as quickly glanced away.

Just then, a hunger pang jabbed at him. He'd been fasting all day and there were those delicious smells wafting over from the table. He knew that Miriam had been fasting too.

"Shall we have our first meal as man and wife?" he asked her with great

34

formality.

Miriam nodded and smiled. He strode to the table and pulled out a chair for her, as he'd rehearsed. He took his own seat opposite. Miriam gently removed the pins from her veil one by one and placed it on the bed, just beside her. Hersh's plate was beckoning to him. First, he made a plate for Miriam and handed it to her. Then, he took some meat for himself, cut a piece, and chewed with enthusiasm.

"Delicious; the puddings look good, too," he said, pointing with his drumstick.

Miriam joined him in the repast. The room was thick with the scent of the foods, mingled with the couple's mixed sense of elation and relief.

Miriam ate a piece of potato pudding, savoring the oniony taste. "Do you like this?" she asked after a moment. "I'll ask your mother for the recipe."

"And she'll approve of you even more than she does now," Hersh replied.

Looking at the table for inspiration, he picked up a spoonful of chicken soup. "Mother's soup is an elixir. You'll have to ask her for this recipe, too," he said, moving the spoon toward her. Just then, Hersh's hand twitched and several drops fell on the shoulder of her dress, the grease spots on the white fabric looked as discordant as coal on snow.

"I can't believe I did that!" said Hersh in an agonized tone, jumping up. He only half-heard Miriam's "don't worry" as he raced out of the room and returned with a damp towel. He came to her side, crouched beside her, and began to wipe the spreading stain.

His hand trembled as he realized he was touching his wife for the first time. He could feel the curve of her shoulder, the give of her flesh just under the fabric. He looked at Miriam, her face inches from his own. Her eyes were downcast, but he could see that they were blinking rapidly. He reached out toward her cheek and moved his fingers slowly down her cheekbone to her delicate jaw and chin. It was softer than he'd ever imagined. Her luminous skin radiated a warmth that stunned him.

"Miriam," he said in a low, aching voice. Her eyes met his and their lips came together gently, barely, exploring each other. After a moment, they relaxed their embrace and Miriam stood, stepped back toward the window, and looked out. She fingered a green pendant about her neck. It caught the light and sent beams scattering across the room, which was strange, since a curtain of clouds had slowly been drawn across the sky, leaving scant sunlight for reflection.

Miriam's face was pale, and her lips, those lips, now curved downward into a frown.

"What's wrong?" he asked.

Scarlet brushstrokes painted themselves across her cheeks. "Everyone knows," she said, twisting her fingers nervously. "Everyone knows we're alone here."

"Then come away from the window," he suggested, extending his arm in invitation. They embraced and kissed again. Then, they each turned from the other so they could undress unobserved. Hersh unbuttoned his shirt, the everyday gesture causing his heart to pound and ache in a way that thrilled him. He could hear Miriam, behind him, disrobing as well. Her breath seemed labored, heavy—unusual, but these were unusual circumstances for them both.

Hersh tossed his shirt over a chair, turned back to his bride—and caught his breath. He didn't understand what he was seeing. His mind couldn't take it in, as though he'd turned and found himself at the edge of a ravine, about to fall in. The shock of it sent sweat pouring from his body. God Almighty! Before him stood a massive thing of bristling brown fur, its enormous yellow-and-black eyes, aglow with evil, glaring at him. Hersh staggered back, wanting to get away, but the were-beast stood between him and the door. It emitted a low growl from its dark, filthy snout and curled back its lips, revealing teeth long and sharp as knives and glistening with saliva. Hersh could feel the intense heat of the creature's breath on his face, hot, putrid breath that made him want to retch. And without comprehending what he saw, he glimpsed the green jewel, glowing now, buried in the thick fur around the beast's neck.

Chapter Eight

Shimen and Sender slouched against the front door of Adam's house, honored to be chosen as wedding guards but a bit regretful that they'd turned down Rabbi Adam's earlier offer of a bench on which to sit. Shimen, tall and lanky, was dreaming of the schnapps he was missing at the wedding feast. Meanwhile, Sender rubbed his belly, still hoping for the mutton and pickled cow's tongue that awaited him at the banquet—if they weren't consumed by the time he got there. When would he and Shimen be able to join the others? Some wedding couples took a few minutes to kiss and eat and then joined the celebration. Others took longer. There was no way of knowing how long Hersh and Miriam would be. He just hoped that there'd be some tongue left for him when he got to the community hall.

They mistook the first cry for revelry, and merely grinned at each other, imagining the scene inside. They made no mistake about the second cry, a long, fearful plea for help. Shimen and Sender looked at each other in confusion, then realized they would have to do what no marital guard had ever done before: intrude on the wedding couple in the seclusion room. They ran into the house just as they heard the third cry, an agonized wail of white-hot pain and terror.

The villagers, feasting and celebrating around the corner at the community hall, had heard the screams too. The braver and more clear-headed among them raced toward the sounds, Feivel and Adam in the lead.

At the house, Shimen and Sender raced up the stairs and flung open the door to their friend's room. The room was in ruins—chairs and table smashed, the bed shattered against a wall, its straw scattered everywhere—and, in the center of it all, a were-beast of immense proportions towered over Hersh, who was sprawled bloodied and semi-conscious on the floor. The creature raised its massive paws, each tipped with a row of dagger-sharp claws, and Shimen and Sender stood transfixed. A half moan, half whimper from their friend brought them to their senses. They couldn't see Miriam—where *was* she?—but they could try to save Hersh. Sender, the shorter and stockier of the pair, swept up a broken table leg from the floor to use as a club. Shimen grabbed the remnant of a ceramic plate from a table as a makeshift knife. They moved slowly toward their prostrate friend, all the while brandishing their weapons. The were-beast swept both them and their weapons aside with its massive paws. The two young men were thrown across the room where they slammed against the wall. They fell onto the floor like discarded dolls, their heads and spines twisted in ways that made life impossible.

The wedding party reached the doorway of Hersh's room. They stared in horror at the destruction, the bloody, mangled bodies, and the were-beast—its muscles flexing under its thick fur, its chest heaving, its nostrils flaring. Feivel turned to Adam to ask if he had a weapon in the house—but Adam was no longer at his side.

He had dashed as fast as he could to his own room, across the passage. He yanked his musket from its hiding place beneath his bed, together with several small pouches. His fingers knew what to do, pouring in powder, then the balls and wadding, and packing it tight.

"Please God, save the children, save the children," he repeated over and over as he pushed through the crowd to his son's room. He raised the musket and took aim at the creature… He would have but a single shot. Should he aim for the head? For the heart? His arms trembled. What would kill the unholy thing? He had never killed a were-beast before—no one in the village had.

A shot rang out. The green jewel flew from the creature's neck. The were-beast looked at the wedding party, stunned and bewildered. It brought up a paw to the blood that was flowing freely from its shoulder and neck, matting the fur across its chest. Its glistening teeth disappeared under its thick, dark lips. The quivering nostrils at the end of its great snout were still. The astonishment dropped away from its face, replaced by a vacant, lifeless expression. The were-beast sank to the floor with a thud that shook the house, and moved no more.

Adam felt for his musket. It was gone. He saw it in the hands of Feivel, smoke wafting from the barrel. Without taking time to piece together when Feivel had taken the musket from him, Adam ran to his son's side. Hersh's chest was a bloody mess, with deep wounds where the beast had mauled him.

Sudden cries from the wedding party jerked his attention from his son. Where the were-beast had fallen was no monster but a woman, Miriam, unconscious or worse, her shoulder torn and bleeding, her limbs twisted ominously. Feivel started toward her, his face gray as the grave.

He was pushed out of the way by Sarah and Dinah. The mothers threw themselves toward their children, holding them, cradling them, screaming for help, not knowing if they were still alive nor, if they were, how long they might remain so. Several of the villagers rushed to their aid, the women trying vainly to comfort them, the men lifting the newlyweds onto the beds, oblivious to the blood seeping onto their hands and clothes. Gimpel Carrots and Eliezer the Bookbinder helped a dazed Adam to a chair. He sat there but a moment.

"No, no," he insisted, unable to say much more. "Hersh... Miriam... Hersh..."

He rose with care, his knees unready for the effort, and collapsed on the floor. One of his hands landed on something sharp that stung his palm. It was a green jewel at the end of a thin gold chain.

Chapter Nine

In theory, it had been a reasonable place to build an inn, midway between the village of Lizensk and the much larger town of Brinnitz. And when the now-ancient inn was young, perhaps there had been sufficient traffic between the village and the town to support an innkeeper and his family. But, if so, those days were long gone. If a peddler stopped for a drink and a meal before nightfall, it was a good day. If the inn was graced by a wagonload of rabbinical students on their way to their academy, or of pilgrims beginning the long journey to the Holy Land or concluding their long journey from it, it was a day to remember. Mostly, though, the inn remained a forlorn outpost on a half-forgotten road, its thatched roof thinning in ragged spots like an old beggar's balding pate, its aging brick peeking out here and there from behind the walls of weathered and peeling dun-colored plaster.

The lack of business weighed upon Yankel, the leaseholder and innkeeper, but mainly because it meant that Reva, his wife, was denied the material pleasures he would otherwise have taken such joy in giving to her. But there was a far graver gap in their lives than the absence of porcelain dishes or silver teapots. Perhaps because of the physical toll of maintaining the inn, perhaps because of some demon curse, perhaps because of a sin of which they were unaware, Yankel and Reva had no children. Reva had miscarriages the way other women had birthdays but, still, they tried. In the meantime, the inn was their child, and a backward one at that.

On fierce, stormy nights like this, Yankel and Reva warmed themselves by the hearth and celebrated the good fortune they had, at least, in each other.

It was said that the Holy One, Blessed be He, found it easier to part the Red Sea than to make a match between husband and wife; if so, He had achieved a great miracle indeed by bringing together Yankel and Reva.

The door of the inn opened and a figure stood in the frame, silhouetted by the curtain of moonlit rain. The inn's lanterns swayed in the wind, sending shadows flying across the walls. Before the innkeeper and his wife could rise, the figure had stepped into the inn and closed the door.

As the figure moved closer to the lights, it took on both age and sex: it was an old woman, short and shapeless in a coarse brown cloak that reached to the ground and a hood that shadowed and obscured her features. When she dropped the hood, Yankel and Reva saw a well-lined, jowly, and squarish face. Her brows were gray and bushy, and her small, twinkling eyes were framed by heavy lids above and heavy bags below. A pair of perfectly round spectacles were perched atop her great mound of a nose. Below it was one of the smallest, thinnest mouths that the innkeeper and his wife had ever seen. The old woman wore a dark kerchief from which strands of gray hair sought to escape. The same thought occurred to Yankel and Reva at the same time: it was remarkable that this old woman had made it to their inn on such a night—and from where could she have come?

The woman approached them, moving with a deliberateness of purpose that seemed at odds with her many years, and making her presence at least somewhat less improbable—although what that purpose might be, Yankel and Reva couldn't think to guess.

"A guest! Welcome!" said Yankel, straightening himself up and stepping forward from the fire. "You've come to the right place. We haven't had the opportunity to welcome a guest in several days."

The old woman turned a bit to face them, as if seeing them in the dimly lit room for the first time. She scrutinized them—first Reva, then Yankel, then Reva again—and then she smiled. "Yes, quite; for a moment, I wasn't sure," she said, somewhat cryptically, in a gravelly voice. "But I do expect this is the right place."

"We've been busier, that's true," said Yankel, oblivious to the discordant note in her reply. "But no matter. A guest, a guest!"

He lifted his black skullcap with one hand and ran his other hand through his unkempt black hair as though to comb it. He plopped the skullcap back down on his hair, which remained unkempt. "Delighted to have you here—and, especially, *in* here, when it's so inhospitable outside."

Yankel introduced himself and his wife. "Pleased to meet you," said the old woman, removing her cloak to reveal a squat frame almost as wide as it was tall.

Reva stepped forward. "You must sit down. Would you like something to drink? Some tea to warm you, perhaps?"

"May the Almighty repay your kindness through a hundred generations," said the old woman appreciatively. The sad look that passed between the innkeeper and his wife was so quick that the old woman could not have been expected to notice it. Yankel took her cloak and ushered her to a table. He offered to take the parcel she carried but the old woman declined, keeping it at her side. She took a quick glance about the room as she eased her great bulk into the chair. "So I'm your only guest?"

"Tonight, last night, the night before… but we manage."

Reva was pouring tea for the old woman as the door burst open again.

The peasant who entered strutted to a table, his muscular body evident under the filthy, torn clothes that flapped about him. He dropped into a chair, its thin legs creaking with an audible gasp under his weight.

"Innkeeper, some ale!" he barked, pounding the table. He scowled and his unwashed face looked even more malevolent than it had a moment before.

The old woman raised a bushy brow and glanced at her hosts, who shared a knowing, wary look. They were familiar with Henrik and, even given the paucity of business, were not particularly happy to see him. Henrik was probably as unhappy to see them, since he would much rather have been in his own bed, rattling the walls with his snoring. It was only an errand for his employer, the Polish duke who owned all the land for miles in every direction—including the inn—that could cause him to be out on such a foul night. But nothing, apparently, could cause him to be happy about it. Henrik snorted. The best approach to keep him from breaking the furniture, Yankel knew, was to humor him.

42

"Ale. Of course. Coming right up."

"And some food!" Henrik bellowed, just as Reva was bringing a bowl of stew to the old woman. Henrik grabbed the bowl from her and set it down before himself.

"But that's meant for this lady," protested Reva, without thinking of the argument she might be provoking. Henrik looked at her, his eyes narrowing as though he were considering whether to snarl at her or strike her as, indeed, he was.

"That's quite all right, my dear," the old woman interjected in a voice that was calm and matter-of-fact, as though they were talking about a few drops of tea spilled on a tablecloth.

"See?" said Henrik with a broad smile that displayed as many gaps as teeth. "It's quite all right. And more ale, keep it coming!"

Henrik laughed, a deep braying sound that filled the room. For the next half hour, Yankel and Reva brought Henrik ale, and mead, and wineskins, and every bit of food they had. The man was insatiable and ate like an animal, lowering his head into the food as though at a trough and tearing at it with his teeth. Through it all, the old woman sat impassively, almost as though she were not there.

"More, more!" Henrik growled after a lull in the arrival of bowls and dishes containing the last of the stew and some chicken that had been broiled in the fire.

"There is no more, I'm afraid," said Yankel, wiping the sweat from his pale, high forehead. "We weren't expecting so much... business."

"And you call yourselves innkeepers!" Henrik rose and started for the door. "I have half a mind to tell the duke to throw you two out of here."

Yankel thought that Henrik's estimate of his intellectual capacity was probably generous, but it was a thought he knew to keep to himself. There was another matter, however, that he did need to broach. He coughed meaningfully. "Um... about the bill?"

"You can get it from the duke," Henrik replied, snorting at his own joke. So that would be that. Yankel and Reva looked down, afraid to make the situation worse.

The old woman hoisted herself up from her chair. In a voice that was as soft as Yankel's, but with unmistakable authority, she said simply: "That's not right."

"What's that, grandma?" Henrik came threateningly close to her. His massive bulk towered over the short, squat woman. She appeared not to notice.

"Please don't—" began Yankel, knowing this could not end well for the old woman.

"I said," she repeated to Henrik in her matter-of-fact tone, "that's not right. You took their food. You owe them payment. Surely the concept is not beyond you?"

"If you weren't an old woman…" Henrik's nostrils flared and his face reddened as though her age and sex might not be sufficient to keep him from fulfilling the unexpressed threat. Then Henrik saw a coin on the old woman's table. He picked it up, wondering for a moment about the strange marks on it. It wasn't a groschen or a kopeck. It certainly wasn't a ruble. It didn't even look valuable. But a coin was a coin. "You're so concerned that I pay the innkeeper, *you* loan me the money," he leered at her.

Through her nose spectacles, the old woman held his gaze as though he were no more a threat than an unruly schoolboy. "You don't want to use that coin."

"And why not?"

"By the grace of the Holy One, Blessed be He, it sets things right."

"All the better!" Henrik mocked. Then he squinted at the coin. "What do you mean: *Sets things right?*" he asked.

"A little something I picked up in my travels."

Henrik was unimpressed. "And now it looks like *I've* picked it up."

The old woman appeared to make a decision. "As you prefer." She turned away.

Henrik turned to Yankel and Reva and smiled. Paying them with a worthless coin that wasn't even his seemed like the perfect joke. "Here's your payment." He tossed the coin to Reva and started to leave. He didn't get far. Henrik began to gasp, and then to shake, and then to convulse. He jerked about the room, stumbling into tables and benches as though he were being pushed and pulled by invisible hands. His ears and nose began to twitch, to change colors, and to grow. His eyes grew large and black and moved to the sides of his elongating head. His hands became misshapen, big black things that clawed at the air. Something long and thick and dark dropped down from under the back of his shirt and hung there: a tail. He fell to the floor and began to run about on all fours. His clothes fell away from his body, which was now covered with gray fur. Henrik was a donkey.

Henrik brayed and brayed again, the sound a bizarre parody of the aggressive tone he'd taken before. He glared at Yankel and Reva with his large black eyes, half threatening, half imploring. They stared back, unable to move, let alone to help him, had they been so inclined. He ran into a table and, with a toss of his massive head and crest, threw it across the room. The sound of it crashing against the wall sent Henrik galloping in panic toward the old wooden door. He burst into it without pause, sending it off its hinges, and disappeared into the night.

For a long moment, all was still in the little inn. Then Reva ran to her husband and clutched him for safety. Only then did the couple remember that they were not alone. They turned to the old woman, who stood across the room, and stared at her in awe and trepidation.

"Now the outside reflects the inside; that's all," she said calmly, looking out through the broken door into the night, with an expression that could have been a smile—*would* have been a smile—had they known her better. "Sometimes the coin makes the inside reflect the outside. He'll be back to normal by morning. But perhaps the experience will give him something to think about. One can hope."

Reva looked down at her hand and her face grew pale. "*I* have the coin!" she cried. "I've got to get rid of it!"

The old woman hadn't been standing next to them—or had she?—but there she was now. She closed Reva's hand over the coin. There was no mistaking her smile this time.

"If you have the coin, then no doubt you were meant to have it," she said, putting several kopecks on the table. "And here are a few more coins to pay for your charming hospitality."

Whatever worries the couple had were washed away by the old woman's soothing tone and generosity. But something else was on Yankel's mind.

"Surely you're not leaving in the middle of the night," he objected. "It's still raining. It's dangerous. We could make up a room for you."

"I'll be fine – and there is somewhere I need to be," she countered, casting her head upward a bit and tilting it to one side, as though listening to a sound they couldn't hear. "I'm already late. I just hope I'm not too late."

She went to the doorway, adjusted her nose spectacles, retrieved her parcel and her cloak, and turned to her hosts. "May the Almighty repay your kindness through a hundred generations," she said and left.

Yankel and Reva went to the doorway—Yankel would have to put the door back on its hinges before they could sleep, *if* they could sleep—and watched the stranger disappear into the darkness. They realized at the same moment that they were holding hands and leaned into each other.

What they did not realize, could not realize, was that in nine months' time, Reva would give birth to a boy, whom she and Yankel would name Gershom, meaning "a stranger there." A remarkable student at an early age, Gershom would grow up to become a renowned scholar of holy books, a master of kindness, and the founder of a rabbinic dynasty lasting for a hundred generations.

Though they knew none of this, they continued for a while to watch the spot where they'd lost sight of the old woman. Then Yankel smiled with tenderness at Reva. She returned his smile and gently squeezed his hand.

Chapter Ten

"Mendel! My God, Mendel!"

Adam's voice, hoarse from hours of calling out in the darkness, was a low rasp, a saw pulled with great effort through hard wood. He held his lantern high, trying to dispel the shadows that closed about him, but the stubborn light would travel no farther than his voice. He had been down Synagogue Street and Mill Street and School Street and almost every other street in the village in the hours since the calamity, without result. Other Lizenskers punctuated the night with cries of the boy's name that sounded like echoes of Adam's own pleas. But as the night wore on, fewer and fewer villagers seemed to be abroad. Who could blame them? They were terrified. What should have been a day of joy had turned into a day of horror such as the villagers of Lizensk had not experienced in a generation.

"How could this happen in our village, a righteous village?" they asked each other in hushed tones. Had Hersh committed a grievous sin? Had Miriam? Had—the thought skittered through their minds, though none gave voice to it—their rabbi? They might also have asked if their own sins were to blame, but this thought did not occur to them.

Some blamed a sorcerer; one might well have taken revenge for a long-forgotten slight. Some feared a demon. "But what type of demon goes about in daylight?" worried Eliezer the Bookbinder.

Daniel the Tanner had a more practical concern: "And how do we protect ourselves against a demon like that?" The men nodded: The tanner had identified the crux of the matter.

But on this night, these whispers fell short of Adam's ears.

"Rabbi Adam, any news?" It was Gimpel Carrots, good old Gimpel Carrots, lantern in one hand, walking stick in the other, making his way toward Adam, his thin, red hair, whipped by the wind, flying about him like a halo.

"No." The word fell from Adam like a stone. It was too much for him to bear. Mendel gone. Leah unconscious and nearly dead. Hersh and Miriam, unconscious too, though whether from their physical wounds or the spell in which they were caught, who could tell? Shimen and Sender, may their memories be for a blessing, already buried, as tradition required. Who could withstand such sorrow?

Gimpel Carrots touched Adam's arm. "Don't worry, Rabbi," he said, looking up at Adam with something approaching conviction. "We'll find Mendel." He smiled a near toothless grin with evident effort to comfort the rabbi, then wandered off down the street and disappeared around the corner of the inn.

Adam continued to stare after him, even after he was gone. Dread coiled in his stomach like a snake. Sporadically, he heard cries of "Mendel! Mendel!" from villagers down by the river, by the mill, by the square, like birds calling out with resignation to mates that could not hear them. Adam feared that Mendel was as lost as the feathers of Chelm, scattered in the wind.

Would the other children slip away from him as well? Just hours before, Ezra, the grizzled old doctor, had dressed Hersh's and Miriam's wounds and dispensed amulets liberally, yet he was powerless to reverse the spell that kept both newlyweds cold and still. Sarah had hovered close by, her face continually shifting between faint hope and outright despair, waiting for the doctor to offer a word, just a word, of optimism. But he'd declined. "I'm a physician," he told her grimly, "not a false prophet."

The cold night wind stung Adam's face, undeterred by the meager protection of his wispy black-and-gray beard. His hands were numb. He held each in turn close to the lamp to warm them then, holding the lamp in his left hand, stuffed his right hand into his coat pocket to preserve its renewed warmth. His hand brushed against something cold and smooth. Ah, the green jewel from Hersh's room.

Adam looked out into the night. He could see lanterns and their dimly illuminated owners returning to their homes. One by one, the lanterns were extinguished. The search was over, at least for the others. He thought of Sarah, at home, tending to Hersh and Miriam and Leah, changing bandages, applying compresses, sitting and fretting. She had said nothing to him. Well, this was no time for conversation, he had told himself. There was too much to attend to. He kept walking, calling, searching. There was nothing else for him to do.

What time was it—one, two in the morning? And how long had he been there? Adam didn't remember fleeing to the little wooden synagogue but there he was, a massive tome of the law open before him. A pair of candles, along with his lantern, threw a small circle of light on the words and the worn wooden surface of his reading stand; beyond that lay the dark. Adam leaned into the book before him, letting the page become his entire world.

A ritual booth that is taller than twenty cubits is invalid. Rabbi Judah says it is valid.

Adam moved his finger and his gaze across the text, from the passage to the commentaries in smaller type along the margins, then back to the main text.

A ritual booth made thirty days or more before the Festival of Booths, the school of Shammai declares it invalid. And the school of Hillel declares it valid.

Adam continued in this way, his focus shifting between the law and its commentators, following their debates across the centuries from Babylonia to Europe as they worked out the meaning of the holy instruction. Its rhythms enveloped him as they always did. Unlike the world in which he lived, the law was knowable, the disputes clear, the controlling opinions decisive: pure or impure, permitted or forbidden, kosher or not kosher. This was the attraction of the law to Adam: a clarity of which he was very much in need.

A shadow fell across the page and Adam looked up.

Sarah stood before him, the light casting deep upward shadows across her round face and giving her narrowed eyes a harsh glow. He hadn't heard her enter the synagogue. A gryphon or even a ziz could have flown in the front door without disturbing him, so immersed had he been in his studies. Given what he saw in her face, Adam would have preferred the raptors.

"Where have you been?" she said, her tone making clear that she was not really asking a question.

"I looked everywhere for Mendel, we all did," he said without expression. "There was nothing more to do until morning, so I came here. Perhaps in the merit of this study, the Holy One, Blessed be He, will return Mendel and save Leah and Hersh and Miriam," he said after a moment.

"'In the merit of this study!'" Sarah muttered. She looked upward as though beseeching the rafters not so far from her head. "He studies and he studies and he studies while our family is destroyed."

Adam stared at her in astonishment. He had never seen Sarah like this before. *It's the suffering*, he told himself. *That's what's making her speak like this. What mother would be any different?* He recalled the words of the Sages, that parents ushered children into *this* world, while children ushered their parents into the world to come. That's the way it was supposed to be. Not like this.

"Sarah," he said, rising from his place and stepping out from behind the reading stand. "I know how difficult this is. I—"

"Listen to me," she interrupted him, her voice rising, her short body trembling. "For our entire lives together, I've been a good wife. I've tithed. I've gone to the ritual bath every month. I've kept our kitchen according to the dietary laws. I've baked the Sabbath bread and kindled the Sabbath lights. And as the affection went away, I've consoled myself with the thought that at least I have a husband who studies the holy texts.

"But now I ask you," she continued, taking a step closer, her hands pressed in tight, white fists against her stained apron. "What good are your books? Has your study helped *any* of our children?"

Adam felt a throbbing in his jaw. He was clenching it so hard he could imagine it breaking.

"No, it hasn't." He swallowed hard. "Still, there is a reason for everything. There must be a reason this is happening."

"Reason?" Sarah snapped, her arms dropping like weights to her sides. "You think you live in so ordered a world? This isn't the world of your books." She lifted one of those arms now and waved it in the direction of the shelves, sagging with their holy tomes, as though she could banish them with a motion. "Look around you: death, disease, demons everywhere you turn. There is no reason here."

He shuddered. Something strange possessed her. He saw abject woe in the sharpness of her eyes, the darkness of her cheeks, the deepening lines in her brow and around her mouth. But he saw something else too: a depth of feeling of which he had forgotten she was capable. That raw emotion had died within him and he had thought it had died within her, too.

The little synagogue was silent, except for the labored breathing of its two occupants.

"I have to believe there is a reason, even for evil," he said, holding out his hands as though the gesture might persuade her. "If I could only find it..."

He left unspoken the converse: *If, on the other hand, there is no reason for this, then perhaps there is no reason, no meaning, for anything.* That, perhaps, was the ultimate blasphemy, and it would not emerge from *his* lips.

Adam turned toward the bookshelves and the very books Sarah had mocked as ineffectual. *Turn it, turn it, for everything is in it,* the Sages had said of the holy books. His hand passed along scores of volumes, books tall and short, thick and thin, books bound in fine leather and embossed with gold and books bound in crumbling parchment and cloth, books with gilt-edged pages and books with pages untrimmed, books written in the holy tongue, in the vernacular, in the language of the ancients, in languages spoken throughout Europe and beyond. But these were not the books he needed now. That was becoming clear to him.

He could feel Sarah's eyes like dragon's breath on his back as he pulled a dozen volumes from the uppermost shelf, beyond the reach and the notice of most worshippers in the little synagogue. Some were as small as a finger's-breadth, others large enough to strain both his arms. These were not books often consulted by the villagers, for these volumes were too powerful and too dangerous for most. Adam had always included himself in the category of those not ready for such instruction so, although he knew their names, he knew little more than that. These were the books of the Kabbalah: the Zohar, the Book of Creation, the Book of Brightness, the Sword of Moses, the Book of Raziel the Angel—said to be written by the first Adam—and more recent works by Rabbi Judah Lev, also known as the Maharal of Prague, and by the Arizal, the Ramak, and other Kabbalists of the mystical city of Safed in the distant holy land.

He peered sideways at Sarah, who was watching without comment, her skepticism perhaps checked by his burst of activity. He skimmed through first one work and then another, searching, searching. His intense gaze did not alight on any page for more than a moment as he compared the texts from book to book. As his study continued, sweat appeared on his brow, which he brushed away with his sleeve like an automaton.

The Kabbalistic books contained many intricate drawings and charts, of the ten divine emanations through which the Holy One, Blessed be He, reveals himself to humanity, of the forty-nine distinct connections between the lower spheres and the upper spheres, of the power of the alphabet to transform reality. But one drawing made him stop.

He stared at an image of a jewel in a triangular cut, the facets of which seemed to continue on and on inside the stone, without end. It was mounted in a filigree setting that held it at five points, two at the top, two at the sides, and one at the bottom. He bent over and squinted to examine the drawing.

After a moment, he reached into his pocket and pulled out a length of metal chain. On the chain was the green, triangular jewel in a five-point filigree setting. He set it down on the yellowed and mottled page, next to the illustration and sucked in his breath. They were so similar, the one appeared to have been drawn from the other.

Next to the drawing were small, densely packed words that extended down the entire page. Adam bent low over the book to read them. After a moment, he mouthed a single word and fell back in his chair as though he'd been pushed.

"What is it?" Sarah asked, bending over to see the page for herself. She looked first at the drawing and then at the jewel itself. And then she read the name of the creature to whom it belonged, a name that all the village—all the world—knew, but that none dared utter:

Lilith, Queen of Demons.

Sarah shuddered and put a hand on Adam's desk to steady herself. "Adam, is *she* responsible for all this?" She said in a whisper.

Adam nodded, but only with great effort.

Sarah's face went ashen. "How are we to save our children from *her*?"

He had no answer. He looked down and began to finger his thin beard.

"I don't know," he murmured after a while and glanced up at her. The taut face, flush like a bonfire, that had signaled Sarah's anger, was gone. In its place was a look all too familiar to him, a face pale and lifeless. No, not devoid of life: devoid of hope. She looked... old.

"So the children are gone," she said without emotion. "And they won't be coming back."

"Sarah..." Adam started to say. Sarah looked at him, the rancor gone from her eyes, and shook her head. Then, she began to shuffle toward the door.

"Sarah!" he called again. He watched as she left the little synagogue.

Alone in his chair, or as alone as one could be in a room infused with the spirits of generations of Lizenskers, Adam's mind drifted to a dark and unforgiving place: Lilith.

She was a demon who had existed from the dawn of creation; of course Adam knew the lore. Lilith had been the mate of the first Adam until she rejected the ways of the Holy One, Blessed be He, who had created them both, and was expelled from the Garden of Eden. Taking the form of a serpent, she ensured that Adam and Eve, too, were expelled from the Garden, condemning humanity to toil and pain. From there, her evil only grew. She knew her prey well, knew the weakness within each human heart and used that knowledge to advance the doom of humanity.

Indeed, a piece of her was already lodged deep within every person: the piece that inclines one to evil rather than to good. Just as she had enticed Eve in the Garden, she used the evil inclination to tempt, to taunt, and to embolden the weak, the envious, and the ambitious. The young and innocent—that is, the most vulnerable—were her particular prize. She would snatch a child's soul, or the child entire, in a heartbeat, as she had done to poor Leah and Mendel. She could steal away the souls or lives of bridegrooms, or leave them as good as dead, as she had done with dear Hersh. If she could only spur a soul to a minor sin, that was enough. Lilith was patient. Once the soul was tarnished, the bigger sins would come and the soul would be hers.

Adam started to rise, then let his weight fall back into the chair, and glanced again across the old wooden walls and furniture of the little synagogue. At the academy, Adam's teachers had prohibited him and his fellow students from delving into dangerous knowledge. It was best left to older, more experienced minds; a younger man could go insane, they cautioned him, or fall under the spell of the very thing against which he was seeking protection. Well, now he was forty, wasn't he? Now he was married; now most would say he was well-versed in Scripture and law. And now he had a lot to learn and little time in which to learn it.

He needed a way to destroy her. What had the Sages said? That the Holy One, Blessed be He, creates the cure before the disease. If so, then surely the instrument of Lilith's destruction had been created before the she-devil was born. There had to be an amulet, a prayer, some force to be used against her. He went back to the volumes on the reading stand before him and scanned page after page, book after book, as a precious hour passed. But neither the Sages, nor the Ancients who preceded them, nor the Latter Scholars who followed them, had anything to suggest.

"Master of the Universe," he prayed, his lips moving, but no sound emerging from them, "Help me."

Help, he knew, would not come this night. Better to sleep for the few hours before morning prayer and start again. Adam rolled up his coat to use as a pillow and put it on the end of one of the benches. It would be best to sleep in the synagogue, so as not to disturb his wife further. He blew out the lantern and did the same with the candles on his reading stand. But the darkness was still held at bay by a candle burning in the back of the room, near the door. Odd. Sarah had brought the only other light into the room with her lantern, and she had taken it with her when she left. Groaning from his growing fatigue, Adam rose to investigate.

Ah, it was one of the synagogue's candles resting on a bench; he saw. He just couldn't remember lighting it. Next to it was a small wooden box—that hadn't been there before, either. The box was lacquered in the purest, deepest black Adam had ever seen, a black that seemed more like a border between two worlds than the cover of a box. He opened the lid and beheld an oval-shaped hand-mirror about the size of his palm, framed in polished white stone, marble he thought, inlaid around the edge with symbols of gold, silver, and a blue metal that Adam couldn't identify. Its back was smooth and unmarked. He marveled at the mirror's loveliness. It had to be valuable, but what was it doing here?

Adam set it aside and his eyes fell on the other object in the box: a book, well-worn, leather-bound, and closed with an intricate metal clasp. He touched the clasp and it sprang open, causing him to pull his hand back as though stung. There was no title page, no clue to the book's contents, just small, dense writing that filled the page from edge to edge. He touched the yellowed and mottled page and could feel it yearning to crack. Page after page, the entries were written in many hands and many languages, and with many inks and pens—reed, quill, and others he didn't recognize. He understood little, words here, phrases there, but enough to know he was glimpsing secrets long thought lost. One page seemed to explain the transmutation of elements, although the formulas remained beyond his grasp. Another seemed to explain the exorcism of dybbuks, a remedy for which he did not yet, thank God, have need.

Adam turned the page and stopped. On this page, the crammed, complex writing jostled for space with equally obscure drawings: the figure of a naked man, elements of his body labeled with the ten emanations of the Holy One, Blessed be He. About its head hovered the first three emanations, Crown, Wisdom and Understanding. Love was associated with the right arm, Strength with the left. The figure's trunk was labeled Beauty and Compassion, the result, it seemed, of tempering Strength with Love. The legs, right and left, were given over to Eternity and Splendor, and the male organ to Foundation. The emanation at the base of the figure was labeled

Kingdom.

Another drawing contained circles within circles, divided into an extraordinary number of minuscule geometric shapes, within which the letters of the alphabet were repeated in seemingly endless combination; in another, a man, lying prone, was surrounded by a host of angels.

As he held the book in his thin hands, Adam felt a tingling sensation in his fingers. The page seemed to glow. These words, these drawings, *he understood*. Unlike the other pages, this one withheld none of its secrets from him. What had been incomprehensible was now profoundly clear. The formulas and incantations: he knew not only what they would do, but also what he would do with them. From everywhere on the page he gained new insight into the ways of the Holy One, Blessed be He. Adam felt a pulsing energy singing throughout his body. Its song consisted of but a single word: Deliverance.

Chapter Eleven

The bank of the San River was so muddy that, in places, Adam's boots sank into it up to his ankles. Above, an iron shield of clouds blocked out the moon and stars and Adam stumbled and stumbled again, the rocks and roots tearing at the hem of his black great-coat.

An inhuman cry shot through the night like an arrow. Adam lifted his lantern and peered into the darkness. Surely it was an owl, unless—Adam felt a frisson ripple through his body—it was something pretending to be an owl? Adam could feel his heart beating hard and fast, but he pressed on.

Adam stopped at a spot along the riverbank clear enough for easy digging and secluded enough to avoid prying eyes. He got down on his knees, the cold, wet earth a shock to his legs, and began to turn over the mud with his hands. The earth, under a layer of mud, was hard, tugging at his fingernails and sending sparks of pain along his fingertips. A shovel, that's what he needed. But on this point the journal had been clear. This was to be the work of his hands alone; as with the construction of the holy Temple, iron tools would play no part. He continued to bring up scoopful after scoopful. His great-coat was soon streaked with mud, as was his face, but still he worked, piling the earth into a mound and then a series of mounds. Finally, he pushed them into a single, oblong shape. His arms ached from seldom-used muscles called to so rigorous a duty.

Now to refine this muddy mass. He started at one end, carving the legs, then stood back to assess his work: two shafts, like sturdy tree trunks. Such legs could outrun a stallion, he felt certain. But could they outrun a demon? Knees. He had forgotten knees. He shook his head in disbelief, imagining the result if he hadn't caught the mistake. The feet were incredibly difficult and after several failed attempts, he left a rounded mound, shaped like a loaf of Sabbath bread, at the end of each leg. He couldn't imagine that toes would be necessary, so he ignored them. As he worked, Adam wiped his hands on his coat and withdrew the journal from his pocket to consult it, confirming that the dimensions of the figure matched the dimensions dictated by the secret text in every respect.

He knew that golems had once trod the earth, but none had been seen in generations; the secret had been thought lost. Could he succeed like the Sages Rava and Zeira? It was said that more than a millennium ago, the Sage Rava had sent a golem messenger to test his fellow Sage, Zeira—but when it proved unable to speak, Zeira detected the test and returned the golem to the earth. Just a few hundred years ago, in Moorish Spain, the philosopher and poet Ibn Gabirol, a leper, had created a female golem as a companion to console him in his solitude—until suspicious and fearful townspeople had forced him to destroy it.

Adam shuddered to think of the most famous, and dangerous, golem of all. Not two hundred years ago, the great Rabbi Judah Lev, the Maharal, had created a golem to protect the Jews of Prague from pogroms and other catastrophes during the time of Emperor Rudolph II. The magic had worked—for a while. But perhaps the role of vigilante was too much even for a golem to bear, for the Maharal's creation had run amok, causing death and destruction throughout the ghetto before it could be returned to eternal rest. And he, Adam, was no Maharal. What would his golem do to his enemies—and to his own people? Doubt crept further into his thoughts, then he shook it away.

Strength would be required, so he made the arms and chest thick with what he hoped resembled muscle. Fingers would be needed, and knuckles, so the hands could grasp and carry—and make fists, the better to defend against the things of the night. The shoulders were a challenge. First he made them too thick, then too square, then too narrow. Were they even, he wondered, or was he creating a hunchback? There, that was better. The neck he fashioned to support a strong, commanding head. But not as large as a watermelon. He removed some of the earth, particularly where the cheeks looked puffy and the chin an afterthought; the head and face would have to convey power and seriousness, and perhaps be somewhat threatening. More angular lines in the face helped.

Using two fingers like a small spade, he hollowed out two deep sockets for eyes, then used the clay he'd extracted to make a long, angular nose. He drew his index finger across the face; the horizontal gash it left would serve as a mouth. Adam stopped and stepped back. Mud covered his coat, his thin beard, and his usually pallid face; with a grim chuckle, he realized that he didn't look quite so different from the motionless figure before him.

Now came the penultimate steps. He knelt by the figure's head, his arm trembling, and extended his forefinger. He took a deep breath and willed his arm to be steady. Using his fingernail, Adam inscribed an *aleph*, the first letter of the alphabet, on the figure's forehead. Then he inscribed a *mem*, the middle letter, and finally a *sof*, the last letter. Together, these letters spelled the word *emmes*, or truth, a reference to the Holy One, Blessed be He, the ultimate truth and the source of all life.

Hours after he'd started digging, Adam looked down on the figure of a man, a massive being at least a head taller than he was, with strong, thick limbs and a broad chest, lying on its back. Something about the ears now struck him as off. Were they different sizes? They would have to do.

Ah, but the ears weren't the only imperfections in the figure. It was riddled with them: with parts that were too small or too thick, or not symmetrical where they should have been. Could a golem with such imperfections be brought to life? Now Adam wasn't so sure. Nor was he still sure that, even armed with the book, he could create life. After all, he was attempting to succeed where holy and learned men had often failed.

He was struck anew by the thought that he was attempting to create life from earth. Wasn't that the preserve of the Holy One, Blessed be He? The wind was blowing hard; Adam turned up his collar against it and pulled his fur-trimmed hat more firmly upon his head. He knew that the first golem had been created not by man, but by the Almighty. That was the first Adam, then God breathed a soul into him, elevating him to a unique level of creation: humanity. Now, Adam, in creating a golem, was acting in the image of the Almighty Himself. So perhaps he was doing God's work, he thought, as he bent over again to smooth a stray lump in the figure's arm. Or perhaps he was merely playing God.

Either way, he had come too far to stop. He stood up and began the final step, reciting the holy words of Scripture:

"And the Lord God formed man of the dust of the earth and breathed into his nostrils the breath of life. And man became a living soul."

He uttered the words with his eyes closed and with all the reverence within him. He opened his eyes and looked down. The mud and clay lay just as he'd shaped it. He placed his hand on the figure's chest to see if it was breathing. It was as still as death.

Scowling, Adam consulted the journal again. Had he made a mistake with the words? With the construction of the figure? With the inscription on its forehead? No, everything seemed in order. He recited the verse again, and again. Nothing happened. No turn of its head. No intake of its breath. No lifting of a finger. *It is no more than it was, clay and mud,* he thought with resignation. Images of his darling Leah and sweet Mendel, of Hersh and Miriam, flooded his mind. He saw Sarah standing in the doorway upon his return, her eyes, her whole body, full of reproach, or worse: the sleepwalker with the dead stare.

His limbs felt impossibly heavy. He lowered himself to the ground and sat against a willow as stooped as he was. The lateness of the hour... the grueling work to dig and to sculpt... the disappointment of failure... they stole away the last of his strength and will. His head slumped onto his chest and sleep began to weave its way into his bones.

After a moment, it started to rain, a soft, gentle rain, barely more than a mist. The water cut little rivulets through the earth caked on Adam's face and hands, creating streaks of pale flesh that looked like scars against the dark mud. *Let the rain do as it will,* he thought only half sensing the water falling on him. *Let it return that pile of mud where it belongs.* A golem! Maybe *he* was the only golem on the riverbank this night. If Adam had any other thoughts, he wouldn't remember them, for soon he was asleep.

Adam started to turn in his bed, his mind teeming with disturbing dreams. His bed felt hard and cold… and wet. He half-opened an eye. He wasn't in his bed at all. He was on the riverbank. With the approach of the sun, color was returning to the trees and boulders and brush. It hadn't been a dream; he had tried to do it. He opened his other eye, rubbed them both with the palms of his mud-caked hands and attempted to sit up. Oh, how his sinews and bones ached with every movement.

He tried to focus his gaze. Beside him, he saw his figure of mud and clay lying on its side. The figure's chest, in slight, almost imperceptible motions, was expanding and contracting. Adam leapt back, almost hitting his head against a tree, and cried out.

The golem rolled over and, with his great empty black hollows of eyes, stared back at him.

Chapter Twelve

The golem rose with great effort and little grace, putting a massive, rough-hewn arm on a nearby boulder to steady himself.

He blinked. He heard sounds he couldn't identify, but he could identify their source: His hands rose to the bumps on either side of his head and he touched them in wonder. What were these things? *Ears.* The word came to him from… somewhere. He sensed other sounds too. The roar of… what? A *river*, the word came to him just as the other had. He heard high-pitched trills and warbles coming from… a *bird*.

Now he brought his hands to the front of his face. Everything went was dark. He removed his hands and the light and shapes returned. He felt two deep depressions in the center of his face. *Eyes.* Many more sensations, sights, and sounds were coming at him. *Breeze, cold. Leaves, rustling. Frogs, jumping. Sky, blue.* The words flew at him, too, faster and faster, in a terrible rush. *Grass. Legs. Big. Insect.*

He could not see the sounds, which confused him. But he could see a creature standing before him, a creature of roughly his own shape, although smaller, making its own sounds.

"Golem, I am your creator," he heard it say.

The golem peered at the creature. Like him, it had ears and eyes. And a *nose* and *mouth.* But it was not like him. Its skin was pale and enclosed in something black. Black and gray hair hung from its face, and in a long curl in front of each ear. The golem reached out and touched the creature's *beard* and *sidelocks.* The creature moved with a sudden jerk, but then held still, allowing him to feel the beard with his fingers.

The golem opened his mouth as the creature had, to acknowledge its words with words of his own. But no sound emerged. He looked without expression at the other and froze, unsure of how to continue. After a moment, he nodded his head. This was his creator. But not just his creator. This was his *master*. He would *obey* his master, always. His fingers, his ears, his torso, his legs—this was the reason he was created, every bit and part of him: to obey his master.

Then the golem saw the rising *sun*, and he reached out with his great dark paw of a hand to touch it but felt only air; it was too far away. The brilliant ball of fire seemed to warp the very sky around it. It cast long, harsh shadows across the landscape. He turned toward his creator.

"Come with me," said his creator, motioning with a hand that was small and soft compared to his own. The golem gave the slightest nod of his great gray head, hunched his massive shoulders, and lumbered forward. He followed the *man* away from the riverbank, remaining two paces behind him all the way.

Sarah awoke as the sunlight streamed into the bedroom of her eldest child and his bride. She had slept, if it could be called that, in a chair by the side of their beds. Once upon a time, she could fall asleep by counting the stars—her father had taught her the names of all the constellations—but those days were long behind her. She sighed, but found no relief in doing so.

Without thought, she reached over to the basin on the table next to her, toward a tin cup filled with water, and performed the morning ablution. Then she rose with a faint groan and gazed at Hersh and Miriam, lying side by side in what was supposed to be their matrimonial bed, not their sick bed. Her large, muscled son was heavily covered with blood-stained bandages that she would soon have to change again. Her daughter-in-law appeared thin and ashen, as though she might crumble if touched. With trembling fingers, Sarah put a hand on her son's chest and held still while she sought evidence of his breath. She felt a slight, rhythmic movement under her hand, so faint that it took her a minute to be sure she wasn't imagining it. She moved to Miriam and, afraid of touching one so fragile, checked her breathing as well. It was the same as Hersh's: there and yet only barely so. The skin visible through their bandages was pale, almost gray, so different from the vibrant glow they had had under the wedding canopy just the day before. What if they never recovered, never lived their lives, never had children of their own?

Attempting to blot out the thought, she went to her daughter's room. Poor little Leahele lay in her bed, her freckled cheeks plump but colorless, her big brown eyes—always playful—now fixed and dull, useless eyes, seeing nothing. Sarah's heart raced. She knew what death looked like—she served in the women's burial society—could she be looking at it now? Sarah bent over Leah, her face a hair's breadth away, held her breath, and waited. The slightest wisp of warmth, only a suggestion of breath, touched Sarah's cheek. A bit of life remained, but for how long? Oh, to think she had gone through the pain of childbirth and so much more with these children, only to lose them now.

Sarah heard a noise from downstairs, probably Adam moving about. She frowned and sighed, remembering the harsh words they'd exchanged the previous night and the emptiness she'd felt inside afterward. They had run out of intimate conversation long ago but, after last night, was there anything at all left to say between them?

She started down the stairs, still bleary from lack of sleep. Several steps from the bottom, she could make out Adam in the kitchen, his back to her, fussing over something. As he moved around the table, she saw the object of his attention: a statue of some sort, dumped into one of the wooden chairs at the table, facing her. It was huge, in the shape of a man but bigger than any man she knew. What was Adam thinking dragging this into her kitchen? And he had put one of her teacups, of all things, in its hand.

Still unseen by Adam, Sarah crept down the stairs.

Adam said, "Drink." Suddenly, the statue's hand lifted the teacup to its face and examined it, then attempted to drink, succeeding only in splashing the liquid about the kitchen. Sarah screamed and clutched her chest. Then she looked around, grabbed a broom, and rushed into the room, shaking it like a weapon.

"Go away!" she shrieked to the statue. "Leave us alone!"

Incredibly, Adam just stood there, staring at her. Now he was waving his arms, motioning her to stop, to back away. Sarah stared back, stupefied. What did he want: for this monster to attack them, to destroy what remained of their family? Just then the monster's mouth dropped open. The black holes that were its eyes widened, sending crease-lines across its brow. She gazed, transfixed by the three letters, *aleph, mem, sof*, inscribed there. The statue hunched its shoulders as if anticipating her blows with the broom. The teacup slipped from the monster's massive hand and shattered on the wooden floor. It stared at the pieces, then at Sarah, then back at the pieces. Adam came around to its side of the table and put a comforting arm around the gray-brown mounds of its shoulders.

"There, there," he said in reassuring tones. "It's only my wife, Sarah."

The monster's huge shoulders relaxed and it nodded its large, brown and gray head.

"Adam," Sarah croaked, still pointing with the broom. "What is that thing?"

"A golem," he said simply and with a touch of pride.

Her taciturn husband followed this declaration with a torrent of words. Sarah listened, dazed, while Adam explained about a box, a mirror, and a book he'd discovered; about the formulas and incantations to create the golem; about his adventure on the riverbank. She could hardly take it all in, his words spilling over like water from the ablution cup.

"We must be very precise in the commands we give to the golem," Adam was telling her. "He will do exactly what we tell him—what we say, not what we intend to say. The golem made by the Maharal of Prague was once told to fetch water from a well, but not how much. He brought water all afternoon—the furniture was floating in it—before the Maharal returned and ordered him to stop."

Sarah shot a sidelong look at the golem. His meat-slab hands were pressed against the table as he leaned forward in his chair, his lipless mouth pursed as though in concentration. Her breath caught inside her. "What does this all mean?" she whispered.

"What this means," said Adam, "is that we're not alone anymore. Someone or something sent the instructions to me because the golem can help save our children."

Not alone, he had said. Yet, alone is just what she felt. She shuddered a little. "How?"

"I don't know, exactly," he admitted, drawing a hand through his wispy, unruly black-gray beard. "But whatever I must do, I can do better with him at my side. I feel it. I've been testing him. He's as strong as ten men, maybe a hundred. And he doesn't feel any pain. That has to be a help."

Sarah looked unconvinced. She glanced at the pieces of teacup lying on the floor. "Was he drinking?"

"He refused food," said Adam with a slow shake of his head. "And he didn't seem interested in the tea. He may not need food or water." Adam looked at the golem and smiled. "That will make him a very easy guest. Now, the question is where he should stay. Golem, stand."

The golem rose, straight and slow, to his feet, his chair falling back behind him. Sarah flushed and turned away.

"Well, if he's going to stay with us, he can't stay like that," she shrieked, looking anywhere but at the golem.

"Like what?" asked her husband.

"Adam!" said Sarah, feeling color flooding her cheeks, "he's not wearing any clothes!"

"I hadn't thought of that," Adam admitted, his face reddening. "But how will we clothe him? My clothes won't fit him."

"No," agreed Sarah, "but Hersh's might, he's broader than you are. At least he might get them on."

Adam followed Sarah upstairs, and looked in on Hersh, Miriam, and Leah as Sarah considered a wardrobe for their guest. "The children look the same," said Adam in a tone that suggested he'd feared to find them worse.

"Yes, but 'the same' is terrible," Sarah said.

Adam swallowed. He turned away and took a few minutes to wash the caked mud off himself with water from the basin, and then to change his clothes. Now it was time to dress the golem. Sarah hurried behind a tall wardrobe to give the golem privacy. She could hear Adam grunting, muttering, and the sound of cloth scraping over something hard as he ministered to the golem.

Finally, Adam called out, "The pants are on, though I can't say they'll stay on." Sarah poked her head out from around the wardrobe and stifled a laugh—but only just. The golem was indeed in Hersh's black pants, but it was hardly an improvement. His legs, thick as posts, strained so against the cloth that she couldn't imagine them ever coming off. Adam looked red-faced and out of breath.

"Let me help you." Sarah opened the wardrobe and selected one of Hersh's old shirts. As she and Adam pulled at the white fabric to button it over the golem's broad, brown-gray chest, they heard a distinct ripping sound. The split went straight up the back of the shirt. Sarah considered it for a moment.

"The jacket will cover that," she said, taking advantage of the slack created by the tear to button the shirt-front.

They worked together to get the jacket over the golem's thick, cylindrical arms, one pulling, the other adjusting, the two falling into a natural rhythm.

Finally, Adam and Sarah gazed down at the golem's toeless, mound-like feet. No shoes in their household—likely no shoes in Creation—would fit them; he would have to go barefoot. Sarah hoped that Adam was right that the golem could feel no pain. Now, she considered his head. Too bad Adam had neglected to sculpt the golem some hair. His stone-bald pate, like the rest of him, was that unattractive combination of rough, textured browns and grays, and too large to take one of Adam's hats. And his ears were mispositioned, the left level with his eyes and the right a bit higher. That gave him the air, Sarah felt, of a dog that's cocked its head, the better to hear some sound to which humans were oblivious.

"Well, no one will mistake him for a Lizensker," said Sarah, "but at least he's presentable." She glanced at the clock. "You'll be late for morning prayers."

Adam nodded. "Yes, I'd better go. Golem, wait here."

Sarah started. "What, you think you're leaving him with me?"

"He won't trouble you," Adam reassured her.

"That's right," she said, crossing her arms over her chest. "You created him, you take him."

Adam opened his mouth as if to object, but then shrugged and signaled to the golem to follow him.

Sarah fetched a broom and pan and began to sweep the shards of the teacup still on the floor. She shook her head with wonder. To think she had spoken to her husband that way, in such a tone. Forbearance and submission had always been second nature to her. But ever since her children—their children—had been taken, those qualities seemed to have gone deep inside her or who knows, maybe disappeared. She wondered what to make of it as she poured the shards into the dustbin.

Chapter Thirteen

Adam led the golem down the street, toward the synagogue. As they passed through the empty market square, a butterfly flitted about their heads, its blue and gold wings painting their little corner of the sky. Adam looked up at it and smiled.

"You've never seen a butterfly before," he said to the golem. "Go ahead, look, they're quite beautiful."

The golem watched as the little creature flitted about. As it flew close to him, the golem reached out and caught it in one of his great gray hands before Adam could stop him. The golem brought it up close to his face to examine it, then let it fall into his open palm. It lay there flat and motionless.

"No, see?" said Adam. "You've killed it. It's dead."

The golem looked at him without comprehension. Adam sighed.

"It's dead. The life is gone. I know you didn't mean to, but you killed it. You will have to be much more careful with living things."

Adam took the butterfly from the golem and let it drop among the tall grasses. Then they continued toward the synagogue. As they walked, Adam explained about his family and Lilith.

"I created you to protect us," Adam said. "That is your job. Do you understand?"

The golem nodded solemnly.

Still, Adam wondered how much the golem understood and how careful he, Adam, would need to be with his speech. On the one hand, perhaps his broad directive to protect the family would suffice. On the other hand, he didn't want to return home and find his house had become a lake.

As they approached the synagogue, Adam could see the men of Lizensk converging on the small building in preparation for morning prayers. The sight of a man of clay accompanying the rabbi was cause for comment. The villagers swarmed around them, poking and prodding the golem, but clearly out of curiosity, not concern. They lived, after all, in a world of imps and demons, lightning and rainbows, dybbuks and sorcerers. They had all seen stranger things.

"Rabbi Yisroel Baal Shem Tov created a golem too, I hear, over in Tloshe," said Daniel the Tanner.

"No, you smelly beast," corrected Eliezer the Bookbinder. "The Baal Shem Tov *destroyed a werewolf* in Tloshe. Hardly the same thing."

"I th... th... think Rabbi Dov Ber of Mezritch created a golem," said Gimpel Carrots, trying to be helpful. "Or maybe it was Rabbi Luzzatto."

"In Padua?" snorted the merchant Dovid Pots, his belly shaking—whether from laughter or indignation, it was difficult to know—under his great-coat. "What would they know from golems in Padua?"

Adam started to explain that no golem had been created since the time of the Maharal, 170 years earlier, but gave up. Most of the Lizenskers, it turned out, thought they knew someone who knew someone who had heard about the creation of a golem by one or another of the holy men scattered throughout the towns and villages of Poland, Russia, Lithuania, Galicia, Bohemia, and the other assorted kingdoms, duchies, empires, and districts in which their co-religionists lived.

On the other hand, they agreed that Adam—who, they seemed to acknowledge, had depths previously unplumbed and unsuspected—had done a remarkable thing.

"So you're a Kabbalist too, Rabbi Adam?" said Eliezer with admiration. "When word of this spreads, you'll get job offers from the big synagogues in Lodz, Warsaw, Cracow. We'll hardly be able to keep you in our little hamlet."

"Maybe the rabbi could create a golem to take my place in the tannery," murmured Daniel, visions of a fragrant future apparently floating through his head.

Adam suppressed a smile. "Actually," he said, clearing his throat, "I created the golem for one purpose, to help me find Mendel."

The mention of the missing child sobered the villagers, for they knew that when someone was carried off by a demon—praise be to the Holy One, Blessed be He, that it seldom happened, and mostly to those who deserved it—that he stayed carried off. The men began to enter the synagogue. Adam walked toward the weathered oak door, the golem close at his side.

"Wait here," Adam said to the golem before entering the synagogue, pointing to a patch of earth a few feet away, where a scrappy bush struggled to survive. "It's not your place inside."

The golem's black-socket eyes widened and the ridges that represented his eyebrows knit closer together; he didn't understand. Adam patted the golem's arm and was about to explain that his soul existed at a lower level than that of a human soul and thus could not by law participate in a prayer quorum, but stopped. "What would you do inside the synagogue, anyway?" he asked instead. "Inside we pray, we talk to our Creator. That's not for you. You wait here."

The golem moved away as his master had directed. Then, his massive head turned until he was staring into one of the windows, through which he could see the gathering inside.

Adam entered the synagogue and counted the men, who were removing their jackets, wrapping themselves in prayer shawls, and donning their phylacteries. Only nine. Adam sighed. They needed one more. A shame the golem couldn't be included in the quorum, he thought as he draped his prayer shawl over his head, but of course it wasn't possible. His soul was merely an echo of the soul that the Almighty had breathed into the first man. That was why the golem could not speak, speech being a gift that only the Master of the Universe could bestow. And should the golem's life come to an end, he couldn't be buried in consecrated ground, nor could the prayer for the dead be recited in his memory. After all, Adam reminded himself, the golem wasn't alive, not really. He was a magical tool, nothing more.

And nothing less, the thought came to him as Chaim the Tinsmith straggled in to complete the prayer quorum. A magical tool was exactly what he needed to bolster the odds in his favor. Now he need not fear phantoms, were-beasts, demons, and other creatures of the night. He and the golem would search all of Poland, all of Russia, all of Europe, until they brought his son home and defeated the evil that had wrought such destruction on his family. Adam pulled his prayer shawl around his head and shoulders, the better to block out distractions to his prayers.

The golem watched his master enter the... *synagogue*, he had called it, and close the door after him, separating them for the first time. Through the open window, the golem could see the villagers as they wrapped themselves in large white sheets with black stripes, and then put small black boxes, bound with black straps, on their arms and heads. The men began to rock back and forth on their feet. Some bowed again and again. Most closed their eyes. All moved their lips, although little sound emerged from them. Some made no sound at all. *Like me*, the golem thought in a distant part of his mind. Some twirled from side to side, their arms outstretched, palms up, in a gesture the golem did not understand. One man, against the wall, kept stroking a beard that reached down to his chest. The golem raised a hand to his own chest in search of a beard to stroke. He found only air. His hand dropped to his side.

"Prayer for the dead!" announced an elderly man with red hair.

Dead? The golem remained where his creator had ordered but strained to see the dead inside. More butterflies? Or were there dead men in the synagogue? He didn't see any dead. But he did see three men rise, their faces .... *sad*, another word that came to his mind, although this word he felt too in his chest, like an ember in his master's hearth. It was a word the golem didn't like.

The three men intoned: "Magnified and sanctified may His great name be, in the world He created by His will..."

This was *prayer*: the men talking to their Creator. The word was a pure white dove, rising in the air to some unknown place. The men could pray to a Creator they would never see, while he could see his creator just there, through the synagogue window, yet would never utter a word to him. The golem's thoughts would remain trapped in his thick head of clay and mud, unexpressed. He felt the sting of the ember again, for just a moment. It subsided and the golem once more watched, motionless, noiseless, from the spot his creator had directed.

Chapter Fourteen

After morning prayers, Adam led the golem back to the house, his mind already consumed with thoughts of the journey that lay ahead. He collected the things he'd need and brought them into the parlor: his prayer shawl and phylacteries; a prayer book and bible; a volume of law to study in quiet moments; his musket, gunpowder, balls, and wadding; a tin cup, plate, and utensils; a loaf of hard bread.

He went to a drawer in his desk and extracted a stack of rubles, a substantial part of what Adam and Sarah had saved over the course of twenty years. Money might be helpful in his travels when a kind word proved useless. The rest of the coins, left in the drawer, would support Sarah while he was gone. He was moved to see that she had brushed clean his great-coat while he and the golem had been at synagogue. He took it from its peg on the wall and draped it over a chair. His gaze fell upon the mysterious book with the kabbalistic writings. He flipped through it with care and, except for the page that described the making of the golem, its secrets remained hidden from him. But the book might have meaning to someone else, and it could prove unspeakably dangerous in the wrong hands. He kissed it gently as he would any holy book, slipped it into the drawer with the coins, and closed and locked it.

Adam found a sack for his belongings. As he began to pack, he reminded himself there was one thing more he must take: the mirror, which rested now on the parlor table, and over which the golem bent his massive frame, peering into it while touching his eye sockets, his nose and mouth and other features. If the oval-shaped glass had not yet proved useful, perhaps its purpose would be revealed on the journey—if the golem didn't drop it first.

Adam retrieved the mirror from the golem with an apologetic smile. He heard footsteps, looked up, and saw Sarah at the bottom of the stairs. She was tight-lipped as she surveyed the scene: Adam with his traveling sack, books and coins and clothes strewn across the table, his great-coat far from its usual place on the wall, and the golem standing by his side, as though awaiting the next instruction.

"You're going?" she asked Adam, the words hardly audible.

"Of course," Adam replied, returning the mirror to the table and picking up a book to put in the sack. The golem followed the shadow that Adam's sudden movement made across the wall. He reached out and ran his hand across it.

"But..." Sarah flushed and looked down at her hands, as though unsure of where to put them, then straightened her already-straight apron. "*Where* are you going?" she said.

"To find Mendel," he said with a touch of impatience. Where else would he go? "Our son isn't in Lizensk."

Sarah opened her mouth then closed it, took a breath, and spoke. "Do you have any idea where he is? What will your leaving do for Hersh and Miriam? For Leah?" she demanded to know.

"I need to find Lilith to save them all," Adam said. It seemed clear: If Hersh and Miriam were still under Lilith's spell, if Lilith had Leah's soul, then of course he had to find the she-demon to put an end to this.

Sarah turned and went to the kitchen, picked up a thick brush from the table, and began to scrub the inside of an ancient pot that sat, empty, on the cold stove. Her movements were agitated, and Adam didn't know why. The golem stopped tracing Adam's shifting shadow and focused his attention on Sarah.

"Would you have me stay and do nothing?" Adam asked as he followed her into the kitchen. Last night she had objected to his passivity. Now she objected to his... what? His taking action? It didn't make sense.

"He decides to leave, just like that," Sarah was saying under her breath as she turned the pot over and began to scrub the outside.

The golem turned his head toward Adam with an expectant look.

Adam tried to get closer to Sarah, the better to see her face and understand. But each time she turned away, occupied with the pot which, to him, looked spotless.

"Are you worried about what will happen if Lilith comes back?" he asked, groping for a problem he could address.

Finally, she turned to place the pot on its hook over the stove. "No, not that," she said after a moment's thought. "I know all this won't stop until you've found Lilith and Mendel. It's best that you go."

Then what? Now he saw the hurt in her light brown eyes. Why should Sarah feel hurt? And then as if struck, he understood. He hadn't told her he'd decided to go. It had just slipped out. He hadn't even asked her opinion. And this wasn't the first time.

"I'm... I'm sorry," he said. "I should have spoken with you first."

Sarah stood there, her shoulders hunched. Adam waited for her to say something, anything. The only sound was a random moan from the ancient wooden floorboards.

"Take food," Sarah said in a slow, even, almost whispered voice. "You can't depend on finding inns."

Her voice lacked even a hint of warmth, but Adam recognized it for the olive branch that it was. Sarah withdrew several boiled eggs from a bowl, using a rag to tie them into a small bundle. She produced hard cheese, nuts, and miniature pastries. The three of them carried the food to the parlor table. The golem, under Adam's direction, packed them in the sack. Sarah glanced at the mirror, which now lay on the table. Her curiosity aroused, she picked it up by its gold-and-marble handle to examine it.

"'Lev?'" Sarah wondered aloud, pointing. "Why is 'Lev' inscribed here?"

"Nothing's inscribed there, it's smooth stone," replied Adam.

Sarah pivoted the mirror to show Adam its back. Where a smooth, unmarked surface had been the night before, the back of the mirror now held the letters *lamed* and *vav*: Lev. Adam blinked and blinked again. He reached out and ran his fingers over the inscription.

"Who's Lev?" Sarah repeated.

"The Levites in the ancient Temple?" Adam shrugged.

"That would be lamed-vav-*yud*," Sarah pointed out.

He took the mirror from her and examined it closely, considering. "Lev...
Lev..."

"Maybe it's not a name," she suggested. "Maybe it's a number."

In the holy language, letters also represented numbers. Lamed: thirty.
Vav: six.

"Thirty-six? Thirty-six?" he said, still puzzled, but also trying to recall
something long forgotten. "That number is important, I think."

He knew that thirty-six was twice eighteen, which was composed of the
letters that also spelled the word "life." Thirty-six represented double life:
life in this World of Illusion as well as life in the True World to Come. The
idea stored away in the darkness of his mind began to yield its outline to him.
Thirty-six... Lamed-vav... Lamed-vav... The Lamed Vavniks: the thirty-six
Hidden Saints. A chill went through him.

"Adam! Adam!" said Sarah beside him, pulling on his arm. "What is it?"

A smile bloomed across his face.

"One of the Hidden Saints," he said, "knows he is needed."

Sarah shook her head and Adam explained.

The Sages taught that the world is constantly under the threat of
annihilation because of the evil that men do. The Almighty permits the
world to continue for a single reason: for the sake of the thirty-six holy
men and women who exist in each generation. The absence of even one,
it is said, would forever tip the moral balance of the universe and lead to
obliteration. According to the tradition, the Lamed Vavniks walk among us
in secret, known only to the Holy One, Blessed be He. They might not know
each other, they might not even know themselves to be Lamed Vavniks. But
when they are needed, their presence is felt.

"You think a Lamed Vavnik gave you the book and the mirror?" she asked
him. "A Lamed Vavnik showed you how to make the golem?"

"I don't see any other explanation."

Sarah considered his words and sat on the bench beside him.

"Then you must find him," she said.

He pushed back in his chair. "Find *him*? I must find Mendel and destroy Lilith."

"And you will do it by finding the Lamed Vavnik," she insisted. "I think he can do much more to help us."

"That's a diversion," he said. "Our children don't have time."

Instantly, he regretted his words, his tone. She would shut down again as she'd done last night. To his surprise, she didn't.

"Maybe our children don't have time for you to search *without* the Lamed Vavnik," she pressed. "It's impossible for you to know where to begin to look. But the Lamed Vavnik may know... everything."

He stared at her. Sarah had a point, but did he have the time to search for the Lamed Vavnik? As he went back and forth, another thought, a verse from Scripture, drifted through his mind. The Holy One, Blessed be He, had said to our father Abraham: "Listen to her voice." The "her" was Abraham's wife, Sarah, another Sarah. *Listen to her voice.* Such simple advice. So why was he finding it so hard to take?

Adam looked at the mirror, still in his hands. His brow furrowed.

"S-Sarah," he stammered. "Look at this."

He held the mirror so they both could look into it. Instead of their reflection, it showed a path into a forest, as though it were a window. Sarah snatched the mirror from his hand and rubbed the surface with her apron. The image was unchanged, albeit a bit clearer than before.

"Adam, what is this magic?" she asked in amazement.

Adam recognized the place in the mirror, a spot near the ruins at the southern edge of the village.

"It means you're right," he said with excitement. "I need to seek the Lamed Vavnik and the mirror is showing me where to go."

Adam gave his wife an awkward embrace. Sarah stiffened at his touch but then relaxed in his arms, a bit. Adam, unsure of how to say goodbye, murmured his farewell. Sarah leaned toward him and grazed his cheek with a kiss. Adam put on his broad-brimmed, fur-trimmed hat, slung the sack over his shoulder, and gave Sarah a wistful smile. Then he turned to the door and he and the golem were gone.

From the window, Sarah watched them proceed down the street and out of sight. She stood there a long time. "Be careful," she said to an empty road.

Chapter Fifteen

Adam headed toward the forest with the golem at his side, his sack slung over one shoulder, his musket over the other, the marble-backed mirror firmly in his hand. As the mass of woods and shadows loomed before them, he stopped and looked around, his eyes probing every stand of trees, every bramble, every boulder.

"Hello," he said in a tentative tone; no answer. He abandoned caution and shouted. "Hello!"

No Lamed Vavnik. He glanced down at the image in the mirror. Yes, this was definitely the same spot. Adam took an uncertain step forward on the long-overgrown path. The Lamed Vavnik could be anywhere in the vastness. It would take days if not weeks to search it all, time they didn't have.

Adam pushed back tree branches, stepped over stones, and made his way over and around jagged stumps of massive, fallen trees that loomed out of the earth like wooden stalagmites, their trunks scattered across the forest floor in varying forms of decay, some beginning to submit to the elements, others nearly returned to the earth.

Just then the image in the glass blurred, the trees and path no longer recognizable. The points of light in the reflection dissolved and reassembled themselves into the image of a wide, clear stream, sparkling in the noonday sun like liquid diamonds. Ah, Adam nodded to himself. So that's where the Lamed Vavnik would be waiting for them. He and the golem continued on past clearings and caves and curtains of oak until they found the sparkling stream reflected in the mirror—but their hidden saint remained unseen.

Adam looked into the mirror again. Now the glass showed him dense carpets of ferns out of which grew hundreds of tall, thin, moss-covered trees, standing like soldiers awaiting their orders. They trudged off again in search of the site. Each time they reached a scene depicted in the mirror, Adam looked about this way and that for his secret benefactor but found no one. Perhaps there was no Lamed Vavnik, he couldn't help thinking as he rested for a moment on a gray, ice-cold boulder, the golem standing motionless nearby. Perhaps whoever had bestowed the mirror on him had done so for dark purposes. With an effort, he shook away these unhelpful thoughts and he and the golem continued their search.

The next time they stopped for Adam to rest, the golem's gaze turned to the forest floor and to the shifting shadows cast by the afternoon sunlight as it passed through the leafy canopies above them. The golem kept trying to wipe a shadow off his barrel of a chest, and Adam smiled. Then it occurred to him anew that the golem might be all that stood between him and the trials to come, and the smile disappeared. The golem was undeniably strong, but he was also oddly gentle, a word Adam never thought he'd apply to a seven-foot creature of clay and earth. Adam wondered whether the golem truly was up to the task ahead.

He told the golem to halt at the crest of a ridge so he could recite afternoon prayers. Out of habit, he slipped his well-worn, palm-sized prayer book out of his sack, but held it in his hand, unopened; these were prayers he knew by heart. The golem stood motionless, twenty or thirty feet off, facing him. Adam turned away from the afternoon sun, toward the east and the holiest of cities, Jerusalem, to direct his supplication. As he prayed, he could feel the golem's deep, dark eyes trained on him. He could feel the heat in his gaze and wondered what, if anything, he was thinking. Adam returned to the ancient words of the prayers.

O King, Supporter, Savior, and Shield. Blessed art thou, O Lord, Shield of Abraham. O grant us knowledge, understanding, and insight. Blessed art thou, O Lord, gracious Giver of knowledge...

After the previous night, these words had a new world of meaning for Adam. The Almighty had given him the knowledge to make the golem. It seemed ungrateful to ask for more, but Adam needed more. Hersh and Miriam lay near death, Leah lifeless, Mendel missing. He could not bear any more grief; he could not afford any more mistakes, any more of the indecision he'd experienced when Hersh had so needed him to take action. He could not, must not, allow that to happen again.

He had almost finished the eighteen benedictions, though he couldn't remember saying most of them. In the faintest undertone, he added one more.

Blessed art thou, O Lord, please help me to respond differently the next time.

He took three small steps backward and bowed, like one withdrawing from the presence of a king. Then he kissed the prayer book, slipped it back into his sack, and he and the golem continued their journey.

Now the light took on a fainter quality. The pair scrambled over outcroppings of rocks that left little room to maneuver. The golem climbed over them without effort; Adam was breathing hard as he followed. His body ached from exertions to which it was long unaccustomed. They came to a small clearing, but the ground was treacherous for it had a significant slope upward, as though they had reached the base of a hill or mountain. With a fine veil of fog filling the forest, it was difficult for Adam to see. A brook, heard but concealed by the mist, lay off in the middle distance.

A flash of color, bright red mixed with yellow, darted on the ground. The golem was instantly alert. Adam grasped his musket. The color flashed again, behind a fallen branch as thick and long as a small tree. Adam motioned to the golem to investigate. With a single, swift motion, the golem swept aside the branch, revealing, of all things, a goldfinch, perched in the hollow of a log where it had evidently been trapped. The bird was a stout ball of feathers, with its red face and yellow-striped wings set off against an otherwise drab costume of brown and black.

"Got yourself caught, did you?" Adam asked the bird, lowering his musket. The bird chirped as though offering thanks, its song a series of rapid, piercing staccato bursts that fluttered up and down the scales. Then it spread its wings and rose in graceful swirls to a nearby tree. It watched them for a moment, then fluttered about their heads and soared away.

With no idea where to go next, Adam again withdrew the mirror from his pocket. The glass showed yet another part of the forest, with a blanket of verdant grasses and a low horizon, suggesting a way out of the woods—once they got there. But there was no telling how far "there" was. With the light diminishing, Adam decided to set up camp for the night.

"Golem, we need a fire. Please gather some wood," Adam directed. The golem nodded and began to comply. A vision of the Maharal's flooded house flashed through Adam's mind.

"Just enough for a *small* fire," he called out after the retreating golem. "Please leave the rest." The golem lifted one eyebrow, the *aleph* on his forehead scrunching a bit as he did.

Chapter Sixteen

Before long, the last purple rays of the setting sun disappeared and the dark blue of the sky—what they could see of it through the trees and the fog—turned to black. Adam and the golem sat together by the fire and Adam ate two of his boiled eggs. Meanwhile, the sounds of the night began to emerge: the high-pitched hoots of birds of prey, the rustling of wings passing overhead. In the distance, the howls of wolves sounded then faded away.

Remembering his manners, Adam reached into his sack and pulled out another egg. "Golem, for you?"

The golem stared at the egg as though he'd never seen one before. Adam's hand withdrew. Of course not: The golem neither ate nor drank.

"It's been a long day," said Adam, stretching his legs so they could gather a bit more warmth from the fire. "Are you as tired as I am?"

The golem gave him a quizzical look, shrugging his massive shoulders and straining the seams of his not-quite-adequate jacket. Then a look of sudden understanding came over his face and he shook his head.

"That's another difference between us," said Adam, with a wistful smile. It would have been nice to have the comfort of conversation with the golem but, clearly, it was not to be. Adam's mind drifted back to Lizensk and to the family he had left there. He uttered a silent prayer that the children should be better or, at least, no worse. He wondered what Sarah was doing. She had probably checked on the children one last time, stoked and replenished the stove for the night, recited her nightly prayers, and retreated to bed. She would be thinking of him, just as he was thinking of her. She would worry for him. But would she miss him? He touched his cheek, searching for some remnant of the kiss she'd given him.

"Golem," said Adam, speaking to his companion but really addressing himself. "Do you get lonely?" Another look of puzzlement from the golem. Ah, another irrelevant question, Adam realized even as the words were escaping his mouth. The golem had been alive for barely a day, although it seemed so much longer. Even if he'd been capable of loneliness, for whom or for what would he have had time to become lonely?

Adam, lost in his thoughts, missed it completely: The golem, with the slightest motion, nodded his head.

A sound arrested Adam's attention: a snort from a creature he couldn't identify. It was a ways off, but not that far off. Adam moved closer to the golem. Again all was quiet, for a while.

At first he was unsure he had heard anything at all; the sound almost wasn't there. Then Adam heard it again, a sound different from the one he'd heard moments earlier, this time slight and scratching and rhythmic and low to the ground. The golem turned the higher of his mismatched ears toward the sound. Adam clambered to his feet. The golem, instantly alert, followed Adam to investigate. Something was moving in the underbrush just beyond the curtain of light cast by their fire. Adam picked up a long branch at the edge of the fire and thrust the impromptu torch ahead of them into the darkness.

His eyes snapped open wide. Nothing was moving in the underbrush. It was the ground itself that was moving. It pushed upward in little spurts, as though someone or something was digging from below. The earth continued to fall away from whatever was making its way upward, toward them. A root appeared in the center of the disturbed earth, thick as a man's wrist. But this was like no root that Adam had ever seen before, because no force was moving it: *the root was moving the earth*. Adam could feel his heart hammering at his chest. The root was undulating, rising from the ground and creating a hole of increasing size. With a sense of panic, Adam realized what this was. They had to get away from it *now*.

"Back!" he barked at the golem who, although startled by the urgent tone of his creator, retreated immediately, almost stumbling. Adam ran back too and they reached their fire just in time to see a shape moving out of the hole. It was a hand. Not the hand of any animal, and not quite the hand of any man, but mottled and hairy like the coiled root through which it was rising into the air. The hand opened and closed with great urgency. Another hand punched up through the earth nearby and the pair rose into the night, capped by long, sharp, claw-like fingertips. Adam stared, riveted by the sight. He could see a pair of forearms, elbows, and upper arms. The earth now rose and fell away from the ground between them. What appeared to be a monstrous gourd rose up: gourd it was, but also a head, with mouth, nose, and eyes—hungry eyes that popped open as it sensed its liberation from the ground. The Yedoni—for that was what Adam had recognized the thing to be—planted its two hands on the ground and pushed down on them to pull itself up out of the earth. It did so with amazing power and speed and came to stand no more than twenty feet from them.

The Sages say that the wild beasts that the Holy One, Blessed be He, loosed upon the ancient Egyptians at the time of the ten plagues were not lions or tigers, but the Yedoni, and that this was why the Egyptians grew fearful of the Lord. Scripture warned man against contact with the Yedoni, for such contact meant almost certain death. In Adam's time and place, most towns and villages were safe because the Yedoni grew only in uncultivated ground. But more than one traveler who failed to reach his destination, particularly those who traveled by night, knew the Yedoni, though it was the last thing they knew.

Human in form but in no other way, the Yedoni stood seven feet tall, towering over Adam and fully as tall as the golem. Its body and face were mottled in the colors of the mud from which it had come, and covered with secondary roots, hairs, spikes, and thorns that added to its volume. Worms and beetles and maggots crawled across its moist, mud-covered skin. The hairy root sprang from the Yedoni's abdomen like an umbilical cord and snaked back into the hole in the ground from which the creature had come.

Waves of terror pounded Adam. His legs felt weak and not wholly under his control. Nausea roiled his stomach and brought a putrid taste to his mouth. He fought to control these impulses and succeeded at least enough to draw his musket to his chest, ready to shoot.

For the first time, the Yedoni saw the two witnesses to its birth. It took their measure and then smiled a frozen smile; its teeth were enormous and sharp, like the thorns of ancient brambles. The Yedoni shook its powerful, muscled body like a dog shaking off pond water. Mud flew everywhere, hitting both Adam and the golem and blinding them for a moment. In that instant, the Yedoni rushed at the golem, knocking him to the ground. The two creatures wrestled like behemoths, the ground shaking beneath them as the Yedoni attempted to sink its knife-like teeth into the golem's neck. As they rolled on the earth, the Yedoni's umbilical root twisted around the golem, binding him to his foe. The golem used his massive, shovel-like hands to try to push away the Yedoni's head, to break its jaws, to crack its skull—but the Yedoni was too strong. Nor could the golem get away; he and his adversary were bound together as one.

All this had taken but a few seconds. The golem was pinned on his back, the Yedoni on top of him. At the sight of his companion's plight, Adam shook off his terror, at least enough of it to raise his musket and fire, but the creature absorbed the balls without result. Whatever was inside the Yedoni wasn't blood and wasn't stopped by musket shot. Adam looked about him, seeking something he could use against the monster. His gaze fell upon the creature's umbilical root. With a sound that was half battle cry, half hysteria, Adam ran forward and brought the wooden butt of his musket down on it like an ax. For the first time, the Yedoni made a sound, a soul-piercing howl that Adam would continue to hear in his nightmares for years to come. *So that got your attention,* Adam thought. He brought the musket down again and again upon the root, with a violence heretofore hidden within him, until the root was severed. Disconnected from whatever part of it lurked deep underground, the Yedoni froze and turned as gray and brittle and dead as a dried leaf.

The golem swept off the unholy debris of his adversary and began to return to Adam. But Adam had no time to savor their victory. Another Yedoni rushed from the shadows, shoving him to the ground with a force that sent him sliding across the clearing, the undergrowth tearing at his face and hands. The Yedoni moved toward Adam but the golem knocked the creature down. They fought, the golem trying to avoid entanglement in the root, which stretched back into the darkness. Before Adam could come to the aid of the golem, a third Yedoni appeared beyond the fire, the flickering light from the flames casting a dance of death across its torso and face. This Yedoni, unlike the others, took a slow and steady pace in its approach to Adam. He looked into its face, with its mirthless smile and dead black eyes, and Adam knew that this Yedoni didn't want just to kill him; this Yedoni wanted him to know he was going to die. This Yedoni wanted him to feel fear, and the greatest amount of fear at the moment of his death.

Adam fought to breathe, as though his body had forgotten how. But he hadn't forgotten how to kill the Yedoni. Adam raised his musket and aimed it at the creature's umbilical root—and remembered that he hadn't reloaded the gun. He lowered the musket and groaned. There would be no time to measure and pour the powder, insert the wadding, add the balls, and pack it. The Yedoni had crossed around the fire and most of the way to Adam, the flames now backlighting the creature and turning it into a featureless, black silhouette that moved closer, closer.

Adam gripped his musket to use it again as an axe. But he lacked the advantage of surprise and would get no chance to use the musket as he had before. A shiver raced through him as he realized his weapon was useless. In utter frustration, he hurled the musket at the Yedoni, which swatted it away like a twig. Adam bit his lip in concentration. To run might deliver him into the embrace of other Yedoni. Instead, Adam began to move to his right, just a step, then another. The Yedoni pivoted to match the change in Adam's direction, and continued its approach. Adam moved further to the right, and the Yedoni again turned as it continued toward him, not about to let Adam get away. Just a few inches more, Adam thought.

The Yedoni stopped, a look of shock on its face, and let out a howl to match that of its fallen comrade. As Adam intended, the creature had dragged its umbilical root into the fire as it shifted direction to follow him. The root was now alight. The fire raced the length of the root to the Yedoni and hit it in the abdomen like a cannon blast. The creature was aflame now, shrieking, running through the clearing on its body's final, fading impulses. And then it collapsed, a pile of smoking ash, and moved no more.

Adam could see the golem still fighting the second Yedoni. The golem rolled the creature in its own root, enough at least to keep its hands and feet under some control. He raised the creature into the air and threw it into the flames. It exploded with a crackling sound and they ducked. Parts of the creature flew in all directions, hitting them with burnt, foul-smelling debris.

A loud rhythmic sound filled Adam's ears and he panicked until he realized that it was the rushing of his own blood within him. He didn't move, trying to gain a sense of what was to come. But nothing more came. Gradually, the racing of his blood and the pounding of his heart abated.

The golem rose from the crouch he had assumed when destroying the last Yedoni and joined Adam. There was concern in his expression, but Adam paid more attention to the golem's wounds. The Yedoni had left deep gashes in the rough brown and gray surface of the golem's face, neck, and shoulders and his black jacket was ripped in several places. Adam noticed the injuries with surprise; he hadn't thought the golem could be injured. But the golem showed no self-pity. Instead, the golem smoothed his clay over the wounds with no more emotion than a potter addressing an imperfection in a vessel, and they disappeared.

Now the golem was staring at Adam, his gray brows raised in what looked like surprise. He extended a finger and touched it to Adam's blood-smeared face. He gazed at the blood in bewilderment. It seemed to Adam that this was one more thing that the golem did not understand, or, perhaps, had not understood until now.

Adam dabbed at his face with his sleeve. The gash wasn't serious. It would soon heal, although it would likely leave another scar. He massaged his shoulder carefully, attempting to assuage a sharp pain lodged there, and winced. Well, at least he was alive, wasn't he? He had encountered the Yedoni and lived. How many people since the time of the ancients could say that? He looked over at the golem, who now was bringing another log to the fire. Adam smiled, realizing that the golem had been tested in strong fire, indeed. And he had met the challenge with every limb of his hulking, clay body.

Exhaustion came over Adam like the white cloth unfurled with a flourish across the holy Sabbath table. His limbs were heavy, his mind adrift. Adam slept.

His eyes snapped open. It was still night. The clearing was empty. The fire, low. The golem, gone. But no, the clearing wasn't empty after all. Mendel? Could it be dear Mendel, his precious son, standing before him? Adam struggled to sit upright, unsure of what kept him weighted down. His boy had returned to him! But why was he merely standing there, looking at his father as though pleading?

The boy's gaunt face was stained with dirt and blood and streaked with dried tears. Adam shuddered, not wanting to contemplate where he'd been, what had happened to him.

"Papa, repair!" he cried out.

"Mendel? Mendel!" Adam bolted upright—but Mendel was gone. In his place stood Leah, no longer catatonic but white as parchment. Sweet, darling Leahele! But how had she managed to find him here? He reached out toward her. He had to get her away from this place.

"Papa, repair!" she wailed in a voice that struck him with grief. Then she, too, was gone, a wisp of vapor that melted into the cold night.

"Leah, Mendel! Come back!" Adam ran about the clearing, looking for them in vain. Other mists congealed and he was confronted by his Hersh and Miriam, bloodied and mangled from their wounds, their clothes in tatters, yet standing before him. He had left them gravely ill but alive. But they stood before him now like ghosts. He looked at them, pleading with them in a voice without words, a voice from inside him that begged to know what he should do, what he could do. And he saw the response in their woeful eyes, the eyes of young people that had seen both too much and not enough: *Repair!*

He held out his arms to them but there were no children for him to grasp.

Instead a woman appeared, as enticing as the first fruit in the Garden. Her black hair cascaded like a waterfall to caress full breasts. Her skin, pure ivory, glistened as with oil, and smelled sharp and sweet. He felt drawn to her red lips, which quivered an invitation to be kissed, and to her emerald eyes, which, unless he was careful, would become the only things he could see. He looked into those magnetic eyes but he was not hers, not entirely, not yet.

"What have you done with my children?"

The woman studied him a moment, took a step toward him, then reached out and stroked his face. He couldn't remember ever feeling this overwhelming pull of desire, but he felt it now. Adam wanted to stop her, wanted to raise his hand and move hers away, but that much will he did not possess. Her touch was everything, a power that immobilized him. He was powerless, like a snake in a carnival, charmed by the touch of its handler. His breathing became labored as his mind struggled to control his body. He both dreaded her touch and craved it.

"Be calm," she whispered to him, stroking his cheek again. It was a command, not a suggestion. "There, isn't that better?"

"No. Please. Don't." His body was no longer his own, at least, it no longer answered to him.

"Shhh. It's all right."

She pressed her body against him and put her lips on his. He tried to twist his mouth away, but found it returning to her of its own accord. As her lips pressed hard against his, his body began to convulse, the air, the very life, leaving him. After seconds that felt like forever, she pushed him away and smiled as he tumbled to the ground, gasping for breath.

A hoarse "why?" was all he could utter.

Lilith considered him for a moment. "You."

"I don't understand," he whispered.

"Of course you don't."

Her pearly skin grew dark and hundreds of small shafts broke through the surface like an infantry of Yedoni arising from the earth. But these were scales, not creatures, hard and pointed and oozing pus. They covered her from head to foot, an impenetrable shield. Lilith had become a shiny, slimy thing of scabs and disease. She was as dreadful as she had just been beautiful, her evil fully manifest. She leapt like an animal, a gigantic springing insect, across the clearing and onto Adam, pressing her mouth down violently on his, sucking his soul from him, ripping it out, undeterred by the meager resistance he could muster.

Adam lost consciousness and all went dark. When he opened his eyes, he was on the ground where he had fallen asleep. He was shivering; so cold, yet drenched in sweat and in the tears that flowed down his face. It was still dark and the shapes he could see by the light of the fire seemed all in motion, leaving him disoriented and queasy. Adam felt arms around him and fought to free himself until he saw it was the golem who held him, enveloping him as though to keep him still. But the golem could not keep Adam from trembling and moaning, not for hours.

Chapter Seventeen

Adam awoke. He squinted against the light of the early morning sun. Birds were singing. He was lying on the ground, the golem cradling his torso and head as he must have done for hours. Relief poured from Adam. What had happened, what had been real? His aching shoulders and bruises suggested the reality of the fight with the Yedoni. But the other part, his children, Lilith—was that a dream? Dreams and reality were not always separate spheres, he knew. It could have been both.

But enough. First he must recite the words with which he began each day.

"I thank thee, everlasting King, who hast with mercy restored my soul within me; thy faithfulness is great," he murmured.

Adam looked up at the golem, who was peering down at him, his gray brow furrowed.

"All is well, my friend, all is well," Adam said, to reassure them both.

He rose and rubbed the aches in his arms and back without in any way dislodging them, then followed the sounds of the brook, the golem in tow. He knelt at the water's edge and performed the ritual ablution. Now, he was ready to begin the day. But first he needed his sack. Back at the clearing, he saw much of his possessions were scattered about. He gathered the small, velvet bag that contained his prayer shawl and phylacteries, put them on, and offered his morning prayers.

Together with the golem, Adam gathered the possessions he could see, and searched for the rest. They retrieved the tin cup, plate and utensils, the shot and powder for his now-useless musket, even his remaining supply of eggs, and returned them to their place in his sack. But where was the mirror? He stopped short at a gray mound in a vaguely human shape, and a shiver shot through him. He was looking at the dead husk of a Yedoni. He nudged the shape with the tip of his boot and, eliciting no response, brought the boot down on the remains, sending a cloud of cinder and ash rising and then dissipating into the cold morning air.

The golem saw something glint near the pile that remained of the Yedoni. He bent down and brushed aside the thin, brittle flakes to find the mirror underneath. He picked it up, looked into it, and showed it to Adam. The glass misted over and, as it cleared, displayed the edge of the forest and, beyond it, a small, irregularly shaped area dotted with spire-topped buildings, open squares, houses, fields, and a river punctuated by several mills and bridges.

"Brinnitz!" Adam marveled. "I know this place. We must be near it."

It would mean perhaps hours more of trudging through the forest, but each step would bring them closer to the Lamed Vavnik. Adam was certain of that now.

They started at a brisk pace toward the rising sun. The terrors of the night were far behind them, and good riddance. Today they would see success. The trees and brush, formerly so abundant that Adam and the golem often had to squeeze past them, grew more sparse, allowing for a very pleasant walk. As the trees continued to thin out about them, they let the mirror guide them out of the last of the woods, down the gentle slope of a meadow of green and yellow grasses, and toward the town of Brinnitz.

A town of considerable industriousness spread before them. They made their way down the high street, past ritual slaughterers, bakeries, a school, houses of study organized mostly along guild lines, and the market square. In the distance, rising above the buildings of the Jewish Quarter in which they found themselves, they could make out the occasional church spire, a reminder to Adam that Brinnitz, unlike his own Lizensk, was very much a mixed town.

He got another reminder when they reached the market. The bustling, boisterous crowds included Jews and Christians on both sides of the stalls. Bearded men garbed like himself, in long black coats with black skullcaps peeking out from the backs of their fur-lined black hats, their sidelocks swinging as they moved, conducted business with fair-haired men in shorter coats, jackets, and open shirts in colors that would never have passed muster back in Lizensk. The women of Brinnitz, Adam noticed, wore the same long-sleeved blouses, shawls, cloaks, and skirts regardless of the side of the town from which they came. But he could still recognize his female co-religionists by their elaborate headdresses: forehead-bands, tied scarves, or lace-caps decorated, for those who could afford it, with pearls.

"You're trying to rob me," complained an elderly woman whose eyes burned bright beneath a white mob cap. "The ironsmith across the way charges half as much for his pots!"

"Then buy from him," offered the besieged tradesman, a heavy-set man sweating as though he were still at his forge.

"He's out of pots," conceded his customer.

The tradesman drew himself up to his full height. "Madam," he said with calculated dignity, "when I'm out of pots, I also charge half price."

Adam and the golem passed through the throng as best they could. They were assaulted not just by the shouts and the crowds, but also by the bleats and neighs and moos of the livestock for sale—and then by the pungent odors of their hairy bodies and their waste. At least, Adam was. He looked up at the long, straight, almost triangular nose he had carved for the golem and wondered if he, too, had a sense of smell.

"Look, Mama!" cried a boy of five or six, holding tight to his mother's skirts and pointing to the golem. "It's a goblin!"

His mother, distracted from her purchase of radishes, looked up at the golem in his hatless, ill-fitting black suit and bare feet, scowled, and looked down at her son. "Goblins be red and better dressed," she sniffed. "Whatever it be, it no be a goblin."

Adam paused at the end of a row of stalls, where he would attract less attention, brought the mirror out of his pocket, and consulted it before anyone around him could see what he was doing. The mirror directed them past the fishmongers and tinkers and booksellers, and out of the market. The sounds and smells chased after them down the street but eventually gave up. Now they stopped short at the sight that loomed before them:

the Great Synagogue of Brinnitz. The majestic structure sat in the center of the Jewish Quarter like a dowager surrounded by her poorer relations. Adam gazed up in wonder at the building—all of wood, mostly horizontal timbers—which soared into the brisk Brinnitz air, daring the wind to make it budge by so much as an inch. It hardly seemed possible to him that this magnificent building could have been built for the same purpose as the humble, one-story synagogue of Lizensk.

Now that they stood before the mighty synagogue of Brinnitz, Adam looked back to the mirror for further instructions. There were none. The image in the glass still showed the enormous prayer house and a small structure next to it.

"So the Lamed Vavnik is in the synagogue," he said to the golem. "I'd say our hidden saint won't be hidden for much longer."

The golem nodded, his lopsided ears making the movement almost comical. They entered the synagogue through the men's entrance into the one-story vestibule that ran the length of the building. Against the whitewashed walls were rows of bookshelves holding thousands of well-worn volumes, more than Adam had ever seen at one time in his own synagogue or anywhere else. Before them stood a long table and chairs which no doubt hosted the weekly meetings of the town councilors, and a one-cell jail for the occasional thief, but no Lamed Vavnik. No anyone.

Moving through the vestibule, they pushed open a pair of wooden doors—big, dark, and heavily lacquered—and stopped, awed by what they saw. The purpose of the soaring exterior of the synagogue was revealed to them: here was a vast, nine-vaulted chamber crowned by a giant cupola. Directly below it stood the spot from which the prayer leader would conduct services, most likely surrounded by hundreds of worshipful Brinnitzers: a six-sided wooden platform, topped by a latticework canopy and surrounded by a graceful balustrade. Who had carved and built and painted all this? Adam wondered. And, of course, he knew: simple, hard-working people, artisans and laborers of Brinnitz who, lacking material wealth, showed their devotion to the Holy One, Blessed be He, in the only ways they could.

Rows of wooden benches surrounded the platform and covered the floor of the great space. The women's balcony ran along the back and side walls in an echo of a similar balcony in the ancient Temple in Jerusalem. His gaze swept back and forth throughout the hall, seeking, seeking, but finding no one.

Adam's gaze went to the far wall, the eastern wall, the wall closest to that most holy of cities. It was the wall against which stood the Holy Ark, which would contain the scrolls of the law and other most sacred scrolls and ritual objects of the Jews of Brinnitz. Could the Lamed Vavnik be hiding behind it? Adam went to investigate; the golem lumbered close behind.

The Ark, a chamber rising a dozen feet toward the cupola, was the most ornate structure in the room, as befit its purpose. The giant curtain which screened its sacred contents was a burgundy velvet, embroidered with gold thread and decorated with glass stones arranged into a shimmering mosaic of springing lions holding the tablets of the law. Here, Adam knew, was the loving work of the women of Brinnitz, who turned their talents with needle and thread to a holy pursuit every bit as impressive as the craftsmanship of their husbands.

Adam's gaze followed the pair of Corinthian columns that soared to the top of the Ark. Upon them sat sculptures of two cherubs, the child-like angels that, to this day, guard the entrance to the Garden of Eden. Above the Ark, too, hung the oil lamp that the congregation kept continuously lit as a sign of the Divine presence. And above all of this, seemingly surveying the scene with majestic repose, stood a representation of the Ten Commandments that the Almighty gave to Moses on Mt. Sinai. Adam saw majesty everywhere he turned. He just didn't see the Lamed Vavnik.

"Hello!" he called out in a last attempt to find his benefactor, his voice swallowed up in the vast space. "Anyone here?"

Only the silence answered him.

Through an open window, Adam saw a small wooden house. It took him a moment to recall that this, too, had been depicted in the mirror. Surely this was the rabbi's house. The smoke from the chimney suggested that the rabbi was at home. Perhaps...

Adam and the golem were at the front door in a moment. In response to their knock, it was opened by an elderly woman who peered at them through small, heavily lidded eyes and a pair of thick spectacles pinched to the bridge of her abundant nose. Her short, stout frame was planted in the middle of the doorway, an effective barrier to unauthorized entry. She gave them a look that suggested she was accustomed to visitors—and didn't think much of them.

"Yes, what do you want?" she said in a voice that could chill porridge.

"We've come to see the rabbi," answered Adam.

"Oh, the rabbi, is it?" she replied, wiping her hands on the apron. She tilted her squarish, heavily lined face up and then down to inspect them more thoroughly, her copious jowls bobbing a bit as she did so. Then, one of her thick, gray eyebrows popped upward, as though to suggest that her opinion of visitors hadn't changed.

"Rabbi Zusman doesn't see just anyone. Who"—she peered again at the golem—"and *what* should I say is calling?"

"Rabbi Adam, from Lizensk and his… friend," Adam answered, turning to include the golem. His companion seemed puzzled at the word, then flashed a look of recognition, and a smile.

"Very well. Wait here." The door closed before them.

After a moment, the housekeeper reappeared and waved her hand in what might charitably be taken for an invitation to enter. They followed her in. Everywhere he turned, Adam saw books: books on tables, books on chairs, books on anything that could hold them, books rising like little towers of Babel from the floor. Amidst all these books sat Rabbi Zusman, a shriveled little man almost lost in a massive armchair, who seemed as ancient as the enormous volumes open before him. He had the barest wisps of white hair that peeked out from his skullcap like escaping steam, a face so lined, furrowed and jowled that it cried out for inflation, and ears that looked as though they could double as wings.

"Rabbi Zusman, here are your visitors," the housekeeper shouted, bringing her own wizened face close to his ear. Rabbi Zusman looked at her without comprehension. With a slight shake of his head, he picked up a large ram's horn twisted in two loops and put it to his ear.

"Eh, what?" replied the old rabbi, whose ears apparently made better wings than they did organs for hearing. Adam noticed the golem reaching up to consider his own mispositioned ears.

"Visitors. You have visitors. I told you. From Lizensk. Rabbi Adam and his... whatsis," she said, gesturing toward the golem. Then she turned to Adam. "Now would be a good time for you to speak your peace."

The housekeeper withdrew, snapping shut a door behind her. They had reached the object of their quest. Their Lamed Vavnik sat before them. Adam closed his eyes and mouthed the ancient words of thanksgiving.

Blessed art thou, Lord our God, King of the universe, who has granted us life, sustained us, and permitted us to reach this season.

Relief poured out of him and he took a reverential step forward.

"It's a great honor to meet you," Adam stammered.

"Eh?" asked Rabbi Zusman, who had let his horn fall to his lap. He retrieved it. Adam stepped closer and repeated his words into it.

"It is?" said Rabbi Zusman, incomprehension filling the deep cracks and crevices of his face.

"We know who you are," Adam shouted into the horn.

"You know who I am?" laughed the other, the laugh turning into a dangerous-sounding cough from deep within his shallow chest. His face grew red and round and Adam feared the worst. When the cough subsided, Rabbi Zusman continued. "My whole life I've been wondering who I am. And you know. So. Tell me." He looked up at Adam with eager anticipation.

Adam nodded. Of course Rabbi Zusman would not drop his mask in an instant. This was a test. "You don't need to pretend," Adam assured him. "We've come because we need your help."

"A lot of people think I'm my late Uncle Lazer's son, Berel," said Rabbi Zusman, not particularly in Adam's direction. "Apparently, we look a lot alike. Frankly, I never saw the resemblance. Still—Shayna!" he boomed, arms waving.

The housekeeper opened the door from the back room and poked in her head.

"I'm not my late Uncle Lazer's son, Berel, am I?"

The housekeeper adjusted her glasses as though considering the matter, replied in the negative, and withdrew, closing the door.

"Aha! See?" said Rabbi Zusman.

What a wonderful disguise, thought Adam, *perhaps it's necessary while the housekeeper is within hearing.* He played along with the wily Lamed Vavnik, waiting for the moment when they could speak without guile. He gave the rabbi opening after opening to reveal himself, but Rabbi Zusman continued to talk about his seemingly endless supply of relatives, many of whom, Adam began to suspect, had never existed. His head began to swim. It dawned on him, with more than a sinking feeling, that Rabbi Zusman wore no disguise. This old man was incapable of pretense, Adam realized with a groan. Hearing himself through the roar of his disappointment, Adam made his apologies for having bothered the rabbi. The old man lifted his ram's horn and smiled as Adam and the golem left.

They stopped on the street and Adam looked back at the rabbi's house in disbelief. He tried to puzzle out where he'd gone wrong. He had followed the mirror. He had done everything that was asked of him. He had nearly been killed, only to have his journey end... like this? It didn't seem possible, but there it was. As they walked down the dirt street, Adam's long, thin legs moved of their own volition. The golem walked in an awkward manner, unaccustomed as he was to a pace slow enough to keep him at Adam's side. They came to the market but this time the stalls, the people, the animals—to Adam it was all a blur. It really didn't matter where he went now; he had nowhere to go. The golem took his arm, steering him away from collisions with the townsfolk moving everywhere around them.

Hadn't the mirror brought them to Brinnitz, to the Jewish Quarter, to this rabbi's modest home, for a reason? There had to be a reason. He had said that to Sarah just two nights before. He had staked everything on it—but what if he had been wrong?

Adam stopped short so suddenly that he almost tripped. People continued to move about him in every direction but he didn't see even one of them.

"Follow me," he told the golem. He turned around and trotted, almost ran, back toward Rabbi Zusman's house. Now the golem rushed to keep up with him. As Adam approached the house, the housekeeper, wrapped in a long, brown cloak, the hood on and falling almost to her face, was leaving with an armful of books for the synagogue.

"Madam!" Adam cried.

"Something else to ask Rabbi Zusman?" she asked as she bustled past them toward the synagogue. Adam and the golem trailed after her.

"No, something to ask you: Can you forgive me?"

The housekeeper paused, turned, and regarded him. The compressed lips of her small, thin mouth might have been curling at the ends into a smile, but he couldn't be sure. And then she was off. She entered the synagogue and Adam and the golem followed her into the vestibule. She put the books down on a nearby table and lit some candles. She began shelving the volumes with a precision that arrested Adam's attention, returning each book to its proper place without a moment's hesitation, though most of the bindings were nearly indistinguishable and the number of tomes vast.

With a single, smooth motion, the old woman slotted volume three of *The Path of the Just* unerringly between volumes two and four at the far end of a low shelf. Rashi's commentary on *Exodus* almost flew to its place between his commentaries on *Genesis* and *Leviticus*, like the water that flew from the well into the pitcher of the matriarch Rebecca. And so it went with the other volumes on the table. A juggler in the market square could not have performed with greater skill.

The room was silent, except for the soft swooshing sound of the reshelved books. Adam was about to repeat his question when the housekeeper, her back still to him, interrupted his thought.

"Why Rabbi Adam, forgive you for what?"

Adam blinked and cleared his throat. "For assuming that a holy person has to be a rabbi," he said.

The sound of the books sliding against the wooden shelves stopped immediately. The old woman turned and gave him an appraising look.

"That *is* quite a leap," Shayna agreed.

Chapter Eighteen

Shayna walked to a bookcase twenty feet away, her stout frame rocking from side to side like a metronome. She reached toward an upper shelf and extracted a book—almost identical to those around it—that had been shelved upside down. She turned the book right side up, gave it a gentle kiss, and returned it to its place.

"We mustn't let the words of the Holy One, Blessed be He, be stood on their heads now, mustn't we?" she asked. Adam wasn't sure if she was addressing the book or him. Shayna turned and looked at him, eliminating his doubt. "It's a small slip, but from small slips grow the greatest of tragedies"—What was she talking about, Adam wondered, what did she know?—"and the Evil Inclination misses few opportunities for mischief. Any chink in the wall, Rabbi Adam. Any chink in the wall. A party invitation goes astray, and, the Temple in Jerusalem lies in ruins for 1,700 years."

It took Adam a moment to recall the reference. In the days of the Roman rule over Jerusalem, according to the Sages, a party invitation was diverted in error from one of the host's friends to one of his enemies. When the unwitting guest showed up, the host ordered him to leave. Seeking to avoid embarrassment, the man offered to pay for his meal, for half the party, for the entire party—to no avail. Humiliated, the man sought his revenge by telling the Roman Caesar, falsely, that the Jews planned to revolt. The Caesar made sure there would be no revolt by destroying the city and her holy Temple, murdering most of her people, and sending the rest into slavery, exile, and dispersion.

Adam knew the story, but he had always understood it as it had always been taught: as a warning against the forces unleashed by baseless hatred. To this remarkable woman, however, it was the story of a minor and accidental wrong, the misdirection of a piece of mail, and the calamitous tear it ultimately rent in the nexus of the lower and upper spheres. Were the worlds truly as fragile—no, as *sensitive*—as that? Perhaps they were.

Shayna removed her nose spectacles and squinted as she used her apron to clean them. For the briefest of moments, she seemed illuminated by a glowing whiteness that appeared to contain all the colors seen and unseen. Adam blinked, merely for a second, but long enough for Shayna to return the spectacles to their perch on her mound of a nose, the lenses magnifying her small, sharp eyes and the wrinkles around them. Whatever light Adam thought he'd seen was gone.

"There, that's all a bit clearer now, isn't it?" she said. "We might as well sit down. I believe we have a good deal to discuss." She motioned to the chairs around the council table, and they all took seats, the golem settling himself with care in a chair not meant for his bulk.

"So I'm right?" Adam asked. "*You* are the—"

"Labels, names," she said, batting his words away with a wave of her wizened hand. "I never had patience for labels. Perhaps I see a little more, know a little more, than the next person"—she glanced again at the golem—"or whatsis. That's all."

"Please, you must help us."

"I know," answered Shayna without inflection. "That's why I brought you here. I believe you have a book and a mirror of mine."

So that was it: His Lamed Vavnik, his hidden saint and secret benefactor, was the short, stout housekeeper of a senile rabbi. Whatever he had expected, it wasn't this. So many questions rushed at him; where to begin? If Shayna had been in Lizensk, why hadn't she just spoken to him there? And why had she sent him on an almost-fatal journey through the forest?

As though sensing his thoughts, Shayna said, "The dangers you face, Rabbi Adam, believe me, are far worse than anything you have faced yet. If you couldn't make it this far on your own… but you *did* make it this far." She pointed a small, plump finger in his direction. "That was the first test."

"And you passed through the forest *twice*, unharmed?" he countered. "How?"

Shayna gave him a sly smile. "One picks up a few tricks in my line of work."

"Your tricks alerted you to... Lilith?" Adam asked, his voice falling to a whisper upon mention of the Demon Queen's name.

"I can sometimes see the past, and my vision is pretty good as far as the present goes," she replied, tapping her thick nose spectacles. "Yes, I sensed Lilith as soon as she made herself manifest. How could I not?" Shayna rocked her head in sorrow, her jowls moving like pendulums.

She looked up and stared at him, but there was no twinkle in her eyes now. "Do you know what it felt like? As though all the joy had been snuffed out of existence like"—her hand groped the air as though she would find her phrase there—"like the last candle in the world.

"And yes, I saw what she did to your family," she shuddered as though reliving the memory. Then, she leaned toward him, her hands palm down, fingers splayed, on the table between them. "Your family didn't stand a chance."

"And the future?" he asked. "Can you see that, too? Can I find my son, save my children?"

Shayna's thick, jowled face clouded. "The future is a book closed even to me. I'm afraid that the Master of the World keeps that volume on a shelf too high for me to reach."

"Then at least tell me why," Adam insisted. "Why is she persecuting my family?"

Shayna looked at him as a not particularly patient teacher might regard a slow student.

"She's not persecuting your family," Shayna corrected him. "She's persecuting *you*."

Adam shivered. That thought hadn't occurred to him. He asked: "What have I done to her?"

Shayna sighed. "Ah, well, there's the question, isn't it?"

Adam could bear the riddles no more. He jumped up, his chair falling over behind him. "Then what's the answer?"

Shayna regarded him with great earnestness, and then, with the subtlety of a passing shadow, her expression shifted to reveal great kindness and empathy. He righted his chair and sat down.

"I'm not toying with you, Rabbi Adam," she said. "There is much here that is unclear, even to me. But this much I do know: This didn't start with Lilith's attack on your family. There is a grave injustice connected to this affair. I can feel it. I can sense it. Can't you? The feeling is almost overpowering. What once went wrong must be set right. It must be repaired."

"Repair," he repeated, retrieving something he had nearly let go of. "In my dream, they kept telling me to repair."

Shayna leaned forward, encouraging him. "Repair what?" she asked.

Adam's face fell.

"I... I don't know," he stammered. "They wouldn't say." He paused and looked down, unable to meet Shayna's gaze. "And I wouldn't know where to begin."

Shayna gave him a sympathetic look, and then she was all business again. "And the mirror told you nothing?"

"The mirror?" asked Adam. "I thought it was just to show us the way here."

"For that, I could have left you a map," said Shayna with a wave of her arm. But was she dismissing him or his suggestion? He would have to learn to read her better—though he was beginning to think that Shayna herself might be a book on a shelf beyond *his* reach.

"The mirror doesn't just show what could be," said Shayna, "but what could have been."

Again, Shayna was talking in riddles. Adam reached into his pocket and extracted the mirror. All he saw was his own reflection. His face was as gaunt and pale as ever, though there were perhaps more gray hairs in his long, thin beard and sidelocks than he'd remembered. He supposed that battling the Yedoni could do that. But what "could have been" was there about this image?

As if in answer to his unspoken question, his reflection faded away, replaced by... nothing. Adam stared into the mirror and saw only a void, a grayness, the absence of both light and dark, that seemed to stretch back into the glass as far as he could make out. It occurred to Adam that the glass was showing him a moment of eternity frozen between his World of Illusion and the True World to Come. After a moment, a crack opened in the nothing and a young woman of sixteen appeared in the glass. Cascades of golden hair framed her pale, luminous face, large, hazel-colored eyes, and lips turned up in a subtle but unmistakable smile.

She was beautiful, perhaps the most beautiful woman he had ever seen. And it wasn't just her physical beauty. She had a bearing, a grace, that radiated from her like the light from the sun. Surely her physical beauty was a reflection of an equally pronounced spiritual beauty. Adam knew this too, though he knew not how he knew it. The young woman looked out of the glass, seemingly straight at him. Her smile deepened. And then, Adam understood.

His skin grew cold and his body lost its sense of balance. He felt the sweat on his face, his chest, his back. His instinct, now as then, was to run away; but this time he knew there was nowhere he could hide, not even within the unilluminated corners of his soul.

He sensed he knew this young woman, though he didn't know how—just as he didn't know much about his past. The two, this woman and his past, were forever connected. She had been wiped from his memory with a completeness that included his childhood, his family, his village. But he knew her. The memories came slowly, with the strain of long-atrophied muscles recalled to use, but come they did. Images passed across the mirror or, perhaps, across his mind. There was a village, the two of them playing by the water, and under a table on the holy Sabbath. Then there was a man—his father?—showing him how to wear phylacteries. There was a woman—his mother?—making simple gifts for friends on Purim. And always, there was this perfect young woman.

He tried in vain to recall the last time he had said her name, or even thought of her. It had been a lifetime ago; it had been a moment ago. He had left her behind in a time and place that no longer existed. And now here she was. The world in which he lived, the life he had created, had never prepared him to see her again, to open the book he'd long ago closed, buried, and run away from as far and as fast as he could.

"Rachel," he said to the figure in the mirror, with a tenderness that surprised him and shocked him too.

As his breath touched the glass, the image changed. Now he saw a synagogue. It seemed familiar, but he couldn't put a name to it, and then he could. "Miropol," he said, tasting the long-unused name on his tongue. The synagogue was packed with villagers. He struggled to recall these strangers who seemed as familiar to him as his palm. He shivered as he stared into the glass, now hungry for clues to a past that had been a blank to him for all of his adult life.

The villagers were wearing their Sabbath finery, but this was no Sabbath. In the front of the synagogue four young men—friends of his, it came to him, although he couldn't remember who they were—each held the pole of a wedding canopy. Below that canopy stood Rachel in a white satin dress pleated and embroidered with flowers. She brought her hand, partly obscured by the long, lace ruffle at her wrist, to her neck. There, she fingered the single strand of pearls that lay atop her small lace collar. As she moved, the light was caught and reflected by the gold and silver filigree crown that held her white veil in place. She was an angel in human form and Adam's heart melted anew at the sight of her.

Only now did he notice the young man standing next to her under the canopy, the tall, slightly gangly youth in his Sabbath caftan. His face was long and pale but his features regular and almost handsome, his rich black locks not quite contained by his fur-trimmed black hat. Adam was taken by the winsomeness of his expression, his eyes wide and his smile easy, conveying his obvious joy. Like the others, this groom too was familiar and, like the others, his name eluded Adam.

Adam's breath caught in his throat. He was looking at the only person he should be able to see in a mirror. He couldn't recall ever looking, let alone feeling, as happy as that young man. Yet he was convinced that this was him, his younger self. A wave of sadness passed through him at the thought of who he had been on that day, and who he was now. Who he had been on that day... he realized with a sudden sting that this was *not* how he had been on that day; this had never happened. He had never made it to the synagogue, had he? Yet he was there now in the glass, under the wedding canopy, exchanging glances of the greatest love with his bride as she circled about him seven times. Adam witnessed the wedding that had never been, the reading of the marriage contract, the placement of the ring on the bride's finger, the blessings over the goblet of wine.

And he witnessed something more. Adam saw shapes in the synagogue, shapes that were moving not among the villagers, but *above* them, hovering over the wedding canopy. As he watched, they took on form and coloration. They were people, or what people would look like if they were made of mist and fog. And they were crying, their faces, as Adam began to make them out, distorted in anguish. Their grief was so great that Adam could not bear to look at them. He forced himself to lower his gaze, to return to the happy couple beneath the canopy, to pretend that the sorrow he saw above did not exist.

The wedding ceremony was completed. The officiating rabbi put a goblet on the floor before the groom, who raised his right foot and brought it down with a sharp bang. The goblet shattered with the violence of an explosion. Glass shards flew in every direction and Adam was blinded by the light they reflected.

When he could see again, the mirror was blank. All of it, Rachel, the synagogue, the wedding, himself—all gone. Nevertheless, Adam continued to stare at the mirror. Where else could he look? The vestibule of the synagogue of Brinnitz was so quiet that Adam could hear Shayna's breathing, and his own, like thunder. And even without looking up, Adam could feel the full force of the golem's gaze trained on him, begging him to explain what Adam himself did not understand.

Adam heard a rattling sound that he traced after a moment to his chair tapping against the uneven stone floor, animated by his trembling body. Gradually both his trembling and the tapping died down, at least enough for Adam to speak.

"What did I see?" he whispered.

Shayna did not answer him and Adam wondered if she did not know or would not say. Then he saw her eyes glistening. And then she spoke.

"I believe you saw what should have been, what was destined to be," she said in a quiet, deliberate tone, one corner of her small mouth twitching. The golem looked down at him with sympathy, his simple black eye-sockets larger, and his gash of a mouth thinner, than Adam had remembered them.

"I don't understand," he said in utter bewilderment. "If I was supposed to marry Rachel, why don't I remember it? Why didn't I have any memory of her or my village until now? Am I crazy? I must be crazy."

"No, not crazy, Rabbi Adam," she replied. "I think you saw the plan that the Holy One, Blessed be He, had for you from long before you and this Rachel were born. Did you notice the souls in attendance? Of course you did. The souls of the dead return to celebrate the weddings of their descendants. But these souls cried out because, like you, they witnessed a wedding that should have been, but never was."

Adam felt his cheeks burn from the tears running down them. He thought of the embarrassment, the shame, he must have brought to Rachel by abandoning her at the wedding canopy, a wrong that the tradition regarded, he knew, as tantamount to murder. While he was absorbing this dreadful thought, another occurred to him.

"But I *am* married..." he began and broke off. If Rachel was the intended bride he had abandoned, what did that make Sarah? She was the wife who was never meant to be. Their marriage had never been meant to be. His stomach grew tense and sour as that horrible truth came to him. This was what he had done to Sarah, an innocent and kind girl whose only mistake had been to smile at him across her father's Sabbath table. He had somehow condemned her to a life of coldness and emptiness. He felt a wave of shame.

Then the abyss opened before him again, only this time deeper and blacker than before, because now his thoughts turned to his children, his dear, sweet children, who did exist, and whose existence was now so much in doubt. Adam groaned. Were his children also never meant to be—and was what was happening to them now a kind of reckoning?

"This is making more sense to me. Yes… yes…" Shayna said, her short, bulky frame and weighty forearms pressing against the table. "You were destined to marry Rachel but didn't. Somehow, that one act has set in motion all the evils that beset you now. From a single spring, many rivers flow. This was the misdirected invitation. This is what you have to repair in order to rescue your son and restore your children, and you must do so before the consequences tear at both heaven and earth."

"I still don't understand," he pleaded. "How can who I did and did not marry have such an effect?"

Shayna looked at him with those small but penetrating eyes and let out a sigh. Adam didn't like the sound of it. "By running away," she said, "you denied existence—however inadvertently—to the generations that were to come from you and Rachel until the end of all time."

Adam grew pale. His eyes widened as Shayna's words began to sink in. He heard her continue as though speaking from far away. "Great leaders, great teachers, righteous men and women destined to help perfect the world and complete the work of Creation," she said, with broad sweeps of her hands that consigned Adam's destined progeny to oblivion.

Shayna squeezed her eyes shut as though the pain of it was too much even for her. "All gone before they could even be born," she whispered, as from the grave. "Who can begin to measure the loss? The world will forever be the poorer for it."

The Sages say that the enormity of Cain's sin was that he killed not just Abel, but all the generations that were otherwise to come from him, and that it was this blood of infinite generations that rose up to accuse the world's first murderer. Now, Adam saw this same blood of generations on his own hands. This was the tear between the worlds that he had caused on that confused, half-remembered day so long ago. He could only begin to grasp what he had done.

"I never knew," he said, his voice without strength. "How could I have known?"

Shayna slammed her fist down on the table between them with a force that sent its sound reverberating throughout the synagogue.

"You. Know. *Now*," she said, her gravelly voice more emphatic and freighted than Adam had yet heard it. "There's no time for self-pity, Rabbi Adam; there's a world to set right and you are the one who must do it. The wrong you committed is a stain on your soul. It has imperiled your destiny and your family and I fear it threatens to do far more than that. You must repair it. Find Rachel. Ask her for forgiveness and repair your wrong as she directs."

"That's all?" Adam asked with incredulity. "Rachel's forgiveness will defeat Lilith?"

A rueful smile flitted across Shayna's thin lips. "No, it won't," she said. "But it will remove that stain on your soul so that you have the strength to defeat Lilith, rescue your son, and save your family."

Adam weighed what he knew about the Demon Queen against what he knew about himself. "How can I possibly succeed against Lilith?"

Shayna's face softened and, looking into that face, Adam thought he just might succeed after all.

"I have an idea about that," she said to him. "It came to me when I saw the light from the shattered goblet in the mirror. Where our father Jacob dreamed of a ladder of angels journeying between earth and heaven, there is a city, a city called Luz."

"Luz?" he asked, aware of the stories of the flourishing city in the midst of the desert, and of its inhabitants who were said to be... immortal. "Surely Luz is a legend."

"One person's legend is another person's reality," Shayna said.

Chapter Nineteen

A dam was about to ask Shayna what she meant when his attention was diverted. Something from the far corners of the synagogue... a sound? No, a smell, an acrid smell: smoke, coming through the double doors between the vestibule and the main hall. Adam put the mirror down on the table. Shayna's head was tilted toward the door, her great mound of a nose high in the air. Even the nose of the golem, who apparently had a sense of smell, was twitching. Adam rose and ran to the large wooden doors of the main hall, the other two close behind. He went inside.

The fire licked at the beautiful carvings on the prayer leader's platform and table. It covered the balustrade and canopy like deadly ivy. With an evil ferocity, it ran across the benches and up the walls. Now it roared through the hall and came perilously close to the holiest place in the room: the ark and the sacred scrolls it contained. And everything in its path was wood. Everything was its nourishment.

"You have to get out of here," he shouted to Shayna as waves of heat assaulted them.

"What about you?" she asked, the sounds of cracking beams and exploding windows making it difficult for Adam to hear her.

"We'll save the scrolls first, then we'll get out," Adam yelled back. "Golem, help her."

The smoke came lower and thicker, stinging their eyes and throats. Shayna brought her apron up to her face as the golem scooped her up in his massive arms and hurried out past the blazing pyre that had been the central canopy. Adam ran toward the Ark as fire rained down from the roof and surged up from the floor. He ran past the women's balcony, which crashed down before him under the onslaught of the fire. A moment later, the golem was again at his side. The shimmering mosaic on the curtains vanished into the growing flames. Adam found a section of the drape still unscathed, gripped it with both hands, and tore it down. The ancient scrolls of the law, wrapped in velvet and topped with silver crowns, lay just beyond. Adam lifted them, one at a time, out of the Ark and passed them to the golem, who carried them as if they'd been sticks.

The smoke was clawing at Adam's throat now, the heat smothering him. The black clouds came at him again and again, taunting him, daring him to move forward. A massive beam, covered in flames, crashed down from the ceiling with the roar of Behemoth. Another fiery beam fell. The fire raced across the hall, engulfing everything in its path.

"Get the scrolls out of here!" Adam cried above the thunder of the destruction.

The golem started out toward the doors. Adam struggled to follow him, flames leaping up to engulf him as though from ambush, the jagged remains of benches and railings tearing at his clothes and threatening his face. Adam's eyes darted everywhere, seeking a route to safety. He saw several volumes of law on a table, about to be consumed. Adam grabbed the books and scanned the hall for the golem as best he could through the flames and the smoke. But his companion was gone. So was any route to escape.

"Always time for something to read?" mocked a voice. Adam turned. There before him was the woman of his nightmare, deathly thin, her emerald eyes glowing from a pale face with cheekbones that could cut parchment. Lilith, dressed in unspeakable leather, seemed untouched by the destruction swirling about her. Adam looked past the crumbling ark for a way out. There had to be a way out.

"What?" Lilith continued. "Time for books but no time for the girl of your dreams?"

"Stop this," Adam pleaded, the bitter taste of the smoke heavy on his tongue. "Please. Give me my son."

"A family reunion? At a time like this?" Lilith moved closer to him. "That would never have occurred to me. What a delightful idea."

"Then you'll return him?" asked Adam, struggling to remain upright as the smoke and heat continued to attack his senses, disorienting him.

Lilith shrugged. "I was thinking more that I might take you as well."

All about him, the remaining ancient wood moaned and creaked as it was torn apart by the fire.

"You would do well to forget your son, rabbi," said Lilith, a mixture of advice and scorn in her voice. "No man has defied me—and lived."

"Why are you doing this to us?" he demanded. "Why?"

"'There has to be a reason,'" Lilith smiled, her voice now delicate and sweet. "Isn't that what you told your wife? Maybe she was right: the world has less reason than you think. Or maybe you'll just have to reason it out yourself."

A furnace blast of dark, acrid smoke clawed at his eyes and throat and Adam doubled over. He felt two hands lift him high in the air. His body was whirled around by the golem, who picked him up as easily as he had carried the holy scrolls moments before.

"Golem, it's—" Adam pointed to Lilith, but now there was nothing but flames. Lilith was gone. Part of the vaulted ceiling exploded above them. The golem sheltered Adam with his great clay body from the flaming debris that fell around them. He hugged Adam to his chest and barreled through the fiery furnace and toward the doors. Through the flames, smoke, and ruins, Adam glimpsed the mirror on the table, where he'd left it, now in shards. Adam reached out as though to grasp the pieces, the futile gesture all that he was capable of. The fire hurtled toward them with terrifying speed. The din of exploding and collapsing walls grew louder and more triumphant. Adam closed his eyes and prayed.

The next thing he knew, he felt sunshine on his face and heard a din, not of destruction, but of voices. He opened his eyes. He and the golem were now in the street, far enough from the blaze to be safe. Wisps of smoke blew before him as though the fire sought one final way to attack him. He could just make out the scrolls, farther up the street, resting in the back of a wooden cart like wounded soldiers dragged from the battlefield.

The golem set him down on his feet. Adam took a lungful of air and then another. Behind him, the fire continued to rage. Scores of villagers had formed bucket brigades from the river, attempting to put out the flames. Many more were gathered about, safeguarding books, candlesticks, goblets, and other precious objects they had managed to save from the fire.

Adam scanned the villagers, seeking a face he didn't see.

"Shayna! Shayna!" he cried out. Where was she? He staggered toward the crowd, almost tripping over tots holding fast to their mothers' skirts, nearly crashing into the bucket brigade.

He caught a glimpse of a familiar apron. Pushing through the thick mass of people, he moved closer, the golem in tow. There was Shayna, sitting on a tree stump, her shoulders bent, her breathing labored. A trickle of blood ran across the deep lines of her brow. Now he could see two village women tending to her, giving her sips of what he took to be ale and daubing at the cut on her forehead.

Shayna threw him a look that might have meant she was pleased to see him. Then, with a swish of her hand, waved away her attendants like a cow's tail swatting flies.

"The excitement," she said in her gravelly voice, "a little too much for me." She coughed, a thick, harsh cough that Adam didn't like. "What possessed you to stay inside?"

"Lilith. She was there."

At the mention of *her*, Shayna's eyes burned brighter and her lips set in a thin line.

An enormous explosion burst behind them as the roof, with its giant cupola, finally gave up its last resistance and crashed into the flaming hulk of what had once been the Great Synagogue of Brinnitz. Adam could barely take in what he saw: The spiritual home to tens of thousands of his co-religionists over the preceding five centuries, into which they had poured their creativity, their craftsmanship, and their love, was dead. He bowed his head.

"My friends told me you saved the scrolls," Shayna whispered, looking deep into his ashen face. "The rest can be rebuilt."

The golem was riveted by the destruction of the synagogue. His hands fell to his sides and it seemed to Adam as though he was smaller somehow. But for Shayna, the time for grief, if there was ever such a time, had passed. She motioned to the golem to help her onto her feet. She pulled her spectacles, black with soot, from a pocket, wiped them on a clean corner of her apron, and returned them to their perch on her mound of a nose. Adam noticed a slight tremble to her hands that hadn't been there before.

"Well, we survived one attack by Lilith," she said. "I suspect it's a poor idea to remain here and await another. Lightning may not strike the same spot twice but I fear demons are not similarly limited. Shall we go find Rachel?"

"But where?" Adam asked, recalling the slivers of broken mirror left behind in the synagogue.

"I thought that would have been clear by now," she answered him, all business once again. "Miropol."

Miropol. Adam seemed surrounded by silence, though the shouts and hubbub around them continued unabated. He shuddered. His two worlds, past and present, were about to collide—well, collide further. And he didn't know what would be left standing when they did.

"But what if she's no longer there?" he asked. "It has to have been twenty-five years ago."

"Then we'll keep looking," Shayna said. "But is there a better place to start than at the beginning?"

Shayna murmured to the golem and he rushed off, returning moments later with her cloak. Shayna removed her sooty apron, folded it on the stump, and put on the cloak.

Adam looked back toward Rabbi Zusman's house, safely out of reach of the fire. Shayna nodded to acknowledge his concern.

"Don't worry about the rabbi," she said. "My friends look after him when I'm… away. He'll be fine."

Adam nodded and turned to the golem. "You know," he said, "that's the second time you've saved my life. Perhaps I'll be able to repay the favor before we're through."

The ends of the golem's thin mouth turned upward in an uneven smile.

Adam and the golem started down the street, away from the still-smoldering remains of the synagogue and toward the outskirts of Brinnitz. Shayna paused for a moment before joining them. In an undertone barely audible even to herself, she said one word.

"Perhaps."

Chapter Twenty

The golem brushed aside branches, and occasionally whole trees, with a sweep of his arm. His broad chin jutted forward as he walked, his black-socket eyes scanning the forest for creatures that might sweep down from the trees, or up from the earth, or simply materialize before them. An unfamiliar sound would cause his brow to crinkle, the letters engraved there momentarily obscured as he scanned the surroundings for its source.

His creator had told him to protect the one called Shayna and so he did. He snapped away branches before her, lest her cloak snag on them. To keep his eyes on her, he ignored flocks of birds and sprites that otherwise would have fascinated him. He watched her footfalls, prepared to catch her if she fell—which she never did. Her eyes were small, much smaller than his, of course, but smaller even than his master's. But with the barest glance, she managed to convey her thoughts to him.

Watch that hill, golem, as we pass by it.

Don't allow your master to depart from the path here, golem.

Make your steps especially forceful, golem. They need to be heard by what lies below.

She was not his master but, in a way, she was. There was so much he didn't understand. But Shayna seemed to understand him as his creator did not. He would think about this.

Adam trudged onward with the others, his fears surging with every unexpected snap of a twig or throaty *tsk-tsk* of a grackle overhead. Cossacks might appear over any ridge. Thieves might emerge from behind any tree or rock. Were-beasts were certain to appear at night, ready to rip their hearts from their breasts as they slept. Despite the company of Shayna and the golem, his nerves remained as taut as an archer's drawn bowstring.

He watched in amazement as Shayna, despite her age and the weight and bulk of her short frame, navigated thick underbrush and muddy expanses, and scaled rocky hills with the sure-footedness of a billy goat, muttering near-silent prayers all the while. With her hood up and her coarse brown cloak tickling the ground, Shayna looked like another hill—albeit a short and portable one—on the landscape. It wasn't a flattering image, Adam knew, but he didn't think Shayna would have the least use for flattery.

Even without the mirror as a guide, Shayna seemed to know exactly where she was leading them. She moved with urgency while her cloak became coated with burrs and nettles, and her thick dark boots grew muddied and scratched. If her appearance bothered her, she never showed it, not so much as to kick the caked mud from her boots.

They hiked on through meadows and woods, along rivers, and through ravines. As the days passed, Adam's fears subsided, while his exhaustion grew.

"Shayna," he called out to the hidden saint and housekeeper after they'd traveled for several hours without stopping, "let's take a break, a short one."

"'The day is short, the work is much,' Rabbi Adam," she replied.

"'...and the workers are lazy, the reward is great, and the Master is pressing,'" he said with a smile and a nod, completing the saying of the Sages. "I understand."

And so they continued.

"Shayna," he called after they'd been walking for an hour without conversation, each lost in his own thoughts.

She turned to peer at him, her bushy eyebrows arching.

"I've been wondering," he said. "We haven't seen so much as an imp since we started out from Brinnitz. No gryphons. No specters. No were-beasts. Doesn't that strike you as unusual?"

"Are you concerned?" Shayna replied. "I know a spell that can materialize a—"

"No, no," Adam cut in. "Not concerned. Definitely not concerned."

"As you prefer."

The hours on the road gave Adam time to think, perhaps too much time. With each footfall, he moved closer to a past that was still hidden to him. Rachel and Rachel alone had pierced the fog of his memory. But where were the others, his friends, his neighbors, his parents—especially his parents? Would they still be alive and would he know them again when he saw them—*if* he saw them? He struggled to remember but the memories remained just out of reach, no matter how much he worked to regain them.

"We should be going soon if we're to make good time today," Shayna said to him on the fifth day of their journey. They sat resting on soft grasses by the side of a lively little creek. Adam had told the golem he could explore nearby, and his clay companion was now absorbed in the inspection of a bank of wildflowers. The golem held a handful of yellow mudworts up to his nose and seemed to be sniffing them. Adam was about to call the golem back but decided to let him have his independence for a moment longer, there would be plenty more commands to be issued and obeyed.

For a long while, Adam contemplated a pair of smallish fish, darting about in the creek. Now he looked up at Shayna.

"Yes?" she said. "Something's on your mind. I've learned the look."

"You know everything about me and I know nothing about you, apart from the fact that you're a housekeeper," he said to her.

Shayna regarded him evenly. "And that is as it should be, I imagine."

Adam pressed on. "I mean, I don't even know if you have a family, or if you *had* a family."

"You're quite right," she agreed. Adam waited for more until it dawned on him that there wouldn't be any more. The awkward silence was broken by the golem. He presented Shayna with a freshly picked bouquet of wildflowers, all bright petals of reds and yellows and purples. With great ostentation, Shayna received it, smelled it, and held it to her chest.

"Flowers for a lady," she said, smiling enough to show her teeth. "I'm delighted to see we are in the presence of a gentleman." She extended her arm and the golem took it, helping her to her large, booted feet.

"Family, I suppose," she said, turning to Adam as she poked the stem of a silver thistle through the buttonhole at her collar, "is sometimes where you find it."

They spent the Sabbath before reaching Miropol in the village of Venitz, at an inn operated by an elderly couple who were especially pleased to have guests. The wine flowed without reservation. The chickens were roasted to perfection. And the vegetable puddings—carrot, onion, potato, and spinach, among them—were as tasty as the ancient manna in the desert, although they likely contained leaves and roots that could no longer be called fresh. That, after all, was the reason to boil, mash, and bake vegetables into a form that hid their origins—which, Adam reflected, made him something of a vegetable pudding himself.

The puddings reminded him of the ones that Sarah would make for their own Sabbath meals, so many miles away in Lizensk. He could just imagine her pulling the turnips and leeks from the little garden she maintained despite the poor soil, and despite the moles and rabbits and imps that stole as much as they could before she could harvest it. More likely, she would not bother to make a pudding at all for this Sabbath, given the work of tending to the children. The truth was he had no idea what she was thinking, and it had been a long time since he had.

Strange how the golem had known to bring flowers to Shayna. Adam struggled to remember if he had ever brought flowers to Sarah. He couldn't recall. Adam took another bite of the green pudding. What would Sarah say if she knew her husband was on a quest to find the woman he should have married in her place? What would any woman say?

The tin spoon slipped from Adam's fingers and landed on his plate with a clatter that stopped the conversation around the table.

The three left Venitz for Miropol early on the morning after the Sabbath. They walked along a road, broad but muddy to the point of treacherousness, that cut through farmland and meadows and, eventually, a forest. Today he would set things right, Adam thought, as he jumped over a fallen tree with a new sense of vigor. Today he would find both Rachel and his parents and set about fixing old wrongs.

After an hour, the canopy above them became thinner and the sunlight more abundant. Shayna and the golem were well ahead of Adam. Rachel's face was as clear to him as though she walked at his side. But so many other faces were still shadows. His parents, his friends... there had been a Yacov, he now remembered, the butcher's son. They had played ducks and drakes, he recalled with a smile, sending small stones flying across the river to see how many times they could make them skip. He couldn't see Yacov's face, but he could see those stones sailing across the river on a hot summer's day, sending brilliant rings of reflected sunlight glistening atop the muddy green of the river.

For so many years, Sarah and the children had asked him to tell them about his childhood and he had had nothing to offer them. Just as he had had nothing to offer himself. Now, with every footfall, he was walking toward that past and he didn't have the slightest idea what he would find when he got there. But what if his friends and parents remembered *him*—as the man who had abandoned his bride at the wedding canopy, causing her untold shame? As the man who had abandoned his parents, his friends, his entire village? At the thought, everything around him began to spin. The trees closed in on him. The earth seemed to rise up against him. And then all was black.

When he came to, Shayna was loosening his collar and the golem was approaching with Adam's tin cup, now filled with water. The golem passed the cup to Shayna.

"I suppose there's nothing some people won't do for a rest," she said as she helped him take sips of the water. Adam tried to focus his eyes, too disoriented to speak.

She considered him a moment. "So," she said, the low, gravelly tones percolating from deep within her. "The magnitude of what you're about to do has impressed itself upon you? I was wondering when it would."

"What will I say to them all?" he croaked.

"Let me ask you this," she said. She lay her hands flat on the front of her voluminous cloak and looked him straight in the eyes. "If your children's lives were not at stake, would you still seek Rachel's forgiveness?"

Adam looked at her for longer than it took for his voice to return to him. "I don't know," he said with reluctance.

"When the time comes," Shayna assured him, "you'll know the answer to my question—and to yours."

Chapter Twenty-One

The forest gave way to the panorama of a long, deep valley and mountains beyond. The great slope down to the valley had no doubt been a medley of verdant hues just a month before. Now, however, the encroaching cold had begun to paint the leaves with strokes of reds and browns and greys. The grasses had turned dull too. The valley was getting ready to sleep. Or to die. And far off, on the valley floor, shrouded in mist and barely visible, lay the village of Miropol.

Adam glanced at Shayna. She had stopped, her head tilted up just a bit, and her great mound of a nose sniffing the air. Her small dark eyes grew smaller still and her heavy jowls seemed to weigh down the corners of her mouth.

"It's wrong," she said.

"You mean that isn't Miropol?" Adam asked.

"No, that's Miropol," she repeated. "But it's wrong."

Adam pressed Shayna to explain but she declined with the slightest shake of her head.

They began their descent into the valley and, for the first time since they'd left Brinnitz, Adam saw Shayna's steps falter, losing their brisk stride of the past week. The path wound away from the village, which passed from sight before they had any clear view of it. After an hour's descent, Adam saw two stones pressed together by the side of the path. Something about the stones seemed familiar to him. They were each oblong, about five feet long. As he stood there pondering, Shayna, and even the golem, watched him, their questions not on their lips but unmistakably in their eyes. Then he had it. Yes, of course: the "two tablets" stones. He and the other children would play around them, imagining them as the tablets containing the ten commandments that Moses brought down from Mt. Sinai. He could see his playmates still, jumping over the stones and running around them. But he couldn't see their faces, not one.

Adam realized that the path they were on ran north of Miropol—and would take them to what had to be his old home, the little farmhouse alongside the heath. His pleasure at remembering this propelled him to run onward and, for the first time on their journey, Shayna and the golem had to keep up with *him*.

Adam's boyhood home came into view. He took a running step, and another, and halted. An unearthly stillness blanketed the place. Not a cow or chicken appeared in the yard. He stared out at charred ruins, the roof collapsed, the walls mostly ripped away, weeds carpeting the floorboards. A chill swept over him. He gazed past stumps of old oak trees that he now remembered climbing as a boy. And there, in the weedy patch, he could recall a heavy, hunched-over, shadowy figure—his father?—cultivating rows of peppers, cucumbers, and tomatoes.

His home. *This* was his home. Adam shuddered and threw a despairing look back at Shayna; she stood near a bare, withered tree, its trunk hollowed, its branches broken stubs. Her head was bowed and her lips twitched in some private prayer.

Adam turned back to the decimation before him. He walked among the remains of his home, the blackened planks mixed with pieces of crockery, leather, and iron that even the scavengers had left behind.

Everywhere, the evidence of some ancient inferno assaulted him. He struggled to remember something, anything, of his time here. Bits came to him—images here and there: chasing a scrawny chicken in the yard... going to market with a tall, pot-bellied man to sell vegetables... studying the law at a rickety table by the stove. A color came to him, blue, the curtains over the front windows, although now he could see no curtains, nor even blanched scraps of fabric. He thought he could remember the smell of his mother's Sabbath bread emanating from the low iron stove that was no longer there, but it was all wishful thinking, not recollection. Had his mother a favored chair in which she sat while mending clothes? Had his father a favored mug in which to enjoy sweet mead after a day in the field? He didn't know and now had no one to ask. His mother. His father. Gone. The hole that had been his past would now never be filled.

Adam sank to the ground. He brought his face against the charred earth and smelled the bitter stink of weeds that had no business growing in his house, in his home. Had they suffered, these parents he didn't even know enough to mourn? He didn't want to consider this. For a long time, he didn't move. He could sense Shayna and the golem nearby, though neither made a sound. Eventually, he got to his feet. Shayna gave him a sad, respectful look. The golem looked at him with unmistakable pain in those round, coal-stone eyes.

There was nothing for Adam here. But as he looked past his companions at the vast heath beyond the farm, he thought there might be something for him there. There had to be something for him there, please God. He buttoned his great-coat against the harsh wind that he remembered could blast across the barren heath. Shayna called out for Adam to slow down as he strode toward the heath but, instead, his pace quickened. He found his legs running, asking no permission, needing no direction. The village began to take shape in his mind… the little synagogue… the market square… Rachel's house.

The heath gave way to the edge of the village. He came to the Widow Baile's house or, rather, what should have been the Widow Baile's house, and felt nausea rising within him. There was nothing but a large pile of rotting wood, overgrown with weeds and vines.

He moved forward with reluctant steps toward the village square, not wanting to see what lay ahead. He stumbled down what had likely been the main street. Everywhere he turned, the ruins of small, timber-and-plank houses looked like toys smashed and abandoned by a malevolent child. Rachel's house couldn't have been spared—or could it?

He ran about, pushing past one ruin after another, trying to find her house. But fire, it seemed, had done its work everywhere. No building was untouched. The homes, the synagogue, the mill, the market stalls—all lay in heaps of charred, grayed, decaying wood.

Finally he stood before the ruins of one of the two-story walls of what had once been, for Miropol, a grand residence. A bit of the porch remained across the front. Behind that partial facade lay only destruction. He sank onto the stoop.

"Rachel! Oh my God, Rachel!" he cried out to the ghost village, his heart breaking anew. His stomach churned as it dawned on him that now there was no way to repair his wrong, no way to save his children. He wept and retched and wept.

He heard approaching footsteps. He looked up from the stoop. Shayna stood over him, her face paler and more deeply lined than it had been when they'd started this day. But her small dark eyes shone with sympathy from behind her ever-present nose-spectacles. When she spoke, her gravelly voice packed more compassion into a single syllable than he'd have thought possible.

"Come." She held out a handkerchief for him.

Adam took the proffered cloth and used it about his eyes and mouth with the slow, mechanical movements of an automaton. A great roaring sound filled his ears, making it difficult to hear her. What was she saying? How could she even be talking? Everyone here was dead. His parents. His Rachel. And that meant that soon his children would be dead, too, if they weren't already.

Shayna continued to speak but he heard, or at least understood, very little, just words here and there. "Demons... Dybbuks... Yedoni..." Nevertheless, he followed her as she moved away, not always noticing ruts and rocks that threatened to trip him. The golem fell in line beside them.

"We must leave now," he heard Shayna say. "Before dark. Before the evil that resides in these ruins returns."

He looked at her and shook his head.

"What does it matter?" he said. "It's over. It's all over."

"Over?" she said with a long shake of her head. "Not that. Never that. There is always a way. And it's our job to find it. But first, we must get far from this place."

Shayna lifted her nose and sniffed, getting her bearing. "There's a village to the south that we might reach while the light remains. Vinitz is surely too far."

So south they went, Adam plodding along, only partly aware of the untamed fields through which they went. Those fields soon turned to forest, a forest that came increasingly close to the road and, in places, crossed it tentatively. They continued and soon heard the distant babble of a stream, unseen behind a copse of Wych Elms. As they drew closer, the sound grew louder. This was no babbling brook; it was the roar of a sizable river, at least. But surely there was no river that flowed here. After another few minutes of progress, the sound grew not just louder but also more distinct. What had sounded like the babble of water distilled into a babble of voices, many voices, some raised in argument, others laughing—and singing.

Adam strained to see the source of the commotion, but the trees still blocked his view. He thought he might be going mad from the despair that hung on him like a shroud, until he caught the bewildered expressions of Shayna and the golem. A minor relief: whatever he was hearing, they were hearing too. They slowed as they approached the bend in the path that would take them around the elms. If these were demons ahead, the sounds suggested there were many of them. Adam looked over at the golem, whose broad shoulders were hunched and hands clenched, as though readying himself for battle.

They continued around the bend and the mystery revealed itself. People, hundreds of them, men, women, and children of all ages, were crowded into what must have been the Miropol cemetery. The gravestones jutted out of the ground at odd angles, like teeth in the jaw of an aged pauper. The crowds sat on them, leaned on them, lay across them to gossip, argue, and generally carouse with their neighbors. Some stood together in small groups. Some were chasing others around the stones as though through a maze, though whether out of sport or aggression, it was difficult to tell.

Adam and Shayna crept toward the cemetery. The golem went with them, but with an evident aversion that Adam had not noticed in him before.

Beggars, adorned in rags and relying on canes and crutches that increased their pathos, as was likely their purpose, pursued the well-to-do for a few kopecks. These people looked vaguely familiar to Adam. A teacher, reed-thin with a wild gaze and a few odd wisps of beard, attempted to lecture a rowdy collection of children who were paying him no heed. His name… what was his name? A blacksmith worked the tools of his trade, bringing his iron mallet down again and again on a white-hot chain that he pinned to an anvil with a pair of tongs. This man too Adam knew; he was sure of it.

Now, as he stood just outside the cemetery gates, it dawned on Adam that these weren't people at all.

"I don't understand," Adam said to Shayna. "They're dead?"

Shayna peered out over her nose-spectacles at the scene before them. "They don't appear to be visiting," she replied, shrugging.

Adam was mesmerized, listening to their shouts and cries and shrieks, and to the intensity of it all: an entire village packed into the few acres of the cemetery, with seemingly no diminution of the activity that had gone on, day after day, when the inhabitants had been flesh and blood.

They advanced to the rotting wooden gate of the cemetery, the spirits within paying them little heed. Life, or death, continued apace.

"What happened to them?" Adam pressed Shayna. "Why are they all here?"

Shayna raised her head and sniffed the air with her great mound of a nose. "I think you should ask them."

Adam wished that once, just once, this sly, elderly saint of Brinnitz would give him a straight answer; but it was not to be. With a wave of his hand, he instructed the golem to remain with Shayna, passed through the broken-down gate, and entered the cemetery. Shayna got comfortable on a log by the side of the road, pulled a book of Psalms from her cloak, and began to recite them. She did so not in the customary, whispered undertone; she sang them, her deep rough voice ringing out happily if not completely in tune.

The golem stood behind Shayna, at a place from which he could keep both her and his creator in his sight. The spirited Miropolers might not be a threat but the tension across his broad shoulders and down to his clenched fists suggested that he could not be sure.

Adam stepped around an old woman whose triple chins he'd have known anywhere: she was Luba the doctor's wife. Startled by the sudden recognition, he just missed tripping over the prone figure of a young man snoring loudly enough to wake the dead, had they been asleep: Zev the drayman's assistant, who—it occurred to Adam—had never provided much assistance to the drayman nor to anyone else in the village. Preoccupied with this thought, Adam walked straight through a tall, gaunt old man: Chuna-Beryl the butcher.

He approached a wizened water-carrier who struggled with the buckets attached to the ends of the pole he carried on his shoulders. Adam knew this old man too, though his name floated just beyond his reach.

"Excuse me," Adam began, not sure how the sentence would end. "Are… you… Chayim?" The little man looked up at him, frowned, and returned to his buckets. Adam tried again, a bit louder; perhaps sound didn't carry across the spheres. There was still no reaction from the man, who struggled in vain to lift his load. Adam cleared his throat and was about to begin again when the man stared at him, his dead eyes ablaze with annoyance.

"Bah!" said the man, sending Adam back several paces. "Out of my way!" Adam stepped back. Everywhere he turned, faces came back to him: Arele the beadle. Pesach the carpenter. Henna the ritual-bath lady. He looked for his dear parents, for his beloved Rachel. He asked the Miropoler spirits about them. The ghosts saw him; sometimes they even reacted to him. But they refused to answer him.

Adam was about a third of the way through the cemetery when a large, doughy man came into his view. He had forests for eyebrows, dark twinkly eyes, and a beard that hung almost to his waist. He sat on his gravestone, his smock and face dusted with flour, leaning forward and working with great effort to knead the pile of dough before him.

"Uncle Itzik!" Adam called out after a moment, warm memories of this man coming back to him as fast and sure as an arrow.

At the sound of his name, the man leaned back, beamed, and displayed a broad smile that revealed a mouth with very few teeth. That smile! Uncle Itzik the baker had once been a friend to all Miropol and especially to young Adam. He'd had no family of his own, Adam recalled, but everyone had been glad to claim him as one of theirs. Seeing Uncle Itzik, Adam thought he could smell something sweet... chocolate pastries? Had Uncle Itzik brought this tantalizing smell with him across the spheres or was Adam merely recalling their aroma? With a warm grin, Adam realized it hardly mattered. The spirit rose to greet Adam, who tried to embrace him, his arms touching nothing but air.

"We don't get many visitors," Uncle Itzik told Adam, his face darkening despite the flour. "No matter. Adam, welcome! Sit down!" Adam looked around. The only thing upon which he might have sat was a small gravestone; he remained standing. "No matter," said the spirit with enthusiasm.

Adam struggled to connect this jovial man to the fire-ravaged ruins he had just left, to the utter devastation that had seemed to claim all the souls that now surrounded him.

"Uncle Itzik," he said, a quiver in his voice, "what *happened?*"

The baker's mouth rearranged itself into a frown and the lines grew deeper across his broad, thick face.

"I don't like to dwell on the past," he admitted. "It was a long time ago."

Adam shook his head, just a bit. "I'm sorry," he said. "But I must know. You must tell me. Please."

Uncle Itzik eyed him. "Very well," he said at last. "You had left by then, of course, but you hadn't been gone long. Three years, or was it four? It started at night. Evil matters so often do, don't they? We heard the sounds first, the low rumble that became a mighty roar. And then the Cossacks were upon us. Why? We never knew. Perhaps a child in one of their villages had gone missing or died. Perhaps the nobles had sent them our way to divert them from theirs. In the end, does it matter? They were here for three days, Adam. *Three days.*"

The baker stopped and looked across the cemetery and, it seemed to Adam, through the woods to the village that lay beyond it. Adam envisioned what could be unleashed over such a time on the men, the women, the children.

"The fires were so great that the smoke could be seen as far as Venitz," Uncle Itzik continued after a while. "No one survived. By the time the Venitzers came to our aid, they were in time only to bring us here." He shrugged, a gesture that took in all the graves about them.

"And here we're stuck," the spirit smacked his heavy hands together with a sound like a pistol blast. "The pogrom was bad, but here it's not the Garden of Eden either, let me tell you. Hennock the schoolteacher forever chases children to whom he must teach the same lessons day after day. The Widow Baile takes in the same sewing each morning and, no matter how well she mends it, she sees it come back again the next morning. Me, I bake my pastries and cakes and pies and breads, but my sack of flour never empties, and my baked goods go forever uneaten."

Adam shivered, though it had gotten no colder. Uncle Itzik's plight had managed to rouse him from his own. The unrelenting noise from the surrounding spirits continued unabated, but he hardly heard them. This poor man—all of these poor souls!—were condemned to a living death that Adam could just imagine, going through the same motions day after day through eternity, to no purpose whatsoever.

"Uncle Itzik," he rasped. "What can I do for you? There must be something."

The baker's great forests of eyebrows knit together.

"Don't you know why we're still here, Adam, why we haven't entered the World to Come?"

Adam shook his head and said nothing.

"My boy," Uncle Itzik's features beseeched him even before the words emerged. "How can we leave this world behind us for the World to Come when there is no one left to remember us?"

Adam felt the sharp pain of the spirit's words like a wasp's sting. However little these people had had in life, Adam knew, at least they had had the promise of posterity. At least they would pass down the tradition to their children, who would one day pass it down to children of their own, and so on and so on until the end of time. But not now. Now, there would be no future generations of Miropolers. No one even to remember that they had once lived. Adam shuddered at their fate, a fate that, for very different reasons, he realized he might well share.

"Oh, Adam," Uncle Itzik said, sliding down from his gravestone to Adam's side. "I didn't mean to burden you. It's no matter. No matter at all."

"But what about the Venitzers?" Adam asked.

"They were masters of kindness to bury us," he said. "But they never knew us. How could they remember us?"

Adam bit his lower lip. "Uncle Itzik, you *will* be remembered."

Uncle Itzik's eyes widened "What?"

"I will say the Prayer for the Dead for you, for all of you, every year," Adam said.

Uncle Itzik's head shook in disbelief. "You would do that for us?"

Adam nodded. "I didn't before, couldn't before. But now I can."

The spirit's mouth hung halfway open but, for a moment, no sound emerged. Then his eyes again gleamed and his expression changed to one of deepest gratitude. "You do for us the one thing that no one else could do," said Uncle Itzik, attempting to embrace Adam and passing his thick spectral arms through him instead. "Thank you, my boy. Thank you."

The Miropolers had waited so long for this; now, their wait had ended. Adam took note of the position of the late afternoon sun and turned his back to it, his face to the east. He closed his eyes and began to move his lips.

"Magnified and sanctified may His great name be, in the world He created by His will…"

Adam continued the prayer for Uncle Itzik, for his parents, for Rachel, for Chayim, for Hennock, for the Widow Baile, for them all.

He was unprepared for what happened next. Hundreds of voices all around him thundered the traditional response, "May His great name be blessed forever and to all eternity."

Adam, startled, opened his eyes. He saw the Miropolers, all of them, old men, children, maidens, beggars, merchants, scholars, tailors, now stopped in their supernal commotion, all facing east. And then he saw them become mist and become no more. It happened slowly at first, to those farthest from him. Then on and on it went, rows and rows of souls returning to the source of all life. Now spirits much closer to him were ascending to the upper spheres as well. Adam looked to Uncle Itzik to say his goodbyes. The baker of Miropol was beginning to fade before him.

"Wait!" he blurted out, rushing toward the spirit. "My Rachel, please tell her—"

"Your Rachel?" said Uncle Itzik, puzzlement spreading across his fading face. "She's not with us. Her family moved to Okop a year before the pogrom..."

And he was gone. Adam stood among the hundreds of stones in the Miropol cemetery. The breeze didn't dare whisper. Not a blade of grass moved. It seemed to Adam as though time itself had paused to honor the departed.

Chapter Twenty-Two

The town of Okop was generally unremarkable, with its share of houses, shops, churches, mills, study halls, and synagogues. But for two weeks of the year, the annual fair transformed Okop to extraordinary result. Then, all the world knew Okop or, at least, of it, from the British Isles to obscure corners of the Orient. How Okop had been chosen or had chosen itself for this distinction no one could remember; centuries before, a merriment of merchants—glorified peddlers, really—had begun to gather for their mutual profit on the leafy banks of the Tundzha river. Those merchants could never have imagined what their gatherings would become.

Adam and his companions walked down street after cobblestone street, each lined with colorful booths and bunting, and each filled with as many people as could crowd into them. Though Adam knew of the fair, he was unprepared for the thousands of buyers and sellers—of spices, silks, and silver, of produce from nearby farms and priceless fauna from far away—that confronted him. A raucous babel of shouts and wheedling and exclamations assaulted him in languages he understood—Yiddish and Russian and Polish—and in languages he did not, such as French and English and others too exotic for him even to label.

They sought Rachel everywhere, in stalls with wineskins from the sunny vineyards of the Mediterranean and stalls selling the furs of sweet marten and sable from Siberia. They passed merchants selling the most commonplace of items—cheese, utensils, charms—and some the most rare, such as pepper, ginger, cinnamon, and other medicinal elements from the

Far East and said to be harvested from the Garden of Eden itself.

"Excuse me, sir, excuse me, madam," Adam asked again and again and again. "Have you seen a woman of middle age, with hazel-colored eyes and honey-colored hair, about so tall, calling herself 'Rachel'?"

They had seen no Rachel, or they had but she was too tall or too short, or her eyes were blue, or her hair was dark, or she fit the description, but her name was Golda. Adam, however, was not discouraged. She was here. He knew she was here. Now, all he had to do was find her.

The trio came to a booth whose proprietor sold amulets to ward off dybbuks, werewolves, and demons. Adam made his eager inquiry yet again, eliciting the briefest shrug of shoulders from the beanpole of a merchant. Adam turned away and was about to leave when he noticed the amulets. He bent toward Shayna and half-whispered, "Perhaps we should buy some of these. They could be useful for our next encounter with Lilith."

Shayna peered over her spectacles at the jeweled and engraved talismans in his hand and said with nonchalance: "Or, the next time we meet Lilith, you could give her a very mean look."

It was unmistakable: the ends of the golem's thin mouth stretched into a smile. No, a grin.

But not for long. Something small whizzed past their heads and hit the golem. He absorbed the blow without any apparent movement but a red stain soon dripped down the side of his head. Blood? Adam reached up and fingered it. It was a tomato. The golem, unfazed, reached up to explore the remnants of the pulpy mess, then turned his unblinking gaze in the direction from which it had come. There stood an urchin, no more than nine years old, his face as filthy as the rags he wore.

Mud Man! Mud Man!

Look at the big old Crud Man!

The nasty lad shouted his verse in exaggerated singsong that slashed as much as his words. Adam, astonished at the animosity packed into such a small boy, stood motionless. Shayna narrowed her eyes and watched the boy with ill-contained anger as he scampered off. Then she turned to the golem, smiled in sympathy, and helped him remove the bits of tomato that still clung to him.

While this had been the rudest response to the golem's presence, Adam had to admit that the golem had attracted a great many disapproving looks from the fair-goers. His unusual size and color were partly responsible, of course, and about that, Adam couldn't do anything. But the tatters his clothes had become were no doubt also responsible. And about that, Adam *could* do something. Perhaps with less remarkable garments, the golem would blend in better with the other fair-goers. Adam drew close to Shayna and whispered his idea. Shayna looked at the golem, then gave a long, single nod of the head.

At the end of the street, they came to the destination Adam had in mind: a tailor's booth. The proprietor was a bald, gnomish little man wearing a bright blousy shirt with ruffles down the front, under a harlequin vest stuck with the tools of his trade: needles, pins, bits of fabric and ribbon. He rose from his stool to greet them and stood shorter than he'd been a moment before.

"Yes! A new dress for madame, perhaps," he said, smacking his lips at the prospect.

"Madame buys her dresses in Paris," Shayna replied, flipping one side of her slightly bedraggled and thoroughly shapeless cloak over a shoulder with great flair.

The tailor's apparent disappointment was fleeting. "Then something for the gentlemen?" he said, looking from Adam to the golem, doing a double-take at the clay creature who towered far, far above him, and then looking back to Adam.

Adam scanned the rows of fabrics, shiny, soft, in all the colors he could imagine—except the one color he could imagine for proper clothing. And then he saw it, forlorn in the corner, a bolt of plain black wool. The tailor followed his gaze.

"Ah, a traditionalist," he exclaimed. "Can I interest the gentleman in a fine, new black suit or coat?"

"Not for me," said Adam, brushing off a bit of the road that still clung to his great-coat. "I think this will do for a while yet. But my friend could use a new suit."

At the suggestion, the golem's eyes widened and his brow scrunched up, compressing the letters carved across his forehead.

The tailor put his hand to his own brow and stared up at the golem. "This is a big job, you understand," the tailor said to Adam. "But I'm the man for it."

The tailor produced a tape measure like a carnival magician plucking a silk streamer from the air and went to work, taking measurements, muttering to himself, and climbing on his stool to measure the golem's broad shoulders and thick neck. The golem did his best to follow the tailor's instructions to remain still, with uneven success. He was vibrating at the prospect of something made just for him.

The measurements taken, the tailor stood back, his eyes aflutter, his lips smacking, lost in deep calculation. "Come back Tuesday," he said.

"Tuesday?" cried Adam. "We'll be long gone by Tuesday." The golem looked crestfallen.

"Very well," he said, with a long, slow shake of his head. "You challenge me sir, you surely do."

The tailor fingered his harlequin vest. "But I'm just the one to rise to the occasion," he continued. He fluttered his eyes and smacked his lips once more, then snapped his fingers. "All right then. Come back in two hours."

Adam blinked, Shayna shrugged, and a smile passed across the golem's face. Then, the three continued their search through the fair to pass the time. Quick, puckish musical notes pricked their ears. They turned to see a band of minstrels playing flutes, mandolins, and three-holed pipes. They were in the buskers' field, amidst the entertainers who performed for the price of a few tossed coins: the puppeteers and jugglers, the aerialists and rope-dancers and fire-swallowers, the men with trained sprites and calculating animals, the clowns, the men of great strength. This exhibition wasn't entirely new to Adam. The occasional busker had passed through Lizensk on his way to somewhere else, but he had never seen as many entertainers as this, nor entertainments so exotic. Perhaps when it was all over, when it was all behind him, he would bring Sarah and his little Mendel and Leah to this place.

At the appointed time, they returned to the tailor's booth and the tailor presented them with the largest suit that Adam had ever seen. The golem retreated behind a screen to put it on. When he returned, Adam could see that the suit fit to perfection, softening the golem's rough edge, smoothing his bulk, and helping him to look a bit less arresting, all things considered. The golem must have thought so, too, for it seemed to Adam that he held himself with a poise he hadn't shown before.

Shayna's small dark eyes twinkled behind her nose-spectacles. "Apparel oft proclaims the man," she said with approval.

"The Sages?" asked Adam.

"The Bard," replied Shayna.

Chapter Twenty-Three

At mid-afternoon, they sought a moment's respite in an alcove too small to shelter a vendor's stall. Adam and Shayna sat on makeshift benches, which they formed by pushing abandoned crates together. The golem remained standing; he needed no rest. Shayna had bought several pale-yellow fruits which she now set down on one of the crates. Adam reached into his side pocket, withdrew a small silver knife, and offered it to her. Shayna used it to cut several slices, which they shared.

It had been three days' journey since Adam, Shayna, and the golem had left the cemetery at Miropol. Adam looked out at the crowds beyond the alcove, at a middle-aged woman selling books from a cart, a lock of honey-colored hair freeing itself from a tight, knotted bun. Could that be Rachel? Would her hair look the same after all these years? He peered closer. As she turned toward him, he saw her dull brown eyes. No, that could never be the luminous bride of his youth. But how would he know her if he saw her? She might be married and her hair covered. She might be a merchant or a proprietress at one of the inns. She might be a visitor like himself. She might be a resident. She might even be one of the jugglers for all he knew. He wasn't going to give in, not yet, but his frustration was growing.

Adam slumped on his improvised seat.

"How are we going to find her?" he asked Shaya. "It will take a month to cover the entire fair."

"It will have to take less time than that," Shayna said, taking a long, slow sip from a bowl of borscht before completing her thought, "because the fair ends in three days."

140

Yes, of course. He knew that as well, he thought, as he ran his fingers through his thin beard and frowned.

"Never pout, Rabbi Adam," Shayna said, popping a slice of fruit into her mouth. "It solves nothing and ruins the complexion. I pouted in my youth and look at me now."

She chewed the fruit with great relish and swallowed it with an audible gulp.

"I suggest that the three of us split up to cover more territory," she said while extracting a handkerchief from a pocket of her voluminous cloak and wiping the corner of her mouth.

The golem, who had been watching the passing fairgoers like a sentinel, raised his head. He looked from Adam to Shayna and back again.

"Shayna's right," Adam reassured him. "We can cover the fair much faster if we separate. Don't worry."

The golem turned to go.

"Just a moment!" Shayna said, and the golem stopped. She searched the pockets of her cloak and extracted a small piece of paper and a writing implement. She scribbled a note, blotted it with her sleeve, and passed it to the golem, who put it in the pocket of his new suit.

"If you find someone who could be Rachel," she said to him, "hand her that note and I expect she will come with you."

They arranged a time and place to meet, and the golem left them. Shayna turned to Adam. "Well, off we go," she said, shooing him out of the alcove as she might have shooed away an imp.

The golem lumbered through the crowds, searching for the woman his creator called Rachel. He knew the description his creator had recited over and over. But he saw no one to match it. Where was she? He had to find her. His creator had told him so. He looked into the face of each female he passed. So many people and no Rachel.

He watched the crowds as they moved from merchant to merchant. All wanted things, so many things. And the fair provided them: clothes, pots, potions, animals. Why did people need so many things? He was different from them: he didn't need anything. Then he looked down at his new suit, the suit that made him look a bit more like the others, and touched the buttons, each in turn from top to bottom. Well, maybe he too had a few, simple needs that could be met at the fair.

He watched people arguing, shouting, singing. He watched children playing. He watched a young man and woman, sitting on a bench, talking. They sat apart and the golem could see they were careful to keep their arms in their laps, careful not to touch. But when they smiled at each other, the golem could see that they touched in a way that required no physical contact. Something, a feeling, stirred within his deep, clay chest.

He turned a corner and stopped, his attention arrested by a strange figure around which a circle of fairgoers had gathered. It was a figure much like himself: another golem? It was a mixture of grays and browns, apparently sculpted from the earth. But unlike him, it was small, the size of a boy, and it wore a simple white shirt and black trousers, a short-brimmed black cap atop its head. This small golem sat on a high wooden platform from which all the people could see him. It was talking to a young woman in the crowd whose hands lay across her large belly.

"...his life will be long and happy," the little golem was saying in a choppy, nasal tone, not like the voices of the others. "He will be rich, not in possessions of the material world, but in his complement of family and friends."

The young woman beamed and thanked the little figure. The golem didn't understand. This creature was made like him, but it could *speak*. It had somehow become like the people, like his creator. How was this possible? The golem touched the line that was his mouth. No sound emerged. Could he learn from the little golem to speak, too? He edged closer, drawing stares from those nearest to him.

"Why, here is another man of the mud," boomed a short, fat man in shabby clothes standing next to the platform. "It's a denizen of the dirt, a creature of the clay, a golem of the ground, come to join our oracular being in fraternal association, marvel to marvel."

The man motioned to the golem, the plume in his broad brown hat twisting in the breeze. People were dropping coins into the large, wide-mouthed bottle at his side.

"I had thought our homunculus was the only one of its kind, but one of only two isn't bad either," the bottler continued. "Perhaps you have a question to ask of the oracle, too, my earthen entity? Just one kopeck for a question about the past or the present; three kopecks for a question about the future—those answers are harder to come by."

The golem stared at the bottler, his impenetrable eyes turning a dark gray. He had no money, let alone any way to ask his question. He stretched out his arms in a silent plea.

The bottler smiled, but it was a smile as cold as the Tundzha in January. "I'm sorry, my friend. No money, no prophecy." The bottler turned away, shook the bottle so that the clanging coins seemed to mock the golem, and addressed the crowd once more. "Does anyone else have a question for the oracle?"

The golem was overcome by a strange sensation. He needed to go to the mud boy. He *needed* to. He pushed past the heavy rope that hung as a partition between the mud boy and the crowd.

"Back, back, please my friend," shouted the bottler in alarm.

The golem stood in front of the platform, looking up at the creature and opening his crude mouth as wide as his jaw would allow. Nothing came out. The mud boy looked down at him, but to the golem its gaze seemed strangely vacant. Its right eye shook a bit in its socket and then rolled up into its head. And from within the platform, the golem heard a quickly stifled mutter. He looked down for its source and, through a gap barely wide enough to slide a coin, he saw a pair of eyes. They were staring out at him with alarm.

The golem bent over and, with a single swipe, removed a handful of slats from the side of the platform. A lad of perhaps fifteen, frozen with fear, squatted inside. Dangling about him, within easy reach, were a series of wooden rods and controls that extended up through the top of the platform and into the now silent and immobile mud boy.

"Please don't hurt the lad," protested the bottler. "It's only an act. We meant no harm."

The golem didn't understand. He turned his massive head from the young lad to the puppet on the platform above him. Was this all that the mud boy was? A doll? A plaything? He grabbed the puppet and, with an internal sensation for which he had no word, watched it crumble, the pieces dropping to his feet as he squeezed tighter and tighter. The golem returned his attention to the terrified youth and raised his arm. From somewhere behind him, the bottler shouted and pleaded with the golem to leave the lad alone. The golem turned away from the stall and the crowd parted before him. They were afraid of him, he realized. This was not what his creator had told him to do, and it had all gone wrong. Bewildered, sad, he staggered away from the crowd and tried to forget what he'd seen and what he felt.

Chapter Twenty-Four

Adam met Shayna and the golem, as arranged, in front of the large inn just north of the produce market.

"Tell me you found her," Adam pleaded. The golem flinched and looked down.

"If Rachel is here, she's keeping herself well-hidden," Shayna answered with a trace of something approaching disbelief, as though this shouldn't have been possible. "I don't even *feel* her presence."

"What more can we do?" he asked, his voice hoarse from the day's fruitless search.

"We can keep looking," she told him. "We must keep looking."

They arranged their next meeting for dusk.

Adam approached the nearest peddler, a filthy old woman selling vegetables that looked fit only for livestock. "Please, do you know a woman named Rachel? Of middle age, about this high, with wide eyes of brown and green and hair that once shimmered like gold."

"I only know my customers," answered the old woman, scrutinizing him. "Would you be one of them?"

As a hint, it wasn't subtle but Adam took a moment to get it. Then, he reached into his sack and pulled out a coin, handing it to the peddler.

"Gladly. It's very important. Now, do you know her?"

"No, I don't," laughed the old woman, securing the coin in a pocket and turning away from Adam to engage another customer.

Adam was stunned, then felt anger welling within him. "Now see here, ma'am," he began in a tone that was as close to a growl as he could muster.

The peddler never found out how Adam intended to end the admonition because he stopped mid-sentence. He was transfixed by the sight of a woman far down the row of booths, examining a potter's wares: the still-golden hair, now streaked with gray; the hazel eyes, glowing with a familiar warmth; the bearing, which announced the character and charm of the woman who possessed it.

It was an illusion, he told himself. It had to be someone who looked like her, if indeed it was anything other than a trick of the light, or of the mind. Then she passed out of the potter's booth and disappeared behind the canvas. Adam roused himself, shouting, trying to be heard over the constant roar of the fair. "Rachel! Rachel!"

He ran through the crowd, pushing people aside and muttering his apologies as he went. In seconds he reached the potter's booth but it was too late. She was gone.

Adam scanned the crowd and almost missed her. And then he saw her standing near an apothecary's stall talking to the proprietor, who was thin, young, barely more than a boy. This time there was no mistaking her. It was Rachel, older of course, her skin no longer as luminous as he remembered it, but her nonetheless. He called out to her but the crowd shifted, swallowing her up once more. He raced to the apothecary's stall in time to see her stroll down the row of merchants and out of sight. And so it went, through the currents of humanity that flowed through the streets of Okop. Was Rachel playing a game of hide-and-seek with him? Did she know that he'd spotted her, that he was seeking her out? Adam didn't have the inclination to imagine anything other than finding her, of begging her forgiveness for the wrong he'd committed so long ago. He continued the chase but the glimpses of her became farther off, less distinct, less frequent. Finally, they disappeared. Adam stopped running. He bent over, his hands on his thighs, panting as he struggled to regain his breath.

He was still winded when a panicked shout pierced the air, and then another. The press of people in the streets, seemingly constant since they'd arrived, became more urgent. Fairgoers were pushing each other in every direction, no one getting anywhere. Merchants gathered their goods in their arms, their baskets, their carts, and sought to join them. An arm shoved Adam in his side and he struggled to stay upright. Somehow, the crowd in which Adam found himself took on a direction, and he was swept along with it. Was he being carried away from the danger or toward it? All he could see was an approaching cloud of dust and all he could hear was a great roar that, as it grew closer, resolved itself into the battering of horses' hooves upon the cobblestones.

Through the dust burst the horror from which the fairgoers were fleeing: a contingent of Cossacks.

"My boy! Don't let them take my boy!" cried a woman at his side, pressing a child of eight or nine to her chest with such vigor that Adam thought she might smother him.

"Give them gold; give them silver!" boomed a man a bit farther off. "That will sate them."

Adam hoped so. The Cossacks were mercenaries of Catherine II, Empress and Autocrat of all the Russias, likely come to recruit boys for her army, said recruitment taking the form of violent kidnapping. The children would not see their families for twenty years or more and, by then, would be Cossacks, too, lost forever to their families and their faith. Many of the fairgoers seemed to share Adam's thought; he saw parents racing away with their sons, some men and women moving so quickly that the boys whose wrists they held fast were dragged behind them, unable to keep up.

The Cossacks were upon them now, ruddy-faced villains in fearsome red tunics, their heads topped by cylindrical, fur-covered white hats. As much as people feared underworld demons, they feared these human ones. Adam watched from behind an overturned cart as the Cossacks entered the street, people scattering in all directions before them, hoping to be among the lucky ones who survived. Some of the villains were on steeds, others on foot, but all had swords and knives drawn, seeking targets of innocent flesh. An elderly woman stood motionless—where, after all, could she run?—her outstretched hands offering the few coins she had to the invaders. A tall, swarthy Cossack approached her and swiped her coins with one hand while plunging his bejeweled dagger into her chest with the other. A young couple ran past Adam, the boy with his arm around the girl, half sheltering her, half pulling her along. A spear flew through the air and caught the boy between the shoulder blades. He was dead before he hit the ground, the girl screaming, trying to pull him away from further attacks that could do him no harm. A Cossack rode by her, his sword bright like fire and sweeping low as he passed. Adam saw her head drop to the ground and roll a few feet, stopping beside the body of her groom.

Bribes would not work today, he thought, his head dizzy from the shock of what he'd seen. Adam forced himself to stand. He ran, his heart pounding, his head awash in sweat or blood; he wasn't sure which. Where was Shayna, where was the golem? And where, where was his Rachel? He screamed for them all, though his voice carried just a few feet. His eyes darted all about in a futile attempt to glimpse them. Were they safe? They had to be safe. He had to find them.

He almost tripped and looked down to see the body of the peculiar little tailor who'd produced the suit for the golem, his body mangled, his beautiful harlequin vest now a torn rag of blood and mud. Off to the side, Adam saw the minstrels trying to run, to hide, their hands held to their heads and faces in vain attempts to staunch gushing streams of blood. The filthy old vegetable peddler who'd taken his coin and dashed his hopes stumbled past him now, blood flowing from the end of a sleeve where her hand should have been. Nearby, the lifeless body of the amulet merchant was pinned to a wall by a spear; at least a dozen amulets hung around his neck. Shayna, as always, had been right.

The Cossacks, unimpeded, were creating new victims by the moment: poor souls trampled under horses, necks slashed, heads blown away, stomachs eviscerated. The shouts of the Cossacks mixed with the cries of their victims, echoing in Adam's ears as a din of evil, horror, rage, fear, and grief. And through it all the never-ending pounding of the horses' hooves sounded like a violent sea crashing against a defenseless shore. He saw people run as they had never run before, likely propelled by a common thought: that the slowest among them would not see the morrow.

Adam glanced up. The very sky, which had been a brilliant, cloudless blue before the pogrom, was now dark, stained with the thick black smoke from the fiery stalls and buildings all around him. Ash descended like a storm of dark snow, settling on Adam's broad-brimmed hat and coat like a million little marks of Cain. The caustic air burned his nose and eyes. He turned a corner and he knew the terrible source of the stench: a group of corpses ablaze, mostly old men, women, and small children, who were least able to get away in time. Unable to look away, he tripped over a deep rut carved into the side of the road and nearly fell.

There was no defending himself or others: The Cossacks had swords and muskets and a ruthlessness that would not be appeased. He looked about and saw a place to hide under a wagon that had lost an axle and now tipped like a small shed. He crept toward it, staying low to the ground. He was almost beneath it when he saw a mounted Cossack charging toward him. If the hooves of the horse—which looked like a behemoth from Adam's perspective—did not trample him to death, the Cossack's sword, which glinted like a second sun and seemed to grow larger and larger as the Cossack approached, surely would.

The Cossack was thirty feet away, twenty feet away, ten feet away. His eyes were ablaze with fury and his nostrils flared like those of his mount as he raised his sword and swung it down upon Adam.

Chapter Twenty-Five

Must find the creator! the voice inside the golem's head screamed at him.

But the noise, the cries, the shouts, the pleading, the pounding of horses' hooves, the pistol blasts—it was far more than the golem had yet experienced in the brief time in which he'd been alive. And somewhere in this frenzy was the creator. He had to find him. He had to protect him. His black, unreadable eyes swept across the chaos. But where? Where was he?

All about him, bad men—some on horseback, some on foot—attacked the fairgoers with their pistols and muskets, with their swords and knives and whips. The golem saw people fall where they were struck. Some didn't move. The bad men had killed them. Others tried to limp or crawl away. The bad men beat or shot or stabbed them until they stopped. They grabbed women and carried them into side streets and dark buildings. The men laughed. The women screamed.

One bad man, fat around the waist like a boar, stood over a little boy with yellow hair. The man's pistol was aimed at the little boy's head. The child's eyes were squeezed shut. His mouth was open but only a hoarse whisper crawled out: "No... no... no... no... no... no..."

The golem's chest pounded. Every thought in his massive head shouted at him to find his creator. Every thought but one. The creator would want him to save this child, wouldn't he? How could he really know? He couldn't, but pushed the thought away and pounced. The golem twisted the man's beefy arm. It made a cracking sound and the pistol dropped to the ground.

The man opened his mouth in an agonizing *ayiii... ayiii... ayiii...* that chilled the golem. He crumpled to the earth even as the golem kept his grip on him.

Well, not all of him; the man's arm had come off in the golem's hand. The golem stared at the twitching man making small splashes in a mud puddle and then at the blood flowing from the place on his shoulder where his arm had been. The man stopped twitching and the golem felt a sudden coldness as the man's soul fled his body. The golem had killed before—the memory of the Yedoni was sharp in his young mind—but never a human, even a bad human. The severed arm slipped from his grasp and fell with a thud beside the body.

The golem looked away. Several yards before him, a woman with bloody gashes on her arms appeared from around a corner, ran to the yellow-haired boy, and swept him up. They disappeared into the mayhem.

The golem lumbered on, his gray-brown brows furrowing at the sight of all the people killed or wounded. Ahead stood a tall man, clothed in red, peering into a dark, narrow alley. A sword and knives swung from the white sash at his waist. His mouth was clenched. His eyes glistened. Another bad man, the golem thought. The man pulled a dagger from his sash and entered the alley. Then the golem heard a voice call out from its depths.

"Does your mother know what you're doing?"

The golem recognized the low, gravelly tones. He bounded into the darkness.

"You should be ashamed of yourself," Shayna admonished the bad man as she shook her head in disgust. The man pushed his tall white hat back on his head and scratched his brow. Then he shook off his surprise and moved menacingly toward Shayna, grunting and growling like a demon. The golem chased after him and reached them both just as Shayna withdrew a hand from her cloak and threw a dark powder at her attacker. He doubled over, his hands grabbing alternately at his eyes and his throat. "Blasted old crone!" he cried as he fell to the floor, struggling to breathe even as he grasped for his dagger.

"Ah, there you are, my friend," Shayna said to the golem, stepping past her would-be attacker. "I'm glad to see you're unharmed."

There was a grunt behind them. Shayna's attacker, his face red and eyes watery, rushed at them. He let out a battle cry, low and long, his hand clenched tightly around his dagger. The golem swung one of his massive arms and caught the man across the stomach. His eyes went dull and closed as the air *whooshed* out of him. He flew some twenty feet before landing in a jumble of torso and limbs. Blood trickled down the corner of his mouth. He didn't move.

"Well done," said Shayna, her small eyes lively behind her nose-spectacles. She brushed her cloak and some of the dark powder flew off and swirled around her, carried by the wind. The golem took a sudden, awkward step back from it.

"What, this?" Shayna asked, motioning to the powder. "I found it at a spice merchant's stall. It's called pepper. Thought it might be useful. Don't give it another thought."

She pushed her spectacles farther up her great nose and pressed them into place. "We mustn't dilly-dally," she said to the golem. "We can only hope that Rabbi Adam has made his way to the inn unharmed."

They came to the buskers' commons and spied a short, stocky Cossack dragging a limp young woman into a dark building. The golem came up behind him, clamped a hand on his neck, and squeezed. The man dropped the woman as garbled sounds burbled from his throat. Shayna took the woman in her arms and gently lowered her to a grassy mound to recover.

As they entered the market square, a pair Cossacks, red tunics flapping about them like wings, charged them. The golem brought the men's heads together, cracking them like eggshells, and moved on without waiting for them to fall. Beyond the square, they spied three Cossacks leaving a silversmith's shop, their arms bulging with looted goods. The golem grabbed one of the men, lifted him, turned him upside down, and shook him as candlesticks, spice boxes, and a pitcher rained down with a clatter. The golem threw him at the other two, sending them all to the ground, where they lay still.

Everywhere the golem and Shayna went, Cossacks, their sweaty, swarthy faces twisted demonically, sought to kill them. Everywhere they went, they left a wake of red-clad bodies scattered like broken dolls.

Maybe the Cossacks left because the golem was one adversary they could not cow. Maybe they left because their taste for violence and plunder had been satisfied. In either case, the pogrom ended gradually, quite unlike the heart-stopping way it had begun. The Cossacks were gone and so was much of the merchandise from throughout the fair, particularly the horses and other livestock, the precious metals and jewels, and the talismans and amulets. But many people had survived. There were too many of them, even for the soldiers of death. The fairgoers had found places to hide in shops, under wagons, in pastures, the cemetery, dung fields and, in some daring instances, out in plain sight in the street, lying still alongside those who were not as fortunate. In the quiet after the desolation of the Okop fair, a thick silence hung in the air and draped itself like a shroud upon the dead.

The survivors crept out of hiding and, with a sense of confusion that was slowly congealing into grief, returned to what was left of what they had owned and whom they had loved. They assessed the damage to their lives and their livelihoods, tended to their wounded, and began the processions to the cemetery. Those who knew enough to perform the cleansing rituals required by tradition before burial did so. Those who didn't simply dug graves in the holy ground and hoped for the best.

They packed their wagons—the ones who still had both possessions and wagons—and prepared to leave Okop for their own towns and villages. Few still had horses to do the work; most placed their harnesses about their own shoulders. All had a common destination: away.

Chapter Twenty-Six

The sound of wagon wheels was the first thing that Adam heard as he regained consciousness. The sound of moaning, somewhere nearby, was the second. He lay on his back and tasted blood in his mouth. He spat out a tooth. Pain streaked through his skull, bringing with it fragmented memories. The Cossack with the sword. The gleaming weapon growing larger and larger before him. He could feel a warm, sticky substance matting his hair—blood? But he wasn't dead. Why wasn't he dead? Ah, yes: the deep, longish rut by the side of the road, several feet away. With no time to think, he had rolled into it. As the Cossack passed on his steed, he managed only to carve a shallow wound into the back of Adam's head. Now, another spasm of pain surged through him. Adam closed his eyes and hoped the danger was gone.

Someone was leaning over him, attending to him. He looked up into the blur of a face and squinted and blinked, gaining only fuzzy impressions; there were too many clouds still in his head. He could make out a broad swath of blue: not the sky, but the woman's skirt. The woman, for now he could see enough to see that, was pressing a handkerchief to the wound on his head.

He still couldn't see the face of his benefactor clearly, but got the impression of middle age, of light-colored hair mixed with abundant gray. Either she was unmarried or, as was more likely, her headscarf had been lost in the pogrom. Now he could make out bright eyes that seemed familiar. As her face came into focus, he could read the concern in it, adding to what seemed to be her unmistakable beauty.

"Rachel?" he mumbled weakly, squinting at the lovely face before him. She stopped and stared at him.

The mists in his mind cleared as though driven by a powerful wind.

"Rachel!" He tried to get up but was stopped by the pain slicing through his head. "Thank God I found you!" he said through the spasm.

"I was the one who found you, sir," she began, stopping suddenly. She scrutinized his face, one of her eyebrows arching. Then her hazel eyes flashed wide. "Adam?" Her lower lip trembled and she said nothing more.

"Yes. Adam," he said, his gaze dropping from those eyes.

Her voice was a hoarse whisper. "What are you doing here?"

"Looking for you." He tried to rise again, more slowly this time and, with her help, succeeded in sitting upright. His head continued to throb without mercy.

"It almost got you killed." She took a breath and then dabbed the blood still streaming from his head.

"Not finding you would have been worse," he said, then stopped.

"Why? Why look for me after all this time?" Those green-brown eyes that saw so much swept his face, searching for an answer.

His tongue had never felt so dry. "To say what I should have said back then." He stopped talking and she did not rush to fill the silence. When he could not tolerate the pause any longer, he continued. "What I did to you was wrong."

She looked at him for a moment longer, taking in his words. Then, she surprised him by grasping the hem of her blue skirt and ripping off a piece.

"Yes, it was," she agreed, looking no longer at him, but at his bloodied arm, and wrapping the cloth about it as a kind of tourniquet.

Adam waited for the sting in the words, but there was none. He looked at her and could almost see the young woman of twenty-five years before, could almost feel as though he were twenty-five years younger, as though the intervening decades had never happened. But no, that was wrong. They *had* happened: they had happened with Sarah. The thought, unbidden, was a sobering slap. His life that was. His life that should have been. He didn't know what to make of the contradiction, and it sent another spasm of pain through him.

"Adam, why?" Rachel said, with the voice that had once caused Adam's spirit to soar.

In place of speech, Adam shuddered.

"I'm sorry," she said after a while. "I promised myself that if I ever saw you again, I wouldn't ask. After all, after so much time, how could there be any point? But looking at you now, I think that perhaps there is."

His answer came in pieces, the memories—fragmented, distorted—muting his response.

"I was scared," he said. "More than scared. I must have been terrified."

"Of what?" Rachel searched his face, his eyes, for the truth that struggled within him. She was so close that he could feel her breath on his cheek.

He looked down, away from her. Long-ago feelings floated by him like flotsam. He stammered. "I... I was ashamed... so ashamed." Had he known this all along, or was it a new realization, one taking form only as he spoke to her?

"And I was frightened," he continued, his understanding becoming clearer to him, like turning the lens in a spyglass. "Could I be a man, a man to you, in a village where everyone knew me, still thought of me, as a boy? That may seem silly to you now but it was paralyzing to me then. The fear became a sickness, a blackness. It overwhelmed me. I had the usual fears too, not knowing what the future would be like, whether I'd grown up enough, *could* grow up enough, to be a good husband. But this was something else, something more," he trembled, feeling a great cold. "It consumed me. I can't explain. I wish I could."

He shook his head as though trying to fling out the truth, then winced.

"I ran all the way to Lublin and found an academy that would take me without the usual questions and recommendations." His words came faster now. "I thought that if I mastered our holy law, it would make up for... what I had done to you."

He stopped. The shouts and cries, the wails and the moans of the injured and those that the dead had left behind continued all about them. But to Adam and Rachel they were muffled, as though from a long way away.

CHAPTER TWENTY-SIX

"Rachel, what happened after… after…?"

"After you left me?" she concluded for him. She was as matter-of-fact as if he'd asked about a delivery from the dairyman.

"I waited for you, Adam," she said, sitting down in the street beside him. "After the guests left, after my family took me home, after the days turned to weeks and the weeks turned to months and the months turned to years. Other matches were proposed but still I waited for you to return." She busied herself once again with the tourniquet. "Nothing went right for my family after that day. The crops withered. The animals died. My parents thought we were cursed. My brother was sure of it."

She gave the tourniquet another twist, attempting to staunch the blood that had widened the stain across his sleeve. "The Sages say, 'change your place, change your luck,'" she said after a while.

He waited for her to go on. Fires smoldered around them. From the corner of his eye, he could see a small, frail-looking woman trying to drag the body of a man, he supposed her husband, toward a wagon. He attempted to rise, to help her. Rachel eased him back on the ground.

"You're in no state to help anyone else," she said. "Look, others are coming."

Just past him, two men lifted the corpse and deposited it in the back of a wagon.

The living were being helped. More of the dead were being placed in carts and wheeled to their graves. But it seemed to Adam that Rachel saw only a vanished time and place.

He cleared his throat, a sudden, sawing sound.

"Rachel, I came looking for you now, after all these years, for a reason."

He began to tell her the story but he didn't get far—how could he? His vision blurred again as his eyes welled up. The tears streamed down his face, stinging his cheeks. Words, leaden in his throat like pellets, choked him, and only little cries of grief emerged as his body shook.

After several minutes, his sobs subsided. The story of Hersh's wedding and its aftermath emerged, all of it, more than he had admitted to anyone else.

"Please don't punish my children for my wrong," he pleaded.

"Punish you?" Her gentle eyes widened. "God forefend. I couldn't punish you, Adam."

"Still, their fate depends on you. What can I do to repair my wrong? There must be something."

"The Holy One, Blessed be He, has been good to me," she said. "I need nothing from you."

"But I must repair the wrong," Adam insisted.

She considered this, her hands pressed together. "And if what I ask seems insignificant?"

A hint of a smile passed his lips. "I'm learning that the world can turn on what seems insignificant."

"Very well," she said at last, her voice taking on a business-like quality. "I have a niece who is supposed to be married in Koretz in two days' time. But my brother, Anshel, doesn't have the dowry and the wedding will not take place without it. Bring him a hundred rubles for this purpose, ensure that the wedding takes place, and you will repair the wrong. All will be made right and I will forgive you."

"A hundred rubles and all is repaired?" he asked in disbelief. "Some coins? That's all I need to do?" He thrust his hand into an interior pocket of his great-coat. He still had more than enough of the coins he'd taken from Lizensk to meet Rachel's request.

She spoke, without emotion, as much to herself as to him. "For the want of some coins, a marriage never happens. Children are never born..." Her voice trailed off and her features were softened by an overwhelming sense of wistfulness.

"Don't worry," Adam said. "Consider it done." Here was another invitation about to be misdirected, only this time he would be there to ensure its proper delivery, to prevent what was right from going wrong.

They had been sitting in the street all this time. The shouts and the cries had died down but the air, tinged with the stink of smoke and death, still stung. The street was becoming thick now with the survivors of the Okop pogrom. They moved about, some aimlessly, some with the simple aim of quitting the town, as though by doing so they could undo what had happened. Adam saw young boys and girls, separated from their parents by distance or death, sitting in the mud, filthy with it, their anguished tears and desperate wails now reduced to dry whimpers. Others lay in the mud too, the ones that had not been carted away to be cleaned and shrouded for burial. Broken people emerged from broken buildings to attend to the dead as best they could before dark, before the dogs, or worse, could get to them.

Adam rose to his feet in another attempt to help them. Overcome with dizziness, he grabbed at a nearby post to steady himself. Rachel scrambled to her feet to help him.

"Rest a bit longer," she said. "That's what you need."

"I'll rest for just a moment, but I *will* be in Koretz the day after tomorrow," he said firmly.

Rachel's smile was warm but rueful. She gathered her skirts against the mud around them and started to leave. He felt an inexplicable stab of loss.

"Surely you will come with me to the wedding?" he asked. Was their meeting to end like this?

"I will be at the wedding but, first, my business takes me elsewhere, which is why you must precede me with the dowry," she said with a resolve that sanctioned no argument. "Act as my agent and as the agent of the Holy One, Blessed be He. Ensure that the wedding takes place and all will be repaired."

He reached out to her, but his pain was not yet done with him. He winced, his eyes blinking shut for but a moment. When he opened them again, Rachel had disappeared among the survivors and the dead of the Okop pogrom.

Chapter Twenty-Seven

T he morning sun was still low in the sky when Sarah heard the tentative knock at the door. The same knock, always the same knock, and always at the same time of day. Her pulse quickened a bit as she went to open the door. Here at least, for an hour or so, was companionship.

"Feige," said Sarah, welcoming the other into her house with a short, slow sweep of her hand.

"Sarah," replied Feige with a nod. The two women offered each other forced smiles. Sarah had long since realized that an outright greeting would have been inappropriate under the circumstances, as unthinkable as offering a greeting on the Day of Mourning, and it seemed Feige had come to the same conclusion.

They looked at each other, Sarah wiping her hands on her soiled white apron, Feige holding hers by her sides, accentuating her thinness, which had become more pronounced over the past few weeks.

"They're no better—but no worse either," Sarah said, offering the same meager consolation with which she tried to reassure herself.

"Well, that's something, I suppose," said Feige without conviction. Sarah escorted her upstairs to the children's rooms. Feige entered Leah's room first. Sarah watched as Feige patted Leah's small, lifeless, almost weightless hand with her own, much larger, pink one.

"She'll come back to us," said Feige, with a sigh that belied her words.

Sarah gathered the porcelain pitcher and bowl, along with the washcloths, and brought them to Leah's bedside. The women opened the girl's shirt and lowered her skirt. They bathed her, as much as they could. Sarah let the cloth glide over her daughter's face, arms, and body while Feige washed the girl's legs. Her hands lingered over a line along the girl's upper arm, so faint that anyone else might have missed it: a memento of Leah's unsuccessful attempt to scale the family's apple tree two years before. As she washed her daughter's hands, she took extra care with a discolored patch on her thumb, the result of a scrape incurred during one of her games of Blind Man's Buff with Mendel and their father. Sarah closed her eyes as the pain of loss shot through her. She would never get used to this.

The two women dried and redressed Leah and moved her onto her side. They crossed the hall to the next bedroom. Feige stopped in the doorway as she saw Hersh and Miriam lying side by side in their separate beds, with just enough space between them to allow Sarah to pass through as she tended them. Their hands were at their sides not just motionless but looking like they might never move again. Each was pale and bandaged, each deathly still, each lingering between two worlds when they should have been laughing and celebrating their marriage in this one.

Feige let out a small but sharp intake of breath, as she did every morning upon seeing her daughter. Apparently Feige too could not get used to this daily horror.

Each woman washed her child then they repositioned them just enough to prevent bedsores. Sarah and Feige stood close at the foot of the beds, staring at their children as though willing them to look back, to offer some assurance that they would return to them, that they would build their faithful home among their people, have children of their own. But no assurance came. Neither Hersh nor Miriam offered so much as a blink.

With a shake of her head, Feige went around to her daughter's bed and gave it a gentle push until it was flush with the other. Then, she took her daughter's hand and brought it to rest on top of Hersh's.

"There," she said, "that's better."

After a moment, Feige sighed and eased herself into the cane-backed chair by her daughter's side. She took Miriam's other hand in both of hers and didn't let go. Sarah left her to her one-sided conversations with Miriam and the Almighty and went downstairs to make tea.

Later, Feige joined Sarah in the kitchen. The kettle, having long since boiled, sat warming on a corner of the cast-iron stove. Sarah poured cups for them both. They sat and drank. Sarah could hear the clock ticking away seconds that their children would never know.

Feige finished her tea. She looked up and nodded a bit mechanically to Sarah, as though concluding a conversation that hadn't taken place.

"I'll come back tomorrow," she said, rising and moving to the door.

"Maybe tomorrow... it will be better," said Sarah with a shrug of her shoulders as the other left.

Sarah returned to the kitchen, placed the kettle closer to the fire, and allowed herself a second cup of tea. After a while, she slumped in a chair, staring at the tea that still swirled in the cup before her. At least she had Feige. None of the others came. Perhaps they were afraid that the house was haunted, that proximity to Sarah and the children would bring curses down on their heads, too. She didn't blame them.

She gathered the tea things and looked for something else that needed doing. She could sweep the pristine floor, polish the shining candlesticks and samovar, straighten Adam's perfectly organized books.

She had to do something, but what? She paced the small parlor like a ghost within her own home. How could she sit, wait, tend to the children, receive Feige, then do it over and over and over again? How could she sit and bear not knowing if Adam had succeeded or where he was or—she sucked in her breath at the thought—whether he was even alive? Adam might never come back and she would live the rest of her life not knowing what had happened to him, and what might have happened between them had he returned to her. Already his absence of days had turned to weeks. She could see no reason it would not turn to months and years and forever.

She could still feel the presence of her husband and younger son in the house, when she dusted Adam's writing desk, when she found a stray ball of Mendel's under a chair. But while these after-images stalked the house like spirits, she sensed that they too, like her, were worn down by the strain, that they were growing weaker, that they would fade in time. And then Adam and Mendel would truly be gone. Until then, her husband and her little boy would be two more of the living dead in the house, a census against which she was significantly outnumbered.

She glanced at the room's largest memento of her husband: his desk. The aged pine desk stood in the corner as though Adam himself were there, pondering her distress. She could imagine him at it now, hard at work to prepare the sermons he would deliver during the Ten Days of Awe and the Sabbath before Passover. The memory eased some of the tightness in her chest.

The desk beckoned to her. She saw it as it had been on that last day, the day he left. He had sat before it, packing the books, the clothes, the prayer shawl, and phylacteries he would take with him. And he had done something more. He had bent over the desk and put something in the bottom drawer: that book. He had taken the mirror but he had left the book for safekeeping. It was from that book that Adam had learned to make the golem.

Sarah wondered what other secrets it held.

Chapter Twenty-Eight

The next day, they traveled by wagon toward Koretz: Adam in the drayman's seat with the reins, Shayna and the golem seated just behind him on a bench in the wagon-bed. Their wagon was a sturdy, well-constructed affair of recent, if not new, vintage. The previous owner had taken great care of it, had likely taken great pride in it, Adam thought as he regarded the fresh-painted frame and side-walls and even the well-oiled leather bridle and pair of tawny-colored horses that drew it. Adam had found the wagon and horses after the pogrom, and alongside them had found their owner too; he, poor man, had no use for them now, no use for anything but a grave in the Okop cemetery. Adam had seen to it before they left. It was the least that he could do. And it was a true kindness, in the language of the tradition, because it was a kindness that could never be repaid.

Adam could not escape the image of the hundreds of souls in need of the kindness. He saw the streets of Okop veined with rivulets of blood and strewn with corpses and parts of corpses… the diminutive tailor, so proud of his fine if flamboyant clothes, lying like a shattered doll in filthy, blood-soaked rags… the minstrels and players with their throats slashed where they'd stood on the commons, their instruments trampled asunder… the beggars, killed for sport and left in the streets like refuse. Adam felt a sickening in his stomach. He'd nearly joined all of them in the grave, surely would have joined them in the grave, but for the help of the Holy One, Blessed be He, as the Cossack had charged him. But for that, he wouldn't have lived to find Rachel. Rachel… who'd stopped and tended to his wounds even before knowing his identity, rather than run like so many of the others. And even when she'd realized who he was, she had borne him no grudge. How few people could claim so selfless a heart? An angel, he marveled.

And now, he thought with a flick of the reins as gentle encouragement to the horse, he was so close to righting the old wrong. He felt the coins through the cloth of the sack beside him. He had the money and they were on their way to deliver it in Koretz. He was getting closer to saving his children with every turn of the wagon wheels, wasn't he? Yes—so why did strange thoughts keep flitting through his mind?

He stared out at the tied bales of straw punctuating the large, flat, open fields to either side, then glanced back at the golem who was content to watch the countryside pass by; he who saw everything with those pitch-black eyes and said nothing. Adam glanced at Shayna, her eyes closed and her lips moving wordlessly in prayer. Shayna! Her name came to him like a jolt—why had she told him this thing, this unspeakably terrible thing, that Rachel, not Sarah, was the one he was supposed to marry? He shuddered as though to cast off the very idea. What man could be unaffected by the knowledge that the woman with whom for twenty years he'd lived, slept, and had children, was a woman he was never meant even to know? That the angels had decreed otherwise forty days before he'd been born.

Again his thoughts turned to Rachel, his destined one. So different from Sarah... what type of life might they have lived together? Adam shook his head. He couldn't think this, wouldn't allow himself to think this.

But the thought returned unbidden, like a fly determined to share in one's meal. What would have happened if he hadn't run away that day so many years before? He would have been a different Adam, perhaps an Adam who didn't look over his shoulder in doubt, an Adam who cherished, rather than obliterated, memories of his parents and his childhood. For his family and the people of Lizensk, he might have summoned strength where he was weak, resolve where he was indecisive, warmth where he was withdrawn. With one act, one wrong, he had gone on to live an increasingly lonely life that—worst of all—was never meant to be. It wasn't just the generations that were to come from him and Rachel that had been lost. He had been lost as well.

They traveled several miles in the wagon. Shayna was eating a small pastry she must have secreted within her voluminous cloak. When she finished, she reached into a pocket and produced her handkerchief and wiped her lips with a single, straight stroke. The golem, meanwhile, was fascinated by a white sash he had acquired from one of the Cossacks who had no further need of it. He was tying and untying it into a series of intricate knots.

"How do you do it?" Adam asked Shayna.

"Do what?" she replied as she surveyed the fields around them.

"The idea that we're going to a wedding, after what we've seen..." his mouth remained open but the rest of the thought remained unspoken.

Shayna gave him an appraising look, the corners of her thin little mouth twitching for an instant. "Oh," she said. "You think I should be a sourpuss, like you?"

The golem put down the knotted sash and watched them.

"No, I don't—" Adam began, then stopped. "I mean, I'm not a sourpuss."

Shayna looked straight ahead, contemplating the road, which stretched to the horizon. "It must be the light then," she said after a while. It appeared to Adam as though a hint of a grin was evident on the golem's great, carved face.

"You know very well what I mean," he continued. "All the dead of Miropol. All the dead and wounded of Okop. More dead than one should have to see in a lifetime. And now we go to a wedding... We should be mourning, not on our way to celebrate—shouldn't we?"

Around them, the afternoon wind grew stronger, colder. The golem leaned forward, awaiting Shayna's response.

"King Solomon says that everything has its season, everything has its time," she reminded him. "A time to weep and a time to laugh. Who's to say that this isn't the time to laugh?"

"Then when is the time to weep?" he cried out.

"I suspect you'll know it when you come to it," Shayna said. "Let me tell you a story."

Adam sighed, suspecting an evasion.

"Just one story," Shayna promised.

"Very well, then," Adam heard himself saying. The golem drew closer still, his black-socket eyes widening in anticipation.

Shayna shifted about on her seat and drew the folds of her rough cloak about her.

Once upon a time, there was a midwife, *Shayna told them.* She had trained early and well at the side of her mother and none of the women of her village, nor of all the villages around, would go into labor but with her in attendance, if they could help it. She married a cobbler and the pair prayed they would soon embrace a baby of their own.

A few weeks after the marriage, her husband was hitching their horse to the wagon to bring his wares to market. Something spooked the horse—possibly an imp, perhaps a demon—and it reared in the air, knocking the cobbler to the ground. And then it came crashing down on its front hooves, making a bad situation far worse.

"Your husband was very fortunate," the doctor told her several hours later, urging her to a seat in their shack of a home.

"Then why don't you look like the bearer of glad tidings?" she asked him.

The doctor hesitated, folding and unfolding his hands. "I'm very sorry," he said. "You won't... you won't be able to have children."

She sat there, stunned. She never knew how long, but it was long enough for the doctor to make his excuses and leave, long enough for the numbness to recede and the pain to begin to take its place, long enough for a knock at the door.

The midwife was needed. The tinsmith's wife had gone into labor early and unexpectedly and something was terribly wrong. Both the mother and baby were in mortal peril. The midwife gathered her lotions and tonics and ran as fast as she could toward the tinsmith's house.

She heard the cries even before she saw the house. Inside, the tinsmith's wife lay on a straw mattress, a pair of candles unable to dispel much of the gloom, the womenfolk of the family gathered around her. The woman was sobbing with pain and drenched with a sweat that plastered her hair and bedclothes to her body like paste. The midwife went to work, feeling the woman's stomach, probing to ascertain the baby's state. The roundness, the broadness she expected to find, to indicate that the baby's head was about to emerge, was not there. What she felt was smaller, harder, and not at all where it should have been: the baby's bottom. This baby would suffocate, possibly strangle itself, before it could be born.

The midwife, however, would not allow it. She moved her fingers with caution, coaxing the baby to turn, to seek life. She spoke soothing words of encouragement to both mother and child, all the time turning, turning the baby toward life. And when the baby was in its mother's arms, everyone cried and laughed and thanked the Holy One, Blessed Be He, who is good and does good. Everywhere in that room was joy and gratitude. And no one felt that joy and gratitude more than the midwife. She hugged the mother, kissed the baby, and blessed them both.

And then, when it was over, when she was home, when her husband was sleeping, and when she was alone, only then did she cry in anguish for the lives that would not be.

When Shayna finished her story, Adam and the golem continued to watch her. "Shayna?" asked Adam after a while. "Who was the midwife?"

Shayna's eyes blinked through her nose-spectacles. "That would be another story," she reminded him.

Chapter Twenty-Nine

One hour and a small sack of roasted chestnuts later—where did Shayna keep all this food? Adam wondered—brought them several miles closer to Koretz, but in the afternoon light it seemed increasingly likely that they would have to put up somewhere by nightfall and continue at dawn.

Adam's eyes never left the road, but his moody stare was focused elsewhere. "If I'd still had my musket with me in Brinnitz, this might all have been different," he told the countryside.

Shayna was having none of it. "You'd think to destroy the mother of evil with gunpowder?"

Adam broke off his musing and turned to her, starting to object.

"On the other hand, you encountered Lilith both in the world of dreams and in our world of illusion, and survived," she continued without pause, popping the last chestnut in her mouth and relishing the taste. "Not many people can say that."

She continued with deliberation, thinking aloud. "But surviving isn't enough. If we are to defeat Lilith, we must take the fight to her."

"Isn't that what we're doing by going to Koretz?"

"Not at all," Shayna said, rolling up the sack and returning it to the folds of her cloak. "She's acted and we've reacted. We encountered her at the time and place of her choosing, in our world. Instead, we must confront her at a time and place of *our* choosing in *hers*."

"You can't mean going—" Adam started.

"On the contrary," she dusted bits of chestnut off her cloak and looked hard at him. "That's exactly what I mean. Lilith rules the demon underworld. After we conclude our business in Koretz, that's where we must seek her out. She's had the element of surprise long enough. I'd hoped that we could avoid this. It appears that we cannot."

Adam had barely survived his confrontation with Lilith in *this* world. He didn't expect a trip to the demon underworld to present more favorable terrain. He opened his mouth and surprised himself.

"So be it," he said.

Shayna smiled. "There's hope for you yet, Rabbi Adam."

Hope would be a welcome commodity, Adam thought. He could surely use it. Adam glanced back at the golem in the wagon bed. The massive creature had found a companion of his own, a little bird of red and yellow that fluttered above his head. The image was nearly comic and Adam gave himself a moment to enjoy it before turning back to Shayna.

"There's a way for us to get to the underworld?" he asked her, giving the reins a tug just in time to steer the horses around a rut in the road.

"I have an *idea*," she replied. "It concerns a city called Luz."

Adam's grip on the reins loosened and the wagon bench slapped them as one of the wheels went over a small rock in the road. Adam regained his grip and focused on the way forward.

"You mentioned Luz once before," he reminded her. "The place where our father Jacob dreamed of a ladder full of angels journeying between earth and heaven. Can we get to the underworld from there?"

"I think we can, but Luz might be far more important to us than that," she said.

"You're speaking in riddles again."

"Unintentionally, I assure you," she said. "Let me explain, but I have to go back a little, to before the creation of the universe."

"That's going back a *little*?"

Shayna shot him a sidelong glance that forestalled further interruption and took a deep breath. The golem, who had been content to play with his feathered friend, leaned forward, one of his mispositioned ears directed toward Shayna.

"Yes, perhaps you'd better listen as well," Shayna told him. "This concerns you, too."

Before creation—*Shayna told them*—there had been nothing but The Holy One, Blessed be He, everywhere, everything, only The Holy One. In order for the Almighty to create the universe, He had to contract to make room for what was to come into existence. In that space, He inevitably created darkness. And it was out of the darkness that evil came—the evil that they faced now.

As an antidote to the darkness to illuminate it and drive it away, The Holy One, Blessed be He, created the light from which would come all of creation. It was a beautiful light, the most resplendent light that would ever be, encompassing all the colors that the universe would ever know. From this light came the stars, the sun, and the moon. From this light came the planets, the earth, and everything, animate and inanimate, on it. During Creation, shards of this First Light fell to the completed earth, and it is these shards of light that illuminate it.

The golem pointed a thick, earthen finger to the afternoon sun, the constant companion on their journey, and asked a question in the form of a raised eyebrow.

"The sun illuminates the physical world, it's true," agreed Shayna. "But the shards of First Light illuminate the world of the mind and of the heart. The good that we do and the love that we feel, we do and feel when we stand in this light."

"But evil remains," Adam said, his tone making it a question.

"Because the light is mostly hidden," Shayna continued. "We have only its faintest glow. But the direct brilliance of this light—evil must wither before it. Sorrow must turn to joy. I think."

"You *think?*" Adam exploded. He tugged the reins and the horses stopped short with brief whinnies of complaint. He didn't glare at her, but he thought about it.

"Yes: think. *Think!*" she responded with a minor explosion of her own. "I'm an old woman with bunions as big as beets, sitting in a wagon on a rut-filled road in the middle of our Great Exile. What more can I do but think?"

The golem looked from one to the other of his companions. If there was an answer to Shayna's question, it wasn't going to come today.

Adam felt his frustration rush from him like a child's held breath. But if this was another wild goose chase...

"Shayna, first, in Brinnitz, you talked about Luz and now it's the First Light. Where is this going?" Then the answer dawned on him. "Is the First Light there, in Luz?"

"It must be," she said. "You see, the inhabitants of Luz do not die. The First Light is the only thing I know that could confer immortality."

Adam worked to absorb this. Once he'd paid his debt to Rachel in Koretz, they could acquire the First Light in Luz and use it to destroy Lilith in the underworld. It was a plan. It was something, at least. But then he frowned.

"How do we get to Luz?"

Shayna looked out across the fields that stretched to the horizon, as though she might see Luz rather than a sliver of the vast distance between them and the fabled city.

"That I expect is the problem," she acknowledged.

Adam wasn't going to let this defeat them. People did travel to Palestine. Pilgrims did it all the time. One way, he understood, would be to enter the Ottoman Empire through Rum-ili, head south to Athens, and then make the passage across the Mediterranean—if and when sea passage for the three of them could be arranged. True, if pirates didn't get them, they would be at constant risk of encountering the great sea monster Leviathan. On the other hand, they could travel overland, hugging the shore of the Black Sea and passing through the Balkans into the heart of the Ottoman Empire. By that route, they would face difficulties from man and beast that he could just begin to imagine. And if they made it that far, it would only be to search the Palestinian desert for a city that no one had seen in thousands of years.

"Problem" seemed an understatement.

His optimism of a moment before collapsed. He jumped down from the wagon and walked off the road into the tall grass. He came to a small boulder, sank onto it, and took several deep breaths to clear his head. He didn't notice Shayna until she sat down beside him. The golem stood nearby, stepped forward, and rested his massive hand on Adam's shoulder. Adam looked up at him, patted the hand with his own, and smiled despite himself. He turned to Shayna.

"Shayna, if we don't succeed—" Adam began.

"You must succeed," Shayna insisted. Her choice of pronoun surprised him.

"If I do, it will be because of you," he retorted. "Whatever happens—"

"Whatever happens," said Shayna, "it will be—it will have to be—because of *you*, Rabbi Adam."

"But you're a Lamed-Vavnik," Adam insisted. "Your magic, how can I hope to succeed without it?"

"Magic?" replied Shayna with a shrug. "I know a few tricks, that's all. If magic made a Lamed-Vavnik, we'd have to let Lilith into the club. No, what's important is choosing to stand up for what's right. That's what I've always tried to do. The right *choices*. That's the secret of the Lamed-Vavniks."

"The right choices?" protested Adam. "That's it? You make it sound as though anyone can be a Lamed-Vavnik."

"Anyone can," Shayna said, "and look at how few are. *There's* a bleak thought for you. If we needed more than thirty-six of us to keep the world going, I don't think we could manage it. I sometimes wonder how we manage as it is."

"Knowing right from wrong can't be that hard," Adam insisted.

"*Knowing* what's right is easy. *Doing* what's right, when it takes compassion, or courage, or faith... well, that's the hard part. But it's not beyond anyone, Rabbi Adam, remember that."

No, the hard part, it seemed to Adam, would be making their way to the city of Luz.

Chapter Thirty

They found an inn for the night and resumed their journey before sunrise, when the sky was just beginning to turn from black to purple with the first hint of the approaching dawn.

Two hours later, Adam knocked on a cottage door. From the heavily weathered, pitted surface of the door and walls to the thinning thatch of the roof, his impression, however fleeting, was that the door might not withstand a regular rapping. Shayna smiled; no doubt her touch would have been more decisive. The golem stood still behind them; a passerby could have been forgiven for thinking him a statue that the other two had, improbably, carried with them.

After a moment, the door was opened by a short, thin, disheveled man with bags under his eyes. "Yes?" he asked, his voice streaked with resignation.

"Are you Anshel?" Adam asked.

"I live in his house and I pay his bills—as many of them as I can, that is," Anshel answered, folding his arms. "So I suppose I'm Anshel. What do you want?"

"It's not what I want," said Adam, trying for a disarming smile. "It's what you want."

"What is this? Some kind of joke?" Anshel started to shut the door.

"I meant no offense," protested Adam, putting his foot against the doorjamb. "You have a problem. My friends and I have come to help."

Anshel surveyed the three of them, clearly skeptical. He turned a critical eye on Shayna, a shapeless little mountain in her brown cloak and hood, who managed at once to look both like, and quite unlike, a score of grandmothers in that very town. That indomitable woman stared back at him over the edge of her nose-spectacles, as though he, not she, were worthy of scrutiny. Anshel stared at the golem, a towering column of earth in a suit who tried, with breathtaking ineffectiveness, to look inconspicuous.

As for Adam, Anshel's appraising eye apparently didn't think much of him, either. Adam knew he looked as worn as his stained, ragged coat. Anshel gave a shrug as though to ask how things could possibly get worse, and showed them in to a modestly furnished room of rough-hewn chairs with seats of woven straw, arranged around an equally rough-hewn table. A girl's soft sobs could be heard from an alcove beyond.

"So you can help?" Anshel asked, motioning them to be seated. Then he took a chair himself, dropping his slight weight into it as though relieved of the burden of standing. "You know what has happened?"

"Some, but please tell us," Adam said, leaning forward and inducing a whine from the ancient, rickety chair.

"My daughter was to be wed today," Anshel spat the words. "The dowry is one hundred rubles. Three nights ago, I left the money in this cabinet. In the middle of the night, I heard a noise. I came downstairs. The money was gone."

"Did you see the person who took it?" Adam asked, shifting his weight and eliciting another whisper of reproach from the furniture.

"I only caught a glimpse, but I'm not sure it was a person."

Shayna looked grim. "Go on," she urged.

The little man stood and paced across the threadbare rug. "The next morning, news of the theft was all over town. The groom's family sent this letter. The dowry must be paid in full by today or there will be no wedding."

The imminent disaster clouded Anshel's face, but Adam, already reaching into his sack for his purse, barely suppressed a grin. He opened the purse and a cascade of coins hit the table and bounced and rolled about, their sounds reverberating about the small room like the chirping of birds.

"May the marriage bring you and your daughter much joy," said Adam.

Anshel looked at the money as though he had never seen the commodity before. Then, years of strain seemed to melt away. He grabbed Adam's cheeks and kissed him. He moved to kiss Shayna but one look from her stopped him. Anshel glanced at the golem—who seemed intrigued by the opportunity for a new type of human contact—then apparently thought better of it. Instead, Anshel turned around to face the back of the house.

"Esther!" he shouted. "There's going to be a wedding." He ran to the alcove. The sobbing subsided and there were murmured voices. Then the cries continued—only this time they were cries of joy.

Anshel rejoined the others, accompanied by a thin girl of seventeen. Adam and the golem rose as she entered the room. More than thin, the girl looked exhausted, her ashen face stained with tears. But no amount of tears could obscure what Adam saw when he looked at her sweet smile and green-brown eyes, and at the thick blonde hair that framed her radiant face: the resemblance to Rachel was so uncanny that Adam gasped.

"This is my daughter, Esther," Anshel told them with fatherly pride. The girl's smile widened and she nodded.

Shayna drew her ponderous bulk from her chair and embraced the girl. Shayna regarded her as Esther held her gaze. "If your groom is half as worthy as you are, my dear," Shayna finally said, "the Divine Presence will surely dwell among you."

"Thank you," Esther answered, her words soft as dew. She hung her head a bit. "I don't know what to say."

"You just said it," Shayna replied.

Anshel pulled on his beard. "Rabbi Adam, don't think me ungrateful," he said, seeming to search for the right words. "But why are you doing this for us?"

"I'm a messenger," Adam said simply. "Your sister, Rachel, told me to bring you this money."

Anshel's face whitened. "My sister?" he blurted. "When was this?"

"The day before yesterday, in Okop."

Anshel took a deep, steadying breath. The room was preternaturally quiet, a quiet that thickened the air about them.

"Rabbi Adam," Anshel said in a voice that was little more than a whisper, "please tell me: how could you have seen my sister Rachel in Okop the day before yesterday when she died there more than twenty years ago?"

Adam swayed as though to faint. What in heaven's name was the man talking about? He himself had spoken to Rachel, seen her soulful eyes, heard her lilting voice. How could she be...? He glanced at Shayna, who seemed deep in thought.

Anshel peered at Adam and pointed a long, thin finger. "Rabbi Adam... Adam... Adam," said Anshel, his voice rising. "I know who you are. You're the one who broke my sister's heart."

A thousand needles of shame stung Adam's own heart. "Yes I am," he said, feeling the weight of each word. "But if Rachel is willing to forgive me—"

"Rachel never did recover from the shock of that day," Anshel continued his head shaking in sorrow. "Her shame was unbearable. Our family moved to Okop to try to start over but the change made no difference. That year we had such a winter..." He stopped at the memory and shrugged his thin shoulders. "Rachel took ill. Then she was gone. You were in Okop yesterday? She lies there still, in the cemetery."

His reddening eyes stared out at Adam with dull accusation. Adam cocked his head; he couldn't have heard Anshel clearly.

"What do you mean?" he asked. "The Rachel I saw—she was strong, she was real, she was as present before me as you are now!"

Shayna nodded, beginning to understand.

"And she was a spirit," she said to him with sudden realization. "The Holy One, Blessed Be He, surely sent her to you as you expected her to be, so you would listen to what had to be said and do what had to be done. You thought Rachel was alive; perhaps her soul thought so, too."

Shayna adjusted her spectacles atop her mound of a nose. "Either way, it was her final act of kindness to you both."

Adam's stomach churned and he felt he might vomit. That day in Miropol so long ago... his actions on that day... had set in motion the events that led to Rachel's death. She had never married, never borne children, never had the family she so wanted, the family he had promised to her.

The two men turned to meet each other's gaze. Adam's sense of guilt remained, but now it was mixed with something else: gratitude. He knew he would forever be grateful to Rachel for coming so far to give him a way to make amends, and he began to understand the depth of gratitude that this man before him would always feel toward her as well. He and Anshel were now bound together through the kindness of a woman long dead. They would have much to talk about, he knew, but that was for another day.

A furious pounding at the door scattered his thoughts like dust. Anshel jumped up, stunned for a moment, then opened it. A middle-aged couple burst into the room. The short, portly man carried a silver-tipped walking stick and an air of grievance. The woman, her pearl-encrusted headdress askew, panted as she followed the man into the parlor.

"I'm done waiting," the man barked, his face red, his body shaking like a pot about to boil over. "You've had more than enough time. I've come to tell you that the wedding is off."

"Moishe, please," the woman implored, "think of Dovid, think of Esther."

"I am thinking of them, Ruth," Moishe said, although Adam surmised that the man's own position perhaps occupied a larger share of his thoughts. "It isn't fair to them or to us. Anshel, I've torn up the wedding contract. There's nothing more to discuss."

Ruth looked like she wanted to be anywhere but in that room. Not quite looking at Esther, she said, "I'm so sorry about this, but—"

"But nothing, Ruth," her husband interrupted. "A wedding without a dowry is no wedding." He waved his hand in the air, shooing away the very idea of a wedding, then spun back to Anshel. Apparently forgetting that he'd just proclaimed the end of the conversation, he asked: "Do you have anything to say?"

Adam saw Anshel's uptake of breath and, for a moment, thought he might lunge at the other man. But he exhaled and smiled.

"I do," he said. "Rabbi Adam here and his friends have made us a gift of the dowry. I'm in a position to fulfill my part of the wedding contract and I expect that you will fulfill yours."

Moishe dropped his mouth open and deflated like an emptied wineskin. He seemed to take in the information after a time. Then he coughed and his lips turned up in a labored smile.

"Then it's all settled," said Moishe a bit contritely. "Listen, if I got carried away before… Well, believe me, we want the wedding to happen as much as you do."

"Oh, Esther, I'm so happy for you and Dovid," said her intended mother-in-law, giving the girl a brief hug.

"Thank you," Esther replied, kissing her cheek. "Is Dovid outside?"

"No, he's at home," said Moishe.

Adam's night in the synagogue of Lizensk rushed back to him. *Bridegrooms and children are her particular prey.* Adam met Shayna's worried glance and realized that the same thought had just occurred to each of them.

"You have someone there with him?" interjected Shayna, urgency in her voice. The golem's expression changed in an instant from impassive to alert. Adam reached for his great-coat.

"No," said Moishe, clearly uncomfortable by their tone. "Why couldn't he be alone? When we left the house, there wasn't going to be a wedding."

"We must act now," said Shayna.

Adam turned to the newcomers. "Show us where you live!"

Ruth clutched at Moishe's sleeve, she didn't understand what was happening, but she knew it was grave, that her family faced some threat far worse than questions over a wedding.

"You're frightening my wife," said Moishe, who was frightened himself.

"May this be the worst fright she has today," said Shayna. "Hurry!"

Ruth and Moishe fled from the cottage, the others close behind.

Chapter Thirty-One

They ran down the street, across the town square, and toward another, narrow, twisting road. Adam pounded the earth beneath his feet. Trees and houses, wagons and townsfolk whipped by in a blur. Overhead, the sky was thick with birds, seemingly hurtling in the same direction as Adam and the others, urging them on. *Hurry, hurry,* he told himself, demanding of his body every bit of speed it could produce. *O Master of the Universe, protect him!*

"Dovid! Dovid!" shouted his mother as they entered the house, straining for her voice to reach its farthest corners, to touch her son and so make him safe. "Are you all right?"

Her question was met by silence.

"I don't see how anything could possibly—" started Moishe. He was cut off by a crash and a cry from upstairs, a cry that Adam reflexively understood: the scream of someone whose soul was being torn from him.

They ran upstairs. *Not another one, not another groom,* Adam pleaded, visions of poor Hersh invading his thoughts. Lilith had to be stopped and he had to stop her. He got to the landing first and faced the long hallway. Which door? A second scream told him. Adam tried it, but it was locked.

"Golem!" Adam commanded. The golem smashed the door with his thick, solid shoulder and barreled into the room. Adam clambered in after him, filled with dread at what he would find.

The groom lay on the bed, pale and still, as though asleep. Astride his chest sat the Queen of Demons. But this was no beautiful woman, not like the intruder in the synagogue of Brinnitz. This was Lilith as Adam remembered her from his nightmare: a creature of black scales, reptilian green eyes, and the stench of the dead. She was leaning over the boy, her mouth on his, pressing and sucking and licking her lips. She became even more frenzied, attacking him with the ferocity and single-mindedness of a wolf tearing at its prey. When she lifted her head, her tongue, long and blood red, snaked out of the boy's mouth and retracted into hers.

Adam stared, his chest raging, his ears pounding.

It was only as she finished that she noticed the others. She turned toward them and emitted a howl of satisfaction. The sound started low and rose in pitch until Adam felt it wrapping about his heart. Lilith's stare bore down on him and from deep within her came a rumbling growl that dared him to approach her, dared him even to move. Lilith scowled, her tongue flicking out toward Adam like sword thrusts.

From the edge of his vision, Adam saw Shayna step forward, her face transformed by her determination. Gone was the grandmotherly warmth she had shown just a few moments before to Esther. Now, Shayna was a warrior, her resolve writ in the thin, tense set of her mouth, the unwavering stare, the contracted brows. She raised her arms and held her hands up, fingers together and palms outward, toward Lilith. She set her fingers in three peaks, symbolizing one of the seventy names of the Holy One, Blessed be He: the name evoking the power of the Almighty. It was the sign made two thousand years before by the priests of the ancient Temple and passed down through the generations in a line unbroken even by exile and misfortune.

Lilith reared back as though stung, but she didn't flee and she didn't vanish. Her black scales glowed with unholy energy. Her gaze turned on Shayna and burned brighter, while Shayna grew paler. The old woman struggled to keep her arms raised but bit by bit they lowered in front of her. Lilith took a step forward, and another. Shayna's face was ashen, her forehead shiny with sweat. Lilith smiled, just enough to show glistening, rapier-sharp teeth.

No! Lilith would not win, not here, not today. Adam too raised his arms and separated his fingers in the ancient priestly sign. Lilith scowled again and stopped her advance. More. Adam needed to do something more. But what?

"In the name of the Holy Assembly," Adam intoned at the demon, his voice hurtling out of him with a power that no one in the room would have expected, least of all him. "In the name of the Great Court in Jerusalem: be gone!"

Lilith roared like a great, wounded animal and threw herself onto the wall. She clung there by her hands and feet, affixed like a scorpion, fury filling her green eyes. In those eyes, the others saw pure evil, the evil that had tempted the first Adam in the Garden of Eden, and that had bedeviled humanity ever since. Adam held firm, his arms outstretched, his will unwavering. For a moment, nothing moved. Then Lilith's tongue lashed out like a whip and she scuttled across the wall in a motion almost too quick to be followed. She moved across the ceiling in the same way and escaped through the window.

Her departure was the breaking of the spell.

"Oh, God in Heaven, God in Heaven!" cried Ruth, running to Dovid, now pale and unconscious, and cradling his head in her hands. Beside Adam there was a sudden movement: Shayna dropped to the ground, a line of blood across her neck where the Demon Queen's tongue had lacerated it. Shayna breathed heavy, slow breaths but at least, thank God, she was breathing. She was alive. He reached for a shirt lying across a small chest and put it to Shayna's neck to staunch the blood. Her face was drained and damp and her body limp. Adam had never seen Shayna like this and it frightened him.

"I'll be all right," Shayna tried to assure them with a tremulous wave of her hand. "But poor Dovid is not."

Esther's face was a portrait of horror.

"Is he...?" Moishe couldn't bring himself to finish the question.

"No," Shayna replied despite her own distress, in a voice that was weak and quavering. "Not dead. Maybe worse."

Adam wished he could say anything but the truth.

"His soul," he said, looking down at the lifeless boy to avoid having to look Ruth and Moishe in the eyes. "She has it now."

Chapter Thirty-Two

As she had at least six times that morning, Sarah returned to her husband's desk and stared at the drawer where Adam had put that book weeks before. Did she dare take it out? Did she dare leave it undisturbed when she might learn something that could help her to help her children or her husband?

She could feel perspiration gather under the band of her headscarf. What was she contemplating? The Kabbalah was forbidden to women, to the unmarried, to those not yet forty. And she knew what could happen to those unprepared. The great Sages ben Azzai, ben Zoma, and Elisha all met with tragic ends when they used Kabbalah to enter the Garden of Eden. The Sage ben Azzai lost his life, ben Zoma lost his mind, and Elisha became an apostate. True, their colleague Rabbi Akiva emerged unscathed, but the odds weren't reassuring.

And she was no Sage, nor even a man. But the prohibition against women studying the Kabbalah, she knew, was because women lacked the foundation of study in the less esoteric texts. Well, she had that; her father had seen to it. She was married too, another qualification. So what if she wasn't yet forty, the minimum age for such study? She would be soon enough.

And there in the parlor, she remembered something else. She wouldn't be the first woman to expose herself to the Kabbalah. Stories her grandmother had told her so many years ago, stories of Francesa Sarah, who had lived two hundred years before in the holy city of Safed. Francesa Sarah was a student of the Kabbalah and the only woman, before or since, to have controlled the spirit of an angel, with which she could tell the future. Even the rabbis had consulted her on matters of the gravest importance to the community. Nor was Francesa Sarah the only female Kabbalist. Speaking in no more than a whisper, her grandmother had spoken of Rachel Aberlin, whose mystical visions included pillars of fire and the prophet Elijah. Sarah had thrilled as a child to hear the stories of Aberlin, a clairvoyant, who led a mystical sisterhood and even exorcised an evil spirit.

Her own namesake, Sarah the Matriarch, had received revelation from the angels of the Holy One, Blessed be He. Miriam, sister of Moses, had been so great a prophetess that, in her honor, the Almighty gave the Israelites a miraculous well that quenched their thirst through their forty years in the desert. Deborah the Judge had been not only a prophetess but the head of ancient Israel, leading her people into victory against Sisera and the Canaanites. So too there were Hannah and Esther and Judith and so many others.

Sarah took a deep breath and felt her anxiety ebb away. If these other women could do this thing, perhaps she could do it, too, she thought, as she moved to the cabinet in which Adam kept his keys and retrieved the one she needed. Sarah rushed to the desk, her pulse quickening and the room feeling warmer. She stared at the bottom drawer, identical to the ones above it, with smooth light wood and a simple round knob as a handle.

She used the key. Her hand was on the bottom knob, grasping it, pulling it toward her. She removed the prayer shawl in which Adam had enwrapped the book. There it was, just as he'd left it. The ancient leather covers distressed with the touch of countless hands, the gold embossed lettering, the pages yellowed and stiff with age. She lifted the book from the drawer with care, as though it might dissolve in her hands, and laid it upon the table. She looked at it, just looked at it, for a long time. This was not only a book, she understood. It was a gateway to something other, something more, something that could change her—for better or for worse.

Only Rabbi Akiva emerged unscathed.

Now she was seated in the stiff, straight-backed chair by the table, the book before her. It was open and she was turning its pages. She read of gilguls, souls transmigrated across lifetimes, who returned to earth to complete missions unfulfilled. She read of gematria, the transformation of holy words into numbers and the use of those numbers to find hidden truths. She read of the ten emanations through which the Holy One, Blessed be He, makes himself known to humanity, including the emanation of the Holy Presence, the female aspect of the One True God.

She bent over the book as though to inhale its mysteries and read of dybbuks and of dancing in the fields with the Sabbath Bride; of the angels Michael, Raphael, Gabriel and Uriel; of Enoch who was brought alive to heaven and became the angel Metatron and the progenitor of angel armies; of dream assemblies…

Dream assemblies.

She sat upright. She rubbed her eyes and read the text again. She could feel her heart beating faster and scanned the room as though she feared someone or something was watching her.

Dream assemblies.

The enormity of what she was considering struck her anew. Her head felt dizzy even though she was sitting down.

Ben Azzai lost his life, ben Zoma lost his mind, and Elisha became an apostate.

She slammed the book shut, stood up, and rushed to the farthest corner of the room, as though distance from the book could protect her from the danger of the Kabbalah. What had she been thinking? She couldn't take the chance; she had to tend the children and pray for their recovery. If they awoke and she was gone, or worse… What these other women did was hundreds, thousands of years ago. Who was she to think she could match their spiritual achievements? Worse than failure, she could unleash another evil on her family, on the whole village.

There was a reason that Kabbalah was forbidden to all but a holy few.

She didn't think she had moved from the corner but found herself again sitting in the stiff-backed chair at the desk, the book before her. She had shut it moments before. How had it come to be open now? She looked at the page before her and began to read.

From the strange little book that Adam had left behind, Sarah learned that man doesn't dream alone or, at least, he needn't. It was possible to share a dream with another, or with ten or twenty, or an untold number of others. Wonder-working rabbis of old had used dream assemblies to converse with their colleagues despite the vast distances between them. Their disciples had used dream assemblies to sit in the academy of heaven and continue to learn from their departed masters.

Connections flowed between this world of illusion and the true world to come, and they flowed through the world of dreams. The barrier between the upper and lower spheres could be rendered as porous as a fishnet. Time and distance could melt away. Those connections could be accessed by the most learned and the most righteous. Those rare individuals could join together in the world between worlds, the world of dreams, through the dream assembly.

But if one were neither most learned nor most righteous, Sarah wondered, could a dream assembly still work? The stakes were too high for her not to try. The dream assembly might be a way for her to communicate with Adam. If she could call him to a dream assembly, she could ask if he was safe. She could learn what had happened to him since his departure from Lizensk. She could ask him about Mendel, ask about Lilith and if he had succeeded or still could succeed against her, if he could make whole Leah, Hersh, and Miriam. Perhaps there was some way she could help. There had to be. Yes, she would cast off her sense of impotence and help her husband to triumph. And at the very least, she would gain the cold comfort of certainty if the worst had already come true.

Dream assemblies...

Chapter Thirty-Three

They moved Shayna to a bed, the golem picking her up and transporting her as though she were no heavier than a doll. She insisted she was all right, that she would be all right, but she knew that Adam saw something very different in her face, the lines deeply etched, the skin sallow. And he had seen something else: her trembling.

Like an earthquake that starts with distant rumbling, Shayna's trembling started almost imperceptibly, then grew until her whole body shook with the demon poison running through her veins. Her heart pounded, raced, seemingly about to burst. And she was cold, so cold. When the spasm hit her, it was with the force of a Cossack's whip. Her face contorted, her skin blanching to parchment. The wound at her neck blazed white-hot and she tore at the makeshift bandage. The pain. There had to be a way to stop the pain. She pressed her hand against the wound, which only worsened it. She removed her hand and scowled at the blood she found streaked across her palm. She didn't have time for this. Didn't the Almighty know she didn't have the time?

Another spasm and the air fled her lungs and the room spun about her. Maybe the Almighty did know. Lilith's poison should have killed her where she'd stood. Perhaps the Holy One, Blessed Be He, had given her time, a little time, to complete her task. But not much; He was cutting things awfully close, in Shayna's estimation. Still, she had said much of what needed to be said, refraining only from that which was hardest to share. Perhaps just a few moments more would be enough. It would have to be.

She fought with what strength remained, as a drowning man struggles to stay on the water's surface. Then, the pain subsided enough for Shayna to look about her. Adam and the golem were at her side. Anshel and Esther and Dovid's parents, Ruth and Moishe, stood just beyond. All were fixed on her, their faces a mixture of profound alarm and sadness. She had been through much with Rabbi Adam and the golem, but these were expressions she hadn't seen from them before, not in the shadow of the smoldering synagogue of Brinnitz, not in the ruins of Miropol, not even after the pogrom at Okop. She saw hope flicker for a moment in Adam's face, then fade away. The golem was trembling as though the very earth of which he was made might split apart.

Shayna groaned with the pain. "Do I look that bad?" she croaked, attempting to produce a smile that would not materialize. She tried to move, to get up, but her body would not obey her in this, either.

"No," blurted Adam in a voice that said "yes."

He knelt by the bed, gripping her hand as though this could somehow keep her from leaving him. Behind him, the golem continued to move in small, jerky motions: he didn't know what to do with himself.

Shayna winced. "I had thought we'd have more time, but it's not to be," she said through a wince. "Already I see... " Her words trailed off like a wisp of smoke.

Adam's body tensed. After a moment, she continued.

"There must be thirty-six Lamed Vavniks." She pushed out each word with effort. "It is a condition of Creation. Without thirty-six, the world will cease to be."

"That's why you can't die," said Adam, feeling the taste of his tears.

"Of course I can die," Shayna replied in fits and starts. "What you mean is... that I ought not to," she said with more labored breaths. "I agree. Unfortunately, our consensus seems not to be... dispositive."

"But without you, how—?"

"The sun rises and the sun sets," said Shayna. "The Holy One, Blessed be He..." She paused, her lips quivering with the effort of speech. "He does not take away one who is needed before He has prepared a successor."

Adam stared at her.

"*Yes,*" she said, her eyes shining like the last ember of a flame before it burns out. "*You!*"

Adam's felt the blood drain from his face. His tongue, leaden in his mouth, wouldn't move.

"Defeat Lilith," she urged. "Rescue Mendel. Save your children and Dovid. That is your test. It has always been your test. Succeed, and you will merit to become one of the thirty-six.... And Lilith..."

She paused again and her heavy-lidded eyes sagged nearly shut. Adam prompted her. "What about Lilith?"

The eyes opened, only a bit, and only after a moment. "She knows," whispered Shayna. "*She knows...*"

"Knows what?" he replied in a quick, hushed tone.

"That's why she tried to stop you... will do all she can to stop you. If she destroys you before you can take my place, she destroys... everything."

Shayna turned her head a bit and looked past him to a corner of the room. Adam followed her gaze but saw no one there.

"Not yet," said Shayna, responding to words that Adam could not hear.

She looked at him again. "Tomorrow will not dawn, cannot dawn, without thirty-six Lamed Vavniks. You have until tonight ends or..."

Shayna again looked at someone or something that Adam couldn't see and glowered. As she turned back to him for the last time, her face softened. Adam looked deep into her small dark eyes, as though he could find some hold there by which to prevent the inevitable. But Shayna offered none. Instead, she finally succeeded in bringing a smile, however slight, to her lips. She spoke in her merest whisper, the words drifting on the air. Adam strained to catch them.

"Hear thou Israel, the Lord is God, the Lord is One."

Then the angel of death drew her soul from her body as gently as pulling a hair from milk, and Shayna, the elderly housekeeper and hidden saint of Brinnitz, was silent and still.

Chapter Thirty-Four

When Adam could bring himself to look at his mentor and friend, he saw that her body was cradled in his arms. Her face was wet and it took him a moment to realize that it was his own tears that made it so. Still those tears came, like a not-so-gentle rain, falling into the deep lines of her face, onto her well-worn cloak, and onto the glass of her nose-spectacles.

The golem stomped the plank floor so hard it shook, holding his hands to the sides of his head. He looked on like a helpless child and stomped again, this time shaking the walls as well. He turned his head heavenward and opened his mouth, releasing a wail, the power of which was diminished not a bit for being silent.

Adam heard Ruth speak from a long way off, saying something about summoning the women of the Holy Sisterhood to attend to the body, and then she withdrew. Adam felt a gentle tug at his shoulder and turned to see Moishe's large, sad face. He hadn't known Shayna but he and Ruth had suffered a loss as well, one that Shayna had told them was perhaps even worse than death. Adam stood and Esther took a chair, moved it to the side of the bed, and sat. Her lips moved although no sound emerged. Adam knew she was reciting psalms and would remain with Shayna, as tradition taught, until the women could arrive to gather Shayna and begin their holy work. It was time for him to leave the room. He allowed Moishe and Anshel, followed by the golem, to escort him downstairs.

Moishe tried to guide him to a chair but Adam didn't sit, couldn't sit. Instead, he paced, the rapid rhythm of his footfalls not calming him, no, certainly not that, but helping to obscure the outside world just a bit and, with it, a small measure of his immense pain. What he had to do seemed impossible; what he must *not* do—succumb to grief for his friend and to self-pity for his plight—seemed even harder. But it was essential and it was what Shayna would have insisted upon. Neither he nor his children—nor the earth entire, he was coming to accept—had time for anything else.

Shayna had denigrated magic but there had to be some spell or talisman that could transport him and the golem to Luz; weren't there ancient stories about our father Abraham flying across the world in a heavenly chariot? Weren't there legends about tunnels throughout the earth that led to Jerusalem? There were always possibilities. In the day and night that remained, he would find a way.

"May you be comforted among the mourners of Zion and Jerusalem," said a small, high-pitched voice behind him. Adam turned to mutter an acknowledgment, but the only addition to the room was a bird, which had flown in through the open window and now perched on a chest of drawers. Adam was about to shoo it from the house when he noticed its red face and yellow-striped wings: a goldfinch. He had seen that fat little bird somewhere before, quite recently—and again, not so recently, it seemed to him. No, surely not the same bird. Its appearance stirred a vague memory in Adam that wouldn't sharpen yet wouldn't go away. The goldfinch fluttered again and alighted on the table quite near to him. It looked at him and then at the others, cocking its head to one side.

"Your friend must have been a splendid personage, surely to be missed," the goldfinch chirped with sympathy.

"She was indeed," Adam agreed, then stopped as the reality of the situation caught up with him. "I'm talking to a bird?"

"And doing it very well, actually," twittered the goldfinch, its high-pitched words coming across as a sort of staccato melody. "Sometimes people talk to us slowly and loudly, as though we were a bit, er, bird-brained. An infuriating expression, that!" The bird started to stammer and mutter in its indignation.

"Can you hear him too?" Adam asked his companions.

191

"'Her' if you please," corrected the goldfinch.

"Sorry," said Adam.

Moishe and the golem both nodded, a smile appearing on the clay man's rough, sculpted face.

"Yes, we hear her," said Anshel, although his puzzled tone made it clear that he shared Adam's skepticism.

"Why shouldn't they hear me?" asked the goldfinch, taking a moment to pick at a wing-feather with its beak. "I can talk. All birds can talk. Although most of us have the good sense to keep our beaks shut around people. Except parrots, of course, always running off at the mouth, are parrots."

"Excuse me," asked Adam, drawing closer. "Then why, if I may ask, are you talking to me?"

"Just returning a favor," said the goldfinch, soaring in a tight circle in the air above them as it spoke, then landing again on the table. "I was stuck in that log in Brinnitz Woods for quite a while. Thought some cat or boar or demon would come along and I'd be history. But they didn't. You did. And you freed me."

The goldfinch hopped onto Adam's arm and looked up at him with its two black-bead eyes. "Thank you!" It turned to the golem. "Thank you, too!"

The golem nodded his acknowledgment. Adam's memory of the goldfinch and their release of it in the forest outside Brinnitz came to him all at once—as did the image of the bird accompanying them from Okop to Koretz. So they'd had a constant companion of which he, at least, had been unaware. He let out a pop of laughter.

The goldfinch trilled with gratitude, her wings rising as though about to take flight. "It was a very lucky thing for me that you happened to come by when you did."

Adam thought again of his dear, departed friend. "Lucky? Maybe," he said.

"Let it not be said that we birds are an ungrateful lot," chirped the goldfinch. "You do for us and we do for you. I overheard you to say yesterday that you needed to get somewhere in a hurry?" Without waiting for a reply, the goldfinch chirped in loud, clear tones.

"Yes," said Adam. "But I don't see—"

"Come now, rabbi," squawked the goldfinch. "If you can't travel overland, then you'll just have to travel *over* land."

Adam and the others heard a sound so faint that at first they questioned its existence. But the sound grew louder. It was low, sharp, and incessant, like the sound of rain against a roof—except that the bright morning sun precluded the possibility of rain. The goldfinch flew out the window and Adam and the others rushed outside to follow its flight.

It took the four of them a moment to discern the mass far above. It appeared at first like an enormous veil hung across a distant part of the sky. As it came closer, it became clearer: it was a flock of birds, if flock was a sufficient term, hundreds of them at first, and then thousands, circling overhead, of more sizes and types and colors than Adam—or any one person—had ever seen before. There were sparrows, cardinals, herons, doves, owls, hawks, and geese. There were robins, vultures, gulls, pigeons, kingfishers, and even hummingbirds.

As Adam continued to stare at the sight, he saw far rarer birds. Here flew a phoenix, with its long neck and brilliant red and gold feathers. There flew a roc, whose eggs were said to be the size of boulders. In the distance, guarding the flock, as was its wont, hovered a ziz, a bird so large that it blotted out much of the sky even from so far away, so large that it was said to rival the other giants of creation, behemoth and leviathan, which Adam, seeing it for the first time, could now believe.

The flock swept overhead in enormous circles that grew first larger and smaller and larger again, like the beating of a massive heart. The beating of their wings caused a din such as Adam had never heard before. It raised a wind that lashed his face like a storm. But, as he surveyed the sky, so filled with birds that it seemed to pulse with a life of its own, he was filled with a growing sense of awe. In little more than a whisper, he uttered the customary blessing to the author of such a sight: "Blessed art thou, Lord our God, King of the Universe, whose world has such wonders in it."

The goldfinch detached itself from the flock and flew down toward Adam, the golem, and the others.

"These birds will take me and my friend to Luz?" Adam asked the goldfinch.

"Don't talk about us as though we're not here," said an eagle, flying close behind the goldfinch. More birds were joining them, circling just above their heads, almost within reach.

"I beg your pardon," Adam replied, bowing his head. "Delighted to make your acquaintance." The birds alternately chirped, cawed, and quacked in response.

"We'll get you to Luz quickly—and on the house," said the goldfinch. "Cast your bread upon the waters, and all that."

Adam turned to the golem, a smile lighting his face. "Shall we go?"

The golem nodded. Then Adam looked back at the house and his smile faded. There were meant to be three on this journey, not two. Anshel must have understood.

"You haven't time, Rabbi Adam," he said. "You must be off."

Adam nodded. He took the measure of the morning sun, still low in the sky, but surely not for long. He fixed his gaze for one last time upon the house.

"You would have known how to obtain the First Light," he said to the one who could neither hear nor answer him. "You would have known how to find the demon underworld and how to use the Light. You had the strength, the knowledge, the holiness. You had all this. I don't."

Make the right choices, said a voice within him. *You were always capable of it.*

Could he? On the other hand, he had never won an argument with Shayna.

The birds began to land around them. They had carried an uprooted grand fir tree, big as a sailing ship, which now lay along its length on the ground. Its trunk was about fifty feet long and at least eight feet across. Its hundreds of branches stood out at broad angles from the trunk, and covered half its length, with the lowest, oldest branches extending up and out some fifteen feet. Layer upon layer of needle-like leaves served as an impenetrable wrapping. Lying on the ground, it looked like a giant's lance or spear. Adam regarded it mutely, far too numb to marvel, too numb even to approach it.

The goldfinch returned and hovered before Adam and the golem, encouraging them to climb onto the tree. Adam found himself lifted off his feet by the golem, who raised him up and onto the trunk of the tree in a single, smooth motion, then climbed up after him. The companions stepped along the trunk, making their way around branches that rose like small trees themselves. Above them they could see the dense thickets of needle-leaves and, through them, patches of the sky. The golem found a spot with smaller, flexible branches; he bent them into leafy seats and gestured for Adam to sit. Adam sat.

The commotion outside of their arboreal cocoon grew as hundreds, perhaps thousands, of birds descended upon the grand fir. Each grasped a branch as thick as it could hold, from sparrows holding the thinnest of twigs to the mighty rocs bringing up the rear with the roots of the tree in their massive claws. Each bird did its part and, together, they accomplished what Adam would not have thought possible. The tree, with him and the golem ensconced as though in a nest, rose in motions so smooth and steady that Adam was unaware of any movement at all until he looked down at the diminishing landscape below. He could still see Moishe and Anshel by the house and a group of women, presumably the Holy Sisterhood, approaching them. Adam bit his lip and turned away. A world without Shayna. He had known her for so short a time but now the idea that she was gone was unthinkable. His teacher, his friend, his guide, and his spur, too.

Adam saw that beside him, the golem rocked back and forth in his makeshift seat like a penitent, mourning Shayna in his own way. He would mourn her too, till the end of his days. He shivered and drew his great-coat tight around him as futile protection against a cold that came not from without, but from within.

So far, the tree had remained parallel to the earth and had moved only vertically, up into the sky. Now it changed. Adam felt the tree, still horizontal, like an arrow poised for flight, turn, rotating to face the rising sun, the direction in which lay the city of Luz. The din of cries, chirps, calls, caws, hoots, trills, warbles, squawks, shrieks, and other sounds not readily categorized, and which had not abated since the birds had converged on Koretz, grew louder. With a motion that was as pronounced as their ascent had been subtle, the tree lurched forward. Adam reached out for a branch with which to steady himself. The golem showed no similar caution. His head was in continual motion as he took in the sights of the clouds above them and the landscape below. Both whipped past them as they raced ahead. They flew at speeds that Adam knew could be matched by no horse, no ship, no arrow, no musket blast. Even the wind, normally from the east, was at their backs, urging them forward, as though the upper spheres approved of their voyage and were aiding them on their way.

Chapter Thirty-Five

The golem hovered over his creator to protect him as he slept. He shielded him from the great gusts of wind but could do nothing to quiet the roar of the birds' wings. Every time the tree lurched—sometimes to the right or left, sometimes up or down—the golem held onto the tree trunk with one massive hand and kept his creator secure with his other.

His master's mouth twitched and the golem thought he would speak; then it stopped. His master's arms jerked and his great-coat flapped back and forth. The golem could imagine something trapped beneath it: a bird or a squirrel. Of course, nothing was there except for his creator's troubled sleep. The quick movements of his creator's eyelids told him that he was not at peace. He had seen enough to know that when people slept, they entered another world, one as real as this one, but what happened there was a mystery to him. He would never enter that world, for he did not sleep. He wondered what it meant, what his master was seeing and doing in that other world.

The golem heard faint sounds, moans, from his creator. He took him in his arms, nestling his master's head against his unyielding chest. For a long time, neither moved. He wished he could ask Shayna about his creator's troubled sleep. Shayna would explain. Shayna... Of course, Shayna was gone. Not her body, that they had left on the ground. Something else: her soul. He touched the part of his chest where he thought a soul might live. He felt something strange inside him: a tightening of his chest, a great heaviness. He had felt something like it before, at the Okop fair, when he'd discovered that the mud boy was only a puppet. No, this was worse, much worse, a thousand sadnesses pressed into one. *Grief.* That was the word.

He stared down at his creator, asleep in his arms. Maybe that's what he felt, too.

Adam awoke to a slow, back-and-forth motion. He opened an eye: the golem was rocking him into wakefulness. He opened his other eye and squinted. The sun was high overhead. A blast of frigid air hit him like water from a bucket.

"I'm awake, I'm awake, my friend," said Adam forgetting for a moment where he was. He was cold, bone-achingly cold. He felt the tree trunk beneath him, heard the incessant wind blending with the sounds of thousands of wings flapping in common purpose. Holding onto a thick branch to steady himself, Adam peered over the edge of the trunk. Below him, a desert stretched as far as he could see, thick with dunes that cast random shadows like soot on snow. Near the horizon, he saw a thin, moving line—a caravan?—that looked no more significant than a trail of ants.

The golem pointed to a place not far from the horizon that Adam strained to see through a veil of clouds. The tree jolted and Adam pitched back against the branch behind him. Immediately, a great gray and brown paw clamped down on his shoulder and held him fast. He patted the golem's hand and looked again near the horizon. It was clearer now, a bit: a walled city. It was vast, spreading out before them for miles like no other city he had ever seen. He took a deep intake of breath. He was about to enter a place of holiness unlike any he'd encountered before, a place whose inhabitants merited to live forever.

The tree made a slight but sudden change in direction, taking them more directly toward the city. Adam felt momentum slam him backward as the tree pitched forward. The birds tried to coordinate their descent and their omnipresent squawking grew louder and more agitated. Adam craned his neck to see through the latticework of branches. He could see the city a bit more distinctly now; it appeared to be built in a perfect circle. It rose up from the sands in a rainbow of desert colors: browns, tans, golds, reds, oranges, yellows, grays, and whites that harmonized with each other and with the endless desert that surrounded it. Adam slid his hands along the tree trunk as he leaned forward for a better view. He was about to enter what might be Paradise on earth. He could only shake his head in wonder and offer a murmured prayer of thanks to the Holy One, Blessed be He.

The birds carried the tree lower, lower toward the city and Adam realized that it wasn't circular at all; it was twelve-sided and as high as it was broad, with scores of soaring, gold-topped towers that climbed to the clouds, many thin enough to look like needles reaching up into the sky. The birds took them close to the towers and Adam and the golem saw details that were monuments to the stonemason's art: elaborate window frames and delicate balconies festooned with filigree designs. Looking down, Adam could make out smaller squares and courtyards lined by massive pillars and arches and decorated with the same colorful designs that encircled the towers.

Now he noticed something else. Here and there, structures were crumbling, their roofs caved in, their walls cracked or breached entirely. Whatever Adam had expected, it wasn't this. Broken walls in Paradise? Surely the Luzites had time enough to fix all this? The thought flitted away through Adam's mind, crowded out by each new sight and sound.

The birds continued their descent toward the city, circling low around it several times. Adam could make out figures at windows and in the streets gazing at the gigantic shadow of the birds as their tree passed over them. But he was still too far away to see them clearly. Were they the wrinkled ancients of his imagination? Or were they frozen in a perfect moment of vitality? On the other hand, what did their appearance matter? These people, however they looked, would have whole worlds of knowledge to teach him. Just then Adam felt a jolt that almost knocked him off his perch. There was a great squawking and hooting and screeching among the birds as they lay the tree horizontally in the center of a busy, enormous plaza.

The golem didn't wait for instructions. He leaped the ten or so feet from the tree trunk to the ground and landed on his misshapen, earthen feet. Adam peered over the tree's edge. The golem looked up at him; he looked down at the golem. After a moment, the golem opened his arms wide. Adam gulped, closed his eyes, and jumped, landing in the golem's arms like a child's wooden ball landing in the cup to which it is tethered. The golem set Adam down on the cobblestones.

"There is no dignity in this, you know," he told his clay companion, brushing off twigs, evergreen needles, and feathers from his hat and shoulders, his great-coat, side locks, and beard. Adam looked around, expecting people to approach them, to welcome them, to express surprise, at least, at their untraditional arrival. But the many passersby continued passing by.

"I suppose," he said, turning back to the golem and shrugging, "that when you're immortal, you really have seen it all before. Maybe they've even seen the likes of you."

The golem glanced downward self-consciously and plucked a few leaves and twigs off his black suit in an unsuccessful effort to make himself presentable. He fingered a few rips in the jacket, through which his skin, the mottled colors of earth and clay, was visible.

The blast from thousands of beating wings continued as the birds hovered above them, blotting out much of the sky. Their friend the goldfinch landed on one of the branches nearby, close to the ground, puffing with great effort. Her yellow wings were still and so too, after a moment, was her gray chest. The golem plucked a small red berry off the tree and held it out to her in his great slab of a hand. The goldfinch alighted there, pecked at the berry once, then tossed it into the air with her beak and, as it fell before her, swallowed it whole.

"Thank you," she chirped to the golem, who nodded in return. She twisted her bright red head toward Adam. "And once again, thank you for rescuing me."

Adam's eyes glinted. "Consider the debt repaid."

"Getting you here seems like the easy part," the goldfinch twittered. "Sorry we can't help you with what's to come." She plucked an errant feather from her chest and returned her attention to Adam. "May the Holy One, Blessed be He, be with you."

Once again carrying the tree in their thousands of claws and talons, the birds took flight. The flock created a thunderous sound that filled the plaza and produced gusts that threatened to knock Adam and the golem to the ground. Flashes of wings red and green and purple and yellow swirled above them like jewels in a kaleidoscope. Ospreys, bluebirds, eagles, flamingos, nuthatches, cockatiels, woodpeckers, wrens, and sun conures worked alongside the griffons and rocs and rainbirds, all of them contributing to a din that rivaled the babble at Babel. The birds flew higher and the cacophony grew fainter until the birds vanished from sight. They were returning to the world he and the golem had left behind, while they were pressing forward toward... What? Adam really didn't know.

The birds had set them down at the edge of a giant market that filled the plaza. Adam and the golem walked past stalls selling vegetables, utensils, fabrics, livestock, bowls, pots, and much more. Adam was jostled and thrown off balance by a short, thick man in a linen tunic with pleats and a fur-lined cloak that might have been worn hundreds of years before. Adam murmured an apology as the man moved on with an irritated glance but not so much as a word. Adam, chagrined, watched the man disappear into the crowd as a couple, no doubt husband and wife, argued past him in long, loose white robes and sandals, the husband's head topped by a thin laurel crown.

Adam watched in wonder as a half-dozen men shambled past wearing bright silk robes belted at their waists, their clothes surely from the distant Orient although the men themselves were not. He didn't know what to make of this dizzying attire. Some wore clothes that might have come from the wardrobe of the Patriarchs, others perhaps from the time of the Crusades, and still others could have accompanied Adam and the golem out of Lizensk.

A group of cranky-looking matrons came toward them in tight-fitting woolen gowns, their complexions gray as though the very blood within them needed encouragement to flow through their bodies. As Adam and the golem zigzagged through the crowds, many of the Luzites merely shuffled past, many with heads drooped or backs stooped, or else lost in bickering.

Two elderly looking women, strands of white hair peeking out from beneath their hats—one tall and conical, the other a blue turban pinned with a ruby—stopped in front of them, inadvertently blocking their way.

"I do not care what you say," said Tall-and-Conical. "She loves you more."

"She does not," insisted Turban. "Mother loves us both the same."

"Ha!" snorted Conical. "It does not matter what I do. You are her favorite."

"How can you say that?" asked her sister.

"You remember the time that there was only one piece of halvah left and she gave it to you? How I loved that halvah!" Conical's tone softened at the memory. "The honey, the cocoa! The way it melted in my mouth!"

And then Conical evidently remembered the halvah that got away. She fixed her sister with a steely gaze. "At least, I *would* have loved that halvah if mother had not given the last piece to you!"

"That was more than two thousand years ago!" snapped Turban in exasperation.

"Oh, you would like me to forget, would you not?" said Conical, her head nodding in answer to her own question. "It just goes to prove it: mother loves you more!"

The sisters moved on, but the sense of discord remained behind them like refuse. Adam led the golem and they ventured deeper into the market, past a labyrinth of stalls and booths, hoping for some clue to the First Light. But the people around them were no different than the old pair and the others they had left behind. Here, a merchant and customer bickered over goods as they had bickered every day, Adam surmised, since the world was young. There, neighbors argued over which of them was responsible for repairing the wall between their properties, a wall that Adam sensed might have long ago turned to rubble. A woman, her eyes daggers, complained to a hapless man who must have been her husband that he'd forgotten her birthday for the thousandth time.

"Yes, exactly a thousand," Adam heard her say. "Do you not think I have been keeping count?"

Adam shook his head: what cranks! They were older than the people he had left behind in Lizensk, but no wiser. They had lived long enough to absorb every wrong, enshrine every slight, rehearse every argument that had ever passed between them. A sickening feeling stewed in Adam's stomach and he felt his face grow cold and damp. None of these people would harbor—would be worthy to harbor—the First Light. He turned to the golem, who shared his disconcerted look.

"No," said Adam. "I don't understand it either. Something seems very wrong here."

Then an even more disconcerting thought occurred to him: What if the First Light wasn't here at all? It was well into the afternoon and they had only the rest of the day and the night to succeed. They didn't have time to be wrong.

Adam needed some sign to show him that the Light was indeed here, and he needed it now. He plowed through the crowd, deeper into the market, with the golem in tow. They passed merchants hawking a world of goods including shoes, sleeping sand, chickens, amulets, and what looked to be invisibility cloaks, but Adam gave them only the merest looks. A sign. Somewhere there had to be a sign.

"Yeeesss!" said a musket-thin man clad in a dark Oriental robe, conjuring a smile as broad as a ship's bow and as phony as a tin kopeck. Despite himself, Adam was brought up short by the man's enthusiasm—the first display of energy he'd seen since arriving in Luz.

"I can see you are a man of discernment," the man in the robe continued. "And you! We do not get a golem every century, let me assure you. Welcome, welcome! Yeeesss!"

Pleasantries completed, the man got down to business. "May I interest you gentlemen in something? Perhaps gossamer wings harvested from the moltings of Ural fairies? No? Of course not—pretty but impractical. How about a shamir?"

Adam glanced down at the little pots of earth lined up on one side of the merchant's counter. In a few, he could see that the soil was moving, disturbed from below. In one, a small insect, a gold-colored bean with pincers and legs, poked up through the surface, looked about, and burrowed back down into its pot.

"These little darlings can eat through stone," the merchant said. "And my stock is descended directly from the shamir that helped to build the holy Temple in Jerusalem."

Under any other circumstance, Adam might have been tempted. But he just shook his head, murmured a polite "no thank you," and motioned for the golem to follow him.

"I am offering a special, this year only!" the scrawny merchant shouted after them.

The golem shrugged an apology for them both and hurried after Adam, who moved through the market, scanning the crowds for someone who might help them, disappointment writ large in the furrows of his face. Where were the wise elder statesmen, the scholars whose intellects were sharpened by millennia spent in study of the law?

A woman's high-pitched cry punctured the hubbub of the market. Adam and the golem ran to it instinctively, arriving outside a stall selling holy books, all leather bindings and gold gilt pages. On the cobblestones before them lay a young woman, her arms still splayed where they'd broken her fall, a small woven basket on the ground nearby, fruits and bread, and several small, wrapped packages scattered around it. As they approached she began to rise, brushing off her long blue skirt and white blouse as she did so. Several young-looking ruffians were laughing as they disappeared into the throng.

The golem helped the maiden to steady herself and retrieved her embroidered shawl as Adam collected the scattered purchases. She brushed a bit of sand from her full, pale cheeks and tried, with uneven success, to restore her long, black hair to some semblance of order. "It is very kind of you to help me," she said, smiling with appreciation.

"It's only common courtesy," Adam said.

"Around here, courtesy is not so common," she corrected him. "But you are not from around here, are you?" she added, pulling the sleeves of the blouse down over a few fresh scratches.

The golem held out the shawl, which the maiden wrapped about her. She turned her pale face toward him and regarded him with great curiosity. "Thank you. You *definitely* are not from around here."

The golem glanced downward, suddenly shy.

"No," acknowledged Adam. "We've come from a great distance. I'm Adam and this is my... friend." It struck Adam that he'd been remiss in not giving the golem a name. It hadn't seemed necessary before. Now, somehow, it did. But what did one name a golem? The Maharal, Rabbi Judah Lowe, had given a name to his golem almost two hundred years before. What was it? Ah, yes.

"His name is Yossele," Adam said. The golem beamed, his thin, lipless mouth turning into an unmistakable smile and his clay cheeks becoming, for a moment, a bit rounder. He tilted his head toward the maiden, which had the effect of accentuating his mispositioned ears.

"And my name is Zippora," the young woman replied, accepting the replenished basket from Adam and tucking it in the crook of her arm. "Surely you must be tired after your travels. Please, my hospitality is not much, but you are welcome to it." She gestured with her other hand. "Come with me." And then she was off, Adam and the golem trailing after her.

"Does this sort of thing happen to you often?" asked Adam when he'd come even with her.

"I am used to it," Zippora said, her shawl fluttering behind her like wings as she strode away from the market. "It is nothing, really. Some people get bored after thousands of years. They pick on each other. Sometimes they pick on me. Why should I be exempt?"

"Bored?" repeated Adam, his attention split between his new guide and the wondrous, luminous architecture that breezed past them. "Surely the boredom must be offset by infinite joys."

Adam's comment nudged forward a new thought in his mind. Something was missing here. For confirmation, he scanned the boulevard they'd just entered, filled with back-bent ancients, young couples, and middle-aged matrons.

"The children," he said. "Where are the children?"

Indeed, of all the Luzites they saw, the youngest were in their teens. Of babies in their mothers' arms, girls tugging at their skirts, boys playing ball—not one was in evidence anywhere.

"Every gift has its price," Zippora said, then stopped, her glance cast downward. "We do not die, but we do not give birth either. We just... are, like the figures in a tapestry."

"I'm sorry," said Adam. "I didn't realize."

"Of course not," said Zippora, eager to change the subject and turning off the boulevard and into a labyrinth of much narrower streets. "Are you hungry? We are almost at my house. You can rest and refresh yourselves there."

"You live alone? Is that proper?" asked Adam.

The barest hint of color came to Zippora's pale cheeks, then receded. "You are thinking about propriety with a woman old enough to be your grandmother—many times over," she laughed, the welcome little sound spilling out of her like drops from an overfilled goblet. "Do not worry. I live with my father, Rabbi Nisn. He will be very pleased to meet you."

"The rabbi?" repeated Adam, now alert. "Of course. The rabbi. We have something of the greatest importance to discuss with him."

"Then you will soon have the chance to do so," Zippora announced as she stopped before a yellow sandstone building, tall and narrow, built up against the edge of the little street, with mythical animals—at least, Adam *thought* they were mythical—carved into the wide wooden frames of the leaden-glass windows. "Here we are."

Lurking in a doorway a few houses down the street stood a tall, ruddy man with dark hair and burning eyes. He drew his tattered brown cape about him, although the breeze was slight. He had been in the plaza and noticed Adam and his clay companion, had overheard the exchange between Adam and Zippora, and had followed them. Now, as he watched them enter the house, the man worked his jaw and spit against the cobblestones. Strangers in Luz were always after something, always meant trouble, he thought. And these strangers might mean the most trouble of all.

Chapter Thirty-Six

T he room in which Adam and the golem found themselves seemed to be decorated in a dizzying array of styles—and periods. Curious, Adam fingered one of a pair of black and orange earthenware vases painted with geometric motifs and highly stylized human figures. It stood next to a bureau of polished mahogany wood, the centerpiece of which was a carving of an armored knight, his lance buried in the chest of a defeated dragon. The golem, meanwhile, was eyeing a dainty fauteuil chair, covered in gilt and damask-patterned tapestry, evidently with the intention of sitting in it, then changed his mind. Adam relaxed a bit; he'd envisioned the chair getting the worst of any physical encounter with his companion.

"Father!" called Zippora. "Are you here? We have visitors—from the outside."

"The outside? My goodness," said a booming voice from the top of the stairs. Rabbi Nisn was a barn of a man with a thick white beard that descended to his chest and sparkling eyes that glistened from under the thickest of eyebrows. As he descended the stairs, his frame shook beneath his capacious robe, the fabric trimmed throughout with a lustrous fur that Adam couldn't identify. Rabbi Nisn carried several large books and Adam noticed a quill and spectacles tucked into a red sash at his waist that matched the red, fur-trimmed turban crowning his head. A long scroll of parchment trailed behind him.

Zippora made the introductions.

Rabbi Nisn shook hands with Adam and the golem, then realized with chagrin that he'd transferred to them the splotches of ink that covered his own hands.

"Forgive me," he said, handing his handkerchief to them. "I was preparing this week's sermon. Amazing that I can still find something to say after all these centuries, but that is Scripture for you, is it not?"

A laugh exploded from deep within him, his index finger thumping Adam's chest for emphasis, a motion against which Adam braced himself so as not to fall. Rabbi Nisn beamed at them. "I'm delighted to make your acquaintances."

"And I'm delighted to make yours—and your daughter's," Adam added.

"It is not easy to be a rabbi's child," said Rabbi Nisn, giving his daughter an appreciative look. "But Zippora carries it off well, I think. Do you have children, Rabbi Adam?"

"Yes."

"How wonderful for you."

"Not at the moment," said Adam, his thoughts wrenched back to the crumpled bodies that had lain in Lizensk, and to the son who might be dead—or worse.

"I beg your pardon?" asked Rabbi Nisn, puzzled.

"Please, sit down," invited Zippora.

Rabbi Nisn and Adam took a pair of leather-upholstered wingback chairs. The golem was about to sit on a stout wooden stool nearby when a cushion appeared, courtesy of Zippora. He took it from her and squeezed it with no evident idea of what to do with it. Zippora smiled and motioned toward the stool. The golem nodded his thanks, placed the pillow on the stool, and sat, the stool groaning a bit but otherwise showing no sign of strain.

"People do not come to Luz without a reason. What can I do for you?" asked Rabbi Nisn. Adam fumbled for a moment. Where to begin?

"My family suffers under a great evil," Adam said, each word freighted with pain. "One of my children is missing. The others are near death. I'm after the one responsible."

"Who is that?"

"Lilith," Adam spat out the word.

Rabbi Nisn let out a low whistle. The room was silent.

"I intend to save them." Adam leaned forward toward the other man, his hands gripping the arms of his chair.

Rabbi Nisn gave his head a slow, gentle shake. "That means destroying her," he said. "And that is not possible."

"It could be... with your help."

"I am not sure—"

Adam leaned in close to Rabbi Nisn. "We know about the First Light."

"I do not know what you are talking about," Rabbi Nisn said. Again the room was quiet. Now it was Rabbi Nisn's turn to speak in a slow, small voice: "You do not know what you are asking."

"I'm asking for your help to destroy a great evil," said Adam with the simplicity that comes from certainty.

"You are asking my people to give up their immortality."

Adam leaned forward, closer to the other man. "From what I've seen, your people don't seem to value it too highly."

Rabbi Nisn sat back in his chair, his face slack. Although he didn't intend it this way, Adam knew that what he'd said was, inevitably, a personal rebuke of their spiritual leader.

"Some do but many do not," Rabbi Nisn agreed. "It is difficult to blame them. After all, how much is a day worth when you know there will always be another?"

"Then—" Adam began.

Rabbi Nisn interrupted. "But you propose to take the days away."

Adam hadn't fully considered this, hadn't thought about the effect of his request, if granted, on the people of Luz.

"Would they suddenly—?"

"Die? Not immediately," Rabbi Nisn said, brushing off the idea with a shake of his hand. "There have been Luzites who grow weary enough of life to propose to end it. They leave the city and the protection of the First Light and live out their years. Then they die."

Rabbi Nisn glanced at a framed painting on the wall that Adam hadn't noticed before. It was the portrait of a woman who appeared to be of middle age—or what would have been considered middle age anywhere else—and who bore a resemblance, particularly in the liveliness of her blue eyes and the shape and breadth of her smile, to Zippora. Adam looked at the painting and then back at the pain he now saw in the other man's expression. The two faces—one frozen on canvas, the other frozen in the flesh—seemed to behold each other and to tell a tale that Adam imagined would be difficult to hear.

Adam had almost forgotten that he was not alone with the Rabbi of Luz. "Father," said Zippora, her hand lighting on her father's arm. "We have to help them."

Rabbi Nisn rose and walked a few steps away, seeming to look off into the distance: the past or the future? Adam couldn't tell.

"We have been protecting the First Light since it was brought here by our father Jacob," he said, a quiver in his rumble of a voice. "We cannot relinquish that trust now."

Adam exhaled. "I understand," he said, starting to rise. "But Shayna said this was our only chance."

Rabbi Nisn turned. "Shayna?" he asked. "Surely not..." his voice trailed off.

"An old woman of Brinnitz," explained Adam.

Rabbi Nisn smiled, showing a broad row of teeth. "Still working for Rabbi Zusman, is she?"

"How did you... how could you know her?"

"There is no way I *could* know her," Rabbi Nisn assured him. "I have lived in Luz for, well, for nearly an eternity. It is just that I sometimes see a little more, know a little more than the next person. That is all."

Adam had heard that self-description before. He considered Rabbi Nisn again. For just a moment, his host appeared to be surrounded by a brilliant, beautiful light, a light which Adam had seen once before, in the synagogue of Brinnitz.

He blinked. "But then you're also a...? Shayna never said..."

Rabbi Nisn regarded Adam. "Shayna does not know everything. I am one of the oldest of our, er, number... well, *the* oldest by quite a bit, I expect," he said. "I have some awareness of the others, but it does not often work the

210

other way around."

He paused and looked up at nothing that Adam could see, then frowned. "Come to speak of it, I do not sense her now."

"She journeys no more, at least, not in this world," said Adam with an evenness he did not feel. He talked of Shayna, of their time together, and of her death. Rabbi Nisn spoke calmly as well, but Adam noticed the tinge of gray that washed out his cheeks and the seemingly oblivious way he kept running his fingers through his thick white beard.

"She died trying to bring me to this place, to you."

Rabbi Nisn let go of his beard. "There is only one reason Shayna would have told you about herself," Nisn said. "You are among us?"

Adam swallowed hard at the thought. "Well, no. That is, not yet." Adam wasn't sure how to answer. "Destroying Lilith and saving my children is my test."

Rabbi Nisn's eyes grew wide under his wooly eyebrows. "Shayna is gone and you have not yet taken her place? Why did you not tell me this straight away? And this happened this morning? Then there is no time to lose," he said.

Zippora stood and looked from one man to the other and back, her long black hair a sharp contrast with her candle-white skin. "Father, Rabbi Adam, what does this mean?"

"It means we can only hope that we are not too late," her father replied.

He turned back to Adam and the golem. "Follow me," he said, as he moved to the back of the house. The four left and crossed an alley that put them into the next street. As they continued along it, they passed, but didn't notice, a tall, ruddy man with burning eyes, dark hair, and an even darker expression, lurking in the shadows of a nearby wall. He watched them go, disdain painted across his face. Then he spit against the wall and pushed off.

Chapter Thirty-Seven

R abbi Nisn led the others down narrow, warren-like streets that felt like a maze. The oblique afternoon sun and high walls of the city conspired to cast long, deep shadows that seemed to cleave the sandstone-colored buildings and walkways. Rabbi Nisn's furtiveness—pausing at crossings, checking around corners—worried Adam, who ran his palms down the sides of his great-coat to wipe off the sweat that was collecting on them. Rabbi Nisn was a great ally, but what about the others in this city? Would the Luzites, if they knew what he and the rabbi were about to do, oppose them and, if so, how? The four passed under innumerable archways, through alleys, and made their way across plazas paved with the same geometric patterns that Adam and the golem had seen from the sky. Adam supposed his apprehension was written across his face, because Zippora reassured him repeatedly that her father was taking a surreptitious route precisely so that they would not be followed. Adam gave her a smile he didn't feel, then glanced back at the golem, who guarded their rear flank as they continued through the city.

Rabbi Nisn stopped before what seemed just another nondescript building colored in browns and grays and tans. He opened a plain, unmarked door in the back of the building.

"If you'll excuse my absence for just a moment," he said to Adam and the others in a whisper that still managed to boom. "I imagine we will do better if we have the synagogue to ourselves." He entered the building, closing the door behind them. Adam and Zippora waited in silence and increasing anxiety. The golem positioned himself to scan the street for threats and remained motionless. After several minutes Rabbi Nisn returned and signaled for them to follow him inside.

Their clandestine approach had not prepared Adam for the sight he now beheld; likely, nothing could have. The room dazzled. The sanctuary was vast, the largest room he had ever seen and larger than he could have imagined a room to be. It looked like a magnificent palace as, indeed, it was, and Adam felt awe in the unmistakable presence of its King. This synagogue had stood for millennia and, Adam could imagine, would stand for millennia more. The golem, too, marveled at the sight, although Adam wondered if he could fully appreciate what he was seeing.

Everywhere Adam looked—at the pews, platforms, balconies, arches, and columns—he saw white marble decorated with the most intricate patterns of inlaid gold and turquoise. A few feet away, the golem ran one of his great earthen hands over a column into which was carved a fine latticework of interconnected six-pointed stars.

The holy ark, an immense structure of these same materials and designs, stretched across the entire front of the sanctuary. Never had Adam even considered that a holy ark could be so vast. It was reached by a pair of white marble stairs, one at the far left and one at the far right, which culminated in a platform surrounded by a latticed balustrade. Four seven-stemmed candelabras, made of gold and set with rings of turquoise, rose ten feet into the air and stood like giant sentries, one at the base of each staircase and another at the top, to either side of the ark.

Adam's gaze followed the sweeping vertical lines of the candelabras alongside the ark, which was crowned with two massive tablets, dark blue and smooth as glass, on which were carved the ten commandments given to Moses on Mt. Sinai. The reflected light from the sapphires—for Adam knew the rabbinic tradition—was blinding, and he could not look at them without shielding his eyes. Surely, he thought, these replicas must be as magnificent as the originals. And then another thought occurred to him: perhaps they were not replicas.

Above and before the holy ark hung an oil lamp with the eternal flame that represented the omnipresence of the Holy One, Blessed be He. It was a gold-and-turquoise vessel holding a globe through which a flame could be seen burning brightly. The whole affair was suspended by three golden chains that stretched up to the distant, mosaic-covered ceiling.

Rabbi Nisn led his daughter, Adam, and the golem across the sanctuary. As they made their way down a side aisle toward the holy ark, Rabbi Nisn stopped at a small, arched recess, in the back of which Adam made out a wooden door barred with thick iron bars. The older man grimaced at the door and nodded toward it.

"The way you seek to Lilith and the demon underworld—it is through there," he said, the mountains of flesh under his robe quivering a bit.

Rabbi Nisn could read the shock on Adam's face.

"Lilith's world—it's below us here?" asked Adam, unable to conceive of how the holy and the unholy could co-exist in such proximity. "You built the synagogue over such a place?"

Rabbi Nisn's broad, rosy face lost some of its color and his eyes seemed to dim. "Deliberately so," he said. "Our father Jacob brought the First Light here to prevent the demons from using this passage, the largest and most dangerous of all the passages that connect the two worlds. Then he built a little synagogue to house it. The city—and this synagogue—came later."

Adam scanned the room but saw nothing that looked like the object of his quest. "The First Light is here? Is it hidden?"

"Here, but not hidden," Rabbi Nisn said with a great shake of his head. "If you want to hide something of value, Rabbi Adam, keep it in plain sight." He looked up toward the burning lamp above the holy ark, walked to one of the marble stairways, and climbed to the platform. The others followed.

"That little flame in the glass?" asked Adam, unable to hide a trace of disappointment. After what he'd gone through, he expected a bit more… something. Grandeur, perhaps.

"Glass?" repeated Rabbi Nisn. He untied a golden cord affixed to the wall and let it pass bit by bit through his fingers. As the cord passed up toward the vast ceiling, the lamp descended at the same pace. The golem watched the lamp and cocked his head, his lopsided ears exaggerating the gesture. To Adam, the simultaneous upward movement of the cord and the downward movement of the lamp evoked the angels of Jacob's dream, traveling up and down a ladder to heaven. That, he realized with a jolt, had happened on this very spot. He gazed about the synagogue; if there were angels with them now, they remained hidden.

Rabbi Nisn gripped the cord when the lamp finally reached them, stopping its descent. "You think you are looking through glass?" he said. "You are seeing the Light through solid iron an inch thick."

Fascinated, Adam peered at the lamp. The hard metal was readily identifiable, yet the flame burned visibly through it as though it were glass. Rabbi Nisn reached toward the lamp, extracted the iron sphere, and passed it to Adam, who held it in his unprotected hands. Another miracle: it was cool to the touch.

Adam felt his heart pounding, his temples throbbing. He held in his hands a remnant of the first day of Creation: the First Light that existed before the physical universe, the Light that the Holy One, Blessed be He, used to bring the universe into being. It was ancient beyond his imagining and powerful beyond his comprehension. The thought caused his hands to tremble and he drew the sphere closer so as not to drop it, heaven forfend. He looked into the Light and realized this was the closest he had ever come to experiencing the Almighty. The Light seemed to grow stronger, brighter in his hands. Did it grow to illuminate the entire room or was the room itself fading away from him? Until now, the First Light had been an abstraction, a thing, a tool, a weapon with which to defeat Lilith and save his children. But now, feeling the radiance of the Light washing over him, he began to understand how much more than this the Light truly was.

"There, Rabbi Adam, is the source of our immortality," said Rabbi Nisn, his great arms folding across his chest in a gesture of completion. "For the first time in... a very long time, the responsibility for it isn't mine."

Indeed, the responsibility was now Adam's. At Rabbi Nisn's words he felt a cold wave pass through him. But he didn't tremble or show weakness. To do so would betray the trust that the other man was investing in him, the trust that Shayna had invested in him. Adam took a long, slow breath and looked down at the magnificent treasure in his hands.

"'Thank you' doesn't begin to suffice," Adam said, lifting his face toward the larger man. He turned to take in Zippora as well. "When we succeed, the golem and I, it will be a success that both of you have helped to make possible."

Adam glanced toward the enormous stained-glass windows, tall and narrow, each depicting a day of Creation. He looked out through the clear panes of the first window and saw that the daylight was taking on an orange tinge as the sun sank in the sky. Time... time... he had so little. Could it possibly be enough?

"We'll go now," he said to Rabbi Nisn and Zippora, and motioned to the golem.

"Not with that light, you will not," said a harsh voice behind them. They all spun around like weathervanes in a storm. In one of the aisles, halfway between them and the distant doors out of the sanctuary, stood a tall, gaunt man in a shabby cape, his hair a disheveled display of dark tufts, his ruddy skin almost red against the white marble of the sanctuary. Behind him stood several dozen Luzites. In their hands they held swords, wooden beams, and knives. The man who had spoken held a musket. An image of his own musket, smashed and abandoned in the forest outside Brinnitz, came to Adam. It seemed a lifetime ago.

The golem moved in front of Adam and the others, positioning himself between them and the mob. His chest swelled and his oversized hands tightened into fists. Then he stood still, with the intensity of a cat into whose vision a rat has had the misfortune to stray.

"Pinhas," called out Rabbi Nisn, his voice a deep rumble as he moved his ponderous weight forward a few steps. "You have no business here."

"In the house of the Holy One, Blessed be He, I have no business?" asked the red-faced man, his voice a barely restrained growl. He came down the aisle with a swagger, as though daring the rabbi to restate his objection. His followers moved along in his wake.

"Judging from what you are up to, I would say it was *you* who had no business here," Pinhas continued, gesturing with his musket at the four on the platform of the holy ark. "Come down here, now."

The golem, a coiled spring, glanced at Adam, who returned a slight shake of his head. These were people, not demons or Cossacks. Maybe there was another way. But he noticed that he held the sphere of Light as though a fight were inevitable.

"We'll come," Adam told Pinhas. Rabbi Nisn regarded the mob warily but held his tongue. He and Adam and Zippora descended, the golem following them down the marble stairs to the floor of the synagogue.

"You don't know what's at stake here—" began Adam.

"I knew you were trouble the moment I saw you," Pinhas interrupted, jabbing the air with the musket. "And I know all about you. *We* know all about you. I overheard you at the rabbi's house. Sorry about your children—but that is your concern, not ours."

"Yeeessss!" hissed the merchant in the fur hat, with even the dragons embroidered on his robe looking angrier than Adam recalled from the market. The other Luzites nodded and murmured their agreement.

Pinhas spit onto the otherwise pristine floor of the synagogue. Adam blenched and Zippora looked horrified. Rabbi Nisn slammed his fist down on a marble railing with a force that surely would have broken Adam's hand had he tried a similar gesture.

"Pinhas, you are in God's house. Put down that musket," Rabbi Nisn ordered.

Instead, the mob's leader pointed the weapon at Adam. "Go back where you came from," he barked. "You do not get to make decisions about the First Light."

"The decision was not Rabbi Adam's," Rabbi Nisn roared. "It was mine and you will abide by it."

Pinhas swaggered down the aisle toward Rabbi Nisn and the others, the Luzites trailing closely in his wake, like the tentacles of a sea creature.

"Rabbi Nisn, you have no right," Pinhas snarled, the others shouting their assent. Adam saw indecision color Rabbi Nisn's face and, for a moment, he seemed just a bit smaller. Adam was sure that the rabbi had anticipated there'd be trouble after they'd left with the Light, but neither of them had expected to be confronted by something like this before he could spirit it away.

Zippora glanced at her father and then at Adam. She stepped forward and Adam saw indignation in her flushed cheeks and heard it in her labored breaths.

"Right? You talk about right?" she asked Pinhas, with a force that put the Luzites on the defensive. "We had no right all these years to squander the gift of the Light. Think of how long we have had it. Think of how little we have done with it. We could have become so much... *better* than we are."

Zippora paused. The mob was quiet.

Pinhas, his face even more red, again spat. "We did not ask for the Light," he shouted, turning to his followers. "We made no promises. No oaths. We owe nothing—certainly not to *them.*"

"Pinhas is right," said Zippora. Adam swallowed an objection. "We are under no obligation to these two," she continued. "Our obligation is only to ourselves."

The mob was listening. Adam was listening. Pinhas' mouth was open but no retort emerged. Evidently, he was listening, too.

"We know what awaits us if we refuse these two," Zippora continued. "Day after day until the end of time, each day like every other day that has already come and gone."

None of the Luzites answered her. None had an answer.

"Pinhas is right that we made no concession for the Light," Zippora said, speaking more urgently as she pressed her advantage. "But surely we gained no entitlement to it, either. The Light was never ours to keep. Perhaps it was ours to protect until this moment, to help someone with the courage to use it as it must be used—to destroy Lilith, to make a difference in the world."

Zippora stopped and breathed. Adam didn't dare to.

A quiet, tentative voice came from the center of the mob: "I do not want to die."

It was met by another: "Me neither."

And then it stopped. Two people had considered Zippora's words enough to think about their implications. But only two.

Zippora had done what she could do. Now it was Adam's turn. He stepped forward, the little iron sphere of First Light still in his hands. He looked into the crowd and saw one of the Luzite couples he had overheard bickering in the marketplace.

"I'm trying to save my family," he said to them, sweat erupting like dew across his forehead. "It's an extraordinary sacrifice for you, I know, but perhaps you can regain something too: The affection and devotion of a husband and wife looking back together over lives well-lived. The passion that lovers feel when they know their days must someday end. The tenderness of a mother's touch when she knows that her children must grow up and go away. You don't have that now. You can have it again. Please, let's help each other."

He looked out at them, seeking some sign that his words had found their hearts.

One of the Luzites called out, "Even with the Light, there is no guarantee you can defeat Lilith." His objection was met with several voices of assent, but fewer than had protested before.

"In my place, what would you do?" returned Adam.

One of the mob, a thin, young man who looked like he'd seen little of life despite his immortality, answered him in a small, wistful voice. "I would pray for bravery, and for the guidance of the Holy One, Blessed be He." He was met with several murmurs of agreement.

"The Holy One has guided me to you," Adam said.

"Take the Light," said another, an older-looking woman whose words rang with maternal authority. "And may the Master of the World be with you."

This time the Luzites shouted their agreement. A few burst into applause. Although Adam didn't notice it, a shaft of afternoon light pierced one of the synagogue's massive windows, stabbing the polished floor before him and creating a line he needed to cross without delay. The last day of the world was passing rapidly.

"Thank you," said Adam. "There's no way I can repay you."

Zippora stepped toward him and the golem and put her hand on the golem's arm. She looked at both of them as she said "Defeat Lilith. Save your family. That will be repayment enough."

Adam and the golem started toward the arched alcove with its barred door to the underworld when a voice interrupted them. "A fine speech," said Pinhas. The fur-hatted merchant was at his side and his gun was pointed at Adam and the golem. "But we do not care what the rest of you think. We are not ready to die."

The golem stepped toward Pinhas. "Do you want to see whether you are faster than this musket?" Pinhas asked him, looking even wilder than when he'd first entered the synagogue. "It may not hurt a man of clay but I suspect it will do its job against a man of flesh and blood." Pinhas aimed the musket at Adam.

The golem scowled and for a moment the letters inscribed on his brow seemed to glow, but he stopped where he stood.

"Now, put back the Light," said Pinhas. Adam started toward the front of the synagogue. "No, not you. The clay man. I want to keep you close in case your friend gets... unfriendly."

Adam turned to the Luzites in silent appeal. Most looked away. "Maybe he is right," said one, softly. "Maybe you can destroy Lilith without the Light," offered another.

Adam's moment had passed. He could fight, would fight, but if anything happened to Rabbi Nisn or to Zippora... Adam handed the sphere of the Light to the golem, who took it toward the front of the synagogue. The golem climbed the marble stairs and released the cord that lowered the lamp. It took a moment before he finished his task, but when he raised the cord again, the Light was burning brightly within it. The golem turned and faced the others, shrugged an apology to Adam, and returned to his side, the gaze of his black-socket eyes never once straying from Pinhas.

"That is better," said Pinhas. "Now you can go."

The golem frowned and moved toward him. Pinhas again aimed the musket at Adam.

"No!" cried Zippora. The golem stopped, then took a step back.

Adam considered his options for overpowering Pinhas but couldn't envision one that ended well. And he had another thought: If Pinhas killed him, who would save his children? As strange as it was to consider, who would save the world?

"We'll go," he said with resignation. A blanket of defeat settled on him, stooping his shoulders. His mouth was dry. He felt cold. To have come so far...

He turned to Zippora and Rabbi Nisn, his eyes moistened with disappointment. "Thank you both for what you tried to do."

"I am so sorry," Zippora said. "Your family..."

Adam tried to console her, and himself. "There must be another way," he said, the words ringing hollow even to his own ears. "We'll find it."

The golem went to Zippora, took her hand in his, and patted it.

"Take care of him," she told him. "And yourself."

The golem offered a small, grim smile. Now there was nothing to do but proceed to the demon underworld without the one weapon that might have ensured their success. Adam and the golem moved to the alcove that Rabbi Nisn had pointed out earlier and stepped into it. The golem peeled back the bars at the back of the small enclosure as though they were strips of paper and opened the door. Beyond it was darkness. They went in.

The stairs were steep, wooden, and creaked under them, barely supporting their weight. The rough-hewn stones caught at Adam's clothes when he slid against them. They descended twenty, perhaps thirty feet, into a chamber of unknown dimensions. Adam groped in the darkness, while trying to protect his hands from the sharp rocks that jutted out from the walls. He felt no passage to the underworld or anywhere else, no way forward. But then, it hit him again, he had no way forward with his quest even if he found the passage. No way to stop Lilith, no way to save his children. And he felt the little time he had left slipping away. Adam shook his head as though to dislodge the thought. First things first. Find the passage.

As he adjusted to the darkness, Adam could detect the barest light filtering down from the sanctuary above, enough for him to make out, after a while, the far end of the chamber. A pile of rocks against the wall suggested something behind it. That, Adam conjectured, was the way they must go.

"This looks to be more in your line than mine," Adam said to the golem.

The golem approached the rocks and cleared them away like a child shooting marbles, revealing a dark opening beyond. Adam took a step toward it, then stopped. He looked up into the golem's face. The light was much too dim to see clearly but the golem's face, it seemed to Adam, held an impish smile. Before he could question his friend, the golem opened his mouth and brought out a ball of the mud and clay from which he was made. The ball glowed like a small sun with the First Light within it.

Adam didn't understand what he was looking at.

"H... h... how is it possible?" he stammered. "You returned the light to the lamp."

The golem shook his head, then smiled. Adam recalled what he had seen, as best he could. When the golem had lowered the lamp and replaced the Light, his back was toward Adam and the Luzites, obscuring the lamp as well as his motions. It was only after he had turned to face them that they could see the Light burning within the lamp. The golem had put back only some of the Light, keeping the rest... and improvising. Apparently, improvisation was an unexplored talent of his.

"Well done!" cried Adam. "You'd better hide it again." The golem placed the Light back into his mouth. With effort, he eased it down his throat. The golem smiled and patted his stomach. The First Light was safe there. Adam beamed with admiration.

"I don't know what we're about to face—but I do know that there's no one with whom I'd rather face it," he said, bringing his hands up to the golem's arms in a partial embrace. The golem seemed unsure of how to respond, finally finding a place for his hands on Adam's back. Now it was Adam's turn to smile.

"Let's go."

Adam started to enter the passage. The golem stopped him and entered first, signaling for him to follow. The golem steadied himself by placing his hands on the narrow walls. They were covered with a luminescent slime that stuck to his hands, though he tried to shake it off. The floor of the passage began to angle downward, just a bit at first, then more sharply as they continued.

Adam saw the golem throw his arms into the air and disappear. He called out to him but received no gesture or sound by way of response. He lost his footing and grabbed at the slimy, slippery walls. Panic seized him and he threw his own arms into the air as he fell down an almost vertical drop. Now he could see the golem, falling too, barely ahead of him. They continued to fall, not just through space, but through dimensions that saw them pass away from their world of illusion.

Chapter Thirty-Eight

Adam's mind clouded and he felt himself moving in and out of consciousness as the sides of the passage hurtled up past him with dizzying speed. He had no idea how long he and the golem had been falling. After a time, the passage became narrower and Adam felt its sides nipping at him, shoving him, catching and tearing his clothes, painting him with the foul slime that covered the walls. His shoulder smacked hard against a protuberance and, with a searing pain, Adam was jolted to full consciousness. He shielded his head with his hands but sensed that if he were thrown against the side, or if the passage became just a bit narrower still, he would not survive it.

He could see a faint light far below. They hurtled toward it and Adam smashed against the floor of the passage, sending shockwaves of pain through his body. He rolled out toward the source of the light and collided into the body of the golem, sprawled before him. Adam lay there, disoriented and unable to move, but relieved that the torture of his descent was behind him. He squinted and saw the portal through which they'd just emerged; it was a large, rotting hole in a huge, ancient tree that held no leaves, nor any other signs of life. Its trunk was bent to the point of deformity, its branches jutting out like the disjointed limbs of an old beggar using a pair of sticks to steady himself.

Get up. He had to get up, though his aching body insisted he lie still for just a few moments longer. *There must be thirty-six*, Shayna had told him, *or the world will cease to be. Get up now.*

Groaning, Adam rose to his knees and found the golem at his side, helping him to his feet. He took his first full look at their surroundings. They were on a moor, a dismal jumble of dark grays and reds, with jagged rocks scattered like dead men in a desert. It stretched out in all directions, punctuated by the occasional tree, or skeleton of a tree, which stood like a knife stabbing up through the ground. Where grass or weeds lay—nowhere could they be said to be growing—they did so like wisps of hair on a desiccated corpse.

There was nothing here, but somewhere in this barren world they would have to find Mendel and Lilith. Adam scanned the cold landscape again. He looked up and realized there was no sun, no sky either, not as he knew it, just a thick, heavy grayness that gave him the sense that the moor, despite its vastness, was an iron trap ready to close in on them.

Just beyond the cold, rocky field in which they'd landed was a shallow gully with a river bed nearly, but not quite, dry. The golem bent down and fingered the mud thoughtfully, trying to get some clue, Adam imagined, of which way to proceed. Adam moved closer and was assaulted by a putrid odor rising from the gully. Bile climbed his throat and he bent over and retched, his body trembling and shaking. The attack on his senses dissipated and he regained control of his chest and his throat. He felt in his pockets for a handkerchief that wasn't there, then reluctantly wiped his mouth on the edge of his sleeve. The thought flickered through his mind that this was the final insult to a great-coat that had been clawed and torn, covered in mud and ash and slime, and nearly incinerated—with him in it. He smiled.

The golem was again at his side, his knitted brows signaling his concern. "I'm fine, fine, Yossele," said Adam, as much to reassure himself as the golem. But he knew he wasn't fine in this ungodly place. All around them, nothing stirred. Nothing sang. Nothing lived. He'd been sickened not just by the absence of life, but by something more: This place was the opposite of life. It was permeated with a smothering sense of death.

Then he saw an extrusion of sorts from the dead terrain, several miles in the distance, and tough to discern from the hills from which it rose. A palace, he realized with unease stealing over him. The palace's ramparts and towers jutted up from the hills, stained in layers of the same dark grays and reds he saw in the landscape before them. They stood not quite upright but angled toward the central keep, as though in subservience to it, or to what it contained. That keep, in turn, rose like a gauntleted fist, seemingly a manifestation of raw power and something more: of contempt for any force that was not—yet—under its control. Adam grew cold.

"That way," he said, his voice a whisper but laden with determination.

In the world above, evening had banished day. Sarah put down the mysterious book she'd been reading for hours; she looked out of the window into a night that surrounded her and the village like a blanket, perhaps protective, perhaps suffocating. Here and there candlelight peeked out from behind the shuttered windows of other homes. It was past time to close her shutters as well. Sarah started to do so and glanced up at the night sky. It was a cloudless night but something was odd, and it took Sarah several minutes to realize what it was: the stars.

The night sky, normally filled with stars like candles twinkling in windows during the Festival of Lights, seemed to hold fewer of them now, though that was plainly impossible. Sarah sought to orient herself by finding Orion, the Great Bear, the Little Bear—all the constellations her father had shown her as a child—but none of them appeared to her. The stars she saw looked random and unfamiliar. She looked for Orion's Belt, the first constellation she'd learned and one which, once glimpsed, was impossible to miss. But the three stars she sought, though they were among the brightest in the night sky, were not to be seen.

And then she realized that she *was* looking at the belt, or what remained of it: two stars, beaming low in the eastern sky. The third star, which should have been to the west of the pair, was not there. Maybe her eyes were playing tricks on her. Maybe the missing stars were somehow hidden from view, although the lack of clouds gave lie to that possibility. But what else could be hiding them? One thing was certain to Sarah: she had enough on her mind without worrying about the heavens. She gave the phenomenon little thought and turned back into the room.

As she did so, one of the two remaining stars of Orion's belt dimmed and was gone.

Chapter Thirty-Nine

Although the golem never tired nor sweated, Adam did both. They ran for as long as Adam could stand it, then walked at the best pace he could muster until he'd regained enough strength to run again. Throughout it all, the palace loomed forever before them. It beckoned to them, mocked them, as though its malevolence was sentient. Adam could feel the sweat coating his body, his heart pounding to express what he wouldn't allow his mind to put into thoughts, let alone words. No time, no time. They had to move onward.

They came to a valley covered in dense vegetation—more shrubs, more trees, covered with vines that stretched out over them like canopies—and all of it dead. They would have to find their way through it; the palace lay on the hills beyond. Adam surveyed the wretched valley grimly. It mocked his hope to get to the palace, to destroy Lilith and save his son before the world ceased to be. Unlike the moor, which laid out its barren nothingness like a dare, this valley was like a crypt, dark and hidden, promising secrets and none of them welcome.

"Maybe there's one bright spot, Yossele," said Adam. "At least, if we can't see what's down there, then Lilith won't see us approaching, either."

The golem nodded and took the lead scrambling down into the depths before him. Adam followed. Desiccated vines crumbled in Adam's hands as he grabbed them to steady himself and he stumbled on the untamed terrain. The golem was quick with his massive hand to keep him upright. Down, down they went, pushing their way through a dead forest that was increasingly dense, unyielding, and ominous. The light changed too, the shadows longer and seeming to move on their own. Surely that was a trick of... of what, Adam was unsure.

As they struggled across the valley floor, over dense underbrush and under thorn-covered limbs and vines, Adam couldn't help feeling that something lurked nearby, that something was watching them. More than once, he thought he heard a sound, something apart from the noise of their own efforts. Was it a faint whisper, something slithering perhaps in the rotting undergrowth beneath their feet? He didn't know, couldn't be sure, but the back of his neck prickled a warning.

They began to climb again, trekking up the other side of the valley. The climb was as treacherous as their descent had been, the ground equally slippery, and hand-holds equally unreliable. And that damnable sense of being watched! Adam swung around but saw nothing. It was possible there was nothing to see. Or nothing that would allow itself to be seen.

After what Adam judged to be two hours since they'd picked themselves up from the cold, hard moor of the demon underworld, they left the valley behind them and found themselves on a ridge overlooking the palace. They hid behind an outcropping of rocks to shield themselves from view. A road of beaten earth ran along the ridge, one end leading off into the distance and the other snaking among the rocks and sloping toward the palace.

With a nod of his head in the direction of the palace, the golem let Adam know he was ready to face the enemy. Adam wasn't, at least, not quite yet.

"We need to know what we're going to face," he whispered to the golem, as though the inhabitants of the palace could hear them from a hundred yards away. Maybe they could. "You blend in better with all this than I do," he said, gesturing to the boulders around them, which might have supplied the raw material for the golem's creation. "Peek around and let me know what you see."

The golem seemed pleased to be uniquely qualified for the task. He leaned around the side of the rocks, the browns and grays of his clay looking like they had always been a part of this desolate lookout. After a moment, he turned back to Adam.

"Are there guards?" Adam asked, "how many?"

The golem held out two fingers.

"Well, that's not too bad," Adam said, a bit relieved. "Perhaps we could distract them and sneak past. Do you think they can see us from down there?"

The golem gave this some thought, then shook his head.

"Good." Adam peered around his side of the rocks to get a better sense of what they were up against.

Adam saw two creatures in the distance, just in front of the palace. They stood and moved like men but could never be mistaken for men, with their greater size and their tusks and tails. These were the creatures that Adam and his co-religionists, indeed the whole world, had long feared. He had met their queen, and now he saw her subjects: Demons, the soulless step-brothers of humanity, monsters that combined the cunning of men with the ferocity of predators. They were the children of Lilith, or perhaps of her mother, Naamah, the witch of the seas who invades men's dreams and lures them to their deaths. The Sages were uncertain; some questions were too dangerous to pursue. These demons were too far away for Adam to see them distinctly, but he could sense an air of evil rushing toward him from the pair like a river breaching its banks. He shuddered.

Adam watched as the demons held their heads high and turned them from side to side, as though sniffing the air for the scent of intruders. Would they smell Adam and the golem from this far away? Adam's heart pounded against his ribcage.

They had indeed sensed something and turned to face it—and turned away from the rocks behind which Adam and the golem were hiding. Adam let out the breath he hadn't realized he'd been holding and followed their gaze toward the horizon. There, another demon was on horseback, riding toward the palace. It carried what looked to be a thick cord or chain, the other end of which was wrapped around a human, a man of indeterminate age and unenviable condition, judging by the way he walked, stooped and limping, struggling to keep up with his captor.

The demon on horseback reached the palace with its prey and conferred with the guards, their snouts shaking, their tails thumping the ground with atavistic excitement. Then one of the guards turned toward the palace and apparently shouted an order. The dark, stained iron portcullis of the palace slid up with a labored, clanking sound audible even to Adam and the golem in their distant perch. The demon on horseback entered with its prisoner. The portcullis slammed down behind them with the finality of the grave.

"Two guards," whispered Adam. "With the element of surprise, I think we can take them."

The golem motioned to his stomach and looked at Adam, his eyes asking the question he couldn't bring to his lips.

"I don't think so, not yet," Adam replied with a shake of his head. "We don't dare risk it until we've found my son."

Adam pressed an eye up to a gap in the rocks. A dozen demons were now taking up positions around the palace entrance. Adam swallowed hard.

"At least," he said, lifting his hat to wipe a line of sweat from his brow, "we still have the advantage of surprise."

He jumped in shock as the tip of a spear tapped his shoulder. Another spear tip thumped the shoulder of the golem. They stared up into the fierce, brutish faces of two demons, faces Adam could not have conjured even in his nightmares. The guards glared at them with eyes that were black points of polished onyx glinting on dark, mottled faces. A pair of yellow tusks, stained in spots to dark brown, rose inches out of each mouth, dripping congealed globs that splattered onto their leather tunics. Only their round snouts were moving, nostrils flaring, as the demons seemed to take the scent of their prisoners. Their heads and bodies were round and thick and coated in the matted, stinking fur of wild boars. Again, Adam was seized by the impression of both human and animal, or of something that wasn't quite one or the other. He could sense the profane wickedness lurking behind those black wells of eyes and thought that this moment might indeed be his last.

The taller and broader of the two raised a well-muscled, lizard-like arm and motioned for them to get up. They did.

How foolish he'd been. Adam would have smacked his forehead if he hadn't feared the reaction a sudden movement might elicit from the demons.

He'd been so focused on the guards at the palace that he hadn't considered that others might be about as well, perhaps on patrol. And now they were captured.

But there was no time for recriminations. He had to think of something, do something, though escape seemed impossible. The larger demon motioned them forward. Adam didn't move. An idea had begun to take shape. The golem looked at him quizzically. Adam brushed himself off and drew himself up to his full height.

"Well," Adam said to the guards, thrusting out his chest, glaring at the demons, and summoning as much indignation as he could, "I'm used to grander welcomes than this, but I suppose this will have to do."

The demons' eyes grew and growls began to swell from deep in their throats. They stared at Adam then looked at each other. Their enormous green tails were now still. They sniffed Adam from his head to his knees and back as though they could glean insight from the scent of this stranger. The golem tilted his head in silent query to his master until Adam stopped him with a furtive glare.

"You *are* here to escort me and my creation to Queen Lilith?" Adam demanded.

The demons turned to each other and argued in grunts and growls, their snouts again flaring. As they did, their spear tips lowered by several inches.

"Don't tell me you don't know who I am," said Adam, casting aside their spears with disdain and warming to his impersonation. "I am Motl the Sorcerer. I have endured the journey from the human world to bring this creation," he gestured toward the golem, "to Queen Lilith as a tribute. And this is the welcome I receive? Surely I was expected!"

The demons made higher-pitched sounds, more moans than barks, and shook their heads. One of them looked down and kicked the dirt with a scaly, clawed foot. The golem watched his master in awe.

"Then that explains it," said Adam with apparent magnanimity. "Someone will be held responsible, mark my words, but I'll make it clear to Queen Lilith that the two of you are not at fault."

The demons grunted and Adam interpreted it as a sign of appreciation.

"To show you I harbor no ill feelings," said Adam, his voice lowering to a conspiratorial whisper, "let me show you something I've brought for the Queen."

Adam opened his sack and held it toward them so they could peer in. The demons leaned forward to get a look inside. Adam raised an eyebrow in the direction of the golem, who didn't need more of a hint. He raised his hammer-like fists and pounded each demon on the head. They fell to the ground, unconscious.

Adam didn't enjoy even a moment for self-congratulation. The golem was tapping his shoulder and pointing. Still at a great distance, a horse-drawn wagon was moving along the road, evidently on its way to the palace. Shielded by the rocks, the two of them wouldn't be visible to whoever was at the reins, at least not yet. But the wagon's course would bring it directly to them. Adam drew in his breath.

"It's always something, isn't it?" said a slight, raspy voice from somewhere nearby. Adam jumped. It took them a moment to discover the voice's source: a mouse-sized, slimy green creature in the ragged, patchwork suit of a vagabond Harlequin. The imp looked from Adam to the golem and back again, his broadening smile seeming to suggest that, despite the abundant evidence to the contrary, all was well.

Chapter Forty

The wagon approached the outcropping of rocks and stopped. A tree trunk lay across the road, blocking its progress. The demon driver and its front-seat companion glared at the obstruction, then grunted and growled at each other. Finally, the scar-faced driver climbed down, its barrel-like frame making a thud that vibrated along the road. Its wiry companion, the smaller of the two, also hopped down, using its thin, long tail to help it land upright. Behind them, in the bed of the wagon, four more demons guarded their caged human prey: a dozen men and women drenched in despair.

The first two demons growled and snorted as they struggled to drag the tree trunk out of the way. The larger demon lost its grip on the trunk and fell backward with a roar. It barked to the smaller demon, who strained with its long, thin lizard arms to get the other upright. They returned to the trunk. Their shoving and pushing, with great bellows of complaint, succeeded in rolling it to the side of the road. They returned to the wagon and climbed in. The wagon, the demons, and their prisoners rattled on toward the palace.

Beneath the wagon, Adam and the golem were holding tight to the undercarriage, their faces and bodies pressed against thick wooden cross beams and iron rods and hooks, their feet wedged above the rear axle, their backs just inches from the uneven ground. The imp had found the breast pocket of Adam's coat to be a snug but sufficient fit.

"See, it's what I told you," squealed the imp. "You don't want to have to outfight a demon, but outsmarting one is a different story. Those thick skulls don't allow for much in the way of brains." They were hanging on almost directly below where the driver and its companion were seated. Adam shushed the imp and tried to find a better handhold among the uneven planks and hardware of the undercarriage. The golem glowered his disapproval of the imp's conversation and, perhaps, of the imp itself.

"That lot won't hear me way down here," the imp continued, nodding toward the demons above them. "We imps don't get noticed unless we choose to, don't you know? Which brings up the question of why I chose to—be noticed by you, that is."

Adam flashed the imp a questioning look. Much as he'd appreciated the imp's suggestion to get them out of a tight spot, imps weren't known for their helpfulness.

"You think you're the only ones with a grudge against Her Royal High-And-Mightiness?" asked the imp, its harsh little voice rising in indignation. "Well, think again. I know I'm just a forgettable little speck in the machinations of evil, but I do my part. Always have. Or, at least, I *did*. Causing the drayman's horse to go lame… launching the washer-woman's laundry down the stream… stealing the coins out of the charity box… I'm good at what I do. But some people are never satisfied, if you know Whom-I-Mean. And that's the problem. What am I supposed to do? Bring about the fall of humanity all by myself?"

The wagon drove over a rocky patch and Adam felt his back slam into the ground, sending a bolt of pain surging through his body. The golem, though impervious to pain, frowned with surprise at the jolt. He flexed an oversized hand to get a better grip on one of the rods that made up the wagon's supporting framework.

Adam's pain subsided and he regarded the imp without sympathy, wishing it would let him endure the rest of the journey in silence. This chatty creature might still bring about their discovery and downfall. He just had to hope that the knocking and clanging of the wagon wheels on the rough ground was loud enough to mask the imp's unending complaints.

"If you want to embarrass the local rabbi—sorry, rabbi; it *is* 'rabbi' isn't it? Yes, I thought so, you have that look about you—or tempt the local school teacher, I'm your imp," the creature started up again, warming to its subject. "But I wasn't impish enough, apparently. Not like the good old days, when a small but stylish bit of mischief was appreciated for the art that it was. And you don't want to cross *her*, let me tell you that. *I* did and look at me now: wrenched back to this wasteland! No chance for any fun. No chance to redeem one's self. I'll die here, alone and forgotten—if I'm lucky."

Then the imp stopped talking long enough to scamper toward Adam's shoulder, its little claws clinging to Adam's coat as it did so. It craned its neck to note their progress and returned to the pocket. Its brief silence allowed Adam to hear more clearly the cries and moans from the human prisoners above them in the wagon. *God willing, we'll save you, too*, Adam thought, tightening his grip on the makeshift handholds.

"… as I said, she may well get me in the end—probably will—but I won't go without getting a little bit of my own back, first," the imp croaked with determination. The wagon hit a rut in the road, sending the three stowaways slamming into the undercarriage. Adam lost a grip and was saved by the golem, who caught his loose hand and guided it back to a handhold.

The imp held on tighter to Adam's coat but was otherwise unfazed. "That's why, when I see the two of you, I see my chance and I take it," it resumed. "Don't know that you'll succeed either—you probably won't, if truth be said—but whatever you're doing here, you can't mean her Royal Malevolence any good, and that's good enough for me. Glad to lend a hand. The enemy of my enemy, don't you know?"

So in the demon underworld of all places, he and the golem had gained an ally, Adam marveled. But before this thought could warm him, it reminded him of the ally he had lost, and of what she had taught him: that epochal change could hinge on the seemingly insignificant. She was right; this imp, whatever else it might be, certainly seemed insignificant.

The wagon pulled up to the palace. Adam twisted in place while still holding fast to the undercarriage. He could make out several pairs of slick, scaly demon's legs approaching. There was barking from above, presumably from the driver, and a snort of assent from a demon that must have been standing quite close to the wagon. Adam heard the portcullis creak open and the wagon began to pass the phalanx of guards between it and the entrance. *We've nearly made it*, Adam thought, but his clenched stomach confirmed what his mind was reluctant to admit: This wasn't over. It was just beginning.

Turning in the other direction, Adam heard barks and growls and could just make out what must have been several more demons running toward the back of the wagon. He shot a glance along the undercarriage and felt sick when he realized the cause of the commotion. The golem's two large bread-loaf clay feet extended a few inches beyond the end of the wagon, putting them in plain sight. The golem too realized his error and pulled in his feet but it was too late.

The roars and snarls grew louder and more vicious as the demons' blood lust grew. Adam could feel the wagon shake as the demons pushed and pulled to get at them. Demon arms, all green scales and claws, reached underneath the carriage and latched onto the golem's feet, seizing him, attempting to wrench him out. The golem held onto the wagon's front axle but the demons made slow but steady progress in pulling him out. Adam grabbed the golem's sleeve with his nearest hand, trying to help and cursing himself for knowing it would make no difference. But under the sleeve, he could feel the clay muscles in the golem's arm tighten. He could see the set of the golem's jaw. The golem turned to him and nodded, and Adam understood that his companion wanted him to brace himself, which he did.

The golem kicked with all his might. The boards at the rear end of the wagon exploded with a roar, the force propelling a shower of debris and demons. Looking down the end of the wagon, Adam could see the casualties land in heaps that set the ground grumbling. Their screams tore through the air. Now they mixed with another sound, from above, in the wagon. Murmurs grew louder and became shouts, shouts of joy and urging, shouts of freedom. The wagon resounded with pounding. The human prisoners were running for their lives, jumping off the back of the wagon and fleeing down the road, away from the palace. Adam heard the growls and grunts of the demons as they rose from the ground, their sounds gradually growing fainter as they chased their escaping prey.

"Master of the universe, help your children to escape their pursuers," Adam murmured as he listened. He nodded to the golem and they dropped to the ground, rolled over and crawled out beyond the front of the wagon. No demons. They rose to their feet and ran toward the palace entrance.

The golem was just ahead of him when Adam sensed the evil springing up behind him. In the same instant he felt knife-like claws rip into his shoulder, creating a white-hot explosion of pain and stopping him dead, the sudden loss of momentum almost throwing him to the ground. He was spun around and faced the thick dark snout, tusks, and shining black eyes of the barrel-chested wagon driver. So not all the demons had run off after the humans. One of the demon's arms rose before him, the claws splayed and held just above Adam's face.

Everything happened in a single moment that seemed to pass in slow motion. Adam shouted "Yossele!" in a whisper that was meant to be a shout. The golem turned toward him, horror at Adam's predicament written across his clay countenance. The demon's claw began its descent toward Adam. And from Adam's shoulder, the imp appeared and threw a handful of dirt up and into the demon's glistening jewel eyes.

The demon stumbled back, trying to wipe away the dirt with its great green claws. The golem was at Adam's side, helping him run under the half-raised portcullis and into a vast courtyard, the imp all the while hanging onto Adam's shoulder to avoid being thrown off.

More demons poured out of arches to their left and right and charged them, tusks glistening, claws raised and fury in their boar-like faces. The golem took aim at the demons and charged them, leading with one of his outsized, muscled shoulders. Flesh and bone—even demon flesh and bone—proved no equal to the golem's earth and clay. He rammed his adversaries, hitting them low and hard. He brought down those still standing with a pounding of his fists that was too fast to follow clearly, bashing heads, knocking the air out of lungs, and scattering the rest of the demons like nine-pins.

With the way momentarily clear, he and Adam bolted from the courtyard into a vast, dark hall, its outlines just visible by the candlelight of a few sconces and chandeliers. The imp tugged at Adam's collar and pointed to a distant arch. Adam ran toward it, the golem at his side. They burst into a corridor of quarried stone walls and floors stained over the millennia by—by what, exactly, Adam had neither the time nor inclination to contemplate. The bitter, caustic odor of the place assaulted him, burning his nose and throat and lungs. Blood raced through him like a tidal wave pounding a shore, creating a deafening roar in his ears. Yet on he ran with the golem at his side, through air thick with evil, cruelty, and misery.

Guided by the imp's excited instructions, Adam and the golem navigated an impossible maze of corridors, losing every sense of where they might be but continuing on in an exercise of blind faith. They felt the floor vibrate. They heard the bone-chilling growls of the demons and the pounding of their feet and tails against the stones, sounds that only grew louder. They were nearby now and would be upon them in seconds.

"There! Turn there!" urged the small, raspy voice at Adam's ear. At the imp's urging, Adam flung aside a threadbare tapestry. He and the golem squeezed into a small chamber behind it, the imp firmly in Adam's breast coat pocket. Adam pulled the tapestry back into place and they were motionless, breathless, awaiting the onslaught. The stale air took on the bitter taint of the approaching demons and Adam stifled a cough. The demons' savage growling shot towards them like a cannon blast and the tapestry shook as though imploring the demons to look behind it.

Adam felt himself pressing against the back of the chamber as though another foot of freedom between him and the demons would make a difference. The noise and the stench and the vibrations reached a crescendo—and diminished. In the chamber, no one moved. Adam listened with intense relief as the demons raced past them and, finally, around a corner. The first sound in the chamber was Adam's struggle for air.

The golem put his hand on Adam's shoulder reassuringly and left it there as Adam's breathing began to ease. Adam patted the golem's hand and looked up at him.

"You saved me again back there," he said in what was almost a whisper. "Thank you."

"And what about me?" squeaked the imp, climbing out of Adam's pocket and onto his shoulder. "If not for me, you would be demon food by now." The imp did a double-take at the golem. "And I don't know *what* they would have done with you."

"I do owe you an apology," Adam chuckled. "It looks like we've found the one imp that *is* up to some good."

"You're welcome. It's nice to be appreciated, don't you know?" wheezed the imp, buttoning its little Harlequin coat and taking a bow. "Now that we're inside, what's next?"

"My son," Adam replied. "We must find him."

Now it was the imp's turn to chuckle. "I like a family man," it said. "And I happen to know where her Regal Painfulness keeps her prisoners."

Adam pulled back the tapestry part-way and looked up and down the corridor. Without making a sound, he eased himself out of the chamber and the golem followed. The imp directed them again until they came to an intersection of corridors.

"Which way?" whispered Adam.

"I hear something," the imp hissed, turning its slimy green neck in all directions. "I think they're coming back. There, quick!" it urged, pointing to the corridor to their left before slipping into Adam's breast pocket.

They took flight down the corridor as the din from the demons grew louder. Adam glanced back as they ran and saw a horde of demons far behind them. The monsters sped toward them like a pack of hungry wolves, closing the gap, their vicious roars rattling out of their chests and chilling the air. Adam turned and saw more demons barreling toward them from the opposite direction.

There was nowhere for Adam and his companions to go.

The golem pushed Adam into the nearest alcove. The mystical letters on the golem's forehead began to glow as he half-crouched in anticipation of the attack. The demons were just a few yards away on either side of them, growling and grunting, beating their tails against the floor and each other, their pinpoint eyes flashing like hot tar. They hurled themselves toward the golem, insane with bloodlust. The golem grabbed the first demons to reach him, one in each of his outsized hands. He spun like a whirlwind, using the two spinning demons to knock the others against the walls and floor. The golem released the demons in mid-spin and they flew down the corridor, one in each direction, bringing down more of their fellows.

Yossele was invincible, Adam thought as he watched with a growing sense of awe. If demons were capable of shock, Adam saw it now in their brilliant black eyes. Clearly, they'd never before encountered the likes of the golem. Yossele fought with ferocity, his fists slamming demons against the stone walls and pounding them to the ground like nails into soft wood. His black hollow eyes were narrowed to slits, his clay face set in grim determination even as more reinforcements joined the fight against them.

"Stay back! Don't let them see you," croaked the imp from the safety of Adam's pocket.

Instead, Adam pulled a large knife from the belt of a demon lying dead just a few feet away. He looked up to see a tall, muscular demon lunging toward him. He held the knife out before him with both hands. In an instant, the demon was upon him and its momentum brought them both crashing to the floor. The creature lay atop Adam, its weight crushing against his chest before it rolled onto the floor beside him. A hot stench assaulted Adam: a wet, sticky goo substance that oozed from the demon's belly. The creature issued a deep, husky moan and began to stir. Adam reached for the knife, still embedded in the demon, and gave it an upward thrust and twist. The demon's eyes dimmed, its body stilled, a great pool of thick dark ooze spread beneath it.

As Adam rose another demon was upon him, its claws tight about his throat, choking off his breath. An awful rushing sound roared in his ears. He tried to use his knife again but it came up uselessly against something hard protecting the demon's chest. The demon's claws pressed tighter and a throbbing in Adam's head threatened to explode. Fighting to hold the knife steady, he brought it up higher, under the demon's chin, and thrust it in with all his strength. The demon was still for a moment, then it crumpled at his feet.

More demons streamed into the corridor. The passage was thick with them, so much so that they climbed onto and over each other in their haste to get at the golem. As one, they pounced on Adam's clay companion, knocking him to the floor and pinning him there. Their countless reptilian claws latched onto every part of the golem's body, his arms and legs, his feet, even his head, and succeeded in holding him down. Adam watched with horror as the golem, overpowered, struggled without success to break free.

"Yossele!" he shouted, although he could hardly hear himself above the unholy commotion of the demons.

"There's nothing you can do for him!" hissed the imp in his ear. "Save yourself!"

The golem was covered by a seething mound of demons, a mass of dense brown fur, enormous snouts and tusks, reptilian arms, legs, and tails. Try as he might, Adam couldn't get so much as a glimpse of the golem.

"Run! Now!" rasped the imp hysterically.

In a moment, the demons would turn on Adam too and there would be no one left to save Mendel—and the world.

He turned and ran up the corridor, away from the demons, and away from his friend.

Chapter Forty-One

Must help the creator. Must find his son.

So many demons, too many. The golem tried to free one of his thick, solid arms but the demons held him against the stone floor. He tried to kick them away but too many claws dug into his legs. They prodded him with their long, dark tusks and ran their rough snouts and leathery black tongues over his body. The golem couldn't throw them off. He couldn't even move his head.

But he had seen his master escape. That was a relief.

More commotion. Through the horde of demons pressing against him, holding him down, he heard one demon howling and growling louder the rest. The others snorted and then grew quieter. Then they grunted their sonorous assent. The golem felt more talons clamp onto his legs and his feet. He did not feel pain, as he knew his creator would, but a relentless binding, a squeezing, a pressure that reminded him there were limits even to his strength. They were dragging him down the corridor. The golem struggled harder but couldn't shake free. The demons he passed kicked him again and again. Each blow from their talons jabbed him like sword tips.

Now he heard the harsh sound of metal scraping against stone. Along the floor just beyond him, the demons pulled away a grate, revealing a wide hole. They dragged him toward the edge, the hot, fetid breath of the nearest demons pouring over him.

Something was beneath the floor, waiting for him. The golem steeled himself for whatever it was, but nothing came. Instead the demons, grunting and bellowing from the strain of dragging their captive, kicked and shoved him over the edge of the hole. A long, dark shaft lay beneath him. The golem tried to grip the rim of the hole but the demons stomped at his hands. As he felt himself slipping into the hole, he grabbed one of the demons by its scaly ankle, and he and the demon were both sucked down into the nothingness.

The golem plummeted down along with the demon, which was squealing and shrieking like a mad animal, its arms, legs, and tail all flailing uselessly. The golem tried to grab at the stones that projected from the shaft's walls. Again and again his massive hands slipped past them; he was falling too fast to gain a handhold. Just above him, the demon's body spun and turned like a child's top. Its cries bounced off the walls, multiplying into a chorus of terror.

The golem hit the stone floor with the sound and force of a great blast, the impact slamming into his head and back like a battering ram. Then, nothing.

The golem's coal-pit eyes snapped open. Had he been sleeping? He didn't sleep but he had been overpowered by something much like it. He was lying on his back on a floor. Where? He raised one of his outsized hands but found nothing to grasp. The hand sank back onto his forehead, where he felt the shapes of something carved. Yes, of course, letters: *aleph, mem, sof.* He began to remember who he was and where he was. And what he had to do.

His other hand, splayed out beside him, felt something long, hot, and sticky. He brought it to his face and it took him a moment to realize what it was: a dismembered arm, green and scaly, ending in talons, and covered in a hot, black liquid that was now oozing onto his own forearm. The golem turned his head and saw the rest of the demon, most of it close by, the body looking like a torn, mangled wineskin, the head and a leg farther off. This brought a moment's satisfaction, but no smile, to the golem.

Where is the creator?

The golem struggled to sit up. He should have thought this first, upon awakening; his purpose after all was to obey the creator. He would find him. The golem stood. At his feet lay the naked, bloodied body of an old man.

Large patches of his chest and arms were colored deep blue and purple. A look of anguish was on the old man's face still.

The golem looked around him and shuddered. There were bodies everywhere, human bodies, strewn on the cold stone floor or piled haphazardly against the dark stone walls. The bodies of men, of women, of children. Many of them looked as old and dry as the desert of Luz, their skin flaking off like bits of worn gray parchment. Others were bones, just bones. He was standing in the middle of a graveyard. No: a dumping ground.

He had been among people long enough to know that a prayer must be said, the Prayer for the Dead. But who would say it? Not him. A golem did not count for prayer. He had learned that outside the prayer house in Lizensk. Nor would this prayer ever be said for him. His soul was not human. His creator had taught him that. But now the prayer had to be said. He had to find the creator.

He would do one thing first. He knelt by the body of the old man, straightened his broken body, and reached for a rag with which to cover his face.

Chapter Forty-Two

Adam ran through a maze of corridors, his lungs stinging as he sucked in air, the imp shrieking to go this way, then that way, and always faster, faster. Now, the passage in which he found himself was narrower than the others. He scraped against its stone walls as he struggled to maintain his balance. The ceiling pressed down against him; it was lower here as well. Adam held down his fur-trimmed hat with one hand as he ran for his life.

"Is this the right way?" Adam shouted at the imp for at least the tenth time.

"If Lilith has your boy, he'll be in the dungeons," the little creature did its best to shout back and poked Adam's collarbone for emphasis. "Faster, faster."

The ceiling threatened to rip away Adam's hat—and his head. He bent forward now as he ran, the awkward posture slowing his pace. As he progressed, the ceiling dropped even lower and he dropped to his knees to crawl forward. Walls and ceiling were all closing in on him and he struggled for air. The pain in his knees burst anew every time they slammed into the hard, wooden floor. Through his mind flashed a vision of the passage as his tomb.

"We're almost there," the imp bleated from Adam's shoulder.

The floorboards creaked as Adam pushed his tortured body onward. Ahead, rays of light jabbed up through random cracks in the floor; there was something below him, something lit. Adam slowed as he heard voices coming from the floor; he pressed his ear to a crack and listened. He was just above another room. He pressed his ear harder against the crack, straining to hear what was being said and inadvertently pressing the imp against the floor.

"Hey!" the imp yipped in pain. "That's my leg! I need that!"

Adam mumbled an apology and shifted so the imp could withdraw the injured appendage. He returned his ear to the crack and listened anew. His heart quickened at the sound. It was the voice of a boy—*his* boy, his Mendel. A wave of joy swept through him. All his travails, all his journeys and risks, had not been in vain. Mendel was alive and he was here.

Adam looked at the imp, hanging halfway out of his breast pocket and massaging his leg. "That's my boy!" he whispered.

"Don't mention it," the imp rasped, his eyes never leaving his leg.

Adam returned his ear to the crack but heard only muffled sounds. He saw another, wider crevice just a few feet away and crawled to it. Now, at least, he could hear snatches of what was said below.

"...don't believe it," he heard Mendel say. "My father will come and..."

Yes, yes! thought Adam, *I have come!*

"I hope he does..." cooed a female voice. It was her. Adam fought the bile rising within him. He had to see what was going on in that room. He saw more light piercing a wooden board just ahead and crawled to it. Its missing knothole was a perfect peephole—although when Adam peered into it, all he could see was a stone floor far below him.

"You do?" he heard his son ask with bewilderment.

Adam imagined Lilith smiling at his son, a smile as dead as the moors. "Of course," she replied. "What sort of wedding would it be without the father of the groom?"

"Wedding?" Mendel could hardly get the word out. "What wedding?"

"Hasn't anyone told you?" Adam heard Lilith respond with mock surprise. "You're going to marry my daughter, Lamia."

Adam felt a shock ripple across his skin. He strained to see his son, to see anything. Someone moved and stood below him. He could make out a pair of shoes, pink satin shoes, and dark hair. The figure took another step forward. Yes, clearly a girl, and young from what little Adam could see, perhaps Mendel's age. She wore a simple, pretty red dress that wouldn't have been out of place among the children of Lizensk.

"Hello," he heard her say in a sweet, shy little voice.

"Hello," Mendel mumbled back.

"I know mommy can be scary," the girl said. "But you needn't be afraid. She won't harm you. I won't let her."

"Th… thank you," stammered Mendel.

"You're welcome," Lamia said with a chuckle. "After all, that's *my* job."

It took Adam a moment to register what she'd said. Lamia tilted up her face—not at Adam, but close enough to jolt him from the peephole. When he returned to it, he could see her brown eyes sparkle then turn a deep green around black, slit-like pupils. She gave a malevolent little laugh and threw her head back further, revealing rows of glistening, finely pointed teeth, over which slid a serpent-like tongue. Her skin was now covered in dark, glistening scales. Adam pressed his eye hard against the peephole, tilting his head first one way and then the other, desperate to see the son who remained just out of sight. Then he heard a single high-pitched cry, brief as a bubble.

He had to do something, anything. No, he needed a plan. His plan had been to find the palace dungeons and steal his son from whatever captivity Lilith had devised for him. But Mendel's predicament was worse than captivity and Adam didn't even have the golem at his side. There must be some other solution, some other way. Surely the Holy One, Blessed be He, hadn't brought him this far for him to fail now.

He heard more sounds from below, footsteps this time. He couldn't see anyone, but he sensed that Lilith was now closer to his field of vision.

"I'm going to be your new mommy," cooed the Queen of Demons. "Let me give you a kiss."

There was no reply from Mendel. Adam heard a slight smacking sound and a cry and then a hiss like the sound of forged iron plunged into cold water. Adam caught his breath listening for his son.

"Doesn't that make you feel better?" Lilith asked, her voice solicitous as any mother comforting her child. Adam's face was moist with tears.

"You don't like mommy's kisses?" Lilith continued. "What a shame, because mommy has so many of them for you."

There was another moment of quiet, then Lilith's voice grew stern. "Take him away. Lamia and I have a wedding to plan."

Two pairs of heavy footsteps crossed the room. For the blink of an eye, Adam saw two demons march below him with Mendel, half dragged, half walking, between them. He thought he heard Mendel sob. Was he hurt? How badly? Adam shook his head. He needed to find a way to the dungeons—was it ahead, or behind?

The imp knew! Adam felt his breast pocket, then more frantically his shoulder, his back: no imp. Where was it? Before he could turn around, voices again reached him from the room below. He returned to the knothole and saw the sweet-looking child standing below him.

"Mother," cried Lamia. "I like him."

"Of course you do," he heard Lilith reply. "You share your mother's taste in humans. Trust me, you'll find him delicious. There'll be others, many, many others for you once the humans destroy their world. But I wanted your first time to be special. I want you to always look back on this night with fondness."

Adam gasped as Lilith entered his field of vision. Her long black hair cascaded over her shoulders and down her back. The dark leather suit she wore was tight enough to be her second skin; against it, her stone-white flesh seemed to glow.

Mother and daughter embraced as tenderly as Adam had ever seen Sarah wrap her arms around their little Leahele. Lilith gave Lamia a playful squeeze. The girl hissed and extended her tongue several inches from her mouth, waving it like a banner. Lilith slid out her own tongue, which oscillated in the space between them like a viper. Then it slithered out farther and the two tongues touched and entwined. Adam closed his eyes, unwilling to see more.

He heard another sound, much closer to hand. A small, slight sound. A scraping sound. Something clicked in the back of Adam's mind and he realized that the sound had been going on for some time now, a minor distraction to which he'd paid no attention. He opened his eyes and turned as best he could. There was the imp, working furiously at one of the boards on which Adam lay. In its hand was something shiny and metallic. With a shock, Adam recognized it as his own knife. He fumbled in his pocket, which was of course empty.

But what was the imp doing? Adam had no time in which to guess. The floorboards beneath him gave way, shattering with the sound of thunder. Splintered pieces of wood rained down on the throne room, followed by Adam himself. He hit the floor and pain surged through his body, excruciating pain as though he'd been smacked in the chest by Leviathan's tail. As he began to lose consciousness, he saw the imp jump down from the ceiling, land before Lilith, and kneel.

"Your Malevolent Majesty," it said. "Look what I found outside the palace. I believe you said something about a reward?"

Chapter Forty-Three

The golem pounded his hammer-like fists against the wall. Not a stone moved. None even made a sound. There was no way out. And no way in, either, except from above. He turned his gaze to scour the pit yet again. Besides the human remains, its surface was thick with rubbish—with capes and cloaks, pouches and sacks; with splintered stocks, frayed ropes, and rusted chains; with knives, swords, pistols and muskets. So many weapons, he thought, but none had saved the people who'd possessed them.

Creator, he thought. *I will find you. I will do your will. I will not fail you.*

Something behind him went *thump*. He turned but saw nothing. Another sound whispered from a far corner, a scratching sound, something scurrying under the pile of wooden planks, iron rods, and old bones. No, he realized after a long moment, the pile itself was moving. The rubbish and remains slid menacingly around him. He had seen leaves in the wind move like this. The Yedoni had moved like this. But never pieces of iron and wood, bones and cloth. They started moving at a deliberate pace, then gathered momentum and began to converge on a spot about twenty feet before him.

The point of the gathering was rising to a mound, and then to a tower. It continued to grow. Skulls and shoes and canvas and wooden wheel spokes flew across the pit. They attached themselves to the rising shape. The shape itself took on more form, rubbish hanging down each side and moving much like arms jointed at shoulders and elbows. At the end of each were knives and spears, swords and bayonets arrayed like petals on the end of one of the flowers that fascinated the golem so. Rags, wood strips, and clumps of mummified flesh converged on top of the thing, resembling a head. The head looked down at the golem and glowered.

Adam's chest sizzled with pain and he tasted blood in his mouth. He felt dizzy, as though spinning, but realized after a moment that he was lying face down on something hard and cold. He struggled to turn his head—thank God his neck wasn't broken—and saw a figure standing over him, regarding him as though she'd found a stain on a rug. Lilith, he groaned to himself. Her eyes widened when he stirred and her grimace was replaced by a smile, albeit one that showed a bit too much of her dagger-like teeth.

"How nice to see you again," Lilith said in velvet tones.

Not the response I'd use, he thought. He wouldn't allow himself to lie prostrate before this evil. He worked, despite the pain, to draw himself up and held out his arms for balance as he worked to stand on his own. The searing ache in his chest began to subside. He touched his ribs and arms tentatively; miraculously, none of his bones seemed to be broken. He glanced about the enormous room, with its tapestry-clad walls and unspeakable trophies illuminated by the gray light filtering through a row of narrow, arched windows.

Two demons stood at attention on either side of an ornate, carved doorway, but there was no sign of the imp. The blasted creature was gone. Oh, how naive he'd been to trust it! But the golem hadn't been fooled; Yossele had accepted the creature only because Adam had done so, and of course Adam's wishes were inviolate to him. Adam groaned, but not in pain; Yossele had paid the price for his obedience. Only the Holy One, Blessed be He, knew what the demons had done to his friend.

Amusement danced in Lilith's eyes as she watched Adam get up. She brought her pale, nearly translucent face just inches from his own.

"Perfect," she trilled. "I like to look a man in the eyes when I talk to him."

And she did like to talk to him, for some reason he couldn't fathom. Perhaps that was something to go on.

"You can talk to me all you want," he told her, "after you give me back my son."

"I'm afraid I can't help you with that," Lilith said with what seemed a tone of genuine commiseration. "And I must insist that you're not leaving any time soon—or any time at all. There's no way out, not for you. Is there perhaps anything else I could do for you? No. I didn't think so."

She turned with an exaggerated pivot of her hips and sat on her throne.

Adam recoiled. What he had assumed was its polished, dark wood wasn't that at all. The throne was composed entirely of black snakes that pulsed and glistened, snakes that hissed, rattled, and rubbed against each other to make a dry, raspy sound, all of them slithering in and out and around each other, and all of them serving their queen.

Lilith looked down and stroked one of the snakes that supported her arm. "I have something special in mind for your son," she said, her expression relaxing as she regarded her pet. He's going to marry my daughter, Lamia. You should feel honored, Rabbi Adam. We'll become family."

She returned her attention to Adam, uncrossed her legs, and leaned forward as though to impart a secret. "Well, not for very long, of course. We demons believe in an... all-consuming passion."

Adam felt rage rising within him and he swallowed hard to contain it. Think, think... Could he cause the snakes to scatter, creating a diversion? He had neither weapon nor bait. If there was a spell for this, he didn't know it.

"But consumed or not, the vessel is really not the important thing," continued Lilith, rising like the royalty she was. She moved toward him, her long, thin legs taking their time. "All of you have something much more delectable than flesh."

Lilith brought her hand to his chin and held it as though she were about to pluck an apple from a tree. Adam yanked his head away but Lilith twisted it back and her grip tightened. Pain shot through his jaw and he thought it might shatter. He was forced to look into her green, slitted eyes, eyes filled with images that flickered in rapid succession. They moved and changed, and it took Adam a moment to realize what they were: the souls of Lilith's victims, impressions of the people they had once been, mostly children and young men in infinite number. They were all tortured, all screaming and pleading in silent agony, all condemned to eternal imprisonment within the Queen of Demons.

Adam could feel the pain of each soul touch his own, each another twist of knife-like agony. Soul after soul... Lilith had taken them over the ages like a fire that devours everything in its path. He shuddered as he realized she did so for the same reason as the fire. The souls of others fed her, warmed her, and gave her strength.

In Lilith's deep wells of eyes, Adam glimpsed the soul of a young man who looked familiar. He stared intently... yes, the face thin, the eyes a bit close together... and recognized Esther's bridegroom, Dovid. The boy was screaming silently and writhing with pain. The image faded from Lilith's eyes and was replaced by another. His breath left him as though by a blow to the stomach: he was looking at the image of his daughter, Leah. Her soul was here, his little girl, her mouth open with cries he could not hear, tears streaming down her trembling face, her hands holding her head as though to keep out the pain. He shouted to Leah, unwilling and unable to contain himself. But the girl, imprisoned in a hell he couldn't imagine, was oblivious to him.

Lilith relaxed her grip and released him. His knees buckled and he almost crumpled to the floor before catching himself. Lilith gave a brief, staccato chuckle and returned to her throne. The snakes pressed against her, embracing her, slithering across her arms and across her shimmering black hair.

"Now, if you'll excuse me, Rabbi Adam..." She swept her hand before her to indicate the interview was over. A snake by her arm, startled, snapped. It was the barest, slightest movement, quickly aborted. But not quickly enough. A dot of Lilith's black blood glistened on her arm.

"What a naughty little creature you are," Lilith cooed to the snake, stroking its head. "We mustn't let that happen again."

She flicked her wrist and Adam heard a crunching sound as the snake's head lolled to the side. Lilith dropped the dead creature at her feet. Several snakes slithered out from behind her legs, wrapped themselves around their deceased fellow, and drew it within the mass of undulating snake-flesh, where it disappeared from Adam's sight.

Adam stared at Lilith's arm. "You bleed," he said, a touch of discovery in his voice.

"Yes, of course," she cocked her head. "But it's just a scratch."

"It also means," he said, "that you can die."

Lilith scowled and the hard angles of her parchment-pale face turned even sharper.

"You don't have any sense of what I can do, Rabbi Adam," she hissed. "You think my power is limited to toying with you, to this room, to this palace? Look and learn."

The Demon Queen took a deep breath. Her eyes rolled up into her head. Her body began to glow, and to vibrate. Her head doubled and tripled in size. Her mouth opened wide, and wider still, wider than her entire head had been just moments before. She flung her head back and roared, a bellow that hit Adam like a raging storm.

Like an explosion they emerged, propelled from her mouth like an endless series of cannon blasts: dark, winged things from a nightmare, fangs and fur with dead eyes that Adam could feel boring into his soul. Scores of them, hundreds of them, streaked everywhere, swarming in never-ending circles about their queen, blotting the room itself from Adam's view. One of the things flew close to Adam, a wing brushing against his face. The pain seared him like a hot iron and he backed into a corner of the room, drawing his arms to his face against the onslaught.

The roar of the creatures grew lower and harsher in tone, like ungreased cogs. The black hair of their faces was falling away, raining down on the floor like soot. The faces themselves were becoming lighter, the features changing to look almost human. They were molting, their bodies cast off like chrysalises. Skin replaced fur; arms and legs replaced wings and claws. Each grew as big as Lilith and took on her shape and form. Now Adam understood. Each of these was a manifestation of Lilith, a spore or a seed or an echo of the part of her that was temptation and weakness, hate and fear.

Lilith raised her hands, a silent but apparently explicit command to her doppelgangers, who shot upward like javelins, headed toward the human world. Adam's breath stalled in his lungs. He knew what just one of these creatures could do.

Because man had free will, they wouldn't all succeed. Lilith knew this as well as he did, of course, but it didn't matter. Any success they achieved was enough to reduce the amount of holiness in the world. One creature would convince a butcher to maintain a false set of scales; another would persuade a scribe to let an error pass uncorrected in holy text; a third would assure a farmer there was no wrong in hiding rotten produce at the bottom of the barrel. They would encourage gossip to spread in the marketplace, neighbor to envy neighbor, and student to mock teacher.

Adam knew their influence would be felt too when parent resented child, when master shortchanged servant, when servant stole from master. They would succeed when men chased after honor, when they looked without sympathy upon the poor, and when they gave up hope. And they would succeed most of all when they created a gulf between husband and wife, for such was the only force that could drive the holy presence from a home. Oh God, he thought with anguish, how much damage had his own demons done to his marriage and to his wife, his woman of valor, his Sarah?

Lilith, restored in shape and size, watched her emanations depart, sighed with evident satisfaction, and turned to the two demons still standing watch by the doorway. She gestured at Adam, her emerald eyes alight with fire. "Take him."

The demons slavered in anticipation, their tusks glistening.

"No, not yet," she dampened their enthusiasm. "He will be an honored guest at his son's wedding. And after we consume the boy, after he *watches* us consume the boy, *then* we will enjoy the rabbi's company."

Chapter Forty-Four

T he golem stared up at the hulking amalgamation of moldy clothes, chains, bodies, bones, and planks that clanked and scraped its way toward him. The golem reached down and grasped a wooden beam, holding it like a club. The thing raised its sword-encrusted arm and appeared about to test the strength of the golem's clay and earth. The golem crouched, ready for battle.

Instead of a battle, a bayonet broke off from the end of the arm and clattered to the floor. The chains, like the beads on a noblewoman's necklace, snapped apart and tumbled down as well, hitting the stone floor and sounding like the strikes of a hundred hammers. Torn and darkly stained clothes fluttered away. Bones snapped apart like sticks. The thing was spinning, throwing off parts of itself so quickly that the golem brought his arms up again and again to shield his face. The thing was shrinking, collapsing into itself, changing color and shape and form. Then it stopped spinning. What had been a blur became something else: Lilith, the Demon Queen. She gave him a long, considered look.

"Yes, it's just me," she said, as though she had entered matter-of-factly through a door. "Nothing you need to do combat with. In fact, I have something special for you."

The golem further tightened his grip on the beam. Lilith moved closer, in a movement so fluid it seemed to preclude steps.

"Cat got your tongue?" she cooed. "Oh, of course, Rabbi Adam didn't give you a tongue. All those thoughts inside your head and no way to get them out. No way to voice your hatred for me. Or your love for him."

The golem stared at her, confused. What was she saying? Why was she talking to him like this? He glanced at the beam in his hands. Her words must be a trick, but his weapon would be of no use against it.

"Yes," she continued. "I know how you feel about Rabbi Adam. He needed your help but he made sure to make you... inferior. Why is it again that you love him?"

She shrugged, as though the answer eluded her too, and continued her approach.

"You're stronger than he is," Lilith murmured. "Braver than he is. You have more of a right to be human than he does."

The wooden beam slipped from the golem's hands and clattered to the ground. Her words were bad, but were they also true? He felt his head throb.

Lilith reached out and stroked the golem's broad, rough-carved cheek. He wanted to move away but his thick clay legs seemed rooted like tree trunks. "You're more of a man than Rabbi Adam will ever be."

She brought her hand to his temple and let it slide over the side of his face. He saw gentleness in her smile and in her eyes and was shocked to realize that it seemed genuine. He brought his hand up to the cheek that Lilith had just touched. Instead of feeling cold and hard, unyielding, it was warm and soft. He could sense the flow of blood just below its surface. His hands moved over his brows, ears, and nose. He checked his arms and legs, and ran his hands over much of his body. With increasing excitement he realized that his clay and earth were gone, replaced by flesh and bone, hair and blood.

Lilith's tongue undulated forward and caressed his outer ear, an ear that a moment before had been cold and dead. The golem felt a powerful sensation surge through his body. He couldn't tell if it was heat or cold, pain or something else. What had she done to him? He searched for the word and it came to him: *pleasure*.

"I can give you what he can't," whispered Lilith into his ear, her warm breath a new and equally pleasurable feeling. "I can make you human. At least, the semblance of it. Do you really want to love him and hate me?"

The golem felt a warm breeze tickle his arm and felt the small thin hairs that now appeared on it. No longer in the pit, he was standing on a hillside, a pastoral palette of wildflowers extending off to the horizon to greet an egg-yolk sun. A sweet scent wafted about him. On impulse, he thrust out his chest. The flowers, the breeze, the sunshine, they were all part of him now; they added to him. They *delighted* him.

Lilith stood beside him, her arm locked in his, enjoying the landscape with him. He stood still, wanting it to last forever.

"Can you feel the warmth of a loving body against your flesh?" she asked, pressing close, even her words wrapping around him. "Is this what you want?"

The golem closed his eyes. He saw the men of Lizensk leaving him so they could pray in the synagogue... the mud puppet at Okop fooling him into thinking that he too might speak... the young couple there who, with just a touch, knew a closeness that he'd thought would never be his.

Yes, what Lilith offered was exactly what he wanted. He looked at her and opened his mouth to answer, but no sound came out. Lilith pouted, seeming to share his disappointment.

"Not yet," she told him. "But come to me and this too can be yours. Rabbi Adam and his children need not concern you again."

The golem blinked, stunned, as though a Cossack or demon had punched him hard in the face. *The creator and his children!* What Lilith offered, what he longed for, didn't matter, at least, not enough. He had to obey the creator. The golem stepped away.

Lilith looked at him in surprise—at first. Then her pale skin darkened and her eyes flared. Fury raged across her face. The golem heard everything around him stop; not a leaf stirred, not an insect dotted the sky. Even the wind was still. The flowers blurred and faded away like water on sand. The hillside melted away. The very sun grew dark and dead. In place of it all appeared walls of stone, wrecks and ruins from long ago, and the remains of what had once been people.

Lilith too was gone.

The golem reached for his jaw, then his hands flew to his face, his neck, his arms, confirming the truth he already knew. It was all cold, lifeless clay and earth. His warm flesh was gone. He blinked in the dim gray light that filtered down from above, then slumped onto a rusty hulk of an ironwork and was still. He lay his head against the decaying metal and rested it there, not moving. He remained without motion for a long time. Without motion, but not without thought.

With effort, he roused himself back to action. He pushed himself off the iron wreck; he could not help the creator or his children from the bottom of a pit. He took stock of his surroundings once more and glanced up the shaft. He saw a pinpoint of light; had someone lit a lantern at the top? It might mark a passage of some kind out of the shaft. His hand moved up to his chin and felt for a beard that wasn't there; he realized after a moment that it was a gesture he'd copied from his creator.

The golem pressed his hands against the wall and moved them about, feeling the surface. The rocks were fitted together and mostly smooth. But here and there, the golem felt gaps in the wall. Some rocks were missing, some were cracked, some extended out from the wall; they created spots where he might insert his hand, might grab onto a protrusion. He reached up with his right hand and found a stone to grasp. He did the same with his left. Now what? He fished around with his foot until he found a foothold and pulled himself up. He reached up and grabbed another rough rock extending a few inches from the wall, and then another foothold. Again and again, in slow and painstaking motions, he climbed higher.

The demons smacked Adam with their heavy, unyielding tails and sent him tumbling into the blackness of a cell. He hit the floor hard, the rough stones ripping at his palms. The thick wooden door slammed shut behind him like a coffin lid and Adam heard the demons stomp down the corridor. He lay where he'd fallen and sucked in air. The acid smell clawed at his throat, causing him to burst into a fit of gagging and retching.

Adam sat up and wiped his mouth with his sleeve. He reached out and felt the stone walls on either side of him, and then the wall behind him. The cell was barely bigger than a grave. But he would not let it become his grave.

His eyes started to close and he shook his head, forcing them open again. Now he had a new enemy to confront: exhaustion. As much as he thought of throwing himself against the door, he couldn't bring himself even to stand. All right then, he'd give himself a few minutes to recoup his strength. A few minutes. Just a few minutes.

A face appeared to him where no face had been a moment before. Was he imagining it? Sarah, in this place with him? He was instantly fearful that Lilith had captured her too. But no, Sarah was smiling, was safe, at peace.

No, she wasn't safe. None of them were safe. I have to get up right now, he insisted silently to himself, as he fell soundly and utterly asleep.

Chapter Forty-Five

Sarah studied the ritual for the dream assembly, the prayers to recite, the actions to take. It could work. Of course it could work. She thought again of Francesa Sarah, Rachel Aberlin, Miriam, Deborah, and all the others who came before her. Not that she needed her name to be added to such an illustrious list; she just needed to find a way to her husband.

After tending to the children for the last time that night, Sarah prepared. In her bedroom, she reviewed the well-worn book yet again. She checked her fingernails and toenails, removing what little bits of dirt she found so that the waters of the ritual bath could envelop her body without even the most miniscule obstruction. That done, Sarah disrobed and redressed in white. Her cloak and a lantern were by the door. She took them both, lit the lamp, and made her way through the village to a modest, inconspicuous structure partly obscured by a small stand of willow trees. She entered the one-room building of the ritual bath and locked the door behind her. Then she removed her clothes and folded them on the only furniture in the room: a single, small chair.

By the light of her lantern, the still water of the ritual bath looked like a mirror. She saw her reflection in that water, who she was and, she thought, who she might become when she emerged from it. The water of the ritual bath—water that had come directly from heaven, untouched by wells or human hands—would purify her, washing away the spiritual impediments to the journey she hoped to take. She brought her foot down on the first stone step carved into the bath and felt the water lap at her toes. It was stingingly cold. She braced herself and took another step, and another, walking deeper and deeper into the bath until the water covered her body up to her neck. But it was not enough. She moved to the center of the bath, held her breath, and sank below the surface. The water engulfed her, eager to surround her as completely as a mother's fluid surrounds the child growing within her. With not a speck of dust to block its way, the water came in contact with every point of her body and purified her.

Later, in her bedroom, Sarah lit the candles and set them on the floor in the arrangement depicted in the book, designed to evoke the ten emanations of the Almighty. She sat on the side of her bed, once again dressed in white. She had committed the words to memory and called upon them now.

"Grant that we lie down in peace, O Lord," she recited as she brought her legs up onto the bed, the straw beneath her making a slight crunching noise as she shifted her weight. She lay down, on her back, her hands folded over her stomach.

"Assist me with thy good counsel," she said in a whisper, her head now on the pillow. She thought she heard a sound, a voice, answering her, but she was unsure and then it was gone. Most likely the wind, or a night animal.

"Guard our going out and our coming in," she said in a voice that was no more than a murmur. Her eyes had closed of their own accord. Gradually, the sense that she was in her own bedroom, in her own bed, left her. With every breath, the physicality, the reality, of her world drifted farther from her reach. She was in the nothingness, the void, the place between worlds.

She opened her eyes, expecting to see Adam. In this she was disappointed; she was alone. She stood in the middle of a garden that stretched as far as she could see in every direction. The landscape was punctuated by trees, lush with leaves and fruit atop thick straight trunks, standing like great, green balls atop massive pillars. Rose bushes—yellow, white, red, purple, burgundy, pink—grew in cultivated rows, their flowers daubs of bright paint against verdant backgrounds. Great patches of the garden, stretching for acres, were filled with banks of flowers—lilies, irises, tulips, giant sunflowers off in the distance, and more—that swayed and bowed their heads in unison, this way and that, in a pas de deux with the gentle breeze.

The remarkable vividness of the flora blinded Sarah at first to the realization that the garden was also filled with fauna. Birds trilled and cooed in the trees, calling to one another and feeding their hatchlings. Rabbits watched her as they munched without pause on the grasses. Swans glided across a pond like skaters across ice. Horses galloped in the distance, streaks of browns, blacks, and grays rushing with joy against the cloudless azure sky. As she walked along the well-tended paths, Sarah saw many more animals, some she knew—including wolves and bears though, strangely, none molested her—and many she did not: birds with iridescent feathers, large cats with stripes and spots, creatures with horns, with elongated noses, with even more elongated necks.

None of this alarmed her, she found to her surprise. Her sense of alarm, honed to rapier sharpness over the past weeks, seemed to have dropped from her as effortlessly as a snake sloughs off its skin. Instead, she felt a quality so alien that she could not at first name it. Then it came to her. It was peace, a sense of calmness and completeness—or, rather, near-completeness—pervading her mind and body.

Chipmunks and squirrels dashed through the undergrowth. Sheep and cows grazed in a pasture. Ducks light and dark and speckled, some with caps and cravats of red or green or blue, made sport as Sarah walked alongside their riverbank. She passed through a grove of white birches whose wind-chime leaves sang out to her. She followed their sweet melody and came to a clearing, well, almost a clearing. It held one tree, but what a tree. More massive than any other she had seen in this place, the tree was broad as a house and soared far into the sky. Its trunk shimmered, casting emanations of gold that made it seem even bigger than it was. Its leaves were so plentiful as to be impenetrable. Thick among them were golden spheres, hundreds of them, each as large as a fist. They were fruit, she knew, though they resembled no fruit she had ever known.

Sarah walked toward the tree, its emanations warming her, inviting her approach. The dense foliage hung in a cascade from the lowest branches, obscuring her view. As she drew closer, she saw a figure standing by the side of the trunk, a man, facing away from her. He was tall and thin, his black fur hat adding to the impression of height. The man turned but his face remained veiled by the leaves. No matter. She saw his gray-speckled ear-locks and his beard, long and wispy, shifting this way and that in the breeze. Adam's hands were cupped before him and Sarah glimpsed something small and animated moving within them. He opened his hands and it popped up briefly, even levitating several inches: a white dove. The bird peered at him then flew away. Adam looked up to follow its ascent and that's when he saw Sarah. His eyes widened, first with incomprehension, then surprise, then delight.

Sarah felt herself flush and a frisson race through her body. He was alive. He was well. He was here. And he was real, as real as the ritual bath in which she'd immersed herself, as real as the world from which she'd come. Her prayers for his welfare had been answered. She murmured her thanks to the Holy One, Blessed be He.

Husband and wife started toward each other. Not running or rushing, but walking, as though they were making the best possible use of all the time in the world. Sarah didn't quite understand why this was so, why she didn't race to him, but she trusted the pace at which her legs carried her.

She would finally get her answers. She would know what had happened to Adam, every bit of it. She would know whatever he could tell her about Mendel and about whether Leah and Hersh and Miriam could recover from their living death. She would learn about Lilith, whether Adam had defeated her or had hopes of doing so. And she had much to tell him too, not only about the children, but about herself, about how her feelings of that last day had not died but had endured like an ember that refuses to go out long after the hearth grows cold. And about how that ember had reignited, how she had labored to find a way to communicate with him, this way, and how she prayed that his feelings for her had also continued aglow since that day weeks before.

They each stopped when they were about ten feet apart, Adam's identical impulse validated her own. He turned toward a dark green shrub nearby and stooped to pick a flower. It was a damask rose, its petals a ragged, vibrant pink halo encircling a golden stamen. He brought it to her and fixed it in her collar. They sensed the sharp, sweet fragrance, like honey, at the same moment.

They looked at each other, really looked, in a way that Sarah had not looked at her husband for years. She saw the gentle lines webbing out from his eyes and the corners of his mouth across his thin, almost hollow, face. She saw the slight, straight scar that ran across his cheek, like a road leading to nowhere in particular. And his eyes, kind, scholarly eyes, eyes that had once struck her as weak, but that now seemed wise and loving and, yes, brave. For an instant, she wondered why it had taken so long for her to truly see into those eyes.

Her smile grew wider as she realized that Adam was looking at her in the same way, thinking the same thoughts, conjuring the same question. Now was the time for her to ask, to learn, to know. But which question to ask first? How to begin so momentous a conversation? What should she say, what should she leave to him? The contentment and completeness she'd felt since discovering him here filled her in a way she could not have thought possible. There was no distance between them, not even the distance of their bodies. They were one and that oneness was the answer to all her questions, the ultimate answer, even to the ones she hadn't thought to ask. It was enough.

And she could see that it was enough for him as well. In his warm, tender look, in the liveliness of his deep brown eyes and the breadth of his uneven smile, she saw the boy from the academy that she had met at her father's Sabbath table so many years before. That boy was now hers again and she, the young, brash girl filled with Scripture and big ideas, was his. The faults and slights and hurts of the past were swept away for them both, as though by a cleansing spring rain—or by the waters of the ritual bath.

She didn't know what the fate of her husband and children would be, but she would trust in this man, in her own strength and will, and in the Holy One, Blessed be He, who had created them both.

Chapter Forty-Six

L ilith watched the commotion in the Great Gallery rising around her like a dust storm. With approval, she noted the demons everywhere scuttling about fixing black wreaths to the walls, arranging black drapes and bunting and garlands from the pillars that ringed the room, fixing hundreds of torches into the iron latticework chandelier and hoisting it into place, putting arrangements of dead flowers in vases, tuning the cacophonous band, and laying out the unspeakable buffet to follow the ceremony. Soon enough, the gallery would become a wedding hall. She turned to admire the centerpiece for all that was about to happen: the platform topped by a black wedding canopy.

The decorations, if not the food, were unnecessary flourishes, Lilith knew, but they delighted her so much that she saw no alternative but to indulge herself. With each inverse semblance to the weddings of humans, she mocked them. It warmed her, not as much as their souls, of course, but she would have her fill of those as well, and quite soon.

Her guests began to arrive and she motioned them to take their seats. The demons and ghouls, the witches, wraiths, and shadow men, the werewolves and chimera and so many others—these were all her armies, her servants, her messengers. If truth be told, she loathed them all. It was not loathing mixed with fear, as the humans regarded them, but loathing born of contempt. They were useful in their way for how they could serve her; that was all. And when they stopped being useful...

Lilith heard a high-pitched, raspy voice. She looked down and saw an imp twitching in nervous little jolts in the front row, its green skin glistening in the candlelight from above. Oh yes, this was the little mound of putridness that had delivered Rabbi Adam to her. A clever little creature. Later, she might see what else it might do, or how it might taste. She loved imps.

But now she was eager, no, anxious, to begin the ceremony. Where was the clergyman? she wondered with rising anger. She was contemplating an unpleasant spell when the demon, old and stooped, limped through the front of the crowd and ascended the wedding platform. His robe and cowl were far too big for him, possibly inherited from his predecessor an eon before, but he would have to do. It wasn't as though the underworld was rich with clergymen. She waved at him with impatience and the old demon bowed in acknowledgment. Then he began to flutter about the wedding canopy, nearly tripping on the hem of his robe, peering through nose spectacles perched low on his snout as he prepared for the ceremony.

The golem succeeded in climbing almost halfway up the side of the shaft. The circle of light above him was larger now. Though his hands couldn't bleed from the rough rocks in the shaft's wall, they could ache, and ache they did. He reached up again. This time the stone came away with his hand. He almost lost his balance but managed to hold tight with his other hand. He pulled out another stone and then another, letting them fall into the pit.

There was some sort of passage behind the wall. He pulled away more rocks and climbed into the crawlspace behind them. A demon rat, the size of a small dog in the human world, scampered out of the darkness, bared its fangs at the golem, and hissed. The golem glowered and scowled in return. The surprised animal squealed and ran back into the darkness from which it had come.

The golem continued down the crawlspace. He heard muffled sounds and followed them. What he heard was a mixture of grunts, growls—and music.

What was that sound? Adam heard it again, low, rumbling, like a saw being dragged through timber. Demons? But surely there were no demons here.

Adam opened one eye and saw a rough stone ceiling not far above him, then walls, even closer. This wasn't right, this wasn't where he was... wherever he was. His head throbbed and he closed his eye again. The scent of something sweet, like honey, was in the air. He struggled to remember where he could possibly be, but the clues made no sense.

An image, something of green and gold, teased the back of his mind and then disappeared wherever dreams go. Had it been a dream? Perhaps he was dreaming now. He opened one eye again and then the other. Another throb of pain. Oh yes, the dungeon. But he had the distinct sensation of having left the cell, of having been somewhere else, somewhere wonderful, somewhere real... somewhere with *Sarah*. He was certain. The exhilarating sensation remained with him, but everything else was gone. No, not everything else: not his determination. He had been with Sarah, and at peace. And he would be so again.

The snarls and growls of the demons brought him fully back to the cell. With clanks and groans the heavy wooden door opened and two demons stood in sinister silhouette in the doorway. They barked at him and Adam struggled to stand, using the wall as a support. They grabbed him without warning, one by each of his arms, and dragged him away.

The demons forced Adam through a maze of twists and turns that he hardly noticed. In his mind's eye he saw not his surroundings but his Sarah. She was in their garden, pulling turnips and onions for the Sabbath stew. He could see her as she worked, hear her as she sang. He could almost smell the garden. Had he been here with her, too? He didn't think so, couldn't even tell if what he was seeing had happened, would happen, or was happening now. But it felt as real as the cold floor beneath his feet and the demons' breath burning his cheeks, as real as the demon claws digging into his arms.

These latter sensations all felt real enough but Adam came to notice that they were unaccompanied by the degree of pain he would have expected. The demons' breath was a sting soon dissipated, their pinching claws unwelcome pressure but no more. Had he changed, or was his mind simply preoccupied by something far more vivid than pain: Sarah? Despite all the confusion and misadventure of the past few weeks, Adam realized that the extraordinary woman he could see so clearly in his mind's eye was the constant in his life and would remain so for as long as they both drew breath. He had ventured forth and she had remained to attend the children, but she had been with him too, every step along the way. She was his strength, his shield. He would succeed in his quest for the sake of their children but most of all he would succeed for her. For them both.

The demons stopped beside a pair of massive, carved wooden doors, flung them open, and dragged Adam through them and into a great hall alive with the activity of hundreds of demons and night creatures. Adam jerked one way and then another, trying to shake loose. But he was no match for his captors, whose vice-like claws continued to hold him so tightly about his arms that thin lines of blood appeared on his sleeves. They hauled him through the vast space to the wedding canopy and shoved him onto the platform.

Lilith stood there, gazing at her subjects and giving him the barest glance. Lamia, in a black wedding dress, stood next to her. A third demon, old and nearly lost within an ill-fitting cowl and robe, flanked his queen on her other side. Lamia kept fidgeting with her dress, and the Demon Queen kept swatting away the girl's hand with her tail.

Lilith turned to Adam and caressed his cheek, her eyes glowing with pleasure, the tip of her forked tongue darting toward him in anticipation. Adam felt his every muscle tighten and his blood turn hot. Perhaps Lilith didn't like what she saw, for her tongue flew back into her mouth and she dropped her hand to her side. She turned to the crowd.

"Silence! The wedding is about to begin!"

The unholy creatures remained as unruly as before. Lilith fixed her indignant gaze on a bellicose werewolf in the second row, snapping at a witch sitting next to it. Lilith's eyes blazed green and fire engulfed the beast, incinerating it as it howled in agony.

Everyone else quieted down.

"Thank you," Lilith resumed in regal tones, as though she'd gotten their attention with nothing more intrusive than a nod. "That's better. The groom will now approach the wedding canopy."

Lilith signaled to someone a few yards away. Adam saw a demon quartet armed with drums, fiddles, and flutes. They began to play a mean, soulless song, its discordant notes a continuous shriek of anger. It seemed to Adam that even the abundant torchlight from above grew harsher in response. The torchlight... Adam looked up at the immense iron latticework holding hundreds of torches. If he could somehow douse those lights... if... if...

The gallery doors opened again and another pair of demons approached the wedding canopy with Mendel. The boy was pale and trembling, his clothes torn, his eyes wide in fear. Adam's blood raced and his heart broke anew at the sight of his son. He nearly screamed Mendel's name and tried to rush toward him, but choked back the scream and forced himself to be still. He could do nothing for Mendel by struggling against his guards.

Mendel, stunned by the sight of his father, froze, then tried all the harder to free himself and run to him. Adam saw Mendel's joy vanish as he realized his father was as much a prisoner as he was. The fight left Mendel and he went slack in his captors' arms. Adam looked about without success for anything on the platform that he might employ to effect their escape.

Lilith smiled at Mendel. "Pre-wedding jitters? That's understandable. And quite all right. A rush of excitement always enhances the... flavor. But we can't allow anything to interfere with the ceremony, can we?"

Lilith locked her eyes with the boy's. Mendel tried to look away. Lilith's eyes took on their green cast and the boy was entranced and still.

"There, that's better," she said to the boy, then turned to his father. "But you, Rabbi Adam—there'll be no spell for you. I want you to be fully aware of the proceedings. After all, I'd never forgive myself if I didn't give you the opportunity to congratulate your son—and to say goodbye. Any last words for the groom?"

Adam felt sharp pains in his palms, then realized his hands were balled into fists so tight that his fingernails were digging into them. Whatever he was going to do to save his son, he needed to do it now. He looked out into the hall for inspiration, any inspiration. Demons, ghouls, were-beasts... and something else: something near the back of the vast gallery, moving along the wall toward him. Adam caught his breath and stifled his excitement. He nodded once, just barely, and Yossele nodded back.

A smile wanted to creep onto Adam's lips. He stopped it just in time and answered Lilith. "My last words to my son will come many, many years from now."

Lilith responded with a half-laugh, half-snort and turned to the demon clergyman.

Adam returned his attention to his friend. He could see Yossele scanning the front of the gallery. Adam's eyes almost betrayed his alarm. What was Yossele thinking? To rush the demons and night-creatures and storm the platform? It was well-intentioned, but madness. Adam gave his friend a small, slight shake of the head. The golem's shoulders sagged, but he nodded in reluctant assent.

On the platform, Lilith signaled to the demon clergyman to begin. He coughed to get the assembly's attention, failed, tugged at the collar of his robe, and began.

"Dearly unloved," he intoned. "We are gathered here today to join this demon and this human in the bonds of unholy matrimony. If there is anyone or anything that knows reason why these two should not be wed, let him or it speak now or…"

He looked at Adam, expecting him to object. Adam didn't stir. Lilith motioned with impatience. "Get on with it!" she bellowed, her eyes beginning to glow. Worry etched itself across the clergyman's face and his tail went limp.

"Very well," he resumed, looking at the couple before him. "I now pronounce you prey and wife." He turned to Lamia and added: "You may now consume the groom."

Lamia squealed with delight. Her face took on a sudden, brutal malevolence. The end of her tongue slithered from her lips, toward Mendel's face. It drew a line of dark red blood across the nearly white cheek. Despite his trance, Mendel cried out in pain. Lamia's tongue, now tipped in the boy's blood, shot back into her mouth. She savored the flavor of human blood and the sound of human agony and anticipated the taste of human flesh.

Chapter Forty-Seven

Above, in the human world, the stars continued to disappear and Sarah was far from the only one who noticed. People who would never know each other and never speak the same language came to a common conclusion: the stars weren't being obscured; they were being taken away, snuffed out, sent back to wherever they had been before the Almighty hung them in the night sky on the fourth day of creation. And then, when they expected the worst but still were unprepared for it, the moon itself melted away like a demon before the dawn.

The sense of doom was palpable everywhere, in the unnatural silence of the great cities of Europe, to the becalmed waters in which sailing ships sat as though anchored. It filled the air like the smothering humidity that precedes a summer storm. Even the crickets felt dread and knew better than to chirp on this night. People kept inside their huts, mansions, farm houses, slums, cottages, and even palaces, not from a misbegotten sense of safety, but with the hope that they could hold onto each other for just a moment longer.

People prayed, in synagogues and churches, mosques and temples, forest clearings, and sanctuaries. They prayed on floors of dirt and of marble, in overcrowded cities, and the loneliest outcroppings of humanity. They prayed in congregations of thousands and with only their own hearts and terrified thoughts for company. Some prayed for the world's salvation. Others had more modest goals, praying only that they be saved from whatever was to come. Still, they prayed. And still the end continued to envelop them.

With no moon to restrain them, the tides began to overrun the shores, leaving a wake of destruction. Homes, stores, entire towns and their inhabitants were washed away. Once-fine edifices were reduced to rubble and washed over the landscape and back to the sea.

Earthquakes erupted and children screamed as their homes shook and they realized that not even their parents' arms were big enough to hold them safe. Lightning strikes illuminated the horror and set fire to towns and forests. What had taken thousands of years to grow was being consumed in mere hours, the massive curtains of red and orange providing a distant warning to the many millions as yet untouched by these first waves of disaster. But it was a warning on which they were powerless to act, for what could anyone do when the world itself was receding back into the chaos from which it had come?

Chapter Forty-Eight

As the thread of blood appeared on his son's cheek like a magic trick, Adam's hand flew by instinct to the matching scar on his own cheek. A torch flared inside his head, its blinding light burning away the Great Gallery, the demons, and the wall that had been erected inside his mind so long ago.

He is seventeen years old and today he is to be married. His stomach aches and not because of the bridegroom's fast. His doubts about marrying Rachel have swelled throughout the day, from the moment he awakened. No, even earlier, in his dreams. But that doesn't matter now. He will run back to his house, retrieve the ring, and get to the synagogue in time.

What a fool he is! Forgetting the ring for his own wedding! What would Rachel think of him if she knew? He rushes into the house, his lungs pressing hard against his chest, his face slick with sweat. Where could the ring be? Yes—there it is, on the parlor table. Maybe all will be well after all.

He starts toward it, then catches a glimpse of himself in the mirror: his hair disheveled, his cheeks burning. He stops. His fears and doubts press in on him once more, like water pushing a drowning man down, down, to his doom. Again he wonders: who is he to think himself worthy of such an angel? What will happen when Rachel realizes, as one day she must, that he is so much less than he appears to be? She will grow to hate him. They will grow to hate each other. He is about to make a terrible mistake, a mistake that will ruin not only their lives, but the lives of their families as well. He feels weak and bends over, his hands on his knees. The room seems dimmer now. He can't think. He can't even breathe.

With effort, he rights himself and sees the woman standing before him in the parlor. He is too stunned even to say a word. He takes in her kind face, her beguiling green eyes, her hair so black and long and shiny that it seems a living creature of its own. The woman extends a slim, pale arm toward him. He stares at it, at her. He doesn't understand what she wants. She smiles again, a smile that warms him and eases his anxiety.

He steps back, not much but enough to convince himself that he can. But his eyes take in her curves, her flesh, her forbidden places. The room grows warmer. He can feel perspiration bud anew on his forehead and his chest grow tight. The woman's fingers play about her hair, her shoulders, her breasts. Somewhere in his thoughts, he knows this is wrong. He shouts "no," but makes no sound. He tries again, but it comes out "yes." He takes a step toward her, just one step. Her smile brightens and her dark green eyes gleam their approval. He takes one more step forward.

In a bound, the woman is against him, on him. He feels himself shoved to the floor, his black satin caftan coming off him. Is he taking it off? He isn't sure. The only thing he knows is that he wants this woman, wants her flesh against his, her smell mixed with his own.

They bump against a cabinet; they knock over a table. The woman laughs and throws Adam against his father's favorite chair. It breaks under the force of his fall. He is oblivious to the pain, or maybe he wants that, too. He rushes back to the woman and the two of them careen about the room. She is above him again, pinning him to the floor. She smiles lovingly as something long and thin and blood-red slides out from between those lips. Her tongue, impossibly long, reaches down closer, closer to him, a predator enjoying the domination of its prey. It caresses his cheek, drawing blood with its knife-like edge, and retracts. The woman tastes his blood and laughs.

A strange, revolting smell assaults his nostrils, an astringent smell of rot. The woman's smile turns to a sneer. Her face darkens and viridescent patches erupt all over it. They are scales, blooming like mushrooms after a storm. They cover her neck, arms, body. Now he knows what she is, but it is too late. Her face is close to his and he cannot escape those dreadful eyes. Within them he sees souls writhing in agony and he knows he will soon join them. He is paralyzed, his body a stone. He belongs to her now.

Her hot, rancid breath stings his cheeks. Her lips, now ancient leather, cracked and blotched, descend and make a seal over his own trembling lips. He feels his breath being ripped from his lungs. Something else is being torn from him: His love for his parents, for Rachel, for harmless mischief, for learning the law by his father's side, for secretly delivering wood to the widow Baile, for whistling—his soul. His hands make weak, useless grasping motions. He is emptying, disappearing into those deathly eyes.

Blackness... stillness... nothingness...

A jolt. He breathes, swallowing great gobs of air. Something has broken the seal of death. Dimly he is aware that the she-demon has pulled away her scaly lips. Her enormous green eyes blink in confusion. She appraises him anew and frowns. She reaches a decision and leans forward, all business. She brings her awful lips close to his ear and whispers a single word: "forget." And then she vanishes.

Reality has collapsed into a series of disjointed moments. He can't understand what has happened, what is happening still. But in his distress one idea becomes clear: he can't let his parents or Rachel find him, not here, not like this. He runs around the room like a caged animal, instinct smothering reason until he is left only with panic. He throws himself out of a window not minding the breaking glass tearing at his skin, not minding the excruciating impact of the fall. He rises with unexpected energy and races into the woods. He doesn't stop running for a very long time.

He hadn't stopped running, he realized, until he found himself under a wedding canopy in the palace of the Queen of Demons.

His hand still grazed his cheek, fingering the faint line that lingered there after all these years. They were years he'd lived without joy, without love, despite the blessings that the Holy One, Blessed be He, had bestowed upon him. Now, his son stood under the demons' wedding canopy, just feet away, about to endure an even worse fate, and not just for a lifetime, but for all time.

"No!" the word erupted from his throat. The suspended world around him—Lilith, Lamia, the unholy congregation, even his Mendel—jerked back to life.

Adam strained against the demons holding him. With the slightest nod of Lilith's head, they relaxed their grip. He shook his arms free and stepped away from them.

"I'm afraid we don't entertain objections to a wedding, Rabbi Adam," she explained. "I thought you understood that."

"It was you!" He spat the words. "All the shame I've carried since that day." He heaved a breath. "It was because of you."

Lilith gave a little trill of delight. "Well, well. The slumbering lad awakes," she said, extending a bloodless finger toward him. "I was there, certainly. But you acted on what was in your heart. All of you act on what is in your hearts. I just make it easier for you to do so."

"You do more than that," Adam snapped. "You take our souls. You—" He stopped as a jolt of realization surged through him.

His voice dropped. "No," he said. "You didn't take my soul."

"Some souls I take," Lilith answered with a wave of her hand. "Others I prefer to destroy over time."

Adam shook his head. "You came to take my soul that day," he said, gathering his thoughts like bits of gossamer before they disappeared. "But something stopped you. Something you saw in me stopped you."

"You're deluded, Rabbi Adam," Lilith replied, but her mocking tone faltered.

No, he thought, *not deluded, maybe for the first time in my life.* He saw the past with a clarity that had eluded him for twenty-five years. His soul—the soul of a potential Lamed-Vavnik—had been too strong for Lilith to take outright, but not strong enough to ward off the damage she could do to him, damage that would keep him from fulfilling his destiny. She could be patient. She could wait for the day there would not be thirty-six Lamed-Vavniks, for on that day the world entire would cease to be and all the souls in it would be hers for the taking.

"You wanted to prevent what I might become," he said to her and to himself.

"What you might have become is irrelevant," Lilith said with a quick shrug and a smile. "I took care of that a long time ago."

"But you couldn't be sure," he continued. The demons at his side—indeed, all the unholy guests in the Great Gallery—were motionless as they watched him. "You attacked my children, you foiled my chance to redeem myself with Rachel, all to break my will, and my soul."

Lilith sneered but said nothing.

"I couldn't—I *didn't*—stand up to you all those years ago," he continued, with depths of controlled force behind each word. "But I stand up to you now. You have no power over me because I give you no power over me."

There was fire in each word he uttered next.

"You *will* give me my son."

Lilith's pale skin grew even more taut over the pronounced bones of her face. She shook her head.

"I have no power over you that you do not give me," she conceded. "But your son and the others, the weak ones, they're another matter. You believe in choices, Rabbi Adam. Here's a choice for you: Your son can go—if you choose to remain, as *my* mate." Her words were measured, her tone calm, yet her fury unmistakable.

Adam nodded in acknowledgment and appeared to consider the offer. His gaze fell again on the enormous iron latticework high above their heads. Its thick hoisting rope descended far across the hall, where it was tied against the wall. And just a few yards away, Yossele stood watching him, still awaiting his cue. With every other living and dead thing in the gallery fixed on the wedding platform, nothing paid the golem heed.

Adam nodded toward the rope. The golem's black-socket eyes widened in response, but he made no other movement. Adam nodded again, as much as he dared given Lilith's glare. But the golem didn't, couldn't understand him.

Yossele! Adam shouted the unspoken thought so loudly within his head that he was surprised the entire assembly didn't gasp. *Behind you! The rope!*

"Rabbi Adam, look at me!" cried Lilith. "Your answer!"

Before he could reply, Lamia stomped her foot with such force that the wedding platform shook. "Mother! You can't let the human go! He's mine! You promised!"

Lilith swatted her daughter aside. "There are plenty more where he came

279

from," she said. "We'll find you a nice, plump one. Mommy promises."

What else mommy might have promised, Adam never learned, for the clamor of clanging iron exploded above their heads. The unholy assembly looked up as one, startled and confused. The massive chandelier plummeted toward them, the heavy rope that had held it in place racing through its pulley like a fox from hounds. Some of the demons were quick-witted enough to climb through or over the others to momentary safety. Most were not, standing gape-mouthed as they got an increasingly close-up view of the last thing they would ever see.

The ironwork sliced through the demons and slammed into the floor, sending floorboards and tables flying into the air. Clouds of demons and dust made the air thick with death. The uncountable number of torches in the chandelier scattered and the Great Gallery was plunged into chaos. The creatures that hadn't been felled were screaming and fleeing for safety. The torches, rolling across the floor, found tapestries, drapes, and wood that welcomed them. Fires burst out throughout the hall, which filled with acrid waves of smoke, confusing and trapping the demons further.

Chaos, not the Queen of Demons, reigned. From her overlook on the wedding platform, Lilith turned this way and that, shouting to her subjects to remain calm, to no result. When she turned back to where Adam and Mendel had been standing, they were gone.

Chapter Forty-Nine

Amid the darkness, smoke, and confusion, Adam scooped up his son and leapt from the wedding platform. Mendel moaned in his arms, a trickle of blood running down his pale cheek to his chin. At least his dear boy was awakening from his trance. Adam held him against his chest and hustled him through an archway in the back of the Great Gallery and down a dark passage.

Adam bruised his shoulders and arms again and again as he misjudged corners and skittered against the stone walls. One jounce caused Mendel to blink and flash open his eyes. Adam hugged him closer and gave him a reassuring squeeze.

"It's all right, it's all right," he whispered to his boy.

As they turned a sharp corner, a pair of powerful hands appeared out of the darkness and yanked Adam aside. He looked at the massive brown and gray speckled hand clamped on his forearm just as Mendel opened his mouth in a prelude to a scream. Adam brought the palm of his free hand up to his son's mouth to muffle the sound. Then, he turned his gaze to the craggy, heavily shadowed face of the golem.

"Yossele!" he rasped, the syllables laced with joy. The boy, trembling, squirmed out of his father's arms and pressed himself flat against the stone wall. His eyes, wide and bright with terror, fixed on the hulking giant beside them.

Adam stroked Mendel's head to calm him. "Yossele is our friend," he said, then turned to the golem. "You did very, very well."

The eight-year-old regarded the clay creature with skepticism. The golem raised the ends of his thin mouth into a self-conscious smile. His eyes seemed to soften and, for a moment, the carved letters on his forehead seemed to glow. Mendel returned the golem's smile with an uncertain one of his own.

A demon's snort, distant but clear, sounded behind them. Adam's heart quickened. "Run!" he roared.

Adam and the golem each grasped one of Mendel's arms. Buffeting the child between them, they raced down the corridor, turning down one passage and then another, chased throughout by the reverberating grunts and growls and stampeding footfalls of their pursuers.

Mendel cried out. Adam turned and saw what was wrong: the golem was no longer at their side. Adam swung around looking for him. He saw his friend several yards behind, his broad shoulders and thick torso nearly filling the space of the narrow corridor.

"Yossele! Come!" Adam shouted, waving his arms at his friend.

The golem looked over his shoulder at them, then turned back toward the approaching frenzy. He was still, implacable, his tense muscles showing in the strains of his plain black suit.

The growls and barks grew greater and more urgent as the demons no doubt smelled their prey. Certainly, Adam smelled *them*. Mendel began to cough.

"Yossele, come with us!" Adam cried, struggling to be heard above the braying of the approaching demons.

The golem shook his head. He pointed to himself and then in the direction of the nearing onslaught. He would hold them off; Adam and Mendel would get away.

Adam raised his arm toward his friend. "Yossele, I command you!" he exploded. "You cannot disobey!"

The golem's midnight eyes widened and Adam saw in them a depth they had not had before. The golem shook his head, a refusal mixed with profound regret. Adam didn't understand—the golem couldn't refuse him, it wasn't in his soul—and then he did. Whatever the golem had been, he was no longer. And Adam, *Rabbi* Adam, had been his teacher. Adam nodded, an acceptance mixed with profound regret.

Adam felt Mendel pulling on his side, moaning. The acrid smell of the demons and their cries, louder and more distinct, signaled their imminent arrival. Adam looked up into the golem's gaze, which seemed almost sorrowful. Before the golem turned away, his eyes seemed to say one thing more: *goodbye*.

Adam again took up his son's hand and they sped like a pair of stags through the woods. Adam glanced back and saw the golem face the approaching demons, a dozen, no, a score of them. Adam's eyes stung; he brushed aside his tears with his sleeve. He and Mendel kept running. The golem and the demons were lost to sight, though Adam and Mendel could still hear fierce, deep throaty growls behind them. As the two continued their flight, the pain in Adam's chest growing, they heard howls of triumph, faint but unmistakable, behind them.

The demons carried their prize back to their queen, navigating the smashed tables and benches, the shambles that was the Great Gallery. Dozens of claws held the golem immobile; dozens of green scaly arms and legs strained under the weight of so much earth and clay. They needn't have bothered; the golem offered no resistance.

They unloaded the golem at Lilith's feet. She glanced at him for but a moment, her fierce green eyes and pale, almost translucent, skin a marked contrast to the motionless earth and clay that lay before her.

"I'm not interested in this one," she spat at the demons. "The rabbi, the boy—where are *they?*"

The demons let out low moans and grunts.

"Find them!" Her command penetrated the vast darkness of the room and a great contingent of demons charged out in search of their prey.

Lilith returned her attention to the demons holding the golem. "And this thing," she said with disgust, "put it out of my misery."

The demons threw the golem on the floor and pounced on him, tearing into him with their claws and tusks and animalistic fury. They gouged deep wounds into him, gashes and holes that no creature of flesh and blood could have survived. Then they went to work on what remained of him, sending chunks of earth and clay flying across the room. While he still had limbs, the golem didn't resist, didn't even move. After that, he closed those black, hollow eyes that had seen so much in so brief a time. The demons continued to savage what remained of his body, eventually slicing deep into his stomach.

Then everything changed.

The darkness was pierced by a ray of the brightest light in all of creation. The pandemonium faded away as the demons watched, transfixed by the First Light, a brilliant beam that didn't just cut through the gloom of the Great Gallery, but obliterated it. Another ray joined it, then another and another, lights blazing in all directions. Wherever the light hit, it burnt through the evil that was the palace and its unholy inhabitants. The imp was among the first to be incinerated; its bright, harlequin-hued suit burning merrily as the slimy green creature within it rasped a final cry of indignation.

The demons and night creatures scurried, hurried, crawled, and flew in vain attempts to avoid their doom. The light cut through them like a mighty sword, its touch engulfing them in flames. Demons screamed and howled as they had so often heard their victims cry and, like their victims, their own cries of terror rang in their ears until they were reduced to heaps of ash.

Pillars throughout the room cracked and crumbled, others exploded. The walls were aflame. The palace itself was melting away. In the midst of it all, Lilith stood tall and still on the wedding platform, her emerald eyes taking in the destruction all about her. She watched her subjects flee like the vermin they were and she sneered at their cowardice. Let them see how their queen faced death and conquered it. The light radiated ever closer to her but still she stood, proud and erect.

Without flinching, despite her imminent doom, she raised her arm. She held her hand flat against the light—the same hand that had destroyed countless souls since her triumph over another Adam—and mustered all the dark powers that fueled her.

You. Will. Not. Take. Me, her mind demanded of the light. At the edge of her vision, Lilith saw the demon clergyman flapping and running in circles like a headless imp, trying without success to escape the flaming robe that encased him. The clergyman let out an unholy wail, a high-pitched cry tempered by futility, then burst into flames and fell to the floor.

Lilith's lip twitched but she remained otherwise motionless as she sought to force the light to her will. *I have prosecuted humanity since the time of Adam, who thought himself my better. I have laid low man and woman by hardening their hearts so that they might do as they will. I will see them destroy themselves, all of them, to the very last one. You may have the others. You will not have me.*

Lamia, partially consumed in flame, ran and clung to her mother, who shook her off without a look or a thought. Finally, the light found Lilith. It pierced her like a rapier and left her twitching, convulsing as her body lit up from within. Her extremities burst into flame next, as though the energy within her could not be contained for another moment. The Demon Queen bellowed in agony, her mouth open as wide as the pit into which she had cast so many of her victims. Now her head was a ball of fire, flames shooting from her eyes, ears, and mouth as though from the windows of a hovel set aflame. The fire danced too along the length of her reptilian tongue, which swung from a corner of her mouth like a flag in a windstorm. She clawed like a great wounded animal at her fiery face and head, to no effect. Then her death cries came, deep and dark, filled not with futility but with rage, her defiance reverberating against what few walls remained of the blood-soaked palace. They were heard too in the human world, where they sounded like the final throes of Death itself.

As Lilith's consciousness burned away, wisps of light, the uncountable souls trapped within her, soared free from the flames and hurtled away from the domain of evil. They did so first in tens, then hundreds, then thousands, like a swarm of sprites painting the night sky gold. They were the last thing holding Lilith together. As they left her, she collapsed in a mound of ash.

Chapter Fifty

Adam and Mendel ran from the palace, scrambling over the rocks and brush of the underworld's moors, their only thought to get as far away as fast as possible. The booms of many cannon blasts knocked them to the ground and they were blinded not by darkness but by light. It took Adam a moment to realize what this light—which he'd only glimpsed once, and then heavily shielded—must be.

"Yossele," he whispered, the sound a mixture of astonishment, admiration... and overwhelming sadness.

Their vision returned but the palace, ablaze in the First Light, remained impossible to look at. The two shielded their eyes as Lot and his daughters—though not his wife—must have shielded theirs from the destruction of Sodom and Gomorrah so long before. Then the vibrations started. Mere tremors at first, they grew so that the very wasteland around them thundered. It was difficult and, finally, impossible to walk, let alone run. Adam held Mendel as the ground seemed ready to explode.

Please God, he prayed, his words but a murmur. He didn't complete the thought. What could he say? The Holy One, he was sure, would complete his prayer as He saw fit.

The waves of First Light flew outward from the palace in every direction, consuming everything that was of the demon world. The First Light reached Adam and Mendel and carried them along with it.

Above, in the human sphere, all was again quiet. Much had been destroyed but much, much more had not. People, huddled in their homes, knew not whether they'd been spared or whether the respite might be revoked at any moment and the destruction take them, too. Across the earth, every tree, every reed, every blade of grass held its breath. Then the rumbling began, a terrible quake that shook everything. Those who felt it, even those who merely heard it, grasped each other tightly, for surely this was the end.

In a valley in which no human had ever trod, the ground cracked open. The First Light poured up through it and splashed the landscape like a tidal wave crashing upon a shore, although this monumental wave brought not death, but life. The meadows became verdant, the trees lush with fruit. Even birds, which had ceased to sing when the apocalypse was nigh, found their throats and chirped as never before.

The First Light carried Adam and Mendel up from the underworld and high into the clean, fresh air. They could see nothing but the Light that surrounded them, cradled them, protected them, much as the Pillar of Light had protected the ancient Israelites in the desert. Adam held Mendel as fervently as any father ever held a child and put his faith in the Holy One, Blessed be He. The Light deposited them on the valley floor, like a breeze depositing a stray feather. Father and son continued to hold each other, determined in this way to blot out whatever dangers might now be in store for them. The Light retreated into the crevice it had carved across the valley. Then the crevice smoothed itself out, vanishing like a wrinkle under an iron, and there was nothing to indicate that the First Light had ever been there.

Adam turned toward the warm, welcome illumination from the sun, which emerged at the horizon to shower the valley with the first rays of its nourishing, orange glow. To Adam, the rays seemed divine reassurance that the end of everything would not come, at least not on this day.

That warmth, however, lasted but a moment. Adam felt it replaced by a sudden wave of cold that prickled his skin and he trembled. It seemed to him like the cold of a light being extinguished, of a soul leaving this realm and returning to the upper spheres from which it had come. Adam knew without need of proof that it was the soul of Yossele. He looked across the valley as though he might gain a last glimpse of his friend, trudging into view after defeating yet another enemy. The Yedoni, the Cossacks, the demons... Yossele had never failed him, even when success could come only at the cost of his own life. Adam again felt a chill, this time deep within him, but he no longer looked across the valley for his friend, for now he carried his friend within him. Besides, his moistened eyes had blurred his vision.

Adam felt a hand on his arm and looked down at Mendel. The boy's broad, full cheeks were stained with dirt and tears and a thin, faint trace of blood. Adam wiped them with his thumbs, cleaning the boy's face very little, but causing the lights in his son's deep brown eyes to burn a bit brighter. A life saved...

... and another life lost. Adam stepped back from Mendel, just a little. There was something else he had to do. His body began bending forward and snapping back like a pendulum as it assumed the rhythm of prayer. He and Yossele... creator and creation... master and servant... teacher and student. But he had been wrong, he realized with a pang, in what he had taught Yossele so long before about golems and souls. A golem's soul, the soul that Adam had bestowed upon him that night on the banks of the San river, could never have defied its creator as Yossele had done. If Yossele hadn't been created with a human soul, perhaps he had found one, or forged one, along the way.

Adam began the slow, mournful recitation of the prayer for the dead, the prayer he had wrongly told Yossele could not be said in his memory: "Magnified and sanctified may His great name be, in the world He created by His will..."

Adam finished his recitation and looked down at Mendel. "Amen," said the boy, looking up with love into the eyes of his father. Adan leaned over and kissed Mendel on the top of his head, then drew him close and kissed him again.

Adam had no idea where they were but he reckoned that walking in a straight direction, any direction, would bring them to a road, if not a town. They walked for hours through meadows and forests, along riverbanks and across fields, before reaching that road. The sun was high in the sky, but now its light was disappearing. Adam looked up to see the sun almost completely blotted out, darkness taking hold of the landscape about them. But this was not night nor was it some new danger. It was a flock. Of birds. Carrying a tree trunk.

As the birds settled beside them, Adam saw his friend the goldfinch fluttering nearby. If a bird could be said to smile, this bird smiled. "You!" Adam exclaimed. "How did you find us?"

"Funny story, that," chirped the goldfinch, flying to Adam and landing in his proffered palm. "Turns out there's an owl who knows a heron who knows an eagle who mentioned it to a certain little birdy."

Adam smiled, shook his head, and motioned to Mendel to join him on the tree trunk. As soon as they were ensconced, the flock took off, flying higher and higher, toward the setting sun.

Chapter Fifty-One

Sarah was gathering flowers from her garden when a shadow fell across her, causing her to look up. The flowers dropped from her hand. The sun was blotted out and for a moment she caught her breath; had the destruction of the previous night started anew? But the breeze was gentle, the earth was still, and the rest of the sky held not a cloud. Sarah exhaled, but her heart beat faster and harder at this enormous, impossible sight.

It was a large shape and it was descending. Sarah watched with a growing sense of wonder as the massive tree, horizontal in the sky, sank slowly and majestically to earth, carried by the largest flock of birds she'd ever seen, and came to rest on its side perhaps fifty yards away, in the village grazing field. There was a great shaking of evergreen branches about midway along the trunk and the most miraculous sight of all nearly made her swoon: her son Mendel, her dear bright, brave Mendel, his face radiant despite being streaked with dirt, sliding over the side of the trunk and running straight toward her with the speed of one of the enormous birds that now flew overhead.

Sarah started running toward Mendel but only managed a few steps before he reached her, threw his arms around her waist, and pressed himself against her. Sarah gathered him up and held him in her arms. His face was now awash in tears, both his and Sarah's, dislodging streaks of dirt that began to slide down his face. The only sound that emerged from his lips was his repeated cries of "mommy, mommy, mommy..." punctuated by sobs and hiccups and deep intakes of breath. Sarah hardly heard him as she covered his face with kisses, warm and wet, that told him what she could not gather the words to express, how he was loved, how she had missed him and feared for him, and how life itself had been restored to her by his return.

Still hugging and squeezing Mendel, Sarah saw a flash of motion by the tree. She looked up and saw another sight that caught her breath: Adam. He was much thinner than before, his clothes hanging from him as though from a scarecrow. His beard and sidelocks and what she could see of his hair were now ashen, their former black-and-gray seemingly drained along with the color from his face. But, like Mendel, he was here. He was alive. He was an answer to a prayer and a dream. A dream... Had he experienced their dream? Would he remember it? Sarah couldn't bear the thought that he hadn't, wouldn't.

Adam strode toward her then stopped and Sarah gasped to think that something, at this last moment, was wrong. She followed his gaze to a dark bush at the side of the path, a bush she somehow hadn't noticed before. He walked to it and snapped off a flower. At this distance, Sarah couldn't quite make it out, but she could make out its color: a radiant pink. He brought it to her: a damask rose. Adam tucked the stem of the flower into a buttonhole of her blouse and the air around them was transformed by its scent, at once sweet and sharp.

Her hands flew around him and held him as he now held her. There were no tears, no words. She had no need for them and knew that he didn't either. She felt his heart beating against her chest, beating along with hers, as though one, and felt at peace. For the first time since he'd left—no, for the first time in many, many years—she felt at peace with herself and with Adam.

Sarah knew that this was more than the joy of a physical reunion. It was the joy of a spiritual reunion. In Adam's bright, loving eyes, she saw that they'd been given a chance, the world had been given a chance, to start over. What the world would make of its chance, she couldn't know. But she knew to her bones what she and Adam would make of theirs.

A shadow passed before Adam's face and his fingers twisted in his beard. "The children?" he asked. "How are the children?

Sarah's wide, warm smile reassured him.

"See for yourself," she said, nodding past him. He turned and saw Hersh and Miriam, followed by little Leah, spilling out of the house and rushing toward him. Hersh's strides were long and firm and he held his bride's hand, helping Miriam to keep up with his energetic pace. Leah, her blonde curls flying behind her like streams of gold, seemed to defy gravity as she raced to her brother and father. Sarah stepped back as they approached. Hersh wrapped his powerful arms around his father and hugged him tight; Sarah could see Adam's eyes widen as more than a bit of air whooshed out of him.

"Hersh, let your father breathe," Sarah said, her caution a mixture of concern and good cheer. Hersh, looking a bit sheepish, released his grip, which was Leah's cue to leap into her father's arms. Adam's grin was broad enough to swallow her whole as Leah planted kiss after kiss on his cheeks, the moisture mixing with the tears that streamed from her eyes.

Sarah embraced them both. "I thought they were lost; last night I thought everything was lost," she told Adam. "But when the sun rose this morning, when it finally rose—they were returned to us. And now, so have you and Mendel."

The reunion was filled with such transcendent joy, Sarah thought, that it was possible to look at them, to look at them all, and have no sense of the evil that had nearly destroyed them. Her heart filled with gratitude to the Holy One, Blessed be He.

"Blessed is the Lord who is good and does good," she said.

"Amen," Adam answered, taking her hand in his.

As they walked back to the house, Hersh and Miriam just ahead of them and Mendel and Leah darting around them like playful pups, Adam squeezed Sarah's hand, then thought wistfully of all the years they had failed to enjoy even so simple a touch. Well, they would make up for the past now. The past… He would have to tell Sarah about his past, about Rachel. How was he supposed to do *that*?

"Sarah," he began in what was little more than a whisper. "There's something I need to tell you."

She cocked her head. "I imagine there's a lot you need to tell me. It can wait."

He took a deep breath and held it while he thought, then exhaled. "There's one very important thing that I don't think can wait."

Her lips twitched for a moment before she spoke. "You mean, about Rachel?"

He stopped and turned to her. He could feel his face flush, the heat rushing through it like wildfire. "You know... about her? How...?"

"Our dream together wasn't the only one I had last night." She brought a soft, pink hand up to his crimson face and cradled his cheek in it. "I know what you did," she said softly, "for all of us."

Adam looked at his wife, his mouth agape. Finally, he managed to blurt: "You are indeed a woman of valor."

"More precious than pearls?" she asked, one eyebrow rising as she continued the quotation from the familiar psalm.

"More precious than anything I deserve," he answered.

Sarah laughed, a wonderful, hearty sound, like angels escaping from her. "In that case," she replied, "I forbid you to leave me and the children again."

Adam considered this. "Then I suppose you'll all have to come with me," he said.

It was Sarah's turn to be surprised. "Where now?"

He looked at her and smiled. "To a wedding."

In Koretz, the synagogue was filled with garlands and bouquets as befitted a wedding reception. The house of prayer was also filled with villagers dancing, singing, and celebrating the wedding of Esther and Dovid. Adam, near the door, surveyed the scene. His gaze lingered on Sarah, whirling and swaying in a circle dance with a dozen other women. Miriam and little Leahele each held one of Sarah's hands and danced in the circle with her. Even from his distance, Adam could sense the selfless joy emanating from his wife like lamplight and his own heart swelled.

Much closer to him, the men danced in their own circle, and Adam smiled to see Hersh moving with the same energy and passion as the rest, his legs flying about but somehow never missing a step. Mendel, looking no older

293

than his eight years even in his Sabbath best, sat atop his brother's shoulders, laughing and squealing with delight and holding Hersh's head for dear life as they flew about the circle.

The band struck up a fanfare and the newlyweds entered the synagogue, surrounded by their friends. The rest of the guests rushed to greet the couple and Adam's family joined them. Adam, however, stayed back and watched, as was his habit. He had thought he would never see his family again. Never see good old Gimpel Carrots and the rest of the Lizenskers. Never see home. But he had come home, he thought with a smile, though his thoughts turned bittersweet: He would, after all, never again see his mentor nor his friend, and how could his home now truly, fully, be home without them?

"You have repaired your wrong and I forgive you, dear Adam, with all my heart."

Adam, startled, turned. A middle-aged woman stood next to him, her hair an affecting mixture of honey and gray, her eyes aglow, her head sitting like a jewel atop a long, still-elegant neck. She had waited so many years for her wedding day, a day that had, in its own and unexpected way, come at last.

"Look at them," Rachel continued, taking it all in before turning to him. "Dear Adam, you and I made their wedding possible. So, in a way, their children will be our children too, the children we were supposed to have together." She paused for a moment and again swept her gaze throughout the room. "Aren't they beautiful?"

Adam didn't understand. "You mean the wedding couple?"

Rachel smiled. "No," she answered. "I mean the children."

Adam strained to see what Rachel saw. He thought he glimpsed a boy and a girl at the side of the wedding couple, where no children had stood a moment before. Then those two were joined by more, many more, and by men and women of every description, many wearing styles of clothing unfamiliar to him, until the room could hold no more. But still they appeared. Through the windows he could see them outside the house, in the street, all filled with joy, all laughing and cheering, all celebrating the wedding of Esther and Dovid and the chance for life that this union had given them.

In the midst of their celebrations, the souls of those yet-to-be turned to Adam and he could feel wave after wave of their gratitude. And in that gratitude he felt a love, a pure, intense love. It filled him, mind and body and soul, and still it came. And then Adam felt another emotion, difficult to label at first because, as much as he could recollect, he had never felt it before. Adam felt at peace.

"What once went wrong has been set right—all of it," said Rachel, once again commanding his attention. She looked up at him and smiled with a radiance that would remain a part of him forever. "And now, dear Adam, you are the man you were meant to be."

Slap! Anshel's hand landed on Adam's back with a wallop. The father of the bride handed his benefactor a goblet of wine. Anshel looked years younger than he had just one week earlier.

"Rabbi Adam, come greet the new couple!" he cried.

Adam turned back to Rachel—but she was gone.

"A toast to the newlyweds," Anshel shouted to the villagers. "To life!"

Adam laughed in agreement. "To life!" he shouted.

For a nearly imperceptible moment, Adam shone with a light that was at once warm and white and every color seen and unseen, the most beautiful light that ever was or ever could be. It was a light that had existed from the first moment of creation and that would forever accompany humanity on its journey, banishing the night and showing the way forward. It was a light that signified that the world was safe, secured once more by the earthly presence of thirty-six Lamed Vavniks.

Anshel stared at Adam but whatever he thought he'd seen was gone. With his hand still on the other's back, he steered the hidden saint of Lizensk in the direction of the newlyweds and the two of them made their way into the joyful crowd.

Afterword

I n a seminal essay in the inaugural issue of The Jewish Review of Books in 2010, Michael Weingrad asked "Why are there no works of modern fantasy that are profoundly Jewish in the way that, say, *The Lion, the Witch, and the Wardrobe* is Christian? Why no Jewish Lewises, and why no Jewish Narnias?" In a reply to critics, Weingrad "wondered aloud how suited the theology of normative Judaism—profoundly demythologizing, halakhic, and without a developed tradition of evil as an autonomous force—is to the making of modern fantasy."[1]

I was already working on *The Hidden Saint* when Weingrad's essay appeared, but it seemed to me then (as it does now) that *The Hidden Saint* is a response of sorts. It has the trappings of Judaism (rabbis, synagogues, Torah scrolls) and even the trappings of Jewish myth (a golem, Lilith, Lamed-Vavniks). But Weingrad was asking a deeper question; I think *The Hidden Saint* is a response to it, too.

Epic fantasy is typically premised on conflict between pagan gods or supernatural beings. Often, the fate of the world lies in the balance. But how can the fate of the world be in doubt when that world is under the omnipresent care of a single, omnipotent, loving God, as normative Judaism posits? The only answer that Judaism leaves open, it seems to me, is that the future can be in doubt only when man exercises the power that God gives him to put that future in doubt.

The myth of the Lamed-Vavniks, the Hidden Saints, is an ancient rabbinic legend. The Almighty created a world that needs a minimal level of holiness to justify its continuance. That level is thirty-six holy souls. As the

296

master Jewish folklorist Howard Schwartz writes, "they are the pillars of existence."[2] What would happen if one of these pillars were to crumble? The bible hints at an answer in the story of Sodom and Gomorrah. God says he will permit the cities to continue if Abraham can find just ten righteous people within them. He couldn't and the cities were destroyed. In the case of the world, the minimum requirement is even more compelling: not the result of a last-minute negotiation, but a condition built into the very fabric of the universe at the time of creation. The Lamed-Vavniks, then, are key to putting the fate of the world in play in Jewish fantasy.

For *The Hidden Saint* to be "profoundly Jewish," in Weingrad's terminology, evil can't be an autonomous force. There's no rebellious Lucifer in *The Hidden Saint* but there is Lilith, and she seems a close substitute. Close but, I hope, no cigar. Lilith has evolved in Jewish folklore over the millennia. As Schwartz notes, the rabbis of the Talmud find hints in the bible to her having been the first wife of the first Adam. The Jewish legend grows in the ninth century and Lilith becomes a child killer, a witch, a cannibal, grafted onto other legends of Lilith as a demon seductress.

For the Lilith of *The Hidden Saint*, I've done some grafting of my own. The idea of the Evil Inclination that lies within man's heart, and of its personification in the Satan, the Adversary, is very old in Jewish tradition (and paired with a counterweight: the Good Inclination). The Evil Inclination is, as Lilith defines herself in *The Hidden Saint*, not just evil, but the impulse to be weak and afraid, to envy, to gluttony, to immorality and more. There is precedent for personifying this impulse. A rabbinic story relates that while Abraham was away with his son Isaac to offer him as a sacrifice, the Satan appeared to Sarah and told her that this act had been completed: her son was dead. She died from the shock. Satan here is a metaphor for Sarah's anxiety and fear; in the world of a single, omnipotent God, he can be nothing else. This is one way I understand the Lilith of *The Hidden Saint*.

Another explanation for Lilith relies on the classic understanding of why evil exists in the world, a question that of course has occupied thinkers, both Jewish (such as Maimonides) and non-Jewish, through the ages. Evil exists to give man the ability to choose good. Evil exists for man to value life. For these reasons, the Almighty created a world with death and disease, war and wild beasts. For those who need Lilith to be more real than metaphorical, she is another of God's creations operating—like a wolf, a virus, or an earthquake—within the destructive parameters that he has assigned to her.

A few other points:

Golems. The golem is perhaps the most widely recognized member of the world of Jewish myth, a favorite of artists and writers both Jewish and non-Jewish. The attraction of creative types to a creation myth isn't surprising. Pinocchio is a golem of sorts; so is Frankenstein's monster. But the Jewish golem is distinctly Jewish, profoundly Jewish, because his creator seeks not to challenge or surpass God, but to emulate him in order to know him better. Creating a golem is a way for its creator to draw closer to The Creator. Only a righteous person operating in submission to the Almighty can succeed.

The Yedoni. I'm indebted to Rabbi Natan Slifkin's *Sacred Monsters*[3] for bringing the Yedoni to my attention. His book is unique, an erudite and entertaining look at both the scripture and science behind unicorns, mermaids, griffins, dragons, and much more. It is *the* work of Jewish cryptozoology and I recommend it highly.

Folktales. Hundreds of Jewish folktales have been told over thousands of years. Fragments of many of these folktales found their way into *The Hidden Saint*, seasoning it like spice in the soup. Shayna's visit to the couple at the inn is an echo of the stories of Elijah the Prophet, who often appears in disguise and rewards the deserving and downtrodden. The little synagogue discovered within the earth and Shayna's attempted exorcism of Lilith are both echoes of echoes, by way of S. Ansky's masterpiece, *The Dybbuk*. And an important inspiration for *The Hidden Saint* comes from the folktale The Dead Fiancée, which Schwartz traces to the 19th century and which is collected in several contemporary volumes.[4] The theme of the broken vow, particularly the broken wedding vow, is longstanding in Jewish tradition. Its origin, according to Ben-Amos, is the Talmud; its apotheosis is *The Dybbuk*.

Rabbi Adam. A pair of nice, Jewish boys—Jerry Siegel and Joe Shuster—created Superman. But they didn't create the superhero. Two thousand years earlier, in the Talmud, Shimon ben Shetach defeated the 80 witches of Ashkelon. More recently, wonder-working Chasidic rabbis were said to battle all sorts of supernatural evil. The Baal Shem Tov, the founder of the Chasidic movement, reputedly bested a werewolf. And there was Rabbi Adam, a wonder-working rabbi whose power, like that of the Baal Shem Tov, Rabbi Lowe (creator of the golem of Prague), and others came from his knowledge of the true name of God. As early as the 16th century, according to Schwartz, Rabbi Adam fought evil kings and sorcerers, although his status as a Lamed-Vavnik is, as far as I know, my invention. I see *The Hidden Saint* as an origin story for this legendary hero: his first adventure but not, I hope, his last.

Mark Levenson

February 22, 2022

[1] "Why There is No Jewish Narnia," by Michael Weingrad, Jewish Review of Books, Spring 2010 and "No Jewish Narnias: A Reply," by Michael Weingrad, Jewish Review of Books, Summer 2010.

[2] "Tree of Souls: The Mythology of Judaism" by Howard Schwartz, Oxford University Press, 2004.

[3] "Sacred Monsters: Mysterious and Mythical Creatures of Scripture, Talmud and Midrash" by Rabbi Natan Slifkin, Zoo Torah, 2007.

[4] "Folktales of the Jews, Vol 2: Tales from Eastern Europe," edited and with commentary by Dan Ben-Amos, The Jewish Publication Society, 2007; "Stories within Stories: From the Jewish Oral Tradition," retold by Penina Schram, Jason Aronson, 2000; "Lilith's Cave: Jewish Tales of the Supernatural," selected and retold by Howard Schwartz, Harper & Row, 1988; "Jewish Folktales," selected and retold by Pinhas Sadeh, Anchor Books, 1989.

Acknowledgements

I wish to thank my publishers, Verena Rose, Harriette Sackler, and Shawn Reilly Simmons at Level Best Books and Denene Lofland at New Arc, each of whom was instrumental in bringing this book to the reader. I wish to thank Ruchama King Feuerman, my developmental editor, who provided crucial guidance in revising the text after I thought it was ready for its close-up. And since I wouldn't have met Ruchama but for Tzivia Gottesman, she has my gratitude, too. Thanks as well to Erin Mitchell and Stuart Schnee, my able PR representatives.

I also wish to thank those who read and commented on the text in its earlier stages, or who otherwise provided support, including Elliot Blair, Justin Brasch and Juli Smith, Jonathan Donath, Esther Gittel Edelson, Larry Engler, Basya Fishman, Jane Glasser, David Goldberg, Bija Gutoff, Micah Halpern, Mark Guterman, Rabbi Joshua Lookstein, Nechamie Margolis, Kenny Sadinoff, Bracha K. Sharp, Chana Shavelson, Sharon Silver, Esther Symonds, Yehudit Sarah Waller, Craig Weingard, Chedvah Wilhelm, and Emily Williamson.

The contribution of my wife, AnneBeth, goes far beyond her thoughtful review of the text, to also include her understanding and patience, her support and encouragement, and, most of all, her love. I also express my appreciation to our children, Zally, Aryeh, and Shira, for out of the mouths of babes ofttimes come things that sneak into books.

The Chasidim teach that not a blade of grass moves but by the will of the Creator. Given that, I gratefully acknowledge the role of the Creator in bringing me to this season.

Mark Levenson
February 22, 2022

About the Author

Mark Levenson is an award-winning dramatist, screenwriter, and short-story writer, as well as a longtime journalist.

His Jewish-themed fantasy writing has won honors from The National Foundation for Jewish Culture and the American Jewish University, as well as a Union Internationale de la Marionnette-USA Citation of Excellence, an award founded by Jim Henson.

Levenson's novel, *The Hidden Saint*, is the culmination of his more than 20 years of engagement with Jewish folklore. Levenson wrote *The Return of the Golem* and *The Wise Men of Chelm* for the stage, and adapted S. Ansky's *The Dybbuk* for actors and puppets. His Jewish-themed short fiction credits include Mystery Weekly Magazine, Kindle Kzine, and Ami Magazine. He also blogs about Jewish fantasy for The Times of Israel.

Levenson began his career as a reporter for *The Miami Herald* and *Dun's Review*. He has written for *New York Magazine, The Philadelphia Inquirer, The Forward, The Jewish Week, the Associated Press, Puppetry International, Stevens Magic, The American Kennel Club Gazette, The Oregonian,* and others. He heads the marketing and PR firm The Levenson Company, whose clients have included Amazon, Microsoft, Intel, and Cigna. Levenson served as director of press relations for The Wharton School at Penn, and director of public relations for the Oregon Art Institute. He also served on the boards of the Jim Henson Foundation and the American Jewish Committee.

Perhaps Levenson's interests in fantasy and folklore are in his blood; his paternal grandmother was a magician, "Lightfingers Ida," whose tutelage sparked his lifelong interest in magic. His great-great-uncle (on his mother's side) was a strongman in a Russian circus who could hold back galloping horses and survive sledgehammer blows by peasants who smashed rocks on his chest, except for the last time.

Although Levenson's physique gives no hint of this lineage, it was a circus sideshow that sparked another lifelong interest, that of puppetry. Levenson writes for and about puppet theatre, was guest curator and catalog author for the exhibition "Winners' Circle" at the Center for Puppetry Arts in Atlanta, and a contributor to the World Encyclopedia of Puppetry. He was the featured *Punch & Judy* performer at the Philadelphia festival marking the 250th anniversary of the first performance of that classic puppet play in America.

Levenson was graduated from Cornell University. He and his family live in Westchester County, New York.

CPSIA information can be obtained
at www.ICGtesting.com
Printed in the USA
LVHW030048210522
719346LV00014B/1156